Acclaim for *Lay My Body on the Line...*

"There's a distinct sense of paranoia pervading this remarkable little book. It comes on slowly and takes off with a rush, as if you had dropped acid 20 minutes ago and now found yourself undergoing questioning at a local precinct house. There is, too, a captivating urgency in the prose. It pins your attention to the action and drives you constantly on to the next page. Together, the two devices make the book both seem shorter than its 206 pages and very hard to put down. ..Leon's paranoia is ..well-drawn and..grounded in the social reality of pot and the politics of the Bay Area in the 60s." Robert Hurwitt, *Berkeley Barb*

"...the first serious novel ...set in the period leading up to and into the strike [at San Francisco State]." Stephen Arkin, *San Francisco Bay Guardian*

"When Andrew Young used the phrase 'American political prisoner,' people were baffled -- how could there be political prisoners in this, the greatest democracy in the world? Berkeley author Floyd Salas understood. His latest novel, *Lay my Body on the Line*, is the story of such an individual, who in the late sixties found himself 'caught between two forces of power, the police and the radical' organizations, voicing a third view of freedom of democracy, of political power...' Roger Leon is caught because his ideals prevent him from co-operating with the establishment or adhering to the 'radical chic,' who often sacrifice the means to the end... *Lay My Body on the Line* is not just another book about the sixties, but about a man trying to speak out in America and finding that it is not the 'land of the free.'" Mary Walker, *The Daily Cal*

Lay My Body on the Line was originally published in 1978 by Ishmael Reed's and Al Young's iconic press, Y'Bird. The sequel to this volume is entitled *State of Emergency*, published by Arte Publico Press in 1996.

"*State of Emergency* is a sequel to Floyd Salas' classic political thriller *Lay My Body on the Line*. In both novels, Salas exposes members of a sinister parallel government out to undermine the liberties of American citizens. *State of Emergency* sustains Salas' reputation as one of our top writers." Ishmael Reed

LAY MY BODY ON THE LINE

A Novel

FLOYD SALAS

AN AUTHORS GUILD BACKINPRINT.COM EDITION

LAY MY BODY ON THE LINE

AN AUTHORS GUILD BACKINPRINT.COM EDITION

iUniverse books may be ordered through booksellers or by contacting:

iUniverse LLC
1663 Liberty Drive
Bloomington, IN 47403
www.iuniverse.com
1-800-Authors (1-800-288-4677)

Originally published by Y'Bird

ISBN: 978-1-4917-4398-0 (sc)

Printed in the United States of America.

iUniverse rev. date: 09/05/2014

Publisher's Cataloging-In-Publication Data
(Prepared by The Donohue Group, Inc.)

Salas, Floyd, 1931-
   Lay my body on the line : a novel / Floyd Salas. -- Authors Guild Backinprint.com edition.

   pages ; cm

   Originally published: [Berkeley, Calif.] : Y'Bird, c1978.
   ISBN: 978-1-4917-4398-0 (sc)

   1. San Francisco State College--Riots--Fiction. 2. Student movements--California--San Francisco--History--20th century--Fiction. 3. San Francisco (Calif.)--Politics and government--20th century--Fiction. 4. Brothers and sisters--Death--Psychological aspects. 5. Historical fiction. I. Title.

PS3569.A459 L39 2014
813/.54   2014914784

LAY MY BODY
ON THE LINE

For Malcolm X
Martin Luther King
and the Brothers Kennedy—
Martyrs for Freedom

And for my father, Ed Salas,
who gave me some bucks to do it
when he was still alive.

PART ONE
A Life Potential

Swung around in a circle by an arm and a leg, flying, the ground swooping by, streaked clouds in the sky, dizziness and nausea and his heart in his mouth, too scared to scream even, then finally set down on his two tiny feet by his oldest brother, Eddy, Roger sees the round damp spot in the soft earth beneath the big faucet slowly come into focus.

The big, graying legs of the tall water tower finally stand still and straight beside it. He lifts his round face straight up from the damp spot to the big faucet to the huge water barrel that towers far above him and sees once again his older brother, Ernie, age eleven, leap from its edge, headfirst, into the air, seem to hang suspended for a moment above the fields on the outskirts of Oakland with his arms in front of him, then turn a circle and land on his feet, collapse in a heap and lay like a pile of his mother's washday clothes.

He sees Ernie again in plaster casts and crutches in the back seat of the car coming home from the hospital and falls to the ground crying. He sees his mother with red eyes the day his brother Eddy's picture is put in the paper for being chosen Head Boy of his highschool and only finds out later that Ernie was in the paper, too, for running away from home, sawing the bars of the juvenile hall and escaping with ten other boys. His mother continues to move back and forth in the kitchen making dinner, sniffling, wiping her red eyes with the back of her hand every once in a while, without speaking.

Rogers sits in church and barely hears a word the priest is saying, but sees instead Christ coming in glory through the clouds of the ceiling, light flowing in multicolored, rainbow patterns through the stained glass, an aura of light that seems to encapsulate the statues, cast a halo around their heads and the head of the priest on the altar, smells, too, the incense, hears the peaceful stillness, and feels the beautiful sense of goodness that fills the church, that simmers in him in an ecstatic, invigorating way, flows up from his body into his throat and over his head with a tingling sensation, makes him wish that some day he, too, can move around on that altar bathed in a beatific glow, in those colorful robes, handling the sacred vessels of the body and blood of Christ, in communication with the Holy Spirit.

He loves to listen to his father tell stories, too. Big man seated by the cash register in his white shirt and tie, broad swath of cloth flowing down and over his big belly, his bald, olive-skinned head glowing, his big brown eyes bright, his neat black mustache contrasting beautifully with his white, perfectly shaped teeth, always bared in a smile.

Roger loves William Tell, too, who refused to bend his knee to the tyrant's cap, who shot an apple off his son's head, and when asked what the other arrow was for, answered, "For the tyrant's heart if I missed."

A warm current of air touches him one day when he opens the front door and walks into the two-story hallway of the big house after a late catechism class. He takes off his wet jacket and hangs it on one of the big coat hooks of the tall cabinet mirror that sits against the wall near the foot of the curving stairs next to the sliding doors of the long front room, then stops and stands there, letting the warmth settle over his damp face and head, letting it bathe his small, eleven year old body, a sense of sweet security rising up in him, hearing his mother's voice somewhere in the front room, catching a scent of roast cooking in the kitchen through the open door of the dining room, then cocks his head in surprise with the first piano notes of someone playing, "Hark! The herald angels sing, glory to the newborn king. Peace on earth and mercy mild, God and sinners reconciled."

Curious, excited, the prayers and incense in front of the altar still fresh in his mind from the catechism class, relating the song to the image of Jesus aloft in the clouds on the domed ceiling of the Catholic church, he slides a door back and steps into the great room from the long hallway to find his mother in her housedress and apron seated at the piano, playing, her spectacled eyes intent on the keyboard.

He stands there in the doorway with wide eyes and an open mouth slowly spreading into a smile at the sight of her, happy, and the big, lighted Christmas tree in the corner of the large picture window beyond her, spider-webbed with tinsel and spun glass, a silvery girl angel at its tip, a small mountain of Christmas presents filling the whole corner of the room around it, and the joyous notes of the song, the warmth of the house, the scent of the roast, and the sense of peace and love that fills him, makes him close his eyes with a deep, quavering sigh.

But the Second World War had already started and his brothers go off to the service, Eddy to a naval officers training school and Ernie to an army military police school. Roger's mother seems to slow down in some ways, seems to lie down on the bed in the afternoon a little more often, seems to get out of breath more quickly, her pale transparent skin turning pink with rosy spots of color from high blood pressure on her cheekbones. Her quick, efficient, almost birdlike motions are still there and her green eyes are as direct and piercing as ever when she looks at him but there is a fatigue she shows now. She often stops her busy activity and sits on a kitchen chair, her hands in her lap, her feet stretched out before her, taking deep breaths through her pink, unpainted mouth. She is forty-one years old, going on forty-two. There are dimples in her slightly puffy cheeks and a pale, doughy color to them and to the soft skin of her neck when she is still. Wrinkles streak down from the sides of her eyes into her cheeks. And it seems that her rimless glasses magnify the webs of wrinkles under her eyes, which have a stillness in them, a pale green deep inside the darker green, fading out in the inner distance as if her thoughts are somewhere else—with her two sons, wherever they are—as if she misses them, as if their absence is killing her.

Then suddenly she starts to bustle around, much more than usual, insists on getting up early and doing her housework in the mornings, then going down to the family's restaurant next to the Leamington Hotel, a neat little place specializing in lunches for the business crowd two blocks from the old lunch counter with higher prices, more fancy dishes, a higher income, and working there all day, then rushing home to prepare dinner for Roger and his younger sister, Belle. At night, she sews or embroiders or bakes something. She is always busy, busy, busy and seems to have people over for dinner every week, laying out her best silver and china, though she always entertains anyway.

Then one morning Roger goes into her room for lunch money and sees her lying in bed with her face swollen and a frown of pain on it. It hurts to look at her, her wavy black hair frizzy against the embroidered pillow. He gets his money out of her purse, doesn't even say goodbye, and slinks out of the house, hurt, but not worried yet. He begins to worry when she is taken to the hospital a couple of days later and doesn't come home right away but seems to stay and stay and stay. And one day after school when he goes to see her, she gives him the candy bars in her drawer and tells him to eat them because she never will and he gets scared. Then he begins to realize when she is in the hospital for more than a month that she might die.

3

Ernie comes home first from Texas on an emergency furlough from the army. From behind the curtain of a front window, Roger watches him step out of the cab in front of their big house and feels emotion rise up from his chest to his throat. He swallows to keep it down. Ernie's leg stretch is short and hesitant. He stops only a couple of steps from the cab near the curb, with his suitcase in his hand, a sunshine sheen on his summer tans across the broad spread of his shoulders. His small eyes in the shadow of his glimmering cap brim are dark and squinting. The Golden Gloves boxing champion of two states, with a small broken knot on the bridge of his strong nose, cheek bones protruding from his taut skin, his full upper lip puffed with shadow, his square jaw sinks instinctively down toward his thick chest from persistent training into the cover of his left shoulder as the cab hums away in first gear, leaving a blue cloud of exhaust, the burnt smell of carbon dioxide which envelopes him in its hazy waves.

Eddy comes home, too, his long aquiline nose hooking strongly over his full lips. His large, soft, hazel eyes are intensified by the black and white of his naval officer's uniform when he asks Roger if he has been eating balanced meals lately. He then puts a box of vitamins in the refrigerator and tells Roger to take one a day until they run out.

Nora always hugs Roger in the morning, presses him against her full breasts, her pretty face creasing in a smile, when he comes into her apartment to tickle the chin of her baby girl with the blond hair and blue eyes who has been born just before Christmas. Roger thinks it is wonderful to be an uncle so young and feels so good when the baby giggles and coos at him that he forgets his mother is sick.

But he wakes one night from a half-sleep to the ring of the phone in the downstairs hall. Nora's footsteps pad down the stairs, the ring stops. He isn't sure if he hears a small cry, the phone clanging down and footsteps running back up the stairs. But his head is still blurred with sleep and dreams. He isn't sure he's really heard anything. He may be only dreaming and he forgets the sounds, sinks back into warm safety. Later, he thinks he dreams of footsteps again. A door creaks. A crack of light shows under his bedroom door. Rustle of footsteps on the hall stairs. The front door opening and closing. Hollow footsteps on the front porch. Whinny of a car starter, whine of it dying. Whinny again. Then the engine coughs and kicks over, is gunned once, twice, three times nervously, impatiently, and then, once, twice, three times more and the car grinds off and away down the street, pop-pop-pops out of hearing. Sleep.

Gardenia scent soaks the air in the funeral home. There is wreath upon wreath of flowers up by the casket. A hundred people kneel in front of their metal chairs. A prayer chant: "Hail,

4

Mary, full of grace, the Lord is with thee. Blessed art thou amongst women and blessed is the fruit of thy womb, Jesus!" reverberates in the room, phrase upon phrase. Its echo lingers like the body heat and the sweet stench of gardenias, overlaps the dry notes of the next phrase, and chanting wave upon chanting wave of prayer and hot breath and echo beat upon Roger, kneeling upon a padded step close to the coffin, pounds in his ears, makes him gasp for breath, long for fresh air, and dizzy, nauseous, feeling like he must either throw-up or faint, he stands, a small boy in a tweed coat, and weaves back and forth over the bowed heads of the kneeling people, hands still clasped in prayer, lips still working, then suddenly lurches across the altar toward the open coffin, arms outstretched, his small figure a blur of motion, shoulders hunched, and grabbing her cold and pale hands, hard as stone, her death-swollen face and the sore on her lip blurring before him, spit spewing out of his mouth with his sobs, he cries, "Mother! Mother! Mother! Mother!"

But the steel gray coffin is closed for the funeral mass and looks as dead as a block of lead in the radiation of stained glass windows, hardly a reflection of light on it. But there is a single fold of white silk lining caught by the closed lid, a single fold of silk that sticks out next to the steel and in Roger's memory for forever and ever.

Cars straggle out behind the hearse for blocks on the way to the cemetery. It is a sunny day in the country. There are sprinkles of many-colored flowers over the green lawns. Gravestones. People stand all packed together. Black hole in the middle of them. Buzz of a priest's voice. Sobs of women, Nora. Coils of sunlight glimmer on little Belle's golden curls as she cries for her mother going down below. Shake belly of his father. Eddy stands in his black and white uniform, unbelieving, an atheist like his father but somber. Ernie lays his hand on Roger's shoulder and Roger squints his eyes in the glare of the sunshine and blinks them to keep the tears down, ashamed of the way he had become hysterical at the rosary the night before.

His father stops for a drink on the way home, walks up to the bar of a roadside nightclub and orders a double. "I just buried my wife," he says. "This is my baby son."

"Well, you're a man, anyway," the gray-haired bartender says as he pours the drink and his father downs it in one swallow and Roger feels proud. Then his father asks him if he wants something to eat, if he wants a hamburger, and finally, if he wants a coke and Roger says, "Yes, a coke," just to make him feel better. Later, at home, Eddy takes him aside and says, "You're going to have to take care of yourself a lot now that Mother's gone. And you must be careful that you don't let Dad spoil you. He loves you and he feels sorry for you, and trying to make himself feel better about it, he might try giving you things all the time. Do you understand me?"

"Yes," Roger says, "Like when we went into the bar and he kept trying to get me to have something although I didn't need anything."

"That's right," Eddy says and runs his hand over Roger's hair.

That afternoon, Ernie walks out of the house and stands in the shade of the front porch, looks up and down the street, quiet and empty, sits down on the top step, pushes up his soldier's cap and stares between his feet, the bulges of his shoulder muscles quivering. Roger opens the door to be with him, to console him, and Ernie's head swivels around and up with the sound, his eyebrows peak in the middle of his brow, then his eyelids go down, close, and he hides his face in his hands.

Ernie goes back to Texas the next day and Eddy goes back to the navy the day after that and their father goes back to work in the restaurant. Roger is supposed to eat dinner with Nora and Phil, though he only eats cornflakes for breakfast and loses interest in taking the vitamin capsules. They sit in the refrigerator and congeal. Except for the time he is with Nora and playing or taking care of his niece, he wanders around alone, sad, unable to forget that sore on his mother's lip. He cries when he is alone sometimes during the day and the hot sun makes his eyes water when he goes outside, and they soon begin to sting and hurt so badly that he cannot open them, not let in any light at all and he can't see to get out of bed. Nora comes into his room and sees his eyes and asks him what is wrong in a high, worried voice and that afternoon she makes their father come home and take him to the doctor. He then spends all of his time alone in his room, with bitterness simmering in him.

"Why didn't God save her?" he says, his thoughts bursting out into words, his head lifting off the pillow with the effort to speak, jutting forward, seeming to hang disembodied above his chest like some strange spaceman's head, goggle-like eyes made of gauze, egg-shaped like a mosquito's, an egg tone to them, a sick kind of yellow glaze from the daylight filtering through the drawn shades of the room. Ulcers in his eyes from the horrifying sight of his mother in the coffin. Darkness behind the patches. Darkness in the middle of the day.

Frightened by the sharp sound of his own words, the condemnation, the judgement of God in them, he lets his head sink slowly back to the pillow, feels the pillow slowly cushion his skull, as if by being careful he might not be noticed by God. For he is fearful. He is afraid God might strike him dead for what he said. He then lies still in the sulphurous aura of orange that suffuses the whole room, the color of the drawn shade that keeps the glare of the sunlight out, the sick cast of eye patches that spreads over his cheeks, and feels conscious of his skull and the bone sockets of his eyes. He has a sense of himself dead, lying still in a coffin, like her. His aching eyeballs are larded with healing salve, which oozes out of his closed lids, glues his lashes together, seals them, but cannot keep him from seeing his mother in the coffin with the sore on her lip. That sore on her lip. He is ashamed of that sore on her lip and her swollen mouth, the puffy look to her face. She looks sick. She doesn't really look like his mother.

He tries to think of something else. Silence again. He can feel tingles of tension with the slight hum of the war port city, the almost imperceptible buzz of noises deadened by the closed room. But the humming silence is too empty. There is nothing to do, and trying to fill the empty space in the room, he reaches for the radio but misses the knob and pokes the soft cloth over the speaker. He drags his fingers down to the knobs, finds the smaller one and turns it with a tiny click.

Crackling static for a second, deep hum, then a voice: "... thousand U.S. planes bomb ..." More static. He switches the dial, catches a blast of music, switches that away, hears: "... heavy task force that destroyed—" and the news of more death depresses him. He turns the radio off with a click and lets his hand drop listlessly down to the bed table. It clings motionless there by the heel of his palm until the table edge cutting across the wrist makes him become gradually aware of the tiny beat of his pulse, a pit, pit, pit, pit, pit, pit, pit.

It is a summer of shadows: shadows over his eyes, shadows in his mind, shadows in the funeral parlor, shadows on his father's face, shadows which fill the big house, the long coffin-shaped shadow of the upstairs hall. By midsummer he can see out again but he cannot escape the shadows within.

In school in the fall, class president, he cannot pay attention. All he can see is his mother's swollen face and that sore on her lip in the coffin and his father sitting by the big picture window in a black silk cowboy shirt, with silver stitching and pearl buttons, all evening, every evening until late at night, with the lace curtain tied back in a knot, something his mother would never have let him do when she was alive, listening to the Red River Valley—and the sweetheart who loved you so true, the song they had courted by, over and over again.

He gets reprimanded for daydreaming in class or for bringing a stray dog into metal shop or for playing with a knife Eddy brings back from the South Pacific or for cutting school to make a polliwog pond for some waterdogs he and his friends have found in a creek. He can't figure out why. He doesn't mean to do anything wrong. He still saves half his allowance every week, goes to confession every Saturday night and to Holy Communion every Sunday morning, though it doesn't thrill him like it did before his mother died.

7

His younger sister, Belle, is sent to live with an aunt and his older sister, Nora, tries to take care of him. She has him eat dinner with her every night, makes sure he eats his vegetables, gives a birthday party for him, is very sweet and motherly to him, and keeps him with her a good part of the time. He spends a lot of time playing with his baby niece. He loves her tow-blonde hair and her big blue eyes and the dimples in her cheeks, and he sobs hard when he lets her roll off the bed once and she bumps her head. He changes her diaper, takes her with him to see friends, pushes her in her baby carriage, carries her picture in his wallet and one day stuffs a big color portrait of her in his belt and peddles to school to show it to his homeroom teacher, Miss McFarland. He is always willing to watch her for his big sister and he is sad if he rushes out to school without going in to tickle her chin in the morning first. But he is sad anyway. He can't shake the sense of doom that hangs over everything. And one evening when he is in his sister's apartment and her baby is crawling on the floor while two young adult couples are watching, he says, "I wish I was a baby and didn't have troubles like her," and everyone breaks out laughing.

But he cries when Ernie finally comes home for good from the war and he and his father walk out to the parking lot from the train depot with him. It is true, really true. His brother, Ernie, is there in his army uniform in front of him, putting his suitcase and his gym bag in the trunk of the car. His husky, boxer brother, who takes him everywhere with him when he comes home on furloughs. He is home for good. For good. "Ernie, Ernie—" he tries to speak, then suddenly bursts out crying, sees his brother through his tears, sees him shimmering in front of him, glowing in the sunshine as if looking through a streaked window pane after a rain.

He sees him in the gym training, then in the ring fighting, sees his brother burst from his corner with the bell, charge the big, black guy at one-forty and after slipping under a long jab, coming in close, suddenly cut loose with a rally to the body and then lift them up with hooks to the head, knock the guy's head from side to side, drive him back across the ring and drop him in a corner with a right hook to the jaw as the crowd goes wild and the screams ring in Roger's ears, loud, loud, so loud it hurts until he suddenly realizes that he is screaming, too, that he is standing up below the corner with his arms raised, shouting, screaming in the glare of the ring lights.

Roger trains too, finally, but Ernie will not let him turn amateur until he gets out of high school. He gets his nose broken right away but he starts getting good with the gloves. He does not do much homework in highschool but reads on his own, reads a history of the Catholic Church by the lamplight of his bedroom and cries over the chapters on the Inquisition for he knows he will never be a practicing Catholic again. But he reads the Bible, too, the New Testament, as well as the progressive labor political tracts of his father, his oldest brother Eddy's books on philosophy and morals, and Nora's Book Club novels. He argues with his father about Jesus.

"By God, boy. You could be a preacher. They live a good life. I'll send you to divinity school after highschool, if you want to."

"I can't do it for money, Dad."

"Do it for any reason you want. They still live good and I'll still send you if you want to go. Think about it. Do you need any money now?"

"I could use my five dollar allowance."

"Here's ten," his father says, holding out the bill.

"I only want five, Dad," Roger says.

"Don't be a sucker. Take the ten. Don't turn down money."

"I just want five, Dad."

"Take the ten or nothing."

"Nothing then," Roger says and turns away.

But he has Dolly now. He loves her and she loves him. She has loved him since she was a plump, little blonde girl with freckles who used to come over and see his sister, Belle, and him, go climbing with him over fences and garages and up trees, over the roofs of churches. She has loved him since he saw a rough girl picking on her in junior high, since he saw the girl hit her in the face, then hit her again and again, though she tried to fight back—little girl who had never been in a fight, had never even seen one, now pawing at the air, ineffectually, trying to defend herself. Then suddenly, all of the pent up suffering over the death of his mother bursts out of him, and he breaks into tears, sobs, sobs and runs and grabs the girl by her hair and throws her to the ground, even hits her on the back until his friends pull him off her and the cops come and take him to juvenile hall. The next morning in the isolation cell, he tells the inspectors what happened and then recites the Boy Scout Oath for them. "On my honor I will do my best to do my duty to God and to my country. To obey the scout law, to help other people at all times and to keep myself physically strong, mentally awake and morally straight," and they let him go.

Dolly is now a very beautiful girl who looks older than her sixteen years, with golden hair which curls into a long pageboy on her shoulders, deep blue eyes, a perfect, pointed nose and a slightly pouting, sensual mouth; full-breasted and well-curved. He meets her at the candy store where she works every night and goes home with her to the clapboard duplex where she lives with her mother. But her mother, a beautiful woman with gray hair who looks older than her age because of her drinking, which always sets them back financially and forces them into poor neighborhoods and shabby apartments, is not home, and they start kissing as they have kissed a hundred times before. But they really kiss this time and he starts pressing her tightly to him, then starts petting her, caressing her breasts, and finally her box, slips his finger into her and soon they are on the couch, where he finally does it. After that they stop and sit in an old coupe that belongs to a friend of his and is parked only two blocks from her house and they do it before he takes her home. They do it one night when he doesn't have a rubber and she misses her period that month, then the next month and finally the third month. The capsules he gets from a friend don't work and they run off to Reno to get married.

But though Dolly gets fat and starts getting irritated and bitchy over every little thing, Roger gets the stomach cramps and morning sickness. Many mornings he throws up on his way to work at the library and has stomach cramps so bad, he thinks he has ulcers. One day, he gets his gym clothes to go to the gym to work out with Ernie, who has quit boxing after fighting out of shape once and getting knocked out, and now hangs around the nightclub owned by his manager, a pimp named Curly.

"You just don't want to be with me, do you?" Dolly says and when he tries to explain that he will only be gone a couple of hours, she locks herself in the bedroom of their apartment in the big house. And when he comes home from the gym, his brother-in-law, Phil, has a funny, commiserating look on his face and Roger finds a note from Dolly on the bed, saying goodbye, that she doesn't want to be hanging around his neck when he doesn't want her and she is going home to have her baby, without him.

Roger gets so mad he goes out and gets drunk with some friends and gets in a fight in a bar when a guy calls him "Sonny," knocks him out with an overhand right, runs outside and is chased by another man, knocks him out, too, with a left hook, and is arrested across the street from his father's restaurant at two-thirty in the morning, where he discovers the second man he hit was an off-duty cop.

Two blue-suited cops who book him beat him with black-jacks to the kidneys, the knees, and the belly. One is balding and his blue-toned face twists with sadism when he slugs Roger. And he keeps slugging Roger until he pretends that he is afraid of them and cringes in a corner. They then strip him nude, order him to turn around, and try to poke him in the ass with a billyclub, but he dodges it and when they order him to turn around again, he refuses and they leave him alone, then take him up to the felony cells.

He doesn't like onions, has never liked spicy food but finds himself making onion sandwiches of old bread by the third day in the dark cells. He doesn't drink coffee either but he starts by the second day just to get warm. The young black trusty who brings the black coffee says, "Yeah, yeah, I know you're innocent," through the bars and so amazes Roger, who was just going to say that, that Roger doesn't even answer, just stares at the young man.

"Say," the trusty says, when Roger doesn't answer, "are you the rich kid?"

And Roger is embarrassed again. His father owns a business and that is the only real difference between him and the trustee as far as he knows. He has worked over a year already and knows what it is to have to earn his own money. He doesn't answer again and the trustee moves off, the big tin pitcher ringing against the guy's tin cup in the next cell.

Two inspectors question him. One is a big, fat cop in a dirty, wrinkled gray suit, with a bald head and beard stubble on the folds of his double chins, who plays the nice guy. The other is a clean-featured, clean-shaven, pink-skinned, gray-haired cop in a neat suit who tells Roger he would have shot him if he tried to hit him and tries to scare him into confessing, then pretends he just wants to get the facts. "Just sign a statement giving your side of the story and we'll charge you with battery."

Roger signs and the next day the cops come in with two warrants charging him with felonious assault, setting his bail at fifteen thousand dollars and facing him with a sentence of one to ten years on each count, if convicted.

His father has just opened a new restaurant and can't afford to bail Roger out and pay an expensive lawyer three thousand dollars, too. Neither can Eddy, who has just borrowed money himself to open a new pharmacy in a medical building, and Ernie's help is out of the question, for he has now become a party boy, whose wife and two kids are fed by Roger's father with food from the restaurant. So, Roger, who keeps expecting to go to trial right away, has to do four and a half months of dead time waiting for trial, always waiting to hear his name called.

It isn't just the waiting day after day, though, responding to the rattle of keys like a guinea pig, tense, alert, head raised, eyes bright, hoping, wanting and expecting to hear his name called, "Leon! Roll 'em up!" or the going to court week after week, building himself up each time for the ordeal of the trial, then finding it postponed again, week after week after week. It isn't just the boredom, the anxious and excruciatingly slow passing of time, in which he learns to tell how close it is to dinner hour, once a day at three o'clock, by the shadow of the bars on the cell floor, or the constant hunger, the bickering over a pan of peaches that is given to the cleanup crew of the tank, until he throws his spoon down one day and says, "I'll be Goddamned if I'll act like an animal anymore," and refuses his share but is hungry enough to argue for his share the next day over the next pan. It isn't just wondering what is going to happen to him, whether he will be found guilty and then sent to Youth Authority or the county farm or even San Quentin, which gives him so much anxiety. It isn't just the violent homosexuals and the fights. It is more being cut off from the people he loves, his family, and especially his wife. Oh, he misses her and is so sorry that he hadn't gone to get her instead of feeling sorry for himself and going out and getting drunk, then getting into trouble when she left him.

When she comes to see him at the county jail, after the baby is born, one of the young ex-convicts says, "That's finger-stuff," and guys start to tease him about her, saying he better look out or he is going to lose her and make him suffer so badly that he writes her sad, accusing letters. He suffers so badly that an oldtime con named Fox takes him aside and says, "Look at the guys who are teasing you. Not one of them has a girl who loves him, who even comes to see him. They're jealous. Now, if you want to live through this dead time, you'll learn to relax and live with it. Now write to your wife and tell her that you trust her, that you understand that she's suffering, too, and that you want her to be happy, and that she has your love, and she'll probably be true to you."

Roger writes to her and she sends him back a love letter saying, "I'll love you forever, Roger, and be true to you forever. I'll never let you down. Believe me. My sweetheart." And tears come to his eyes.

Eddy–A Life Potential

White smock buttoned up to his neck, his round pink face glowing in the bright reflections of light through the window and off the white walls of the pharmacy and the glass jars and vials of the glass-enclosed prescription booth, Eddy stares past Roger out the wall-wide front window, with the blue and green crystal balls hanging in its separate corners and a walnut frame around it like a painting. His slightly protruding eyes are dreamy and moist as if he is seeing nothing but the inner sights of his mind as he says, "I can tolerate Dad now. I no longer hate him. I can say that I've gained that much maturity. Now when he doesn't give me a present or even congratulate me on my birthday or invest any money in the pharmacy when both of his brothers do, I might cry and feel a little sorry for myself after a couple of drinks, but I don't hate him. Mother used to say—"

He turns full face to Roger and looks at him with yellow-flecked green eyes nearly identical to Roger's, pausing as if to pull his mind back from his mother and father to his younger brother and says, "I used to say, 'I hate him! I hate him!' And she'd say, 'Don't say that!' and look through her glasses at me with those really quick eyes. But her face would get soft and pink and her voice would be both kind and stern at the same time and she'd say, 'Some day when all you children are grown up, your father and I will live alone. We'll still have a life to share after you've all gone. He's my man and a real man even if he acts like a boy sometimes—and he's your father. And you've got to become man enough to love him with his faults, his insensitivity, though he never thinks of how other people feel. You've got to see that he's good and kind, that he never means wrong. You've got to see the good in him and not just his faults, or *you'll* never be a man.' "

Eddy looks off through the window again. He looks round and bloated to Roger with those protruding eyes and soft, pinkish skin, almost as if he were decaying. Eddy should exercise, Roger thinks, as Eddy looks out the corners of his large eyes at him.

"I've never become a man, Roger. Because I'm still not man enough to love him."

Roger sits up on the high druggist's stool in his clerk's white jacket, his wavy hair falling in curls over his forehead, and checks an urge to reach out and touch his brother. But still wanting to soothe his feelings, he spreads his hands and, avoiding any mention of their father, says, "Even if you're not a pro boxer like Ernie or had a couple of amateur fights like me, you're still a man, more of a man than either Ernie or me, because you've done more in a man's world. You've succeeded at everything. You've proved to the world that you're brilliant. You won every scholarship that the public schools and colleges could give. You've gone to Cal and Harvard. You've been a naval officer in war time, been decorated for it, studied medicine, published short stories, and have your own successful pharmacy, and you're only thirty. You've proved you're a man to the whole world. You've really lived and accomplished as much as a man in his fifties. You're an exceptional man, Eddy."

"Not to Dad," Eddy says and looks around him at the shelves, neatly stacked with vials and jars and boxes of medication, no sundry goods ("This is a professional drug store, not a supermarket," he always says), then glances down at the new issue of "The Peoples World," a Marxist weekly, lying on the prescription counter with ads from his pharmacy and their father's restaurant in it. He has often told Roger tales about their atheist grandfather, his radical populism in a 19th Century cowtown infested with superstitious Catholics, about their father's union radicalism and about his own Marxism, his belief in The People, enforced by his stay in France. And he has encouraged Roger in his desire to become a lawyer and help people. His round face then gets pink and animated as if a quick glance around his own store has reassured him, but his bulbous eyes become hazy and dreamy again, soft with an inner ache.

"Oh, yes you are. Dad thinks you're a man," Roger says, afraid to reach out and touch his brother now for fear it will make him seem weak. "You are a man, more of a man than either Ernie or me. I'll never be as much of a man as you."

"Oh yes you will," Eddy says. "I'm ten years older than you, Roger, but you're already more of a man. You're more of a man to Dad. You're a man's man, and I'm bisexual. Even if Dad doesn't know that, he knows, he feels that I'm not manly enough. He's always felt that I wasn't manly enough. I used to embarrass him because I wasn't rugged enough as a boy."

"But, Eddy, you were always brave," Roger says. "One of my earliest memories is of you knocking Ernie flat with a bloody nose when he tried to sneak out one night when Mom and Dad weren't home."

A quick smile crosses Eddy's full mouth and he nods, then says, "But you'll surpass me. You'll achieve more."

"Oh, no," Roger says. "At my age, you were already a sophomore at Cal and making straight A's. I haven't even started school yet, got myself all tied down and put in jail. How could you say that?"

14

"Because you're more manly, Roger. I'm not just feeling sorry for myself. I tend to pat myself on the back too much as it is. But you see, men will feel your manliness and they'll give you more respect, they'll open a bigger world for you."

"I don't see how I could possibly surpass you," Roger says, shaking his head. "I'm so far behind, I'll never even be near you at your age."

"I may not even be around when you're my age," Eddy says and turns away again, looks off through the window.

"What do you mean?" Roger says and sits up stiff-backed on the high stool.

"Because I might kill myself, Roger," Eddy says and faces him again with his heavy lips pursed.

"Oh, no, don't say that," Roger says. "You have everything to live for. Nobody has done as well as you."

"Dad doesn't seem to think so," Eddy says, looking off through the window again. "Mother died this day seven years ago."

The conversation bothers Roger badly the rest of the day. He goes about his deliveries, mopping the floor, laundering the smocks, tending the store with a depressing vision of Eddy in the same casket as his mother, looking like her, his face puffy like hers. He then comes back and looks closely at his brother, seeing the sight inside his head and the living brother in his pinkish flesh there in front of him, a glow to him in his white pharmacist's smock, his face broad now, the large hooked semitic-looking nose now gone, cut off by a naval doctor, with a small pink button in its place, giving him a moon face, bloated the way it is, rather than the handsome craggy one he had when he joined the navy. The nose job has been so poorly done that a decaying hole has appeared in the bridge and Eddy now wears a flesh-colored band-aid over it. Yet, even this evidence of dying flesh cannot make him believe that the brother standing in front of him will ever be dead.

The next morning the pharmacy window is dark when he gets to work. There is hardly a shimmer of reflection on it and the wooden frame which encloses it like a picture, with the red and green crystal balls in its upper corners, holds a shadowy still-life. The glass front door which opens out onto the stone porch of the small medical building is closed and locked, too, and pressing his face against the cool glass, Roger can tell that not even the back room lights are on, though it is after nine in the morning and Eddy never opens late, no matter how little sleep he had the night before from being out on deliveries or coming home late from an after-hours place. He drops the pink heart of a dexie pill, washes his face, makes coffee and gets to work. Yet, the green chevrolet that Roger uses to deliver prescriptions with is parked out in front of the store in the reserved white zone and

Roger is confused. For it means that Eddy is inside.

He walks down the stairs and crosses the wide sidewalk to the car to try the door, finds it open, and sits down inside with the door ajar to wait for his brother to appear, expecting him to come down the sidewalk from either direction or out of the medical building where the dentist-landlord has his office and a suite of rooms with his wife, adolescent son and daughter. He is bisexual too, descended from Latin American stock and sensitive about his Indian blood though he is a wealthy, selfmade man of Caucasian features, married to a pale white wife of upper class origin. But Dr. Santos is also fond of Bill, Eddy's lover, and jealous of Eddy because of Bill, because of Eddy's brilliance, and because of the fact that he is an American of pioneer stock before being a Latin, but mostly because of Bill.

Roger stares down the street of the Tenderloin section of San Francisco, a lonely, deserted neighborhood on a quiet sunny morning. The nightclubs and girly shows with their neon signs and dusty showcase windows look a little shabby by daylight and depress him. He begins to worry over Eddy's words about killing himself the day before, and though he continues to sit in the car after the meaning of the conversation first occurs to him, he can't get it out of his mind. Finally, he gets out of the car, slams the door, and goes up the stairs to the pharmacy door again.

He tries it once more, looks past the lettering on the glass: LEON PHARMACY, MEDICAL PRESCRIPTIONS ONLY, and into the interior at the glass-enclosed prescription booth with its chin-high counter, the cash register next to it, and the small passageway between them that leads up to the sleeping alcove where two camp cots sit between walls of books.

He must be upstairs asleep, Roger thinks, but the taut skin of his forehead wrinkles with worry and he tries the door again, shakes the knob, then turns and hops down the stone steps to the sidewalk. He hurries, taking long steps, his arms swinging, his wiry torso in a sport shirt and sweater straight-backed, his curly-haired head up on his long neck, moving with the easy speed of an athlete, past the front window and down the basement stairs of the building into the Turkish Bath below the pharmacy, through the long hallway with the lush, bright tropical flowers painted on its walls, into the big steamy massage room at the back of the building with the separate private booths and swimming pool, where he tries the door to the back stairs of the pharmacy, then tells the small foreign masseur with the rapier mustache and flour-white skin that he is going to climb through a bath window in the airshaft into the supply room window a floor above, then props the masseur's ladder against the building and climbs up to the window, which he knows is unlocked.

He has to lean back at the top of the ladder to open the window, which opens out like a door, then sticks his head and shoulders into the darkened room and steps over the sill into the sink, where he stops when he sees his brother wrapped in an army blanket on the floor with his head to him, and smiles, thinking, "Poor guy, he's wiped out," then pulls his other leg in and lets himself quietly down to the floor so as not to scare his brother, tip-toes past him through the room, past the passageway with the stairs leading up to the alcove, and out into the front room where he turns on the lights and opens the front door to get ready for business.

But he stops with his hand still on the knob of the open door, his right eyebrow arched, listening, suddenly scared for he has been expecting sounds of Eddy awakening and there is only total silence. He stares into the darkness of the back room but can hear or see nothing, then lets go of the knob and steps quickly back past the cash register, through the passageway and into the room where he switches on the light above the desk and sees his brother lying on the floor with deep blue circles under his eyes and his full lips cracked open and dry.

"Eddy! Eddy!" He screams and jerks the phone off the base and, hands trembling, dials the operator, seems to wait minutes for the mechanism to click and the line to buzz, for the operator to finally answer, his brother lying motionless on the floor across from him.

"Send an ambulance, please! My brother is dying! 231 Ellis Street! Hurry! Hurry!" he cries and slams the receiver down and runs past his brother down the back stairs and out the back door into the Turkish Bath where, his face contorted, eyes round, mouth wide, he shouts, "Masseur! Masseur! My brother is dying! Come quick!" then runs back in, but the door slams behind him, and he jumps back out and holds the door open for the little man who runs in his undershirt past him up the short flight of stairs into the room and drops down on one knee, throws the army blanket back, and presses down and up on Eddy's stomach, making his cracked lips part with a moaning groan, "Uuuuuuuuuuh!" The masseur does it again and again with smaller sounds each time. Now Roger's hopes, which rose with the first groan, sink with his sagging face on each succeeding try.

Finally, he hears a siren and runs back up to the front of the store and out onto the sidewalk where he waves at the ambulance, stops it right out in front, and motions for the attendants, who jump quickly out to follow him. He leads them at a run into the store and straight to the back room where they lift Eddy, blanket and all, onto the stretcher, carry him out to the ambulance, let Roger jump in, then shoot down the street to the corner. The driver turns right down Mason for two blocks, then turns right up Market Street, siren wailing, the back doors flying open as the ambulance zigzags in and out of traffic, around cars, over the streetcar tracks, through red lights, while one attendant keeps an oxygen mask over Eddy's face and Roger sits facing the back, his hand touching the cold hand of his brother.

Eyes dry, heart aching, the siren screaming in his ears, Roger watches the wide street waving away from him, the marquees and automobiles, the shiny streetcar tracks, the people on the crowded sidewalks of the main boulevard turning to stare, and knows that he will never forget, that what he sees and cannot stop to think about now will stick in his mind forever. And he has the presence of mind to jump out first when the ambulance stops and hold the doors open for the dark-haired driver who runs around from the cab and says, "Good boy!" as he pulls out the stretcher, then takes the front end with the other attendant carrying the back end and hurries into the emergency ward with his brother.

Roger follows them down the white-tiled corridor to the emergency operating room where a nurse closes the door in his face and makes him stop, turn, and pace back and forth, back and forth in the corridor, his hands in his pockets, his head down, his hair falling over his forehead, his eyes on the small, shiny white squares which stretch endlessly before him, suppressing sobs in his throat, needing, wanting to cry, but unable to while there is still hope that his brother will live, reliving over and over again the moaning grunt which came out of his brother's mouth, counting on it, needing to count on it, though still unable to forget those words of suicide, the talk of their father and mother as he paces back and forth, back and forth, staring at the frosted window of the emergency room door as he walks toward it, glancing back at it after he turns to start back in the other direction.

He has gone halfway back down the hall for what seems the hundredth time when he finally hears the door open behind him, and he spins around to see the young blond doctor step out and walk slowly down the tile floor toward him like some white apparition: white hair, white skin, white smock, white floor, white walls, white door behind him. His head lowered, his tall body slack, but his eyes on Roger, sizing him up as he approaches, his mouth coming half-open when he stops a couple of feet from him as if afraid to speak. Roger looks into his light eyes for a moment, then says, "He's dead, isn't he?" and the young doctor nods.

"I hope he chose it," Roger says. "I hope he did it on purpose." Then he turns away and steps into a phone booth in the hall, drops a dime in the coin slot, dials a number, and waits in the thick, wired-glass enclosure until his father answers the phone.

"Dad," he says. "Eddy is dead."

"Whaaaaaa? Whaaaaaaat!"

"Eddy is dead, Dad! Eddy is dead!" Roger says, his voice

breaking with a sob and he smashes his fist through the glass wall of the booth, tearing big gaping holes in his hand.

His father seems to get old fast, slow down, lose business. He has a lot of gray hair around the fringes of his bald head now, lines where there were none on his smooth face. Jowls. He sits in the garden a lot. He's not his expansive self, doesn't keep everyone entertained at dinner anymore. He eats more, gains weight, moves less. He peeks out the door when Roger goes away sometimes as if he is afraid he won't see him again and wants to get a last look. "I love you, Daddy," Roger says, touched by it and he knows he will never ever tell his father about his last talk with Eddy.

Dad gives Ernie Eddy's car after the funeral if he gets a job and starts training again. But Ernie keeps partying and Dad takes the car back and gives it to Roger, who feels so guilty he gives it back to Dad. But Ernie talks about their father now for taking away the car. He starts chippying with junk. Then he starts to steal. He becomes a booster, boosting out of the downtown stores. He starts to lose his hair and by the fall of the year he is skinny and has dark circles under his eyes and hollows in his cheeks and wears wrinkled clothes with burn holes in them from going on the nod with a cigarette in his hand.

Nora gets sloppy with the house, though less so about her person. She is still a striking brunette with the fine soft features of a very feminine woman, but she gains weight, gets plump, and lets her house get cluttered. She swears now, too, lots of Goddamns and Hells, and talks about divorcing Phil when she has too many drinks. When Roger tells her about it as tactfully as he can, she says, "Mother and Eddy worked hard, were very, very good and both died young. I want to live a long time and enjoy my life."

Dolly works hard at her job as a bank clerk. She cries after the funeral, twists and turns and sobs in bed for Eddy. She gets very thin. Her breasts are only palmfuls. "Feed her!" a friend says once. But she is sad because Roger is sad. She knows he now needs much more out of life than she can give him. Though they love each other.

Eddy's moon face, deep blue circles under his eyes, cracked lips puffing apart with that final breath, "Uuuuuuuuuh!" wakes Roger. The bedroom is a heavy blanket of smothering darkness. Horror. Hopelessness. He is afraid to go back to sleep, afraid the face will come back and haunt him again.

But it stays with him even when he wakes in the morning unrested, feeling light in the brain as if he hasn't slept enough or has slept too much and his mind feels heavy, sluggish. He thinks of his brother on the floor wrapped in that army blanket and fights the guilty feeling that comes over him for not realizing sooner that something was wrong and for not going through the back window right away, maybe getting in there in time to save Eddy's life, maybe .

"PRIVATE—Edwin Leon, Jr." the small bound notebook says on the green cover.

"Each person has a life potential," it says on the first page and Roger has to stop and pause and wait until the picture of his brother dead on the floor passes, then swallows and begins to read.

"Each person has a life potential. Each person has a purpose for being here—good or bad. Each person is a minute cog in the way of life. The length of this potential may be influenced by the activities of one's life, environment and *friends*. Everybody has to work. Always while on earth a person must work—see physics definition (i.e., a transference of energy from one body to another.)—the idea to approach is a state where one is content with the work one does. The real way to live is to live today! Upon passing on, there are no regrets for oneself. Life may have been full and the purpose served—but was he happy? Define word happiness. When one passes on the dirt claims you. A death when one suffers a major death—as of Mother—if one doesn't believe— the suffering is harder. There is no faith, no belief, no beautiful talk of that great day to heal or ease the suffering or tightening within one's rib cage. When life has ceased—it has ceased to be forever—you become part of the hillside. Hope my hillside is green. But after death what matters? A body should be laid to rest if circumstances are such; otherwise the spirit of the individual be allowed to infect the bereaved even if only in a minute degree—then life goes on—the sun still shines, the surf still roars and women still continue to have babies.

"One rule—be happy, it's infectious. Remember, that with each disaster suffered, and each hardship endured, new strength emerges to cope with other stones or pebbles that may rise to hurt one's feet while treading the path of life.

"Won't say life is boring!"

Roger takes the diary with him. He reads it often. He cannot shake off his brother's suicide. One night as he waits for the bus in front of the Terminal building alone, he paces back and forth by the bench, oppressed by the inability of his brother to be happy, to love his father, and the dead-end all his brilliance and goodness has come to. The frustrating pain builds up with such great pressure that he suddenly stops and lifts up his head to the dark, clouded sky and words burst out his lips, pour out of him in a flood. As he speaks, he does not think. He listens, rather, to each emotion laden word that rises out of him, each word that somehow helps to clear his mind and ease the constriction in his throat, the tightening in his rib cage, the ache in his heart.

"I love you, Eddy, and I miss you. I really miss you. And I

swear by your memory and my love for you that I'll try to achieve the image you had of me, that I'll try and live up to that ideal. I swear I'll do good on this earth, that I'll try and achieve happiness in the here and now by your concept of work as the transference of energy from one body to another. I'll work at something which will bring me personal contentment and will help others, too. Something, not law, which is too dry, too unsatisfying, but something in the arts, writing or painting. Something like you wanted for yourself, after Mother's death killed your will to be a doctor, killed the reason you worked so hard, so diligently, killed the main driving impulse to save her and everyone like her, which grew so large during her long years of heart trouble, from the day I was born. I swear that I'll work as you believed not for subsistence but for self-fulfillment, that I'll seek the freedom of the creative artist, the free man, to do significant, meaningful work, the transference of energy, physical and spiritual, from one body to another, work, Eddy, that would have kept you from committing suicide if you had only followed your own advice."

He reads his brother's books as soon as he gets home from work in the afternoon, reads until dinner and after dinner, until the words blur across the page and he falls asleep with a book in his hands. He has already been influenced by his family's reading tastes. Nora loves popular novels, his father history and geography, socialist pamphlets and the Police Gazette. His mother influenced him in a religious direction though she did not read much and Ernie did not read at all. But Eddy is a renaissance man and his library is universal and socially oriented, from novels like "Sons and Lovers," which reminds Roger so much of Eddy, who was so close to their mother, to "Leaves of Grass" to "The Basic Writings of Sigmund Freud" to "Studies in the Intellectual Development of Karl Marx."

Roger begins to believe that there is no contradiction between Jesus and Marx. Both were humanists and both revolutionaries. Jesus was born as a threat to the state and died as a threat to the state, the so-called King of the Jews. Roger goes through the whole New Testament underlining all the words with political meanings. And he feels that Marx's insistence on man living in the here and now, his proposed utopia on earth instead of in the heavens by and by is another manifestation of the Judaic prophecy of the Kingdom of Heaven here on earth, what Eddy believed. And Marx was a Jew, too, descended from a long line of distinguished rabbis.

Roger never forgets his brother, Eddy, answering the phone in the prescription booth, signalling him to pick up the extension in the back room, from where Roger hears a voice say, "I've been a friend of yours and a customer of your store for years. But if you don't withdraw your ad from the *People's World* I will not buy from you anymore." To which Eddy replies in a sharp, articulate tone: "All my friends are intellectuals. So that doesn't include you. And, furthermore, I have only been in the business for less than a year. Thank you and goodbye."When Roger joins him in the prescription booth, he says, "Some rightwing group or the FBI probably."

Roger never forgets that though his father has owned first class restaurants, coffee shops and skid row bars, as well as several houses and has been a landlord all his life, he sometimes dresses in a white, starched, flowery shirt, black tuxedo pants, and a red cummerbund around his wide waist and looks a colorful figure with his bald head and ready smile, bright teeth flashing under a thin, black mustache. When he has a good dinner house going, he always tells stories of his working man days, that middle period of his life, between being a rancher's son and a small businessman, when he was on the road, on the bum, he calls it sometimes, when the whole country was moving from the farms to the cities.

But he never forgets either that his father won't join the Party, that he considers it a trap and that he often warns Roger against all politicians, profiteers and the police, saying, "Politicians aren't worth a damn! People are!"

He never forgets either that Eddy told him that the Russians forced the people into a one-party state and broke any sentimental attitudes he had about Russia and its great socialistic experiment. He sees that Marx, the seeker of freedom, made a mistake, that a dictatorship of the proletariat is a basic contradiction of terms, that if the proletariat really rules it is a democracy not a dictatorship, and that a dictatorship destroys the personal freedom and the individual flexibility necessary to solve the concrete problems, the contradictions of the people on a local level and in the society as a whole. He sees that there is a difference between the economic and the political structures of a society, that socialism might be a better economic policy for the people than capitalism but that democracy is a better political framework than a dictatorship of the people, which is a misnomer, for it turns out to be a dictatorship of the party leader, and that the great thing to fear after a revolution is not just a counter-revolution by bourgeois elements but also the suppression of an ongoing revolution by party bureaucrats, with their vested power interests. The most important thing of all is to have the freedom to fight the fascists of whatever color, flag, nationality or ideology, the MVD or the FBI, Beria or J. Edgar Hoover, the Rockefellers or the party bureaucrats, all the oppressive enemies of freedom. Freedom, that is the issue, that is what is at stake. Political freedom. Economic freedom. Spiritual freedom. Freedom is the key to progress and unfettered evolution, the end result of a genuine peoples' revolution.

But he must work, too, and he spends his twenties on a

hundred jobs, enough jobs to keep him in school, studying, searching for the tools to set him free from menial jobs of pure subsistence, to reach a level where his work will be as meaningful as his studies. There are no movements in the Eisenhower Fifties, so he trains himself, he sharpens his tools. He prepares himself. It is a hard job. He often has to quit school and take full time jobs to make more money, to get them out of the hole. He works hard. His wife helps him. His son grows. When he reaches the first grade, they both quit their jobs and go to school together for a year, until they run out of money again. His father buys him a small apartment house and he keeps working, studying, gets one degree and finally heads for another. But he realizes that he must *do* something socially, that study is not enough, that even the act of writing fiction is not enough if the world is to be made better, if his life is to have some truly significant meaning and not become dead-end, like Eddy's. And he joins the all-night vigil with a crowd of ten thousand people outside the gates of San Quentin the night before Caryl Chessman is to be executed.

He identifies with Chessman (he can't get over that name: chess-man, a pawn in the hands of political forces) because of the short but terribly long time he spent in a cell himself and he gets excited by a black ex-convict's words over the microphone on the suffering he has endured while waiting to be executed on Death Row, before his conviction was overturned by the courts and, pentup, shaking, Roger asks to speak and is given the microphone.

He has no idea of what he is going to say and when he sees the huge crowd and the spotlights poking up into the black night, the blur of faces looking up at him, he stutters, then stops and catches himself and begins again. "I was put in jail for hitting a cop in civilian clothes when I was eighteen. But when I was there I came to know several killers and in almost every case it was a series of misfortunes and injustices which finally led the men to commit murder and even then as much by accident as design, as if they were pawns in the grip of social forces beyond their control. They were as much victims as criminals. I tell you, they didn't even know what they were doing."

The cheers of the crowd interrupt him and his fear leaves him. But the energy, the passion still swells in him, seems answered by the crowd, seems fired by the crowd, and he says, "Governor Brown is a hypocrite and a liar who makes eloquent messages to the state legislature on his opposition to capital punishment, yet refuses to commute Chessman's death sentence to life imprisonment after the Senate has tied forty to forty for the abolition of capital punishment in California. Forty to forty! What more could he want?"

The crowd laughs and claps and Roger continues: "And I tell you that he won't take the chance—and not much of a chance when half the representatives of the state agree with him—because he wants to have complete control of the state's delegates to the Democratic National Convention in Los Angeles this summer, as a favorite son, and he doesn't want to offend the Democratic authorities in Los Angeles, who want Chessman dead. I tell you that the liberal Governor of our state is playing corrupt politics with a man's life for his own personal advancement. He's willing to let Chessman die on the chance he can get on the national ticket as the Vice presidential candidate. This is what he's done to Chessman! This is why we're all here tonight! This is why Chessman is going to die!"

A huge burst of applause rings out and everyone claps and cheers and rises to their feet and when he steps down from the microphone people crowd around him and reporters come to question him and find out who he is and where he came from. A group of radicals ask him to go to Sacramento with them and one older man insists when Roger declines that they can do more good by marching around Governor Brown's mansion all night to convince him to commute the sentence than spending the whole night in front of the prison gates.

Everyone claps when Governor Brown comes out of the mansion in the morning in a handsome brown suit and asks, "But where are you people from?" Roger answers, "They're all students and teachers!" which most of them are but he sees the Governor stop and draw into himself, and he feels he's made a mistake, that he should have said there was a cross-section of the population there, but still trying to fight back, to save Chessman, he adds, "They're saying on all the campuses that you won't commute the death sentence because you want to control all the California delegates to the National Convention as a favorite son this summer!" Brown's mouth falls open. But Chessman dies at ten o'clock and Roger never forgets that either.

He is in line marching with a sign up Market Street to protest the invasion of the Bay of Pigs, escorting the symbolic coffin of democracy to the Federal Building in downtown San Francisco. He even steps out of line when an agent takes a photograph of him so the guy can get a good shot, proud to be photographed by the FBI, proud to be fighting for liberty, for putting his philosophy on the line, no matter how much he thinks of John F. Kennedy personally, and believes that he is being socially useful, that he is a patriot in the tradition of the first American revolutionaries, the Fathers of the Constitution, and that he will someday help bring true democracy to the country and to the world, eventually, a blend of Marx and the Bill of Rights. He believes he is fulfilling his brother's concepts of work and happiness in all aspects of his life, as a student, as an artist, and as a revolutionary. He really believes it when he sees State College and Catholic College fraternity boys snatch signs out of girls' hands and break them, charge through lines of pacifists with V-shaped wedges and knock them down, trample on them. But when the bully boys reach the inner circle around the symbolic wooden coffin, he blocks the path of the little redheaded guy carrying a large American flag propped from a belt around his waist and says, "If you dare to push through this line, I'll bust you in your mouth!" And the flagbearer turns pale, closes his shouting mouth, and stops and then finally backs off into the packed crowd and the charge is stopped. He never forgets that either.

Ellen inspires him. Soft, pretty face, slightly plain, plump, tan skin the color of her pale brown hair. She, too, wants to oppose all militarism, of all the countries, the Soviet Union as well as the United States. She too wants to unite all the splinter groups, who are usually at each other's throats, in a big peace rally and spread love and pacifism throughout the warrior state. She, too, wants to fly the flag of solidarity with all the peoples of the world and only through peace will it be possible. Peace is the most important goal in a world divided by the cold war, peace which will give people a chance to talk to each other, then understand each other and love each other and solve all their mutual problems together. Peace. There must be peace pure as the sacred heart of Jesus. Peace. Peace.

"Yes, we should go to this peace rally," the plump Young Socialist President says, waving his fat hands in the air, "Definitely, we should go." He is speaking at a banquet table in a backroom covered with plastic vines in a restaurant owned by some old time wobblies. He peeks down through the glasses on his nose at his seated disciples. "But we should go with one thought in mind and one thought foremost: to go to this rally with the idea of making it pay off for us. That's the right way to go. Power is what makes the world go round and power is the game we're playing."

Roger stands up to end the furious clapping. "Your Chairman is exactly wrong," he says. "His attitude is exactly what the rally is supposed to try and remedy. You must go to the peace rally because you want peace and brotherhood, not just to feather your own nest. There will never be a change in consciousness from the competitive to the cooperative if you, the young, continue the Machiavellian politics of the old, which has brought the world to a cold war and to the verge of destruction now. Go because you want to be brothers with all the peoples of different persuasions not because you want to rule. Thank you."

One coed claps hard for him but the others sit in silence.

"You're a good speaker," a young anarchist says when he steps out of the backroom, but the Young Socialist Club does not join the rally.

"There are more important things for the Student Political Committee to use their energy on than a peace rally," Slugger, one of the Houlihan brothers, says, but Roger knows it is really because he unwittingly told some other radical leader they, the family, wouldn't join because of the Party, and angry, he shouts,

"That's a cheap political trick, Slugger! Why don't you tell the students why you really oppose it?" Then he walks out of Ellen's house with his wife, gets back in his car and with her driving, says, "I'm glad it's over. It was a lot of trouble for small rewards. It's crazy anyway, trying to join bickering groups together. I'm just going to work hard on my studies and my novel. I'm tired of politics. I didn't know trying to save the world was so sneaky." He notices a Volkswagen with two men in it staying close to them all the way home but he doesn't think much of it until months later.

The next day Ellen meets him in the cafeteria and says, "We won! The rally's on! The vote was nearly unanimous after you left the house! The rally's on!"

When the Russians set off a fifty megaton hydrogen bomb, the Quaker at the school cafeteria table keeps staring at Roger and hinting they should do something about it. Roger knows what the frecklefaced guy is doing but he gets excited anyway, his emotions flame up with the new cause and he says, "Alright! I'll help organize an all-night vigil! Just come to the activities office with me!"

When the school paper gives them front page coverage and a lot of publicity to Roger as the main organizer, several people cool toward him and one girl, who did not stay up the whole night, says, "You enjoy the glory! That's what motivates you!"

"No, it isn't," Roger says and he soon gets a chance to prove it. But in spite of the disillusioning aspects, he has learned from his organizing experience. One, he can speak to and influence crowds. Another, the range of opinions and attitudes of the radical and dissenting groups on any given issue is enormous. Another and often times as important, they are often selfish, narrow-minded and egotistical. Others are really pure, usually those who are not leaders and who do not think of themselves as professionals, especially the anarchists. Another more somber thing is they all live in fear of the FBI and some are very suspicious and secretive for that reason, tending toward a cynical negativeness. Many just follow the party line of whichever party and others are fiercely independent to the point of being excluded from some organized radical activities because they are too radical. But the experiences have been rich and the fire is still burning in him. He has energy to burn and the memory of his brother, Eddy, comes to hurt less and inspire him more, as long as he is busy, engaged in work, in doing and not just existing, when he is sure he is fulfilling himself and living up to the personal and social responsibilities, the radical ideals handed down to him. There is no deep sadness then, just a lingering melancholy when he stops and speaks to his brother's portrait, an oil painting as alive as his dead brother was, and tells him what he is doing and how it is an attempt to live up to him and his ideals.

The Setup

"You know I can speak Spanish well, Roger?" George says and Roger nods, remembering George's reactionary South American friends and their suspicious floor model radio which was turned on though it made no sound during the impromptu debate the night of the Fair Play for Cuba meeting. George is a thirty-two-year-old, one hundred and forty-five pound State College boxer with thickened eyebrows and nose bridge and the broad face of a German peasant, who has come back to school the semester after the Bay of Pigs to work on his master's degree, though Roger never sees him with a book or even hears of one class he is in or of anyone who has ever had a class with him. He joined the Student Peace Union and asked Roger why he quit after organizing it.

"Too many big egos around," Roger says and George says, "People are always jealous of natural leaders. Don't let them make you quit, Roger." He appears at Roger's house that night, coming through the back gate to the back door instead of the front and insists that Roger come outside to talk, as if he wants to get away from Roger's wife. As they stand in the darkness of the backyard, he keeps glancing up and down the street.

"Well, I learned to speak Spanish so I could go down to Guatemala last summer during that revolution." He pauses and smacks his puffy lips, then stares at Roger and says, "We need patriotic natural leaders like you to help keep the peace movement from going totalitarian."

"We?" Roger asks.

George looks both ways up and down the leafy street and says, "The guy you would work with is a beautiful person, Roger."

He looks away again, glances back at Roger from a lowered head as if squaring off with him, though Roger has made him quit in the school gym with big gloves.

"We want you to stay in the Student Peace Union and keep it a peace movement, keep it from becoming violent and dangerous."

"Who's we?" Roger asks again.

George stares at him for a moment, seems to tense himself to reply and says, "He's a good guy, Roger. You'll like him. We know that you're not an authoritarian or violent guy and that you'll be a good influence on the movement. Things can really open up for a talented guy like you: a great future, fame, if you—"

"But what if I don't want to do it? And it's not just being an informer or agent, if you want to call it that. What if I don't want to mess around with a bunch of small-time, petty politicians anymore, guys more concerned with their egos and power than with peace? What about that?"

George looks down the street again, then faces Roger again. "We're going to try and get some CP guys with grass, and anybody at all involved in the movement who uses it could get in trouble, especially any guy who's been in jail before." He raises one bushy eyebrow at Roger.

Roger puts his hands in his pockets and fingers a joint in one of them and says, "Not much of a deal, is it? Sounds more like a threat to me."

"You don't have to get anybody in trouble, Roger," George says. "All you have to do is let us know what's going on. You have a bright future ahead of you. You could become a famous, important person, get a lot of publicity for your books, and you could stay true to your ideals by helping keep the movement democratic. That's what we're interested in—democracy."

He looks away down the deserted street again and Roger in a voice tight with anger, says, "Yeah, I'm patriotic, if you mean loving the land I was born and raised in. But I love the people in the rest of the world, too, and though I want to keep things democratic and non-militaristic, I'm not going to rat on anybody. There's enough militaristic cops around for that!" And he looks George in the eyes.

Roger feels as if he's just escaped with his life, his honor, with his ideals intact, and he settles down to work hard on his novel, ready to drop out of The Movement forever, feeling very wise, sure that he is now choosing the best possible work and way to happiness and that his brother, Eddy, would be very proud of him. But he does not escape.

He begins to get mysterious phone calls. When he picks up the phone there is only silence or heavy breathing on the line. Sometimes it rings in the middle of the night and when he answers, they hang up. Mostly it rings when he is alone and Dolly is at work. Sometimes he picks it up and waits for the other person to speak first. One time, he waits a whole five minutes before the caller hangs up. "Hello? Hello? Hello?" an official voice says once even after he speaks, as if the person cannot hear him. Sometimes, the caller asks, "Is George there?" Sometimes, they just ask for other people. He knows that the object is to harass him and that he has to assume it can happen at any time. He gets apprehensive when the phone rings, a fearful sense comes over him, an emotional flash that makes him weak and becomes almost crippling when he lifts the phone to his ear and hears the silence. He is afraid to say hello. He is afraid there will be no answer. He waits for the other person to speak first. One night, he is awakened out of a sound sleep and without thinking about it, asks, "Hello? Hello?" then realizes by the silence that they've tricked him again and he shouts, "Answer, Goddamnit!" and slams the phone down, knowing that he has fallen for the bait but is too angry at being awakened at four in the morning to care.

He is followed by a man in a car, usually a station wagon, every time he leaves the house. Every time he crosses the bay bridge, a car full of sailors drives alongside him, two with their backs to him and two facing him, as if they are talking to each other. A green sedan with a long antenna, a license plate with the call numbers of a shortwave station and driven by a thick-necked, middle-aging, black-haired man comes by at least once a day. The man slows down on the hill outside the house and stares up at the big bay window where Roger sits at his desk and drives very slowly by. A firetruck starts coming by once or twice a week, too. Roger is amazed to see it every time it comes by. The truck turns the corner from the side street and cruises past the front of the house with all the firemen on the truck staring up at him! It is unnerving, but he gets the point: he is hot!

He is followed around school, too. Everywhere he goes on campus he notices a man in a brown, suede jacket who looks like Jack Dempsey. The guy doesn't look like a student or an instructor but more like a truck driver, a garbage man or a cop and has a square face, with black hair growing straight back from down low on his forehead, close to his thick eyebrows, chin and cheeks heavy and blue with beard shadow, a boxer on a boxer. He appears between the shelves of the library and his eyes are all Roger can see of him. Or he sits at the next table in the cafeteria and sips from a cup of black coffee. Or he shows up in the gym and watches Roger punch the bag or box. And when he gets wise that Roger is wise to him, he comes walking slowly by Roger in the library, heels clicking, then suddenly spins around a few feet from him, meets Roger's eyes and then walks slowly back by, staring all the while, trying to scare him.

But there is more. The picture of the editors of the *Passport*, the student literary magazine, is taken out of the yearbook and a new picture that doesn't include him put in its place, without any mention of him as prose editor. Then the Chief Editor of *Passport* calls him up and tells him there is a shortage of space and that his poem will have to be cut.

"I'm warning you, Dick, if you try to cut my poem out of the magazine, I'm going to the Board of Publications."

"Is that so?" the voice says and Roger can picture Dick's sallow skin and full lips, his kinky hair and swears that Dick has black blood back in his ancestry somewhere, though his father is a professor and he considers himself "upper class white" and the best poet to ever come out of State College.

"And furthermore," Roger says, "you're a pompous bastard who got elected as Chief Editor only because I spoke for you and didn't run against you. And though I'm dropping off the magazine, which ought to make you feel better, you better lay off my poem or you're asking for trouble. I don't care who you're working for!"

There is no answer, only a slight buzz on the line, finally a click and dead silence, and Roger puts the receiver down, feeling brave and perceptive for recognizing what it was all about and fighting back. And though there is a hollow, anxious feeling in his stomach, too, as if the shadows held watching men—he can't forget the veiled threat about grass that George made to him, he goes to bed feeling satisfied with himself.

But he is surprised to find his old friend Ross at Keith's liquor store, slapping him on the back, shaking his hand, saying, "Roger! Roger! Roger! Roger!" pushing the bottle of cheap sweet wine in his face, saying, "Have a drink! Have a drink! Have a drink!"

"What's up, man? I've never seen you so zipped up. You on benny? Something wrong?" Roger asks Ross, who is now married and settled down with two kids, only plays in combos on weekends now, who has told him Keith has pounds for sale. Keith, their bandy-legged buddy from high school, five-six and muscular, with wide fishlike eyes and a big beaked nose, but handsome, who has sold Roger a lightweight pound through a partner and told him to bring it back so they can exchange it when he gets off work, counts the cash before locking up. It is almost midnight.

"Just glad to see my old friend, Roger," Ross says, then takes another sip of wine and squints his eyes and doesn't look at Roger. And Roger feels a quick tremor of anxiety in his stomach when he hands Keith the paper bag of pot. He suddenly remembers that Keith's roommate dropped a plastic vial of grass in a mailbox at the sight of a plainclothes cop in their hotel lobby and they had to move out that night. He could be hot. They could both be hot. He knows that he himself is hot. The whole deal could be dangerous.

"I'll wait outside in the car while you count up, Keith," he says but Ross grabs his arm, pushes the bottle in his face and says, "Stay here and drink with an old buddy. Have some wine! Just like old times."

But when Roger pulls free and opens the door to go out anyway, Ross says, "Okay, you stay inside and I'll go out and wait."

"What?" Roger says and leans back to look at him but Ross

sways a little as if he's drunk, then tries to beat Roger out the glass door and close it on him. But though Roger can't understand why he's acting so strange, he doesn't think it's cute and he pushes by him and goes out to his car, parked in the first space next to the red zone on the corner. Ross follows him.

The boulevard is brightly lit though traffic is light so late on a week night and all the stores in the middleclass business district are closed but the liquor store on the corner of a sidestreet. Roger turns down a sip of wine for the second time when he sees a man drive slowly by in a cream colored coupe with receding blond hair on a bullet-shaped head who stares with hard eyes at them. The man looks closely into the liquor store as he turns off the boulevard and down the side street into the residential neighborhood, watching Keith, who, Roger knows, is counting up the till.

Roger sits up wondering if the guy is the big kilo dealer coming to pick up the lightweight pound or maybe a dealer of Keith's, although he looks too old for that. Or maybe he is an armed robber casing the store? But he is so suspicious looking, Roger says, "That's a strange-acting guy."

"Oh, don't worry about it. It's nothing," Ross says and hands him the bottle but Roger pushes it away and hopes Keith will hurry up, when he sees the guy in the cream-colored coupe reappear on the side street, pull up at the stop sign on the corner, peek at the store, then start backing his car into the red zone.

"Hey! That guy just came back!" Roger says and sits up.

"He's probably a customer," Ross says. "Here!"

"No thanks," Roger says and pushes the bottle away again. "I better go tell Keith."

"Stay here! It's okay! Everything's alright!" Ross says.

"I'm not so sure. Keith's got almost a pound of pot in there," Roger says and opens his door, pulls his arm out of Ross's grip and gets out as the man gets out of his door too. For a couple of seconds they walk straight toward each other: the man crossing the sidestreet, Roger approaching the corner. Then Roger suddenly sees him lengthen his step as if trying to beat him to the door, and he picks up his own pace, barely keeps himself from running and reaches the corner first, turns into the store, snaps the lock on the door as he closes it, and shouts, "Hey, Keith! Some strange man's coming across the street!"

"What?" Keith says, stepping out of the back room, then his bulbous eyes pop open and Roger spins around to see two big plainclothes cops running across the boulevard from a double-parked blue cop car without markings. They hit the glass door hard, try to jerk it open, shake it, rattle it and hit it with their shoulders.

"Don't let them in, Keith! Don't let them in!" Roger shouts and runs past him into the storeroom, grabs the paper bag out of the whiskey case, where he has seen Keith hide it, and with the sound of Keith arguing with the men banging on the door, shouting, "Open up! Open up!" He runs into the toilet and, hands shaking, dumps the weed into the toilet bowl and flushes it, shouting over the rushing water, "Don't let them in! Don't let them in!"

"The store is closed," he hears as the water runs down and a layer of wet grass floats to the top. He flushes the toilet again but there isn't enough water left to carry the layer of grass down. It swirls a little but stays on top, three or four lids' worth. He jerks the handle again to make sure there isn't any more water and sure he is going to get caught and go to jail, he starts scooping the wet grass up and stuffing it into the paper bag with shaky hands, gets all he can out of the water, then jams the bag back into the whiskey case, pushes the case behind some others, and flushes the toilet again. But he still hasn't gotten all the grass and he picks up what is left with his fingers and washes them off in the sink. Then, hands shaking, legs weak and wobbly, he steps back into the display room where Keith is shaking his head and saying no to the single cop in the plain blue suit still at the door. The cop stares at Roger, then turns and recrosses the boulevard, gets back into his unmarked car and drives off with the other cop.

Roger hurries up to Keith, who is still at the door, and looks across the side street to find the coupe now gone. He starts to explain what he saw when Ross comes to the door and says, "What's taking you guys so long? Let me in."

"Don't open the door, Keith!" Roger says. "The cops might still be around."

"Open up, Keith!" Ross insists.

"Don't open that door!" Roger shouts. "Those were narks, man. You almost got busted! You weren't sitting outside and saw what I saw. Ross kept—"

"Hey! What's going on here? Open up!" Ross says and Keith unlocks the door to let him in but Ross only puts his foot in the door and stays outside.

"Make him come in, Keith!" Roger says and when Ross shakes his head as if he can't figure out why he is acting so strangely, Roger grabs his arm and pulls him inside, then locks the door behind him again.

"What's the matter with you guys?"

"Didn't you see those three guys who just tried to get in here?" Roger asks, unable to believe he couldn't have seen them, and looks into his eyes. When Ross looks away, Roger suddenly understands it all and shouts, "You finked, Ross!"

All the color goes out of Ross's face. The freckles seem to stand out like blackheads on his pale skin, and Roger catches him with an overhand right to the cheek, drops him flat on the floor, and breaks a gallon jug of burgundy. But Ross rolls over and covers his head and Roger pounds him on the back with both fists, shouting, "Fink! Fink! Fink!"

Roger wakes the next morning and looks around the room at the walls, the ceiling, the familiar pictures, the open closet door with his and Dolly's clothing in it. The room is like a vacuum, a temporarily suspended space in which his past life and future are balanced just outside him, his living sphere. The past, the good, the familiar, the very room and bed in which he lies are in danger. And the future is a threat, a chance for getting put behind bars, of waking up in the morning to the clang of cell doors, the jingle of keys, a cop marching past his cell to count him, dark steel and dull concrete all around him, prisoners on the make, no privacy, only boredom and monotony and emptiness. His stomach quivers with fear. He remembers the four and a half months he spent in the county jail at eighteen, never knowing what was going to happen to him, sweating it out from day to day, and how his hands used to shake whenever anyone came to see him, like his father, who in a voice close to hysteria, asked, "What are you shaking for?" as if it was his fault he was shaking. Big fat man, he stared at the shaking hands with fear on his own face and unable to reach out and touch his son said, "I've got to go! I've got to get out of here!"

Roger rubs his sweating palms on the bedspread. He has barely escaped. But he sprung the trap too soon by insisting on going outside, by refusing to let Ross manipulate him and keep him inside where he couldn't see anything. Now they are after him in more ways than one, he thinks, and it suddenly hits him. All this is happening because he refused to spy on his fellow pacifists for the "nice guy," since he refused to be a stoolpigeon. Ross is a stoolpigeon, there is no question of that. And the state nark who busted Keith when he was eighteen swore he'd put him in San Quentin if he ever messed with drugs again. They must have tried to kill two jail birds with one stone through a mutual friend, Ross. But that is as close as Roger can come to logic, which is always guess and assumption when it comes to under-cover men. Only a court of inquiry could prove anything and maybe not then. But he does know that he almost went to jail and that his life has been in a tailspin ever since he refused to be an informer and that he can no longer trust a single friend.

Cop-out: to inform to the police. He thinks about that word with the hyphen in the middle. His identity would split like that word if he copped-out. Copping-out would break him. He would never have the strength to create great art. He would kill himself then. There would be no reason for living. He must pursue his ideals, those shaped by his brother, Eddy. He must withdraw into himself for good. He must write. He must write now.

Divide and Conquer

"You are a very promising writer and your intuitive grasp of craft is extraordinary. I can't help you too much with this story, but I am willing to work with you on other stories by mail—I have a weak heart and might not live much longer. I need to keep my schedule small but send me your stories. I think your potential is great." Roger reads and shows the letter to Nora and his dad.

He is beaming. He can barely talk, he feels so happy. "She's a famous woman, Donna Shandy. She helped some great writers, like James Jones who wrote 'From Here to Eternity.' She supported him for nine years. She has a colony of young writers in Ohio. I sent her my last story."

But Nora only glances at him and busies herself at the sink. His father has a doubtful look on his long face, and glancing up at him with dull brown eyes, says, "You could be a good lawyer, son."

Roger freezes with the letter held out in his hand.

He is hurt. His father has encouraged him to go to the Youth Peace Festival in Helsinki and meet with the communist youth of Eastern Europe, and has praised Kennedy for stopping the steel companies from raising their prices and has seemed to back his radical activity, not saying much but never showing displeasure. But this is more than displeasure or even disinterest, this is discouragement. Then he fears it is more than discouragement when he gets his next letter from Donna Shandy: "I regret to say that my work load is too heavy, and I won't be able to work with you as I had written. But let me tell you to keep writing and someday, though I don't know how or when, you will be a well-known, well thought of writer."

Roger takes the letter in to show his father, really hurt, but trying to hold onto her last words, build on them, save himself by them. But before he can speak, Phil, his brother-in-law, an already overweight young man with a pot belly who moves in a world of managers and supervisors and union business agents, says, "The guys you've been running around with, all those peaceniks, are just a bunch of dupes for the communists. Always claiming the Fifth Amendment. The FBI's right to tap those guys' phones. They ought to lock them up or run them out of the country."

When Roger just looks at him without answering, he says, "You high? Still smoking that weed? I bet you've got some hid in the house. Tell the truth. You do, don't you?"

Roger cannot answer. He has never talked about smoking dope in front of his father. It is disrespectful. It is immoral. It is against the law. He says nothing about the dope. He says nothing about the peaceniks. He says nothing about the letter.

"I thought you still had four months to go, Ernie?" he asks, surprised to see his brother home from the county jail farm. He hasn't talked to his father in a couple of days. He is mistrustful of his whole family. They are the only ones who knew of Donna Shandy and now she will not work with him. He is afraid they do not want him to write, that they are cooperating with the police.

"Got out on accumulated good time and some extra good time for doing volunteer work for the Captain," Ernie says, curling his big upper lip in a broad smile, as if he's pulled something over on somebody, trying to charm Roger, too.

"I never heard of that before," Roger says.

"Say! I know where we can get a pound cheap. Why don't you give me a ride? I've got a few bucks. We could go halves. You always need grass."

"I could use some alright," Roger says. "I could use some money, too. I've got cops on my tail."

"Naw, naaaaaaaaw," Ernie says out the side of his mouth, squinting one eye, pushing his snap-brimmed hat back on his high forehead. His face is wide and round from a high-starch diet on the county farm. There are no hollows in his cheeks and no dark circles under his eyes, yet, eyes that never meet Roger's eyes. "Nobody'd be after you. You're too respectable. But if you want some money, why don't you help me plan a big job? You're supposed to be a big brain. We could make a lot of money. You could go off to the mountains and write your book, quit breaking your ass on a job, too."

The idea is tempting. It is just a matter of time before they set him up at the shoe store. With some money, he'd be able to go away and write his novel, get it published and come back a big enough success they'd have to leave him alone. But he's been a front man who talked to the cashier while Ernie tapped the till when he got out of the county farm before, trying to keep him off junk, not taking a penny of the money, staying with him until he started shooting up again, then went back to school while Ernie got hooked and went, eventually, back to jail. He thinks of Eddy, too, and says, "No. Not ever again. We've gone through this before. But I'll go in with you on a pound of weed."

They are smoking a joint as they drive down the big boulevard to the dealer's place when Roger spots a station wagon with four big, beefy men inside, coming up fast behind them, as if trying to pull along side. "Cup that joint, Ernie, there's a car full of cops coming up on us," he says, and without speeding up too quickly, changes lanes and slowly out-distances the station wagon, then turns off the boulevard and goes around a block and comes back up on the boulevard and doesn't see them again. But they don't drive much further when a zipped-up hotrod with molded fenders and a very pretty girl driving it pulls alongside them. She guns her motor and grins at them, then digs out at the green light, trying to get Roger to race with her.

"Let's go party with her," Ernie says but Roger says, "Let's go get the weed instead," and turns off the boulevard again.

He waits in the car while Ernie goes inside a big apartment house and notices a car with a very conventional looking man and woman in it parked a couple of cars behind him. They look too old to be sitting around in cars necking. He waits for a half an hour and finally rings the bell of the dealer and is let in to find Ernie and the connection, a tall man who looks like a truck driver or a bartender, with two full hypos of methedrine ready for use on a coffee table. As soon as Roger steps in, Ernie ties his bicep muscle, bends his arm and shoots into the big vein of the forearm, wipes off the blood, and sets the hypo down. Roger waits for the tall guy to shoot up, too, but he says, "I don't want it. You can have it," and points at the hypo.

"Not me," Roger says.

"I guess I'll have to take it then," Ernie says and picks up the needle and looks at Roger. But Roger just stares at him and he ties up his other arm and puts the needle to the forearm. Then he looks at Roger again and Roger just shakes his head.

The second jolt seems to lift Ernie up on his toes and turn him into a zombie with bulging eyes and stiff limbs. He is so comic that a wave of love sweeps over Roger at his crazy, crazy brother and he lifts him up in the air and says, "You're crazy, Ernie," but puts him down again and asks, "Where's the pound?"

"Let's get out of here," he says, after the dealer gives him the pound, but Ernie only drops down in the sofa chair and stares with glazed eyes at nothing.

"Let's go," Roger says, but Ernie waves his hand and says, "Take it home. I'll see you there."

The couple is still sitting in the car like twin shadows in the twilight and he has no coat to hide the brown paper bag. He knows that they see it and he is in danger. He puts the car in gear and drives toward the stop sign on the corner only a hundred feet away just as a pickup truck parked on the boulevard with two men in it suddenly pulls across the street and parks in the crosswalk in front of him, completely blocking his lane. He stops and glances in the rearview mirror, the car with the man and woman in it has now pulled out from the curb and is coming right up behind him. Fear shoots through him but he swerves his car to the right, bounces up a curb, and speeds across the corner of a service station and out onto Foothill Boulevard, out of the trap between the two cars. But he is being chased by the truck and he speeds up and makes a right turn on the next corner, shoots down a side street to the next corner and turns left. But the truck is still on him and he zigzags from one street to the next, his lights off in the twilight, increasing his distance on the truck until he loses it, then shoots up into the Oakland hills to Joaquin Miller Park and hides the bag in a bush behind the dead poet's little white cottage.

He drives home in the darkness, parks his car in front and steps past the hedge, expecting some cops to jump him. He keeps tense all along the path through the vines and huge, leafy tropical plants in his father's exotic garden, and all the way up the inner stairs to his own apartment, where he turns out the lights, tells Dolly to keep quiet, then watches from his window for only a few minutes before a patrol car stops directly in front of the house. Dolly crouches down with him and they watch a cop get out and shine his flashlight on both sides of the hedge, then walk through the garden to the front stairs where he checks both sides of the staircase with the flashlight, shining the light among the trunks of the big exotic plants, where only Dolly knows Roger hides his dope sometimes, where it could be anybody's not just his.

"How will you hide it if they are cops then?" Ernie asks that night.

"I'll bury it in the back yard," Roger says, and late at night he walks in tennis shoes through the darkened house and out the back door so as not to wake his father in the bedroom behind the kitchen and hides his share of the dope Ernie has picked up for him at the foot of a fruit tree. Two days later, coming home from work at the shoe store, Roger sees his father working in the backyard with several post holes dug for a new fence, with his half pound of dope at the bottom of one of them. He picks it up and opens it.

"Do you know whose bag that is?" his father asks, setting his saw down.

"I'll ask Ernie," Roger says, not afraid to connect his brother with dope since he has been arrested so many times for junk already and it is the most plausible explanation. His father just nods, but when he starts up the back stairs, his father says, "The police are really smart and can use smart men," but starts sawing again when Roger turns around.

Roger does not know what to believe and he is really shocked that night when his father says, "Ernie, show your brother what you've got. Don't keep anything from your brother," and Ernie pulls a pistol out of a kitchen drawer.

"What's that for?" Roger asks, and when neither of them

answers or looks at him, he says, "Since when do you encourage Ernie in crime, Dad? And since when do you want him to involve me in it?" When neither of them will even look at him, he says, "I don't trust either of you. You've sold me out, Dad. You and Ernie. Both of you. That's why you've been talking all this patriotism stuff lately and how the cops can use smart men. What happened to both of you? You, Dad, you're the one who made a political rebel out of me, but now that you're older and tired and the heat's on, you sell me out. You, too, Ernie. You're the one who taught me never to fink, never to rat on anybody, and look at you. You set me up a couple of days ago, your own brother, and I almost got busted. You even tried to get me hooked, though I've never touched anything hard in my life. You're both a couple of rats. I'm getting out of here and I'm never coming back. Eddy would hate you for what you've done. I wish my mother was alive so I could tell her on you. I hate you, Dad! I hate you and this dopefiend rat, here!"

He stomps out of the kitchen, grabs the painting of Eddy from above the fireplace and stalks upstairs with tears in his eyes. He cries again the next day when Nora says, "But if Dad and Ernie and Phil and everybody else thinks differently than you, aren't you the one at fault? Aren't you the one who's causing trouble for our family?"

He stays alone in the new apartment most of the time, refuses to answer calls on the newly installed phone, since half of them are wrong numbers and open lines without voices and/or heavy breathing anyway. He keeps the lights off in the apartment at night, the shades up, so he can see out, and lets the phone ring and ring and ring, hurting and bitter inside, cursing everyone over and over again to himself, out loud, under his breath, or in his mind, pacing back and forth in the darkness, refusing to even answer the door, and determined, if he must, to spend his whole life alone. He has his novel. He has his stories. He has his poems. He will write. He is an artist and he can live in solitude. Someday he will write the whole truth of what has happened; that a police state, faking legitimacy, subverting the Constitution, lurks under the cover of respectability and patriotism. He will tell the truth and in telling the truth will produce lasting art if it costs him his life.

Till Death Do Us Part

Dolly is staring at him again with that strange look in her beautiful blue eyes, as if she is seeing deep into him for the first time and discovering something horrible about him but when he pulls away from the woman in the bar, turns his back on her so she'll go away and faces the crowd of young merchants they had gone to high school with, Dolly suddenly screens her eyes with her long dark lashes.

"Let's get out of here," Roger says and asks her when they are stepping away from the bar: "What's the matter? Don't you like that girl hanging all over me? Why didn't you let me know?"

"It's alright if she lets me know she's doing it," Dolly says and pushes through the thick Saturday night crowd to the door ahead of him. He is completely mystified by her answer. He has seen her looking at him like that several times the last week. One day she called him up and told him she had seen Ernie on the street and that he really looked good. She kept repeating the phrase over and over again until he got suspicious and began to worry that she was getting set up. When she came home he told her that Ernie wasn't trustworthy and she turned her face away. She seemed to be either looking at him wierdly or not looking at him at all lately and it was beginning to bother him. She had gone with him to review a Beckett play, "Happy Days," for the school paper and they had stopped at her suggestion to have a drink at the bar in Jack London Square. The girl, a friend of her boss Wes, threw her arm around him and pressed up against him until he finally pushed her away and got the strange reply from Dolly.

He sees her stop in front of him, then step to one side, then step back and then suddenly turn and cry, "Roger! This guy won't let me by!"

"Step out of the way, please!" Roger says and when the man just stands and stares at him, he steps in front of Dolly and tries to push through but the balding guy throws his arm around his neck and starts choking him. But it is so crowded, Roger can't punch and he grabs the guy by the balls and they stagger out the front door onto the sidewalk, where the guy lets go and pulls away. They stand facing each other in the doorway.

"Get him!" another man yells and the balding guy lunges at Roger, who brings up a left hook from the side just as he gets in range, but Dolly steps next to Roger and blocks the punch with her hip, his fist hits it and misses and the guy grabs him again. But

Roger stays in close, walks him back to keep him from getting room to punch, then just pushes him away and steps back.

"Get him!" the other man says again and the guy charges Roger once more and they clinch and fall off the curb, where surrounded by a crowd of people, Roger rolls over on top of him and pins him down by his wrists. He looks up at Roger without making any attempt to get up so Roger lets go of one wrist and picks up some notes on Beckett that have fallen out of his inner coat pocket. He glances up at a pickup truck that turns the corner and creeps around behind them with two middleaged men in it, both watching carefully, like the two men in the pickup truck who tried to bust him with the pound. But the balding guy throws his arm across his face as if to keep from being hit, and when Roger just looks at him, he brings it down again, leaving blood on his face, something that Roger cannot even remotely comprehend because he hasn't even tried to hit the guy but once and that was blocked by Dolly! But the guy doesn't even move and Roger gets carefully off him, picks up his last note and walks off to the car with Dolly.

"Why did you block that punch?" he asks.

"I know those men couldn't hurt you and I didn't want you to hurt him," she says but he says, "How do you know they couldn't hurt me?" and when she doesn't answer, he stares at her as if he was seeing her for the very first time.

He goes to school to take finals, suffering over her, knowing that she has betrayed him, believing that she set him up for a felonious assault charge, which, with his record, could put him in prison. He sits and aches in the library but studies very, very hard, studies to keep from dying, to keep from flipping out, from going crazy. There is no one, absolutely no one in the world that he can trust. Even his thirteen year old son is sullen with him as if the golden-haired boy believes his father is destroying the family. There is nothing left. He feels like Raskolnikov in "Crime and Punishment."

"Dolly," he says. "I love you, Dolly. We've been sweethearts since we were little kids. If you have turned against me, then it must be my fault. Call up the D.A. and tell him he can pick me up walking down the boulevard smoking a joint. Tell him I give up."

"No, Roger, don't do that," she says and stands up from her chair and walks toward him. "I don't know what they really want yet. Let me go see him tomorrow and try to work something out that will protect you better."

"I'm willing to go to prison to save our marriage, Dolly, our family, our son. We took a vow: till death do us part. You work something out tomorrow and I'll go. Don't be afraid."

"Oh, Roger!" she says and throws her arms around him, kisses him, kisses him, kisses him and he has no fear about tomorrow.

40

Shock Treatment

The psychiatrist, a small, stocky man with gray hair and hairy arms, bends over and stares into Roger's eyes, one eyebrow arched, and says sharply: "What did you say? The police are after you?"

Roger, sitting in a chair below him in gray bathrobe, gray cloth slippers, gray pajamas, wavy hair uncombed and cheeks rough with beard stubble, feeling sloppy and dirty and not himself, nods his head.

"Are you sure?" the psychiatrist asks and leans down even closer, so close that Roger can smell the tobacco on his breath and he gets confused and looks down and hides his eyes and feels like a lunatic. Though he is not surprised to see Dolly testifying against him. She looks very beautiful in a tailored green tweed suit, her cool blue eyes deep as the evening sky, her golden hair swept back close to her ears. "He yells and loses his temper and claims the police are after him. And he doesn't trust me. He doesn't act normal. He's so suspicious all the time."

She has already betrayed him twice, once with the fight and again when she had him taken to the County Psychiatric Ward instead of jail. This is just the capper. But he isn't crazy and when the judge asks, "Do you really believe the police are chasing you?" Roger, who refused to take a sleeping pill the night before so he could be sharp for court in the morning and who stayed awake half the night trying to figure out what to do, glances around the courtroom at the benches filled with young nurses, at the jury in the box, at the prosecuting attorney, and at the gray-haired psychiatrist who had tried to frighten him into silence about the police, then spreads out in the chair, lets one gray bathrobe clad arm hang over the chair back, lets one gray pajama'd leg hang over a chair arm and as nonchalantly as possible says, "Your Honor, I've been smoking a lot of weed lately and I felt guilty about it and began to imagine that the police were after me. I had paranoid delusions from too much smoke, that's all." And Dolly and the psychiatrist both stare at him.

"Now that makes sense," says the bald-headed judge. "But you seem tense and nervous and a few days rest out at the State Hospital won't hurt you."

"Alright, Your Honor," Roger says, a little disappointed but still relieved, for nobody can say he is crazy now. He can even tell about the cops and they will not be after him. He has paid his dues and the fight is over. Everything is still going to be okay. Things look good.

He is interviewed by the director of the hospital himself, a little baldheaded man with a pot belly, long nose and sagging jowls, blubbery mouth and gray tufts of hair over his ears. He looks like Alfred Hitchcock and is just as subtly sinister as the mystery filmmaker. He asks, "You say you imagined the police were after you? Because you were smoking marijuana?"

"Oh, yes. I thought they were tapping my phone, calling me in the middle of the night and bugging my apartment, tailing me everywhere I went, every time I stepped out of the house."

He watches the little man scribble his answer down, playing their game because the first interview taught him they weren't interested in the truth, they only cared about police security, and that they won't let him out until he is not a threat to it. "He who fights and runs away lives to fight another day," he tells himself. He is overpowered and he knows it. But he also knows that no matter what they make him do to get out now, some day he'll write about it.

"But why do you smoke marijuana if it causes you so much trouble?" the director asks.

Roger hesitates, pauses but can think of no lie and says, "Because it makes me love everybody."

And love everybody he does. The long strain of living like a hunted animal is over. He is even pleased to be in a nuthouse instead of a jail. There is an open gate, wide lawns, lots of trees, friends and lovely girls. He sleeps ten hours or more every night and gets up late as possible for breakfast, walks sleepy-eyed into the ward dining room, the last person in line, says good morning to everybody near him, waves to those across the room, patients and staff. He becomes disc jockey and wins the twist contest of the nuthouse with a beautiful sixteen year old partner. He is glad he surrendered. He has lots of hope.

But he has to take sanity tests, including Rorschach and others. They are seemingly very simple but he can see they are designed to test his aggressive impulses. There is a puzzle with some missing parts. A woman is knitting but there is a blank spot in the middle of her lap and a knife, scissors and a ball of yarn beneath the picture. PLACE THE MISSING OBJECT IN HER LAP, the caption reads, and he skips over the stabbing objects and puts in the ball of yarn. Some are designed to judge his logic and common sense and are childishly simple, but a more subtle one is a Rorschach card that has the shape of a satyr with dangerous horns lying in a field of spotted colors. Roger, guessing what they are after says, "It reminds me of Mothers Day, full of flowers."

42

And when an old high school friend takes him around the grounds and points out undercover cops in gray cars with official license plates and says that they work on the grounds, Roger can see that they could be cops or just plain professional workers but doesn't argue either way because his "friend" may be trying to get him to tell what he knows about the police and their methods and also to verify his commitment papers. If he still thinks of cops swarming around him then he must still be having paranoid delusions and should be kept locked up. He doesn't contradict Dolly when Ron, the psychologist with the soft cheeks and sweet smile, asks, "How about those midnight phone calls?" and she answers, "There haven't been any midnight phone calls," because he knows that if he still believes there have been then he is still sick.

"Let me have a couple of dollars so I can go see my girl, Roger," Moresco, a beat poet and patient in the hospital asks, and Roger quickly digs in his pocket and gives the money to him, not thinking much of it, glad to be of help to a guy. He can see a doctor from Ward B standing outside his office doorway in the sunshine. But as he walks into the building to see his psychologist he wonders if the doctor was watching them and suddenly guesses that Moresco has set him up to test his attitude toward authority, whether or not he will help Moresco break the rules and go home without the ward doctor's permission. They are checking to see if he is a sociopath, to see how far he will go, and give him enough rope to hang himself.

When he sits down across the desk from the little Hungarian refugee, he decides to tell him for reasons which only become clear as he talks. He has been cutting a lot of corners trying to keep from getting caught smoking weed over the years, then as a political rebel. He doesn't want to do that anymore. He wants to live in harmony with his society on an honest basis so that he can survive and thrive and not continue on his destructive course. He is now out in front with them on the grass issue. He can be himself and he wants to accept their criticism of him without being defensive so he can straighten out the crooked edges. The gift of the two dollars puts him in a shaky position and jeopardizes everything he has surrendered himself for. Now, if Moresco is in on it, it is foolish to protect him, and if Moresco is not in on it, he will feel guilty if something happens to him when he is gone.

"Yes. I'm glad you told me. But you must go and talk Moresco out of leaving, even if it means taking the money back," the psychologist says, and frowns as if he is really worried. He is a pudgy little man, soft and round with wire-rimmed silver spectacles who escaped from Hungary in 1956.

"It is when the patient is almost well, when he is back in contact with reality and capable of functioning in society that he is most likely to commit suicide."

Rogers hurries out and looks for Moresco, worried that he might hurt himself, runs to the bus stop at the gate to try and catch him. But Moresco has gone and yet when Roger walks back to the psychologist and tells him, he merely smiles and says, "Don't worry about it." He is sure now it was all a trick to check him out. He doesn't know what to believe.

What is real now? He wonders where he is and when the examining psychiatrist asks, "Have you stopped smoking marijuana for good now?" Roger stops with his finger up and his mouth open, looks all around the long table at the doctors, then at the crowd of nurses and technicians seated in the audience, wants to say no but wants to tell the truth, and says, "I—I—I don't know," and knows he has made a mistake. They do not discharge him though he is the only patient in the entire hospital who is not on medication, but they do allow him to go home on the weekend with his wife. He takes his stash of three brown bombers and flushes them down his toilet, wishing he could have done that before so he could have said no at the hearing. Now it is too late.

"You're not an intellectual. You're not even a writer. You haven't published any books," the patient says. He is an ex-prison guard who always brings the group therapy session around to Roger. "You ought to grow up and get a job as a reporter and write something worthwhile and take care of your son like a father should instead of wasting your time on these outlaw stories." His fly is open. Hanging from his neck instead of a religious scapula is an ID of his grown son. "And you ought to wear regulation khaki issue like the rest of us instead of your own clothes. Quit dancing with all the young girls, too, and do something serious. If you think the cops were after you before, they'll never stop following you if you don't conform."

The ex-guard is big and heavy like a cop. He always tries to make Roger take something from him, like a Lifesaver or a cigarette.

"You should try and join the Masons. They run this country. Every president but this guy Kennedy has been a Mason and they'll get rid of him somehow. He'll never serve a second term. Isn't your wife's uncle a Mason? See if he can help you get in. What's the matter? Don't you like what I said?"

"I don't have to join the right wing to be a good citizen," Roger says.

As soon as the session ends, Dr. Smith asks, "Would you like to help with shock treatment tomorrow morning, Roger?"

Dr. Smith, a red-faced man who parts his orange hair on one side and combs it down flat against his skull and wears the same shiny brown double-breasted suit with the same green tie day after day holds the two ends of the electric wires an inch on each side of Hernandez' temples and says, "You saw Hernandez

44

yesterday morning swinging his mop around the ward, right, Roger?"

"Yes," Roger says and notices that Dr. Smith looks at the "Doctor" who is observing rather than at him and smiles.

"Well, let's see if we can calm him down," Dr. Smith says and then touches the vaseline on Hernandez' temples and he jerks once, then twice, then three times, then four times! and Roger cannot believe what he is seeing. All the other patients have only had one jolt each and even the red-headed Okie who tried to fight several guys and who has just come back to reality enough to perform minor chores like tying the wrists of the shocked patients before they come out of the shock and go into convulsions has only had one at a time. Roger rolls the gurney into the bedroom and helps the Okie tie Hernández down on the bed, then turns to push the gurney back for another patient when the Okie says, "I think something might be wrong," and Roger turns and sees Hernández gasping for breath, his face blue, his powerful body twisting and turning to tear loose from the rags that bind his wrists and ankles to the bedposts, unable to breathe because his diaphragm has collapsed from the multiple shocks.

"Doctor! Doctor! Hernández is strangling!" Roger yells and runs into the shock room and grabs an oxygen tank and wheels it into the bedroom and fights to hold Hernández down with five other men while the doctor struggles to keep an oxygen mask on his face. But when he is finally breathing again and they go back into the shock room and start working on another patient, Dr. Smith says, "Tell the doctor about *your* shock treatment, Roger."

Roger is speechless for a moment. Then he looks the doctor right in his cold green eyes and says, "I have never had shock treatment, doctor."

He knows the doctor is trying to see if he has mental deterioration but has been smart enough to conceal it. But he also knows the doctor has tried to scare him by giving Hernández four shocks, because if not a Mexican, Roger is at least a Spaniard, a spic, and is supposedly tough with his fists and uncooperative with authorities.

When Dolly shows up to get him, already tense and unhappy, he sees that she has had her long blond hair bobbed and that *every* nurse and *every* girl in the women's ward of their building with long hair has had it bobbed, too! He does not know why, but he does know he likes young college girls with long hair and *they* don't want him at the college causing trouble anymore. He realizes he can't trust her. She hasn't worn her hair short in their whole married life together! It is more than a coincidence! They are trying to drive him crazy! make him doubt everything he sees! He sits in the passenger seat next to her the whole fifty miles home without speaking one word. He will only shout. He will only hate her. He will only tell everything he knows about them. They will only use it against him.

They are trying to break him and make him cooperate, be a *good* citizen. Then when he gets home and looks out the front window, Ross, his former friend turned fink, gets out of a car right in front of the house but does not come in, walks around the corner instead. He guesses they want him to run out and stop him and make friends with him, prove he carries no grudges. But he is too angry and too worried and too confused to be full of love and forgiveness.

He sulks in a corner so silent and brooding that Dolly insists they go back to see the doctor. She is very calm, keeps a straight face and speaks directly to him, too directly, Roger thinks, as if forcing herself to do it so as not to arouse him, make him start shouting and yelling. He doesn't trust her. He thinks she is only tricking him into going back so he can be locked up, this time for good, no furloughs. But he is so unhappy, he welcomes the chance to bring it all out in the open where he can at least face it. But there are no windows in the doctor's office and he knows he is trapped no matter what happens next. Barely able to keep from yelling, he asks, "Did you or did you not, Doctor Smith, ask me to tell the observer about my so-called shock treatment in order to find out if I had deterioration of the brain?"

The freckle-faced doctor stares through gold-rimmed glasses with cold green eyes at Roger, then without a blink of his pale eyelashes, says, "Yes." And Roger, angry, fuming, ready to explode, so tense he holds one pointed finger down on the desk to keep himself down with, suddenly knows that there is still hope, that with that one word, that one honest word, he has been saved from suicide, from desperate escape, that in spite of everything there is still a slim chance he can survive intact, with all his ideals, with his whole person, as a whole person, and he says, "Why? Why do you play tricks and then expect me not to think cops are after me? How can I respect you if you can't be honest and straightforward with me?"

But the doctor stares with cold green eyes and as if now retreating from out in the open, unwilling to discuss the subject anymore, says, "Calm down or you'll be given a shot to quiet you!" and Roger is right back where he started from.

"You'd like to hook me, wouldn't you? You'd like to make an emotional cripple out of me, huh?"

But though his stomach is as tight as a rubber band and he wants to smash something with his fists, he shuts up and walks out of the office with Dolly.

"Alright," she says, tears running down her face. "You got him to admit it. Why don't you go on and run now? You know I tricked you to get you back here, why don't you run? Go on and run! Run away!"

Now, they want him to run! he thinks. They are going to put the pressure on! Yet he has that one word of truth. That, that one word, can keep him alive.

"Look!" the ex-guard says and flashes a badge in Roger's face. It is gold and swollen in his palm. He cups it and sticks it back in his pocket, then asks, "Have you ever had shock treatment, Roger? Here's a pamphlet on shock treatment, why don't you read it?"

Fear shoots through Roger. He feels weak, helpless. He sees himself strangling on the gurney with no one willing to save him. He wants to fall down on the floor and beg the guy not to give him the treatments. He sees days and weeks and maybe months of horror. They are going to force him to cooperate, prove that he is a good citizen. But he also knows that life is worthless if he has to live in such fear, without joy or spirit, and he stares right in the cop's eyes and says, "If that's what it takes, that's what I'll take. Give me the shock treatments!"

The cop pulls the pamphlets back, holds them next to his belly, stares at Roger, then turns and walks down the hall. Roger, though he is scared to the core of his being, weak in every limb, trembling with fear, knows that he has let himself in for it now but also knows that he doesn't care anymore, that a life filled with that much fear is not worth much. He would rather be dead. He would rather die on his feet than live on his knees. They will never break him. They can only kill him. He holds his breath at breakfast the next morning when the names for shock treatment are read off and they are allowed to drink only black coffee, but his name is not called and it is not called the next day and the next day. The following morning, the doctor lets himself in through a door next to Roger's room and says, "Good morning, Roger," and that day the sixteen-year-old girl says, "That ex-guard did it with me yesterday. He forced me into it. What should I do?"

Roger looks at her. She is an olive-skinned Italian girl, with soft brown eyes. She either wants to screw him or test him. But he trusts no one and he says, "Go tell the security guards."

"Not unless you go with me," she says.

"Alright," he says and goes with her, knowing that the ex-guard, nee cop, did not touch her. That he is behind the whole thing and that Doctor Smith and the girl are doing what he says. But Roger will protect himself, will not go for the bait and also prove that he can *cooperate*. And the next morning when the doctor comes in through the door next to his room again and says, "Good morning," Roger says, "Good morning, Doctor. I'd like to apologize for accusing you of trying to trick me."

The doctor smiles and says, "That's very nice, Roger. Why don't you write a letter to the State Director of Mental Hygiene and tell him about the job you were offered at the Oakland Post and maybe he might let you go soon."

The Collaborator

Alone in the small, two-person suburban newspaper branch office, hs stares out the window at the green lawn and takes deep breaths to relax his tension. He goes around taking deep breaths all the time. He knows that the stress he is still under can lead to a heart attack or an ulcer, even in a young man, and can, maybe, kill him. But even death seems a peaceful release. He is sick to death with sadness. The very daylight is colored with sadness. There is a bleak tone over everything. They are still trying to make him cooperate. The constant conspiracy wears him out. He has no one he can talk to or trust, no one to tell how he feels, no one to love him or kiss him.

Dolly, who always seems to be watching TV in her curlers and bathrobe when he gets home, says hello pleasantly enough but does not touch him. Sometimes, when he gets home in the early evening she is not there and when she does come home she is cold to him. He begins to suspect that she might be having an affair with her boss, his former school acquaintance. She feels no love for him he is now sure, since she asked him to get her keys from her car one night and he found a vacuum cleaner hose curled up next to the exhaust pipe, a nice hint as to how he could end it all. Then a nest of yellowjackets suddenly appeared under the wooden stairs on the lower slope of their property in the Montclair hills and he was reminded of an early short story he wrote about the suicide of a girl junkie with a large jar of yellowjackets.

He gets that hint, too, and he realizes that if things keep up as they he will kill himself. He has to fight for life. He has to stay alive. He has to survive somehow. He has to keep them from persecuting him to death. He must find a way to cooperate so they'll leave him alone. He remembers that Ernie often brings up the name of a latin nark named Lopez as if trying to make him familiar with him, maybe even like the nark so he'll be willing to cooperate with him. He decides to grasp the straw before he drowns and dials the telephone, quivering inside, gets the number of the State Narcotics Bureau and asks to speak to Lopez.

"Ernie who?" Lopez asks, then remembers and says, "Oh, yeah. I went to school with him. Come and see me tonight."

"So this is it. I'm finally going to become a fink," Roger

thinks, suppressing the shame that wells up in him, tells himself that he has a right to live and that he has been betrayed by every person he has tried to protect. Yet, he really knows, deep inside him, that he will write about it someday and tell the truth about himself, too, that he will transcend his own weakness in the end, when he is stronger, that he will get them back for making him do what he is doing now. And nervous, but not afraid, he appears in the basement of the City Hall and is taken to a back room, without windows, with six narks in it, Lopez and his superior, the head state narcotics agent, Colonel Gee, a black man, two county narks and two city narks.

Gee makes a big show of taking off his coat, flexing his muscles, pulling in his flabby belly, unstrapping his holster, taking out his snub-nosed pistol, and putting it in a filing cabinet in front of Roger. Then he turns on him and says, "I've got a memory like an elephant."

Roger guesses he is talking about the bust he broke up at Keith's Liquor Store but Gee doesn't scare him and he says, "I want you to leave me alone and I'm willing to help you, if you will."

"Are you trying to say we've been harassing you?" Colonel Gee says, standing, all six-feet and two-hundred and twenty pounds of fatty beef in front of Roger, who is sitting down.

Roger looks up at him, then takes a quick glance at all the other narks and says, "No, I'm not saying that. I'm saying that I consider it my duty as an honest citizen to cooperate fully with you."

All the narks in the room seem to sit back and relax, though none of them smiles, though one scribbles quickly in a notebook, seems to write everything down that Roger says.

Roger knows a couple of people at the 23 Club when he walks in to score. A thin woman named Joanne, a longtime dopefiend friend of Ernie's, and a couple of other guys who also know Ernie. But Roger senses as soon as he asks Joanne if he can buy a lid that something is phony. He can't really put his finger on it. He just senses it when she says, "He'll be here right away." He makes a phone call from the booth right next to the bar through a connection on the Bay Bridge, where he has been tailed so often, and Gee says, "There are two cars on the block. They will be watching the whole thing to protect you," as if trying to scare him. But Roger isn't afraid and when the so-called dealer walks in and just happens to be a blond Portuguese kid he knows from Oakland High School, everything is so transparent it is almost ludicrous to him. But he goes outside with Joanne and the dealer to his car, where Roger spots Gee parked across the street on the corner in an unmarked car. The guy gets the lid out of the truck and hands it to him in full view of Gee. But when Roger hands him the fifteen marked dollars, he looks deep into his eyes and says, "Be careful, man." The guy ducks his head and seems to freeze with one hand on the money, afraid to take it, as if he now knows he can be double-crossed, and Roger guesses *he* is being set up, *not* the dealer. He is sure of it when he meets Gee and another nark at a pre-arranged spot to give him the plastic bag of dope and Gee says, "Sign here for your expense money." But he is glad it is a trap. For Gee is setting him free, giving him a reason to never, ever have anything to do with undercover cops and stool-pigeon dealers again. He signs but does not show up the next night for the bigger buy and Gee calls him at home.

"Why aren't you here?"

"It's too depressing."

Silence, then: "If you don't come now, I'm going to use your name as an informer in court."

"Do what you want to. I've had it," Roger says and hangs up. And he isn't afraid for he now has enough information on them to prove what kind of games they play. Nobody in any court can say he has imagined it again. The next day Colonel Gee calls at the newspaper office and Roger says, "You tried to doublecross me."

"How?" Gee asks.

"By getting me to sign that blank form."

"You can have it back," Gee says.

"You can keep it," Roger says, aware that the middle-aged female column writer is listening to him and has been ever since he used the word *doublecross*.

"You won't get away with this," Gee says.

"Yeah, I know. You've got a memory like an elephant," Roger says and hangs up, bitter but strong, knowing that they can only keep up what they are already doing, what they have never stopped doing no matter what he has done, even surrendered, and that there is no use ever cooperating with them since they will only doublecross him anyway. He feels elated in a somber, silent kind of way, sure that they have taken him past the point where they will ever be able to break him, and though they may never stop persecuting him, he never has to give in for they are dishonest and always will be, it's in the very nature of their work. Deceit is the name of their game. And when he is driving across the Bay Bridge the following day to sign up for a novel writing class at State College and becomes aware of a blue car following him, he crosses lanes, drops back, comes up behind the car in the very next lane, sees that it is Gee without his hat, stays one car length back so he can see Gee very clearly and follows *him* all the way across the bridge until Gee has to turn off to get away.

Head Shrink

Two days after he follows Gee across the Bay Bridge, he notices a man taking pictures of the junior college campus where he has just interviewed a dean running for town mayor. But just as he closes his car door and turns the ignition key, the man steps next to the window, pokes the whirring machine a foot from Roger's face and takes his picture. Roger is caught for a moment, can't move, then sticks his middle finger up to the camera eye and keeps it there until the man steps back and turns away. When Roger reaches his psychologist's office, Greenelm keeps looking through some papers on his desk, without greeting him, then looks up, looks down at the papers again, still without saying hello. Green eyes, pink skin, thick gray hair waving straight back. Half Scandinavian and half Puerto Rican, he had said, "Because of your unusually high intellect, I will not attempt to establish and maintain a classical, Freudian patient-therapist relationship, which could take years. My whole object will be to get you to live in harmony with your society. If you insist on living by your ideals as an artist, you will be destroyed like Van Gogh or become a mere charlatan like Picasso. You can write and work too, work can be found that can be suited for a person of your ability. You can live a happy life rather than a tormented one."

Now, *he* looks tormented. He scribbles on the papers. He shuffles them again. He stacks them neatly at the corner of his desk, then he looks up and says, "You know, I realize that not all of my patients' claims are untrue. Even some of the more outlandish of them. They might not be exactly what the patients claim they are but the patients often have justifiable grounds for some of their more paranoid reactions and, sometimes, just a little talk will clear them up."

He waits, looking up, wrinkles on his forehead. But Roger won't go for the bait. He knows Greenelm will only try to justify the picture taking, which he already knows about, and that the whole object of his candor is to help the police. Roger knows that if he doesn't accept Greenelm's explication then he still believes the police are after him and he must be crazy. Now the last person in the world he doesn't want to think he's crazy is the shrink so he has no paranoid reaction to tell about, the police weren't tailing him and nobody took his picture, though he still gave the guy the finger.

Greenelm picks up the papers again, shuffles them, writes down some small notation, then puts the papers down in a neat stack, and, staring Roger hard in the eye, says, "Sometimes when an outpatient is unable to resolve some of his 'reactions' in a logical way, it is the responsibility of the therapist to send him back to the hospital for a little rest."

"Hell, I don't need a rest," Roger says, taking him exactly at his word, for he *is* naive, and Greenelm sits back in surprise, then suddenly smiles and says, "Did you read about the rooster that laid an egg about a year ago?"

"No," Roger says, watching him lie, watching him *test* his sanity, look for a crack in his reason they can drive a wedge into, and have a reason to put him away again until he is better trained. Roger keeps control of himself. He doesn't want to explode with anger at the cheap psychology and patent dishonesty of the man. The shrink is to transparently dishonest and evil he wants to shout it in his face. But it can only be used against him. For if he loses his temper then isn't he a danger to himself and to others? And aren't these grounds for keeping him locked up?

"Oh, yes, on some farm back east. They had reporters and TV cameras and all to record the event, to take pictures of him sitting on the egg," Greenelm says and pushes his chair back and stands up and takes off his plain sportcoat. His arms are crooked. They warp out at the elbows. He acts as if there is nothing wrong and walks around his desk to the eighth floor window, then stands in front of it and turns around to face Roger so that the bright glare shines in Roger's eyes. Roger is holding his dark glasses in his hand. The light is bright but does not hurt, though Roger's eyes have been sensitive since he got ulcers in them when his mother died. But he knows what Greenelm is doing. He saw a TV show ten years past about an escaped nut caught at the toll gate of a bridge by a guard who shines a flashlight in his eyes and gives him vertigo. He sees that Greenelm is looking for some sign of psychosis to catch him with and he welcomes it, for it means they will never convince him they are trying to help him when they are only trying to break him and keep him from writing about them.

"Is that true?" Roger says.

At the next meeting, Greenelm tries to be friendly, to be buddies, and speaks at length to another patient over the phone. "Anywhere you like. You choose it. No, we don't have to meet in this office. We can have a drink together, chew the rag." But Roger doesn't go for this either. It's too late. He does not want to be buddies with his enemy. He will keep it formal and at a distance so he can't be tricked. Greenelm is cold at the next meeting in his office.

"But you must be a homosexual. No grown man in our rough Anglo-Saxon society could possibly be so sensitive and nice-looking without being homosexual. Look at your hands. They're so soft and slender they're almost girlish. You like to dance, that's what young girls like to do. And you're so emotional and so poetic, that's feminine, too."

Roger holds his tongue. He thinks of the young James Joyce and his vow of silence, exile and cunning. He knows they are after his balls. He knows they want to get at his guts, he has fought them so long and so hard at such great personal cost. He knows that once they get him to think of himself as feminine, they will be able to make him submit like a female, they will be able to rule him. But he also knows he isn't homosexual. He knows what all his dreams and unconscious urges mean, symbolically and otherwise. In fact, he knows so much about Freudian symbols that Greenelm has had to be convinced he didn't have an extensive education in psychology, that his psychological education consisted of reading *The Basic Writings of Sigmund Freud* when he was nineteen, and that he had an intuitive grasp of symbol and metaphor because he was a poet. The next week Greenelm says, "You must know this is our last visit together. After this visit you will see the Chief Psychiatrist and if she is satisfied that you are of sound mind and able to function with harmony in the society on a socially acceptable level, you will be released."

"Yes," Roger says.

"Of course, you know now no police have ever been after you."

Roger stares at him.

"And no police are after you now. Are they?"

But Roger just stares at him.

"You have to show proof that the psychotic disturbance is now healed in order to be released from state care."

But Roger just stares at him.

"This will have to be postponed. Come in next week," Greenelm says.

Roger waits for the questioning again. He does not know what to say. He wants to be free. He does not want to be locked up again and does not want to have to keep coming to see the Shrink.

"Look, Roger. This is your last chance. Just *say* that the police have not been after you and are not after you now. Just say it!"

"I— I— I want to   I really want to. I— I—" Roger says but he cannot say it and Greenelm says, "For heaven's sake! Come in next week!"

But Greenelm is not there the next week and he waits for two hours on the bench outside the Chief Psychiatrist's office. He knows they are trying to get him to explode. But he tells himself over and over again that he only has to keep calm for a short time and he will walk out of the office a free man, but only if he remembers what is important and what is trivial. He outwaits them and the black female psychiatrist stares at him for several long seconds, then signs without a word and he picks up his papers, says, "Thank you," and walks out.

He is bubbling with excitement when he gets into his Volkswagen, drives up to Mountain View Cemetery and up and down the paths of the small hills with tombs like ancient Roman houses on them, then up to the gigantic cross at the top of a hill where he can see the Golden Gate Bridge, then down a curving road and straight at an unmarked gray state car with three men inside and one standing by a window, making the plainclothes cop on the outside jump out of the way, then up and down some more hills and finally straight down to the open iron gate. But the road is blocked by the same state car, with all four men in it this time, parked sidewards across the road. But he drives straight at them as if he is going to hit them broadside and makes all of them duck down inside, then swerves around them, up on the lawn and down again to the road on the other side and out the gate with tires squealing. Free! Free! They will never put him back in the nuthouse. He will kill himself first.

He quits his job that night. He will return to school and get his master's degree and finish his novel. He will get a JC teaching credential too and try to fit into society that way. The next day he takes his novel manuscript out of a drawer and sits down at his desk and puts a blank piece of paper in the typewriter. But his stomach aches with tension. He knows he is going to have to pay for not admitting the police weren't after him, for driving his car at an unmarked police car, for quitting his reporter's job, and for starting back to work on his novel again. Dolly was not pleased when he called his publisher and quit. She did not smile in the morning or even say goodbye when she left for work. She only sees more suffering in store for her as well as for him. Nobody cares if he ever writes another word, if he puts one single word down on the blank page. But if he doesn't write, he'll die. He'll kill himself. There is nothing else to live for. He will never again expect the love of a single human being to be cause enough for living. He knows better than that now. He knows that the State can break the love of any human being on earth, except for those few rare people willing to die first, of which he knows none and of which only a few will be born in an overdeveloped, technological police state society in which he lives.

He stands up from the typewriter, walks over to the closet, gets out a little .22 rifle his father bought him when he was nine, sits down and takes his shoe off, then tries his toe on the trigger. But it is clumsy. So he puts the barrel in his mouth—it tastes like coin—then reaches down and presses his thumb on the trigger and finds that it works handily. He can kill himself that way. He takes the barrel out of his mouth, sits there for a moment, considers whether or not to put a bullet in the chamber, then puts the barrel back in his mouth and tries pressing the trigger with his thumb again. Today they get the writers and tomorrow everybody, like in Nazi Germany. But he pulls the barrel out of his mouth, puts the rifle down, stands up, walks back to his desk, and sits down in front of the typewriter again.

He stares at the blank page for long, long minutes, a half hour, three-quarters of an hour, an hour, with no energy nor will in him, wishing his brother, Eddy, and his mother were alive, wishing they were around to encourage him, to give him a reason for starting the book all over again. He has to do it. Not just for himself but for every person in the country, in the world, who cares about freedom, about democracy, about a better world. He jerks his head up, swallows, forces his fingers onto the keys and, with misty eyes and without any idea of what he is going to write, types, "Each tear is a crystal heart. I count them: one, five, paper spots, damp, blurring print, streaking my thoughts, but I'll spread them for you, give the why. Why? Because I ache in my guts. Because my intestines cramp with memory and that memory is greased with brain and blood and this is the why of that . . ."

Something Has Died

"You are not going to spank my son! You are not going to beat him with a strap or a belt or, or anything!" Dolly says. Her back is to the big picture window that overlooks a wooded hillside of expensive homes in Montclair. They have moved to their home on the big commission she gets as bookkeeper for West Oakland Junk Company. He has earned an M.A., won an important literary prize, a fellowship, had his book accepted for publication, and has a part-time job as lecturer in English at State College, but she pays the bills. It is her house. His son, Randy, is crouched against the wall of the luxurious front room. He has consistently refused to obey any of Roger's instructions, as if he senses that his *crazy* father no longer has any real authority in the house. Roger has tried to reason with him. Now he is going to whip him.

"Dolly, he's got to be responsible. He can't just run around. He'll get in trouble. As his father, I have to teach him what's right and wrong. Don't you see?"

"You're not going to whip my son."

"I am!" Roger says and tries to step around her but she stops him and struggles with him and when he throws her aside, she grabs the phone and starts dialing the police.

"Put that phone down!" he says, but she keeps dialing and he throws the strap down and snatches the phone out of her hands, slams it down and shoves it behind a leather chair. She stands up, sees he no longer has the strap and stands in front of Randy.

"Dolly, don't you see what's happening to us? To our family, too? I don't have any function in this house anymore. We don't have any love together. You don't even kiss me anymore! You haven't kissed me in over three years! I mean really kissed me! You go out with your boss but not with me. We're up here in this fancy house, with two cars, Randy in a private school and no love in our house! Don't you see that?"

"You're not going to whip my son," she says, her huge blue eyes glittering, sparkling with determination.

"Don't you see what I'm talking about?" he says.

"You're not going to whip my son!"

"Don't you love me anymore, Dolly?" he asks.

"You're not going to whip my son," she says.

"Do you love me, Dolly?" She just stares at him. She does not speak. She just stares at him.

"Something has died in me," he says.

One Dog's Life

The room is clouded with pot smoke. Everyone is sitting around in a slow, coasting mental slide when Roger notices how his dog, Boots, keeps getting up and moving restlessly from one place to the other in the room, with his hindquarters hunched and his tail between his legs. His black, furry head hangs forward with a frown on his face.

"Boots doesn't look good," he says.

"He's just stoned," Craig says.

A couple of people laugh.

"I think it's more than that," Roger says and the next morning he hears him bark and looking out sees him squatted against a telephone pole on the treeless San Francisco street in the Haight-Ashbury District and smiles, thinking he is proclaiming his territory. But the next day, Boots yelps when he squats and tucks his tail between his legs a lot the following week and Roger takes him to a veterinarian. He has a swollen prostate gland, a sign of old age. He is twelve years old already. Roger is afraid. Boots, the curly-haired little black dog, is the only creature on earth he can trust and he has already suffered greatly over Roger. A big, spotted Dalmatian set upon him by a twelve-year-old girl in the Montclair hills almost broke his neck. Then the pet clinic sent him home two weeks later with a big hole in his neck and so weak that when he jumped in the car, he fell over backwards. When Roger went down to the office to complain, two big beefy men in orange hardhats sat on a bench and watched him, ready to jump him. But there was no veterinarian on duty, it seemed, and he told the receptionist with pancake makeup caked on her face what he thought about her company anyway. Then when he drove forty miles over mountain roads to get a fatty tumor cut off Boots' hip, Boots scrambled out the door when he picked him up, away from the vet, and jumped in the car through a window and cried in agony all the way back to the cabin where Roger was writing his novel, and when Roger complained the vet had been brutal to him, Dolly said, "He's not suffering very much," and Roger said, "What's the matter with you? What's happening to your soul? Can't you even admit the truth to yourself?" Then when Boots is put on medication and kept in a dark cell for a month for observation and it doesn't work; when he is given an operation which makes him look so gray and thin and so much older but it doesn't work either; when finally another vet keeps him two weeks and makes him yelp every time he touches him, Roger is sure *they* are at least taking advantage of a natural illness to cut another of his ties to Dolly. He is sure they are trying to kill his dog and he takes him out of yet another hospital. Boots, little guy in the seat next to him, steps over Roger's lap and stretches himself across Roger's chest and presses himself up against him, all seventeen of his furry pounds, and stays there for five long minutes, and Roger knows that he will never put him back in another hospital. He knows that he will keep him with every minute until he dies. Boots will never see another veterinarian.

But Boots is so weak and wobbly that Roger has to carry him around in his dog basket. Every morning and evening he has to give him his pills and stick a long plastic catheter up his penis and drain the urine out of him, then put eggs in milk and chocolate for him to drink since he cannot eat solid food. And Boots' face becomes pretty and soft like a puppy's again. Roger loves him more than anything on earth. And one morning when he walks back into the kitchen after pouring Boots' urine in the toilet, Boots, who is lying on the drainboard of the sink waiting for him, looks up into his eyes and wags his tail, and Roger's heart almost breaks. His eyes fill with tears. That little wag of the tail, that little gesture of appreciation, makes all the suffering worthwhile. But that night Boots cannot make it up a three-inch step from the front room to the bedroom to sleep with Roger. Then he throws up the only thing he can hold down, his milk, and lies down next to his basket, gasping, a blank look in his eyes. And sobbing, Roger takes his dog to the closest vet for a death shot to the bloodstream and by the time the vet pulls the needle out, Boots, who looks like he is sleeping, is dead.

The Real Way to Live

Big green eyes appear in the doorway where he is registering students for creative writing classes. The eyes keep glancing at him as they cross the room, move around students in other lines and finally appear in front of him. He is afraid his eyes are red from smoking grass and keeps them down. He wonders if he should put on his dark glasses, feels that would be too obvious, then suddenly feels conspicuous about the hip way he looks with his hair curling over his turtleneck sweater and his brown hip-hugger cords.

"What grade did you get in freshman English?" he asks.

"A," she says.

"Then you can take the class," he says.

"Don't I have to get a blue permission card signed by the instructor first?" she asks, watching him closely.

"I'm the instructor," he says.

"Oh!" she says and blinks her eyes.

When it is her turn to read one of her poems, he expects a certain amount of awkwardness from her like most freshman students, even if they are honor students. But as she begins to read, he is astonished by the polish of her delivery, the ease and articulation, the perfectly modulated voice that so suits the feminine thoughts and feelings of her poem. He is struck by her soft, childlike beauty; the long sandy hair that drapes her shoulders, the long, long lashes that shade her green eyes, the slight pucker of her lips like a pout as she speaks, and a smile of endearment spreads over his mouth and he shakes his head in disbelief at her loveliness, at the tenderness of the moment, then catches himself and quickly straightens up and glances around the room to see if any students have noticed.

He often sees her waiting by the main door to the commons when he comes through the hall after class, briefcase in hand, heading to the cafeteria for a coke, fearing the police have put her there, though she has a class in a nearby room. Once he raises his hand to wave to her then sees she is with another of his female students and holds his hand stiffly in the air, as if to ward her off, afraid she will stop him to talk. But she writes the guttiest fictional assignments in class and the best paper for the midterm exam and he stops to tell her so one Spring day and they begin to talk and he finds himself wanting to be with her, asking her what she does in her free time. When they sit and face each other on a bench between buildings, she says, "You love life, don't you?"

"Yes," he says, noticing the flaws in her beauty, the nose a little too large in the tip and the slight double chin when she looks down.

"I want to, too, but this engineering student I've been going out with and his crowd seem to look down on too much enthusiasm. They make me feel foolish or like some child if I get excited over something or laugh too much or maybe cry in a movie," she says and looks up at Roger only a couple of feet from her, straddling the bench.

"That's because they live by blueprints and are afraid of emotion. But don't you stop showing it. Remember, you've got to wear your heart on the outside, no matter how much they hurt you," he says, becoming her teacher again. "Remember, if you're emotionally honest, if you show how you feel and don't hide anything, nobody can stab you in the back. Nobody can lie about your motivations or behavior because they're up front for everybody to see. That's the healthiest and strongest way to live and the best way to write."

She watches him while he speaks, then nods her head and says, "He tries to get me to drink a lot, too, though, and 'loosen up that way,' he says."

"And ball you while he's at it," Roger says.

"I'm a virgin," she says, lifting her finger to make her point as if she is the teacher, then glances up at a student who pokes his head out the window just above them and smiles as if he has heard everything.

"Would you like to go have dinner with me?" he asks in a shaky voice.

"Sure," she says and smiles.

Her smiling face appears in the upper half of the window frame of her room as if she is standing on a chair to see him when he walks up the front porch to her door and calms the fluttering inside him at the prospect of having to meet her family.

He shakes hands with both her father and her mother in the front room, noticing the cleancut features of her father, a perfect Anglo-Saxon type with thinning, silvery hair and a pinkish, slightly freckled complexion. He looks like a career cop, yet when Roger shakes hands with him, he is very pleasant and there is a modesty to him that Roger likes, a meekness almost in the spare words of his greeting that show he doesn't, really doesn't think too much of himself.

Her mother has a broad smile on her face and a hint of prettiness still in the wrinkled green eyes behind the rimless glasses, though there is a certain lack of interest in her own appearance, her loose-fitting dress, her apron, the brown hair which hangs in limp curls around her tanned, soft cheeks, as if she doesn't leave the house much and so doesn't dress up.

Everyone stands around in a quiet tense circle, stuck for words, what to do next, while Penny and her mother and her father look at Roger and Roger looks around for something to do, then spies the dog and, leaning down, starts tickling the old dachshund behind the ears. The little animal rolls over on its back and Penny says, "Look at Tilly! She usually barks at strangers!" and everyone smiles.

Penny smiles as they speed down the Eastshore Freeway, her back against the passenger door, but keeps looking at him and then away, and he keeps looking at her, then at the road, then at her, then at the road. Neither of them has much to say and seem locked in silence this first official moment of being alone together, until he can't take the tension anymore and reaches out and clasps fingers with her and holds onto them tightly as they drive, moving along in the light evening traffic, San Francisco Bay shining slate gray and silver in the dusk behind her.

In the Italian restaurant he tells her for the second time to eat her meatball sandwich and pulls his hand back when she says, "Don't act like my father," liking the way she tells him directly what she feels. It makes him trust her and he makes a mental note to watch that teacher's tendency of his, although the eighteen years between their ages—36 and 18—serves to bring it out. Later, he kisses her under a street light in front of St. Francis of Assisi Church, picks her up by her underarms, sits her down on a car fender, then strokes her breast once, softly.

"They're small," she says.

"They're nice," he says, then adds, "I'll probably marry you."

She is waiting for him outside his last afternoon class the next day but starts walking away down the hall when he comes out as if she is just passing by.

"Penny!" he calls and hurries to catch up with her, aware that her being there is no coincidence but not sure whether it is her own strategy or that of the police. It can be either or both. He believes they are watching the romance at the very least and maybe they are encouraging it. He sees signs of it that day when they go into a delicatessen on Ocean Avenue to get some sandwiches made and are dancing while they wait to a slow tune on the jukebox. He turns her in slow graceful swirls, rocking slightly, slowly, with each sliding step, her face next to his, unconcerned with the man behind the counter in the white chef's cap until Roger sees him look up with the jingle of the doorbell and, turning slowly, sees a young, starting-to-sag-around-the-middle man in a blue sportshirt come in, smile at Roger, then walk past him to the counter. Roger pirouettes around, watching him, feeling put-on, guessing the guy is a cop trying to encourage the courtship, this contact with a girl who might bring him back into a family unit again, in harmony with a society he fears and mistrusts. The idea embarrasses him and he slows, finally, to a stop before the music ends.

But he wants her anyway. He is still suffering over Boots' slow, agonizing death, from having to carry him around in the basket, from having to stick a catheter up him twice a day to drain out the urine, from having to wash his rear after he grunted and yelped in the back yard trying to move the mushy little lumps that stuck to him and which he finally dropped around the shrubs. It still all hurts too much: the tape recorder playing "Pictures at an Exhibition," the back yard always damp from the heavy rains that Spring, the lace curtains that hung over the rain-streaked window panes, the smooth spot on the rug in front of the heater where Boots used to lie, his collar in the empty basket in the closet with the little bell that always jingled when he walked. Roger needs love. The writing and the teaching aren't enough. He needs someone to love, has to have someone to love even with cops' approval. It is a matter of life or death. He will kill himself without love, even a compromised one, and he is willing to take the chance that the police sent her into him or, seeing the attraction between them since they follow and spy on him every place he goes, have encouraged the relationship. Still, he cannot accept the romance unless it really includes love and when she throws her arms around him and says, "Oh, I do love you, Roger! I do love you! I really do love you!" he sees the nearly closed eyes, the pucker of her lips with the drawn-out "youuu" and feels it is forced and holds back, keeps himself from squeezing her and returning her words, and she pulls back away from him and asks, "What's wrong?"

"Sometimes when you say that to me, I hear a clang like someone banging a pot against the stove and your face seems to harden in a metallic kind of way. It doesn't seem true."

"Don't you believe in me then?"

"I can feel you trying to love me and I can accept that," he says and she pulls away from him, stares, then suddenly turns away, picks up her purse, pulls a picture of her and her former boyfriend on the night of their senior prom out of her wallet, shows it to him, then rips it in half, tearing her boyfriend out of the picture and hands him the half with her on it in such an obviously symbolic gesture that he frowns when he takes it.

She spins away and pulls a hanky out of her coat pocket, pokes her finger up it, sits on a chair and sniffles and dabs at her eyes as if in a play. When he turns away from her, she leaps up and throws her arms around him and squeezes hard against him and he kisses her hard on her mouth, believing in her wish to love him.

"Ow!" she says the first time he tries it. "Ow!"

He can feel the innerside of her silky thighs against his but with her second cry he feels his hard-on wilt between his fingers and he rolls off her on the couch for the second time. He lies next to her and looks out the curtained window at the frame of the infant's swing glistening with raindrops in the backyard, the melancholy notes of "Sketches of Spain" ringing like bell tones.

"I'm sorry," she says.

"That's okay," he says.

"I really am sorry," she says, "but it hurts."

"That's okay," he says, idly squeezing his now soft and useless prick.

He tries it again a second time about a week later without much hope he will succeed and with her first "Ow!" he lifts his hips over her leg, lies down beside her with a heavy sigh and stares up at the ceiling. She lays her hand on his deflated chest, touches the swell of his pectoral muscle, then looks quietly at him with sloping, almost closed eyes as if near tears.

"Girls who want me touch me, you know," he says and she blinks her eyes, is quiet for a while, then suddenly reaches over and starts fondling his dick. He lies there and looks up at the ceiling as she kneads and caresses it with her fingers, and he continues to lie still, slightly amused. She sits up, leans over, and by the shade-filtered daylight of the windows, carefully examines the folds of his prickly balls, the vein on the underside of his prick, as curious as a child or a monkey at the strange thing he carries between his legs. Then, high and happy, he feels her lift up to meet his charge with her moist box for the first time and he says, "Here goes!" and rams into her, pumps until he comes in a rubber, then hurries into the bathroom and pulls open the shower curtain so she can stand in it nude and watches the blood drip heavily down from the slit of her brown-haired snatch.

"Hooray! Hooray! It's gone!" she cries.

"Are you sure you want to go?" she asks after she shows him the letter from her mother, inviting him to a barbeque and a talk about their daughter.

"Yes," he says, yet on the way, pulling next to her Volkswagen in his MG, seeing her in profile, the turned-up tip of her nose as she peeks through tiny birdseye dark glasses at the road, he feels he is neatly being forced into making a declaration for her hand when he isn't really ready to make any decision about marriage yet. But, skimming along the highway, close yet separate from her in a separate car, he knows he wants to love her and have her love him, and the small flaws in her beauty or even the pat little actions which show the hand of the police aren't enough to deter him. He wants to trust her. He wants to build a new life based on her love and loyalty. He'll take a chance. "The real way to live is to live today," Eddy said.

"I'll marry her," Roger says to her mother, "eventually."

"You seem sincere," her mother says and looks over at her husband, who says nothing.

"There's going to be trouble," he thinks when he nears her house to pick her up and run away to Big Sur with her and sees her father driving down the street in his gray Volkswagen towards him, only a half a block away. Her father's pale eyes stare through the windshield as the cars draw near to each other, as if he is expecting him, though he doesn't wave or nod or make any sign of greeting, and Roger keeps his eyes on the road, glad he is wearing his dark glasses, and speeds up a little after he passes him. But a redheaded homosexual poet with a freckled face, who always comes on outrageously with him, suddenly runs out in the street and waves his arms. Roger gives it the gas to shoot past him, intending to do no more than wave at the guy, when Penny steps out from a hedge behind the poet and waves, too, and Roger spins a U-turn in the middle of the block and pulls up next to the curb.

"What happened? I just saw your father pass by. I thought I was supposed to pick you up at your house?" he says and opens the car door so she can get in.

"My father didn't go by here. He hasn't been home all morning," she says and he starts to insist he saw him until she says, "It doesn't make any difference anyway because my mother kicked me out when I wouldn't tell her what I did with all my clothes."

"For that?" he asks.

"Maybe she sensed that I was going to leave anyway," Penny says. "Bob, here, saw me walking down the street and told me to come in and wait for you. He says we can spend the night here if we want."

"Two blocks from your house?" Roger says. "Get in. Let's get out of here."

He picks her up under the luscious pink blossoms of the passionfruit vine that grows over the porch of the hundred-year-old cabin and carries her over the threshold of their first house together. When he sees her lying, bare-breasted, on the bed in the hot afternoon, her nipples as pink as the passionfruit flowers, her lips as pink as her nipples, waiting for him to finish writing so they can make love, he knows how lucky he is. When he teaches her how to box and punch the fast bag and climb the hills around their cabin, then wrestles with her and holds her down by her wrists on the floor and she smiles up at him, looking as happy as he feels, then he knows how lucky he is. When the smell of charcoaled steaks floats up from the small hibachi in the evening air and he smokes grass with her and dances to the Beatles' "She's leaving home after living alone for so many years, . . . she's leaving home . . . bye-bye," he knows how lucky he is. When they lie out on the sunporch by the bird feed and wrap their arms around each other and stare up at the billions of stars above them before falling asleep he knows how lucky he is, though she first has to get over her fright at the rustling sounds of animals in the Big Sur woods and keeps waking him up the first night they sleep on the porch, saying, "I can hear something! Can you hear it? Hear it?"

He lifts his head and listens and says, "It's only a deer."

But an hour later, she wakes him again and they go through it again and finally, near dawn, when he won't pay any more attention to her, she says, "I'm going in. I'm too afraid," and throws the covers back to get out of bed, he wakes himself up, picks up the flashlight, listens for the noise, then flicks the light onto a small doe eating the green ferns and wild plants on the hillside beneath them. It doesn't even look up and she lies back down and goes to sleep and Roger realizes it is a myth that deer are hypnotized by the headlights of cars. They, like other wild animals, just don't pay attention to the lights.

But he knows how lucky he is, too, when she comes home from town one day when he is still writing with a tiny German shepherd, who is a quarter wolf, says, "We need a family," and insists they take him out for a walk. Omar is a cute, furry little guy who looks like a miniature bear and learns everything very quickly. The first night, he sleeps in a box by their bed and the next morning they find a pile of stools by the cabin door. The next night, Roger hears him whining and scratching and gets up and goes outside with him. Except for a couple of mistakes, he never does it in the cabin again. He is very gutty, too, and hurries after them in the forest, jumps up so high over logs he falls on his back, but whimpers and scrambles up and tries again. But the second day, Penny has an allergic reaction to him and her eyes swell and water and her nose runs.

"I didn't want a dog," he says. "I'm still suffering over Boots' death. I'm afraid I'll be tortured again, whenever they want to make me fall in line. But I'm glad you got him. I love him already. And if you love him and want him, then make up your *mind* that you want him and the reaction will stop."

The reaction stops in a few days. He becomes a very beautiful long-haired shepherd who looks like a wolf but has soft, orange eyes. They give him the care of a child and he is so full of puppy love, he makes them very happy. He makes them a family. He makes their life very beautiful. Roger knows how lucky he is.

He knows how lucky he is when she writes letters to her family and mails them from Monterey, return address care of General Delivery, even though they are strangely formal, even when describing the beauties of the cabin and forest, the view of the ocean three miles away, letters which show him she doesn't really communicate with her family nor they with her, everything between them nice and polite so it doesn't hurt, even when their daughter runs away. It helps confirm the thought he cannot get rid of that they helped her to leave. He tries to train her not to be afraid of the truth but is sometimes too blunt and suffers for it.

He is getting a glass of water from the kitchen faucet at one end of the big, one-room cabin when she steps over to him to get something and he sees pink patches over her eyelids and under her eyes when she looks at him.

"Man, I guess I'm just getting to see what you really look like," he says and when she ducks her head and hides her face in her hands, he feels like a brute and throws his arms around her and hugs her to him as her body jerks with sobs.

"I'm sorry. But don't worry. We'll go to a doctor and he'll give you some medicine and a proper diet to follow and your face will clear up fast," he says and squeezes her to him. But she continues to jerk with sobs and he says, "Do you hear? We'll go today and your face will clear up soon. It's only what you're eating."

She nods her head and when he lifts up her chin and pries her fingers gently down from her face, she manages a small smile but squints her chapped eyes and ducks her head again. Yet, he knows how lucky he is. He knows how lucky he is even when she comes back from town and throws herself on the bed and starts crying.

"What's the matter? Tell me what's the matter?" he asks, laying his hand on her shoulder, feeling her body jerk with her sobs.

"They   They   ." she says, lifting her head from the pillow. "The nurses in the office never gave me a pamphlet on how to use birth control pills. That's why I've been having cramps and headaches, the doctor said. They gave me pills without the pamphlet. Oh-oh-oh!" she cries and bursts out sobbing again, "Why? Why? Oh, why would they do that to me?" she whines, then pushes her face in the pillow again, and sobs and moans.

"That's the way the world is, Penny," he says, stroking her shoulder, and she lifts her head, her eyes red-streaked and glistening and says, "But why? Why do they have to be so cruel? To me?" then bursts out into another run of tears and hides her face in the pillow again.

"Because that's the way it is, Goddamnit!" he yells and straightens up, pulls his hand away from her and steps back to the table where he has been writing all morning. "You ran away with me! You chose to break society's rules, to live out of wedlock with a man! Your English instructor and still married, no less. Now, you've got to pay! You're not a sweet little middleclass coed anymore. You're a whore by the standards of those shrivel-

66

snatched old spinsters in that reactionary town! You've got to pay your dues! You broke the rules, now pay your dues! And quit sniveling. We've been living together for over a month now and you're no cherry anymore. Expect more of this, if you want a life of your own choosing that isn't based upon convention, that has some inner spiritual direction, that suits the mores of your own generation not theirs!"

She stops sobbing and though the tears are still running out of her eyes, lifts her face to look at him.

"You want to be free? You want to make your own life? Then get ready to pay and pay some more. That's the way it is. That's the way it will always be for anybody who's got the guts to go his own way. You've got to be strong. You can't cry. You can't snivel like this. You might as well go back to your family if you're going to do that."

Her tears stop and she lifts her head from the pillow, her reddened eyes on him, the yellowish flecks of his eyes glistening in the bright morning light that streams through the window.

"You're just getting your first taste of what I've been going through for a long time—years! Now you know what it costs to be a rebel, especially a girl rebel. So be strong, take it when it comes, and don't be afraid and don't allow yourself to get hard, to get cynical, no matter how much it hurts!"

He steps back to her again and, reaching out, grabs her hand and pulls her into a sitting position on the edge of the bed. She allows herself to be pulled up, then tries to hold a sob down and hiccups and they both smile, and he knows how lucky he is, even when he hears the news over the radio that evening that Martin Luther King has been killed.

PART TWO Manhunt
Black Panthers

A light afternoon mist has begun to fall in the Santa Cruz Mountains. Yellow road signs that read SLOW and MEN AT WORK glimmer on the curve of the four lane highway and Roger curves his MG roadster slowly and carefully to the right before starting up the half mile incline to the next curve which veers left out of sight. Penny is sitting quietly next to him, her seat belt fastened around her waist, and Omar is asleep on the small shelf behind the seats, under the blurred, plexiglass back window. Only the drone of the motor, the "shhhh" sound of rubber tires on wet asphalt, and the "click, click, click" of the windshield wipers can be heard in the car. All the men wear wet yellow raincoats and the one holding up the SLOW sign looks closely at Roger from under a yellow raincap with steel-rimmed spectacles and light colorless eyes, and his glance is so official that it unnerves Roger and causes the picture in *Newsweek* magazine of Martin Luther King in swirls of white satin, puffy-lipped and shut-eyed and dead, to flash in his mind. The spasm of shock that jerked through him then touches him again with a warm rise of tears to his eyes, eyes large and drooping with a dreamy gaze to them. He looks sad. His skin is smooth, ivory-toned and stretched taut over prominent cheek bones, with subtle lights and shadows on it. He is going back to The Movement after six years. He is risking the peace and security he finally won through his novel writing, but he has to do it. King has been killed only a few days after he prophecied his own death and a rightwing coup in America by 1970. Roger has to do it or he won't be able to live with himself.

He shifts into second, keeps the MG at a low speed, and turns very slowly away from the men performing some kind of road work on the opposite shoulder, then starts climbing the rain-slicked highway, aware that the far opposite lane coming down the hill on the four lane highway is blocked off with yellow pyramid markers the whole length of the incline between the curves. A large diesel truck is droning very slowly up the right lane about a third of the way up the incline on his side of the road. The tips of pine trees and small oaks poke up beyond the truck on the thousand foot drop down into the canyon below and the sky is an unbroken mass of dark clouds clear to the horizon beyond. As Roger begins to gain speed up the hill, taking his time to play it safe on the slippery pavement, he notices a yellow volkswagen come around the curve up ahead and move down the hill toward him, swaying slightly as if the driver is having trouble straightening out.

He keeps his eye on the car as he continues to gain speed up the hill, moving near the truck on the outside lane, then drawing even with its rear trailer. He is nearing the middle of the first trailer when he sees the volkswagen suddenly shoot out of its lane and cross the double line into his lane, jerk once to its right again as if the driver is trying to pull back across the double line, then keeps turning to its right, spinning in a circle as it flies straight toward him.

For a fraction of a second he takes the whole scene in: the volkswagen turning end-first toward him, and the big truck moving slowly, heavily up the hill in the outside lane, completely blocking any chance he might have of swerving out of the way. Then, without another thought, without a single sensation of fear, he stamps on his gas pedal and shoots ahead, trying to clear the truck before the volkswagen hits him, not thinking about whether he can make it or not, just trying to make it, seeing the volkswagen ahead and the truck's left front fender on his right, measuring everything by that fender, his body taut but elastic, total coordination between mind and body, swerving to his right in front of the fender, expecting the impact of the volkswagen from one side and the truck from the other, hearing a crash right behind him, sure it is his own car, but has no time to think about it for he is moving straight toward the edge of the road, only a few feet from shooting out into space, into the tips of the pine trees directly in front of him, gray clouds beyond, and he spins his wheel to the left, feels the car tip to the right as if it is going to start rolling over, then spins the wheel to the right, straightens the tires, hits the brake and brings the MG skidding to a halt with a scraping sound from under the floorboards.

"Quick! Out of the car, Penny!" he says, still afraid the car will start rolling over. She slides out her door, taking Omar with her and Roger slides out her door, too, afraid to rock the car by trying to open his door on the uphill side. He throws a roll of joints into a clump of bushes below the car and climbs up onto the highway, sees with relief that his left wheels have caught on the foot-high, paved ridge on the outer edge of the shoulder and that his car is unmarked except for the bent oilpan underneath, the muffler, and the exhaust pipe. He is amazed to see that the volkswagen has crashed into the left fender of the truck about a hundred feet down the highway from the MG. It is hard to believe he has covered so much space so quickly.

But he is suddenly excited, and mouth open, brows furrowed, he says, "Stay here, Penny! Watch Omar!" and runs down the highway to the truck and the few cars already piling up behind it, where a gray-haired, middleaged man gets out of the volkswagen and begins to talk to the truck driver, a tall man around forty, with graying hair and the rough features of a working man.

"You almost killed me!" Roger says to the gray-haired man.

"I was trying to do a Barney Oldsfield," the man says and Roger stares into his gray, saggy-cheeked face, struck dumb by the words. He remembers instantly that they are the exact words of a man arrested for killing two Bay Bridge workers with a speeding car only a couple of months past. Roger has told a lot of people about the man and he is now suspicious of this man using the same words after almost killing him. He turns away and trots down the highway toward the group of working men to ask them to call a cop when a highway patrol car comes around the curve and drives straight up to the accident.

"I was dri—" Roger starts to say, but the cop turns away from him with a sour expression and while his partner directs traffic around the crash, he calls the truck driver, the driver of the volkswagen and a woman in a black car parked behind the truck into his patrol car, closes the doors and leaves Roger standing out in the steady mist by himself for the whole interview. Then after a tow truck appears and separates the volkswagen from the truck, he gets back into his patrol car and leaves with his partner without giving anyone a ticket and without once asking Roger a single question or offering him any help.

"She'll get you made an honorary Black Panther, Roger," Gary says, after introducing him and Penny to a beautiful black-haired girl and opening the cartons of Southern Fried Chicken and potato salad.

Gary pockets the bite of chicken in his black cheek and nods at the girl as she bites on a leg and balances a plate of potato salad on her slim thigh. Her long black hair hangs down to the nipples of her breasts, which are surprisingly large for her slender build and which poke through the filmy material of her light blouse.

Roger takes another bite of his chicken wing to keep from having to say anything, suspicious, feeling that the offer is somehow related to the strange accident. The road sign SLOW now takes on a symbolic meaning, a warning not to get involved with The Movement again after he has made a separate peace with the powers that be. The whole thing means most of all that he is under surveillance again and has probably always been under surveillance. If *they* will kill a president and a Nobel peace prize winner, they won't miss any sleep over destroying a radical writer who knows too much. He watches carefully as Gary's black cheeks puff up like a trumpet player's with chicken and potato salad, leans back in his chair as if to pull in his belly—thickening from his good life as an EOO counselor, not near the shape he was in when they were in high school together, Roger thinks—all the food in one cheek, and says, "The Black Panthers are where the revolution is at. And she knows Kathleen Cleaver personally and can probably work it out for you."

Roger looks at the girl again with soft eyes that belie his thought that Kathleen Cleaver and this girl might be a fink, then thinks of the possibility of becoming a Panther, something which would put him in the middle of the fight again and he turns to Penny to see what she thinks.

She is already looking at him with her eyes slightly squinted as if she is already thinking about it, too, or is hurt by the presence of the girl. She continues to stare at him without eating, holding a chicken breast in her hand, then as if no one else is in the room, her eyes still on his, asks, "Why do you want to become a Black Panther?"

Roger thinks about that question the next morning at the funeral of Bobby Hutton, the seventeen-year-old Black Panther shot down by the Oakland Police when he sees the pinkskinned, plainclothes white cop sitting in an unmarked cop car just inside the parking lot gate behind the church. He thinks about that question when three young black brothers with naturals step right past him in the lot without looking at him or Penny. He thinks about it when they are stopped by the crowd of hushed, hostile black people at the foot of the church stairs, a crowd which spills out into the street, around double-parked, idling cars in front of the modern church, fills the sidewalk on the opposite side of the street and all the corners of the intersection in the black residential neighborhood.

He thinks about that question when he follows Gary up the stairs of a side door, his full, black cheeks dull in the gray light, his arms hanging forward in his striped sportcoat, his belly protruding and his rear end popping out in back, up the back steps to the balcony, where there are so many black people packed together that he can't see at all at first and tries to edge his way towards an empty chair up against the window on the other side. He thinks about it as he edges sidewards, moving carefully, brushing against a suitcoat back, an arm, a young woman's side, seeing only the side of a black face, the back of a head, not one eye straight on, catching a word over the speaker now and then, moving through them as if he is up to his waist in water and doesn't want to make a ripple that might annoy someone, until he finally reaches the chair and steps up on it.

He thinks about it as he tries to make out the features of the black figure in the coffin, a steel gray, satin-lined box below the pulpit, but can't. He remembers the picture in the *Berkeley Gadfly* of the black kid in the Black Panther outfit behind the bullet-shattered glass with a "What's your story?" arch to his eyebrows and a cocky peak in the center of his cap brim, a kid who was shot down by all the cops when he came out of a bullet-sieved, broken-paned basement full of teargas smoke, where he and Eldridge Cleaver had been cornered by the Oakland Police, stripped to the waist, his eyes swollen and blinded by tear gas, his hands up, trying to surrender. He thinks about Penny's question when Penny finally reaches him after working her way through the crowd and notices that her changeable green eyes are gray now like the overcast sky, looking much too sad, too large for her small face and he squeezes her hand when he helps her up on the chair with him to make her feel better, knowing that she is only there because of him and that she is full of doubts. When she squeezes back and presses against him, he thinks how pretty she looks with her long, gold-burnished hair and her curvy dancer's body in her purple knit minidress and blue tights, and how lucky he is to have her, but he feels the rough, picked skin of her thumb, which she sometimes sucks in private when she is unhappy and he thinks about her question again.

He thinks about her question when he looks back at Bobby Hutton and realizes that he doesn't mean anything to him. When he acknowledges that Bobby Hutton is just a black corpse in a gray coffin no matter how much he might want to care for him. No matter how much he might be capable of caring for any black or white or yellow or brown man, no matter how much he might identify with the underdog of any type, and be able to rise above his own need to protect himself against a pattern of deceit and manipulation, Bobby Hutton doesn't mean anything to him personally. He thinks about this as the sweat starts to trickle from his armpits and bubble on the foreheads of the black people around him. He catches the smell of talcum powder and remembers how one of his black buddies in high school used to splash it under his arms after showering in the gym, a memory which makes him feel something personal with his black brothers.

But he still thinks about her question when the preacher quits and somebody announces that Bobby Seale will now speak and there is a ripple of bodies as the two lines of Black Panthers on both sides of the church snap to attention. He thinks about her question as Bobby Seale speaks, too, says, "Bobby Hutton died to get the hog out of the stream! And that isn't black racism but black realism!" He thinks about her question when the organist starts playing "Going Home" and the crowd starts pushing quietly out of balcony and he watches the people in the pews below pour into the middle aisle to file past the black corpse with the white swirls of silk around it. The rosy hue from the stained windows behind the altar gives all the black faces a somber tone and makes Roger feel more left out of their suffering than when he had first come in with hopes of joining them. He stays up on the chair after helping Penny down and watches the people file past the coffin below, only able to pick out a couple of white faces in the line, which makes him feel even more like an enemy.

When he sees a row of well-dressed hippies slide out their pew into a side aisle and move out the back door instead of going out past the coffin, he feels like a fool for thinking he could just come and join the black revolution or seriously think of ever becoming a Black Panther. He steps down from the chair yet is forced by the slow-moving crowd to watch the people move past the coffin and he feels guilty for wanting to cop out on the black experience, the sadness, the suffering, just because it doesn't fit his preconceptions and he has to suffer for it in a different way than he had expected, without being welcomed into loving black arms.

He moves over to the balcony railing and looks over, his face a frown, his dark glasses giving his sallow face a serious look. He stays up there still sweating from the heat, trying to make up his mind, until the crowd on the balcony files out and Penny presses up against him and upon seeing the quiet but impatient look in her eyes, he suddenly says, "Let's go down there and get in line."

He leads her down the stairs and up the middle aisle to the end of the doubled-up line of black people moving step by slow step toward the coffin in front of the altar and stops, hoping he'll suddenly feel some kind of harmony sweep over him, some intangible thing that will stop him from feeling like an enemy among the black people. But the black people in line and those still moving into it from the pews stare at them, the only two white people in line, and he suddenly remembers that his neck and chin are streaked with blood from his hurried shaving, and he lowers his eyes, keeps them sighted on the soft carpet so he won't have to look at anyone and can concentrate upon how *they* feel, can try to achieve some sense of identification with *them,* some sense of *their* suffering and not get hung up on his own appearance. And he keeps his eyes down all the way up the aisle, only glancing up once to look at Penny, whose face is pinched with concern, as they draw closer to the coffin. Finally the last black man moves out of the way and Roger steps up to the coffin to see the black boy in the middle of all that silk. But he is astounded for there is no slender young black boy with a cocky arch to his eyebrows in the gray coffin. There is only a black, puffy corpse so full of formaldehyde it looks fat, with white streaks of makeup covering the slug holes in the black skin, and Roger gasps and claps his hand over his mouth to stop a sob and sees Penny turn toward him with wide eyes, her mouth falling open and her hands flying up to her own face, too.

The whole dirty, deserted look of Gary's flat gives him an uneasy feeling, as if Gary doesn't really live here. There are unwashed dishes in the sink with blackened food stains on them, only a half-full bottle of tokay wine in the empty, sour-smelling refrigerator. The portable stereo is closed up tight as a suitcase and all the albums are lying around covered with dust. All the shades of the windows are down but the one he is standing by. Ominous shadows hang from the gray pieces of Victorian furniture, flatten a mattress that serves as a bed, slopes across walls, blurs novice paintings and posters and darkens all the rooms of the small flat.

The strange accident in the Santa Cruz Mountains seems a deliberate attempt to stop him and seems, at the very least, a warning of what can happen to him if he insists on getting back into The Movement. He looks around the room for places the police could plant bugs—the Victorian lamp with the porcelain base and the blue-tasseled satin cover, streaked with dust, the checkerboard holes of the metal air vent next to the floor, the mattress itself, even the drawers of the bureau, and, naturally, the stereo, with the natural receiver of its speaker and an unhappy sense of foreboding hangs in his body. If his feelings are right, he is coming under heavy pressure again. He is again being driven outside the law and has to expect that every person or group, no matter how radical, can and will cooperate with the FBI. If it is the Panthers it can mean guns and even death.

He thinks of Malcolm X dead on the stage, his teeth sticking out of his gaping mouth like a dead goat's, of Martin Luther King flat on his back on the motel balcony, of Bobby Hutton's puffy face in the coffin, and John F. Kennedy's body falling forward in the back seat of the limousine. He winces and lowers his head, keeps it down for a few moments, waiting for the pain to pass, his nose bridge a strong, straight line in the harsh window light, his large eyes heavy-lidded and sloping, distant and solemn with his sadness.

Finally, he looks out the window, stares up at the gray atomic energy building on the wooded Berkeley hills, the concrete peak of the campanile bell tower, the gray campus buildings, and all the trees and rooftops and streets and lawns and jigsawshaped back fences of the neighborhood around him, and the whole city as far as he can see is dull and sullen-toned under a flat ceiling of low, gray clouds. Suicide weather.

Gary bursts into the bedroom from the hallway, puffing, his heavy lips sagging open, bright pink and wet against his round, black cheeks.

"Heard a rumor the Vacaville authorities are going to attack us when we show up to demonstrate for Eldridge Cleaver this afternoon!"

"What? Who told you?" Roger asks, searching Gary's dark eyes to see if he is faking it.

"That girl, Lydia, from last night. She heard that the

Vacaville Police, the Sheriff's Department, and all the reserve prison guards they can get from San Quentin and Folsom are waiting with riot sticks, tear gas, and mace to give us the works when we show up."

But Gary won't look at Roger. There are murky discolorations on his shiny cheeks, a brown undercurrent in the darker black that surfaces rosy there and stands out as if the blood has risen to them with embarassment, and he sits quickly down on the bed and starts untying his dress shoe, slips it off, then holds it up and looks inside it, glances past it as Penny comes in the door, then bends down, slips his shoe back on, stands up to force his foot all the way in, twisting his ankle to help, then says, "Let's get to the rally," and bends down to tie his shoe.

Kathleen Cleaver's voice rings in the air over the lawn from the edge of Lake Merritt, "As far as we know then, the Parole Board revoked Eldridge's parole this morning for associating with known criminals and . . ." She is speaking from a microphone on a truck behind a line of Black Panthers, her wild, reddish brown hair a bush of coppery glints in the sun, with a large red PEACE & FREEDOM PARTY banner hanging from the sidegates of the truck behind her. Two thousand people are seated on the lawn that slopes down to the waters of the lake, glittering in the afternoon sunshine. Huey Newton, the Supreme Commander of the Black Panthers, is locked in an isolation cell on the twelfth floor of the Court House across the street from the lawn. And black girls with natural hairdos move through the seated crowd, their bronze arms bared long and smooth as they hand out BOBBY HUTTON MEMORIAL FUNERAL and FREE ELDRIDGE CLEAVER pasteboard signs to hang on car doors and take donations in big, white cardboard buckets.

The girls handing out posters seem to disprove Gary's warning but they only increase Roger's confusion, his doubts and suspicions, though Penny, seated on her blue peacoat next to him, gives him a sense of security she is so calm and serious, intent on Kathleen Cleaver.

"Eldridge is being kept in Vacaville until his gunshot wounds are better, then he'll be transferred, probably, to Folsom Prison. But they're no longer claiming that he's being kept in Vacaville for better treatment in the hospital, while we know through the grapevine that he's in the hole. The pigs have gone and done the thing, baby. We've got to get out there and demonstrate and get them to revoke their own order today or postpone a decision until the Parole Board meets next week."

Roger strains for a better look at her, keyed up by her high-pitched, intense voice, thinking of the pictures in the papers of her, the look of the cat about her, with her slanted green eyes, pug nose and fair complexion, her wild light hair sticking out around her face like a lioness, and claps hard with frustrated enthusiasm when she finishes speaking and a big, plump Panther moves over to the microphone and surrounded by ten other Panthers in black leather jackets, black pants and berets, raises his black-gloved fist and shouts, "Free Huey!"

"Free Huey!" the Panthers answer.

"Free Huey!" the crowd shouts.

"Free Huey!" Roger shouts, too, and jabs his fist in the air with all the others, jabs it with each chant up at the jail on the top floor of the courthouse behind him, where Huey Newton is in an isolation cell only across the hall from where Roger had been in the padded cell at eighteen, naked, living on two pans of water and four slices of white bread a day for five days for breaking the jaw of an ex-convict who grabbed his ass in the jail tank every day for two long months, forcing him to fight or submit.

"Free Huey! Free Huey! Free Huey!" he shouts and snaps his fist like a spear in the air, poking it up at the tall mass of concrete from the safety of the lawn and great numbers of other rebels, fighting back in the open against the police who have haunted his life and taken his woman from him. He glances over at Penny and sees her drop her small fist against her thigh and realizes that she had only jabbed it in the air the first time and had barely made a gesture the second time. She peeks up at him now from over the rim of her chinked sun glasses, her long lashes curling up to her eyebrows, and touches his leg with her hand as if in apology. But her small mouth is drooping and in the pause after the chant, Roger slips his arm around her and hugs her to him.

But girls handing out signs for the procession to Vacaville draw close to them and make him doubt once more the rumor of the planned attack there, until Bobby Seale is announced as the next speaker and there is a quick shifting of men on the platform as a noose of black bodies draws close around the black figure behind the microphone, a noose drawn tight to protect the last free Panther leader from assassination, and he realizes for the first real time that there can be shooting, not only in Vacaville but on the lawn.

He twists around to scan the rooftops and spots about twenty men on top of the three-story library across Fallon Street, and some on a small, one-room concrete city utility building nearby. The men on the roof—some with cameras—are silhouettes moving against a blue sky and Roger can see that a sharpshooter with a telescopic sight would have an easy chance of picking off any man at the mike and if it is Bobby Seale the Panthers will be leaderless. When he turns back toward the mike there is more shuffling and shifting around behind it, a black woman steps to the microphone in place of Bobby Seale and the Vacaville rumor seems even more real.

Roger watches closely as the Panthers around the mike spread out and make a loose half-circle behind the plump brown woman, about forty years old, whose big busts and bumpy hips bounce when she steps to the microphone in her shiny beige dress and begins to speak.

"Wha' choo afraid of?" the tan woman shouts, standing spread-legged behind the mike in high heels, jamming her fist in the air. "Awm fo-ty-fo' years old and I an't scared! Wha' choo scared of? Let me tell youuu that when Bobby Seale and Huey Newton were over at Oakland Junior College trying to get themselves an education, they didn't settle for what they just gave out to them. They tried to get some black history in that school and they took on the whole college and the students, too. And by the time they got through there *was* black history in that school! Somethin' all black students can be proud of! Now how 'bout choo? You want to be a slave all your life? Can't get no education and always endin' up with the dirtiest jobs. When you can *get* a job, that is. Why don't you fight for what you are? You ain't askin' for nothin' but a job to work at and a chance to feed and put clothes on yourself, to have your own house to live in and be proud of what you are. Wh' choo scared of? Help these brave men. You black boys down there. Scared because they killed little Bobby and shot Huey and Eldridge? You scared of that? Well, if your fathers and their fathers had fought like these brave men are fighting and getting shot at, Huey and Eldridge wouldn't be in jail and little Bobby wouldn't be dead now!"

"Yeeeeeeeeaaaaaaa!" the crowd shouts and their cheers drown out her voice and someone starts leading the crowd in a Free Huey chant and Roger joins in, picturing handsome Huey Newton more brown than black up there in an isolation cell but really seeing himself at eighteen in the hole only a few feet down the hall, waking up in the middle of the night, panting for breath, naked, no blankets, the solid blackness of the padded cell crushing down on him, suffocating him, sending him scrambling across the small patch of concrete floor with the toilet hole in the middle to the thick, padded door, where he crushes his face down between the pad and the cold concrete floor and tries to suck air out of the dollar-size air holes in the metal strip between the pad and the floor into his crushed lungs, suffering the icy wind that blows in through the barred windows of the jail hall for the rest of the night rather than wake up screaming and smothering under the crushing weight of total blackness in the cell again, wondering how the world can go round when one innocent person is suffering so much so unjustly.

"Down with the pigs! Down with the pigs! Down with the pigs!" someone shouts and Roger jumps to his feet and jabs his fist in the air with all the other people, his mouth twisted, his whole face contorted, shouting, "Down with the pigs! Down with the pigs! Down with the pigs!'' until his voice is hoarse and he sees Penny shudder down below him, then hold her arms to her sides, lower her eyes from him and sit tensely as the chant explodes around them, seems to boom out in echoes over the choppy waves of the lake behind the truck until someone shouts, "Silence! Silence!" and the cheering dies down enough for a speaker to say, "Marlon Brando will now speak," and there is quiet again.

A gray-haired man appears behind the microphone and Roger recognizes him from that morning in the graveyard, holding his Cadillac door open while two black Panther leaders carry a slim black girl, long legs dragging, hurting so bad, her miniskirt clear up to her crotch, her garter straps showing, moaning as if she wants to die now that little Bobby is dead, over to his car, while he holds the door open, his long graying hair blowing in the wind, his hooked nose sharply silhouetted by the horizon of the hill, the Golden Gate Bridge misty in the background.

"I don't have very much to say," he says, standing very relaxed and calm behind the mike, "not having lived through what you, black men and Panthers, have lived through. I'm just here to learn, to find out what to do, to——"

"Henry Martin! Henry Martin!" a white hippy girl calls, wheeling her baby in a stroller across the strip of lawn near them, irritating Roger by her squeaky voice, displeasing him with her bad complexion, her pale, gaunt look, her mousy brown hair pulled back and hanging between her bony shoulder blades.

"Henry Martin!" she keeps calling, making it hard to hear Brando and people around Roger, including a row of Black Panthers a few feet away by the old white clapboard museum, turn to look at her. One big heavy Panther with a tiny goatee sprouting under his bottom lip squints his eyes at her and smacks his lips in disgust, but by the time she has walked by and her voice has faded, Brando stops speaking, the crowd claps and cheers and Gary comes strolling up the lawn past her, nonchalantly swatting his leg with some folded leaflets.

"Hi!" he says and drops down next to Roger as if he hasn't been gone for all the rally so far and except for a glance out of an eye, just a glimmer of an eyewhite, he doesn't show the slightest sign that Roger might wonder where he's been. But a Panther announces, "Bobby Seale will now speak!" and there is a quick shifting of black-uniformed men down on the truck bed, a tightening noose of black heads around Bobby Seale so that only his face shows in the mass of men, and not even the long stem of the mike can be seen behind their black bodies. Flashbulbs pop and cameras whir when his black-gloved fist flashes in the air, holding his other glove.

Roger turns and looks back at the library through the wide trunks of the eucalyptus trees at the courthouse and the low utilities building across the ramp of Fourteenth Street where, in addition to the men with highpowered rifles, other men huddle behind movie cameras and even more are scattered throughout the crowd, and he can't possibly tell which are legitimate TV and news photographers and which are FBI and police cameramen. But all are pointed at Bobby Seale, the last free Panther leader, his face a mustachioed dark brown, down in the huddle of black and brown faces, black jackets and black berets, on the truck bed.

"Brothers and sisters! Black brothers and the people from the Peace and Freedom Party, all you hippies, let me try to correct one thing!"

He leans closer to the mike, his teeth flashing between his black mustache and his black goatee.

"People are going around saying the Black Panthers advocate violence. That's not true. The Black Panthers advocate self-defense and are willing to fight to the death for a brother Panther. We are willing to die for all our black brothers. But we still don't advocate violence. We advocate self-defense against the pigs. Remember that! Not violence but self-defense against the pigs!"

"Down with the pigs! Down with pigs! Down with the pigs!" a Panther shouts, leaning in over the mike and the crowd takes it up. It seems to burst from clenched fists and Roger nudges Penny to make sure she got the point about self-defense and raises his fist in the air.

Bobby Seale then leans close to the mike again and his whole body shows. The Panthers who had been chanting and jamming their fists in the air aren't crowded around him anymore and Roger sees that the black beret down low on his forehead is a perfect bullseye for a sharpshooter with a telescopic lens.

"Now let me tell you hippies something," he says, pausing, and Roger can't catch his next words because a black girl steps in front of him and holds out a white cardboard bucket for donations and he drops his dollar into it with a smile.

"Now I know that a lot of you hippies belong to the Peace and Freedom Party and that you are capable, even if you are white men, of believing in our cause, like Marlon Brando. But you're not black and though we appreciate your wanting to join us to help the black people, you can't join the Panthers. Only black men can do that."

Roger glances at Gary but Gary keeps staring at Bobby Seale as if he hadn't even made the offer.

"That's another point I want to emphasize. People say that the Black Panthers are racist, that they're anti-white." He shakes his loose glove in front of him. "Well, we're not! We're pro-black, not anti-white! Remember that! Remember that!"

A big cheer goes up from the crowd and the big, plump Panther grabs the mike and starts to lead the crowd in another chant:: "Down with the— Down wi— Dow—" But the mike sputters with static, then fades out, and there is milling and confusion on the truck until it sputters on again and Bobby Seale grabs it.

"What the white peop—" he tries to say but his voice won't carry and he stops as a low mumbling sound swoops over the seated crowd.

People whisper to each other, some get up and stretch and move around and don't sit down until his voice finally comes over the speakers again, fades a couple of times, but he finally manages to say, "Somebody sabotaged this mike and it was probably the pigs."

"Henry Martin! Henry Martin!" the hippy girl with the bad complexion and bony body calls out, coming back by Roger again, still pushing her little blond baby in the stroller, making so much noise that Roger can hardly hear Bobby Seale.

"Why don't you keep quiet?" the big Black Panther with the goatee says. "People are trying to hear Bobby Seale."

"I'm calling for my husband," she says, staring at him through spectacles.

"Find him another way then and don't bother all the people," he says and she pushes her baby away, disappearing among the mass of people down by the truck.

"We need black brothers, young black men, to come and fight with us and help save our people," Bobby Seale says. "What are you afraid of? A sister even came up here and asked you that. Come and join us. And I don't mean any of you Uncle Tom FBI agents either. You good black brothers who care about your people, come and help us save Huey and Eldridge, help us save all the black people. Bobby Hutton was only seventeen years old but he was our Minister of the Treasury, and he died for— He died—" But the mike sputters off again to a few shouts of "Speak anyway, Bobby! Speak anyway!"

But he only cracks his black-gloved fist in his bare palm a couple of times, his teeth flashing as if he is swearing and waits until the mike comes on again.

"This mike has definitely been sabotaged," he says. "And because of that, I'm going to let you all in on some bad news I got about the demonstration for Eldridge at Vacaville today." He pauses and lifts a finger. "There are pigs down there waiting for us with tanks and machineguns. They're going to try and wipe out the Black Panthers today forever! Forever!"

A huge moan rises from the crowd and Penny presses against Roger, leans into his side. He puts his arm around her, feels her shrink up even closer against him and a tremor of fear quivers in his belly. He looks at Gary, almost apologetically, shocked that the rumor is really true and Gary glances back out of a corner of his eyes, his crooked mouth twisted close to a smirk.

"But this mike convinces me," Bobby Seale says. "I was going to take a chance and force the pigs to show their colors. But this mike convinces me how they could stage it all down there outside the prison walls and kill us all. So I'm cancelling the demonstration right now."

A murmur spreads with a restless wave of the seated bodies across the lawn.

"Yes! The demonstration is off! We'll choose our own battleground. I'm not going to give those pigs a chance to kill us all like animals. We're not going to Vacaville today and that's it!"

Land and Liberty

It is quiet over the lawn. Stiff everybody sits or stands, no movement. Squatted down. Upraised heads. Shock on some faces, wide eyes, open mouths. Traffic sounds from the streets the only noise. Silent cars crawling along the opposite bank of the lake, a half mile away. Roger staring at Gary, who sits with his arms resting on his knees, his head hanging forward, a small smirk on his dark lips. Penny huddles under Roger's arm, staring up at him over the top rim of her dark glasses.

"So, it's off," Bobby Seale says, and there is a ripple of limbs and heads along the surface of the sitting crowd, figures standing up, lots of stretching of arms. Some people reaching down to help others up. Coats waving as they are put on. But no sounds. No murmur of conversation. No talking of what just happened. It seems unreal to Roger. People should be excited and all talking at once. He pictures imaginary figures doing that. But in front of him, on the lawn, long-haired hippies and fuzzy-haired blacks move in slow motion, as if in a dream or under water, merely getting up and going away as if it was just the end of a ceremony instead of the cancellation of a great demonstration by one of the bravest of black men because of his fear of a mass police attack. A Panther grabs the mike and tries to lead the crowd in a "Free Huey!" chant, but though he shouts loudly, only a few people down in front join him and the sound is scattered and faint.

Roger gets to his feet and helps Penny stand with one hand, then waits as she brushes strands of grass from her blue peacoat. Gary gets to his feet and stares straight at Roger with hard, black and triumphant eyes, letting him know how powerful he really is. But Roger wonders how he knows so much about the cops. Tense and jittery, he does two knee squats, then hops a little on his toes as if jumping rope in the gym. Bound up inside, he wants some outcry about the cancellation and has an impulse to join a small knot of people, mostly black, gathering around the truck bed when Gary says, "Let's go," and starts across the lawn to the street.

The sun is out. Silhouettes of twenty men cluster on the library roof. The high buildings of downtown Oakland are only a couple of blocks away. It seems like a normal day. Yet the accumulation of fear, paranoia, sadness, frustration and helplessness at hidden police control over everything—the mike, Gary, the wreck in the mountains, even the Panther parade—is overpowering to him. An ominous silence seems to hang over the city. Yet, the traffic hums and honks, the lights change, cars drive by, and the danger of the police seems a distant and almost unbelievable fantasy.

As they drive up past the beautiful lake, the wooded lovers lane section jutting out into the water like a tropical island, his heart aches that he can do nothing about it, that life, action, good wishes can never be fulfilled. He feels like shouting and cursing to break the tension when a Black Panther opening his car door sees the Bobby Hutton placard on their door and jabs up his fist and Roger jabs up his fist, too, and suddenly says, "I'm going to try and write something about the revolution and get it published."

"Where?" Gary asks, snapping his head around to look at him.

But the fire burns in Roger and bursts into flame when he opens the San Francisco *Chronicle* and reads a provocative article on the famous Russian poet, Yevtushenko. He throws the newspaper down flat on Gary's kitchen table and shouts at Penny, still asleep on the mattress in the next room: "Penny! Take a look at this racist shit Yevtushenko has written about Martin Luther King! Look at it! Come here and look at it!"

He leans back in the chair and sees the sleeping bag shift and wrinkle a little and he stands and stalks into the shade-darkened room where Gary has slept and has already left for work, the blankets of his bed wrinkled, then turns and stalks back through the small darkened parlor where he sleeps on the floor with Penny, and into the brightly lit kitchen, his eyeglasses glimmering.

"And that Roy Soames is coming to town this weekend and is always talking that dogmatic party-line shit!" he says, then suddenly turns and stalks back to his typewriter, takes it out of its case, puts it on top of Gary's clothes bureau, raises the shade, pulls the curtain back, sticks a piece of paper into the machine, plugs it in, thinks of Soames and Blum, two great writers he has admired and whom he doesn't trust, who have hurt him, and with all the suppressed hurt and resentment and frustrated love burning in him, he begins to type, hitting the keys hard, the anger in him driving him on, producing a steady, machine-gun-like fire, filled with flame, feeling as if he will rise up and fly like the phoenix from the ashes, not even noticing Penny, just writing, writing, writing . . .

AN OPEN LETTER TO THE MOVEMENT
OR A NOTE ON THE POLICE STATE
"MEXICO CITY—Russian poet Yevgeny Yevtushenko has written

a poem saying the bullet that killed Dr. Martin Luther King 'entered in me . . . and I was reborn a Negro.'

The Soviet writer, vacationing in Mexico, called the poem, published in a newspaper here Saturday, a memorial to Dr. King.

The Ode said:

'He was a negro
But with a pure soul as white as snow
The whites with the black souls
killed him.
When I learned the news
That same bullet entered in me .
And I was reborn a Negro.'

This item published in the San Francisco Chronicle this morning, is a tribute to Martin Luther King—or so the author says. But is it? Certainly aside from the clichés that it's composed of and which is indicative of its sentimental origin, the poem is a classic racist piece of propaganda. Anyone with even a passing knowledge of 'Black is Beautiful' will recognize the unconscious racism in the equating of black with evil and white with good here. But this is from the pen of the great Russian 'rebel' and dissenter, Yevgeny Yevtushenko, the same poet who argued with Khrushchev about art during the Cold War thaw, the same poet who wrote a poem called 'Babi Yar' about the murder of Soviet Jews during World War II, a poem which, purportedly, moved the Russian nation. And Russia is the supposed-to-be 'classless' social-ist society in which racism does not exist in spite of the persecu-tion of the Jews and . . . Yevtuchenko's racism. But racism does exist in Russia as 'Babi Yar' and, in its unwitting way, this poem indicate. Racism exists in Russia after the revolution, a revolution that was led in large part by Jews. Racism still exists in Russia because there has been a change in the economic system but no change in the political system, meaning there is now communism in Russia instead of feudalism in which the state gets the profits instead of aristocrats and profiteers, but the change in the political system has been only from a monarchy, one-man rule, to a dictatorship, one-man rule.

The Marxist objective of the final withering away of the state has not yet been embarked upon, that first step of a thousand miles has not yet been taken, and the attainment of liberty, the ultimate political objective ('The first step in the revolution by the working class is to raise the proletariat to the position of ruling class, to establish democracy'—the Communist Manifesto) has been postponed indefinitely because of pressing 'immediate' problems, the daily battles against the capitalistic world, and the domestic problems of implementing socialism.

The ultimate objectives have been forgotten in the press of the so-called important problems, meaning Russia has racism now because the leaders did not work for the twin objectives of the revolution: land and liberty at the same time. They expected that *once the economic system was changed, greed would disappear and men would be better. That is still a valid idea, but men also change the world, and if the men who implant the new economic structure have the same values in practice, regardless of what they state, as those men they seek to supplant, then the society they bring to light will only be different in quality from the deposed one and not different in kind. The revolution has to be led by saints and not mere politicians or we will end with one form of tyranny instead of another.*

Think: Yevtushenko, this great dissenter of Russia, is not only a racist but does nothing about the hundreds of recognized writers who are locked up in prisons and insane asylums throughout Russia. He keeps totally quiet about them, never dares to fight for freedom of expression though he is a writer, and ends up writing dishonest poems which reflect the reactionary values of the State. The Stalinist bureaucrats still rule in Russia, control the press, and except for a small clandestine portion, all publishing concerns in the country. Writers like Solzhenitsyn and all others who dare to exercise their critical faculties about the contradictions in the existing social structure are put in prisons and nuthouses. And right now they're busting Jews, intellectuals and poets in Eastern Europe, too, under the slogan of international proletarianism.

Yevtushenko's racism is just one facet of a reactionary society which has had a true economic revolution but only a mock political one, not a real one in which consciousness is truly changed, in which people become better human beings because of greater opportunities to fulfill themselves economically, politically, and spiritually. This has occurred because the leaders fought only for power instead of the elevation of man, his continued evolution to a level which would produce the millennium on earth. (Remember that Marx opposed terrorism because the tactics mislead the people from the real objectives, which were to change the world, to make it a better place for all, instead of the privileged few.) A small clique seized power in Russia in 1917, but brought no real change in man's nature because the ultimate goal was forgotten in the struggle to survive at all costs, even at the cost of those ideals which prompted the whole revolution in the first place.

But there's an important lesson for us here, all of us of whatever color, ideology, and faction in the American Movement. We are fighting a revolution here too, and the murder by a white segregationist of Martin Luther King only three days after he warned of a rightwing coup in America by 1970, and the murder of Malcolm X by Black Muslims—the two greatest black men of their time, and probably the two greatest Americans of their time—are inclined to make us want to start fighting with guns for survival at all costs. It becomes almost easy to forget that there are two goals, liberty and land, not just the seizure, quickly or gradually, of power from the profiteers and their military goons. And unless we are careful—even if we win—we will end up with a change in the economic system but no real change in the political system; and greed, racism, and the subjugation of man by man will continue. We might end up with socialism and fascism, too, like Russia. We will end up producing poets who cooperate with the military like Yevtushenko, who are so used to not facing the facts they are unconsciously ignorant and racist.

Roy Soames will speak at State College Friday night, on an invitation from the Black Students Union. Roy Soames is probably our greatest black playwright, certainly one of America's great playwrights, and a fighter for his people. But he is a racist, and in his racism he plays games with the FBI against other radicals, like me, and the system which he helps bring about might be one of reverse racism in which black is good and white is bad.

About a year ago on a TV talk show he said that the mere overthrow of the U.S. government by a government like Red China's would solve the problems of our land, racial, economic, and political, just because it was run by yellow men for yellow men. He also said that the only white man he'd trust was Joe Blum, without explaining whether it was because he was a Jew or a so-called Communist, which he stated in his poem, "Scream," or because Blum was a poet or just a friend.

Well, Soames cooperated with the FBI against me when I was teaching at State College. Citing personal evidence if I may, a few years ago I organized a writers' conference and asked Soames if he would come. He and the Black Students Union stalled until the last day when a student spy in one of my writing classes asked me what I thought of the poetry in THE BLACK WRITER, in which most of the black writers on the campus were published. I said it was mostly hate though there were good things in it, which was no judgment upon them as people but as poets. And though I might not have liked the work in that magazine, I certainly did not mean it was a judgment of all the poetry of black writers or of Roy Soames, either, since I think he is one of the very best and most important poets in America today, black or white.

But when I went to the BSU office immediately afterwards, Roy Soames was there to say no to my request for black writers and black visitors to come to the conference in more than a token amount. He then put a fair, light-haired, green-eyed, handsome black writer on me. But I knew what had happened since there were spies in all my classes, one of whom wrote Mao Tse Tung propaganda in place of fiction to test my reaction, and when I finally confronted her with this, she reported me to the head of the Humanities Department and I was told not to apply for further employment. This might sound far out, though you'd believe it if you saw it in a movie, and I lost my job through just such machinations. My last day of teaching, a student was put in my class to write everything down in case I told all my students what had happened and I had to send her out.

Blum, the Jew, the self-admitted Communist, was run out of Cuba and an Eastern European country because he was a sex-pervert, and he couldn't get a Guggenheim fellowship until he came back and told everybody what happened to him, as well as write a poem about it called 'May Day'—which doesn't say much for the Guggenheim Committee, although they gave Roy Soames one too. Five years ago Blum refused to help me get my first poems on the military-industrial complex published when there were no poems on that subject being published because the FBI was trying to suppress them, and in the process, suppress me to the tune of turning my whole family, including my wife, against me. They put me in the nuthouse until I agreed to quit writing social-protest novels and poems. Blum said, 'Quit talking this secret police talk or you'll scare me,' and I did scare him. He turned the poems down.

So, the only 'white' man that Soames will trust does the same thing he does: cooperate with the police against dissenting poets, those who don't belong to their faction even if all are working in their different ways for the same goal. And the society that he brings into the world will not advance us upon the road to a better world because it will not bring with it a real change in consciousness.

So the Movement has to realize that there are two goals they are fighting for: land and liberty. They must bring true socialism and true democracy into being. But in order to do so, they must be willing to never commit an act that will not be true to the two goals. They cannot bring us true democracy in which the state withers away unless they are willing to remain true to the honesty and virtue which drives them to seek a change in the economic and political structure now. They must bring a change of consciousness in the revolution, not after it. After will be too late. They will have already shaped the conscience of the revolution and all their acts will be predetermined by their attitudes. If they are not better than the men they hope to supplant, if they do not offer a genuinely better world in which men can fulfill themselves then the American people will not follow them, and they deserve to lose. If the Movement is not motivated by people of pure motives, then it will fail even if it wins.

The Age of Aquarius will only come to pass if the people in the Movement remain true to their ideals and refuse to practice the dirty games of the Man. There will never be a millennium, a utopia, there will never be a peaceful and happy world where every man and woman has the right and opportunity to completely fulfill himself, to pursue happiness without interfering in *the happiness of others, in which the state is nonexistent, unless the people in the Movement refuse to play the pig games that have brought us to this state now, all over the earth, since the beginning of time, except for individual great saints like Martin and Malcolm, unless they refuse to let the pigs in power involve them in their secret web of intrigue, of corruption, a web which they use to play all the sides and factions of the left against each other, in which they play divide and conquer.*

If all the Movement people refuse to play the dirty games and keep in mind the overall objectives while they pursue their personal goals, they will inspire the people, and more leaders of the rank of Malcolm and King will come to the fore to lead the people on, all the people, black and white. But if the Movement people only think of their own needs and adopt the Machiavellian attitudes of the oppressor, the people will not follow them, there will be no change in the consciousness of man, and he will continue to be a cannibal, killing his fellow man for material gain and political power.

Remember that the economic object of the revolution is to share the profits so that no man will have to cheat or steal or kill to live, and that he will then have the chance to be good to his fellow man since he will cooperate not compete with him. Then the political objective of the revolution—to achieve a democracy so perfect that the State withers away, so that there is no need for anyone to rule—will be easy to achieve since there will be no need for greed, since people will be happy.

But none of this will come to pass if the attitudes of kill or be killed are adopted from the Man by the Movement people and used with him against each other just for their immediate objectives. The petty battles that have to be fought daily will, if not watched, become more important than the ultimate objectives. We will then end up with a society which, while professing to be classless and without prejudices, produces poets like Yevtushenko who are not even aware that they are racist."

Catching a glimpse of a blue sleeve down at the far end of an empty office out of the corner of his eye, Roger asks, "He's here?" and turns into the office with the white girl's smile and nod, her dark hair curled and teased into a natural. But the thin line of her mouth lingers in his head as he walks with bouncy, nervous steps past the empty desks to the cubbyhole room in the corner, trying to read the answer on Axel's balding crown, the long brown ringlets hanging down the back of his blue working shirt. Penny is closely behind him, almost in formation, holding her cloth bag under her well-shaped arm, her small face set, her green eyes serious.

"Well, Axel?" Roger asks, wanting to get it over with, his mouth set, mournful.

Axel turns to greet him with a small smile on his moon-shaped face, holding out his hand, reminding Roger of Joe Blum in his glasses and wrinkled workman's clothes. But the pale crown of his head, which he covers with a cap on the street, and his wide, gray-streaked brown beard makes his tan face seem gray and wrinkled, though it still has the firm shape of a young man's face. Roger has known him since they both joined the three-month long picketing of the Atomic Energy Commission in 1961. Axel invited Roger to write for him when he first started the *Gadfly*, but he declined, fearing it would take him from his novels, and the *Gadfly* was delivered late every week after that. Now he is asking Axel to publish him, and he's a little pessimistic.

"Huh?" he asks as he takes the hand but doesn't squeeze it very hard, not trusting the smile, a sinking feeling in his stomach, aware of Penny's face over his right shoulder, her standing stiffly behind him.

Axel stops smiling and stares at Roger for a moment, his back to the little slots that cover the wall behind him, filled with tear sheets and photographs, copy for the next edition of the weekly paper. He grins again, showing his discolored teeth, bunching the wrinkles up under his eyes, and the pale yet distinct orange tone to his rimless lenses. But when Roger relaxes his hand instead of grinning back, Axel's mouth snaps back into place again and he pulls his hand free and sticks it up into the wide fan of his beard and fingers a tight curl, and all the old suspicions that Roger had come flooding back to him and Axel's next words seem to only confirm them.

"You know that I've got a readership that I'm responsible to," Axel says and lets go of the curl, barely shows his teeth in a tight smile. And there is just the slightest crease of Roger's brow above his dark glasses, hinting at the tension in him, and Axel's eyes quicken as if he notices it and he looks away with a blink of reflected light on his glasses and starts fingering the curl again.

"Well," Roger says.

"You know that I've got a readership that I'm responsible to?" Axel says again but pauses again and Roger nods with a quick annoyed tip of his head to hurry him up.

"Well, you can cause trouble with the things you wrote," Axel says and turns to pull a sheaf of copy from a slot. He starts leafing through it as if he is searching for the article but stands turned so that he can see Roger, watching him, waiting for his reaction.

"Well, what's bothering you? Come out and say it!" Roger says, his voice tight and testy. "How can I cause trouble?"

Axel turns full face toward him and says, "What good are you going to do by causing trouble between the black and white activists, Roger?"

"Well, what . . . the . . . fuck! Why don't you tell me what's bothering you, Axel? Tell me what you object to?" Roger says and Axel replies, "Because Yevtushenko doesn't know he's prejudiced doesn't mean that American Marxists are!"

"I don't say that," Roger says. "What I tell the reader is the Movement must stay pure, that thinking in clichés like Roy Soames in which Marxism is all good or blacks are all good just because you're red or black is dishonest and sentimental, that this leads to dishonest acts, since Soames is lying to himself, and that what we will get from this is the dishonest sentimentality of Yevtushenko even after a socialist revolution and consciousness will remain unchanged. Soames will be at State College Friday to talk to the Black Students Union and it's important that he not lead them astray. They've got to think for themselves, not follow platitudes and clichés. The revolution has to stay pure so it won't lead to fascism, like in Russia."

A flicker crosses Axel's face, from an inner twinge or just a shift of the sunshafts coming through the window, and he looks off-color for a moment, too, a yellow pallor to his hairy face, like some bookworm radical intellectual of the thirties, Roger thinks, and stares so hard that Axel begins flipping through the sheaf of copy again with exaggerated motions.

"I'm a gadfly, Axel, a critic in the tradition of Marx and Jesus," Roger says, trying to salvage things. "That's my function in life, in society, even in a future revolutionary society. You can't change consciousness *after* the revolution, you've got to change it *during* the revolution. You can't play the same old game and expect to make things better."

"We sort of consider ourselves gadflies, too," Axel says, but keeps working without looking at Roger, takes some folded, typed pages out of the slots and staples them together.

"Then why don't you publish this 'Open Letter to The Movement'?" Roger asks, and Axel pauses, his hands stopping in mid-air over the pages, his wrinkled, lowered eyelids the only part of his eyes that Roger can see.

"It's the attitude of the writer that bothers me the most, I think."

"What about it?" Roger asks, toning his voice down, feeling that they are making progress, that there is still some hope for publication, willing to keep his subjective feelings out of consideration for the sake of better judgment and not only his article but for the sake of the revolution too, for freedom.

"The writer's bitter," Axel says and opening the copy on the counter next to him adds: "See here, where he speaks about what Blum and Soames did to him. The whole piece is bitter like that. So bitter, it hurts to read it."

"Bitter! I've got cause to be bitter! I know so much about the so-called radicals around here, in the whole Bay Area, guys who play that so-called communist line—Stalinist is a better word.

What you're really complaining about is I tell the truth on these guys. I pull the covers on them so people can see what they really are and not be misled by them. So they can judge for themselves and force their so-called leaders to be honest and true to what they say and believe. What you're really objecting to is that I tell how these guys play dirty cop games!" Roger shouts, and feels Penny touch his arm and press up against him. He catches himself and remembers what he is after, what the point of his being here is, and he hears himself say, "I'll cut the things you don't like out, if you'll publish it," and feels Penny squeeze his arm.

Axel turns completely away this time, puts the sheaf of copy he has stapled together in a slot and pulls out a photograph and another piece of copy from another slot, keeping his back, the bald spot, and the long brown, graying curls to Roger. Then he staples the copy and the photograph together and says, "No," without turning around.

Roger keeps his eyes on the bald spot, fights the flood of hot blood in his face and in a quavering voice asks, "Why-y not?"

Axel pauses with his fingers spread inside a rubber band, the bald spot turned slightly out of view with a small twist of his head and says, "Because it would be harmful to the Movement, to the blacks, to the activists, and to myself. It's me people ring up in the middle of the night when they're mad and call a bunch of motherfuckers."

He works very quickly and methodically, taking typed and folded pages out of the slots, marking them with a pen, rearranging them, stapling them together, paper clipping photographs to them, and ignores Roger when he shouts, "That's chickenshit!"

"Roger!" Penny warns, and slips her arms around his waist, but he pulls her arms apart and says, "How're you going to bring a better society into being that way? Suppression helps the police. If we don't criticize our side the fascists will. All we've got to do is tell the truth. Be moral! We've got to keep all the political leaders in line so they won't be playing any sell-out games! That's what democracy is all about!"

"The whole piece is bitter," Axel says again under his breath while pretending to search through the copy slots, his profile to Roger.

"Bitter! What the fuck are you talking about! It's optimistic! It's about love, man!" Roger shouts, knowing he is blowing all chance of getting the article published. Penny jerks him around toward her and he thinks she is just trying to stop him and pulls his arm free but sees two men in summer clothes standing out by the counter in the hall. One is a young man in tennis shorts with a brown butch haircut and muscular legs. The other is a slender graying man in a gray khaki jacket and pants. Both are staring at him. He guesses they are plainclothes cops who have come up to protect Axel and he shouts, "I could document the stoolpigeon acts of famous radicals who play games with the cops!"

"Take it easy, Roger. Take it easy now," Axel says, copy in his hands, a concerned frown on his face. "Don't get in trouble. Try to realize how things are, what you're doing. You endanger yourself, too, from all sides."

Axel's concern for him checks Roger's impulse to rush over and punch one of the men in the mouth. He the same as admits they're cops. But Roger is still angry they're watching him, following him, and he pushes by Penny and hurries past the empty desks and out to the men standing in the hall by the receptionist's counter, her round face silent and watchful, aware of Penny's footsteps close behind him.

"Who are you? What's your name?" he demands of the gray-haired man closest to him and the slender man flushes darkly under his tan as if he is scared but just shakes his head and won't answer.

"What's *your* name?" Roger demands of the other man and he turns his square face directly to Roger and his light eyebrows wrinkling up into his forehead, almost touching the stiff bristles of his crewcut widow's peak, his face red and angry, he answers so quickly that Roger can't hear him.

"What?" he asks, and the guy repeats it just as quickly, as if daring Roger to do something about it. But Roger looks into the square, slightly freckled face and he knows he has been shut up, then turns and stalks back past Penny and the office up to Axel, who is standing in the doorway of the closet-size office, trying to keep his mind on the concrete object and forget his ego, Roger says, "Okay. Tell me what you want to cut and I'll do it."

But Axel's eyes seem soft and unhappy as if he feels sorry for Roger and shaking his head, he says, "You can trim it if you like, Roger, but I don't think I can use it."

"I can try," Roger says. "Tell me exactly what you don't like about it."

"The whole tone's no good, not just the things we talked about. You give people the wrong impressions," Axel says, a frosty glaze to his glasses. "I honestly don't think you can cut it without ruining it, Roger."

"I can try," Roger says and grabs the article off the counter.

Berzerkeley

A warning pulses through Roger's body telling him to be careful, he is being tailed down the street, a street filled with hundreds of students and street people, who line the sidewalks on both sides of the Avenue, who sun themselves in front of shops. He can sense plainclothes cops like shifting shadows in the crowd, cops in all different sizes and shapes, young and old, hip and straight, with long hair and beads, blacks in flashy clothes. *They* are around, even among the bikers out in front of the pizza shop in beards and long hair and sleeveless Levi jackets, rapping their bikes with explosive pops of exhaust pipes, mingling and talking with the gang of long-haired teenyboppers who hang around them. *They* are there just as the squads of riot cops are there, sauntering up and down both sides of the Avenue, plastic face-visors up on their sky-blue helmets, tight straps under their chins, riot sticks dangling from their wrists by leather thongs, stopping guys at random, checking IDs. *They* are everywhere. He knows it. He feels it, and is sure that he is doomed to be fighting shadows forever, that there is no way out. He feels so helpless. It becomes unbearable and he comes to a stop with a mournful look on his face, two crease lines above the black frame of his glasses, his mouth thick and set and says, "I'm not going to cut it! I'm going to get it published like it is or not at all!"

"Try someplace else then!" Penny says, and he wants to throw his arms around her, but the sense that the cops are still there, might even be standing near him on the sidewalk and his sudden fear that she, too, might be playing a cop game, keeps his arm down, yet he says, "Cal! The *Daily Cal!*"

Roger watches the editor so closely that an image of him ten years in the future flashes in his head. He sees the student bald and beefy, lushing, the tip of his tie flopping over his pot belly. He is sure *he* has already been contacted by the cops, too, when the student glances over the first page of the article, then ducks his head and says, "Welllll, it's certainly strong." He then looks up at Roger and says, "Powerful would be a better word. But it's really not our thing. The style being so unusual and the subject matter not a   student-related one   Ah   know what I mean?"

"No, I don't," Roger says. "But I get your point," he adds, and he reaches out with a stiff arm and pulls the article out of the guy's fingers, barely able to keep from snatching it away.

With Penny hooked to his arm and Omar trotting on ahead with his furry body rippling, his bushy tail swishing from side to side like a blond, plumed pendulum, Roger moves down the sidewalk, through the crowds of shoppers and students, hippies, blacks, bikers, and dealers who whisper, "Grass? Speed? Acid?" the scent of grass and incense in the air, going someplace else now, giving it another try.

"Don't give up," Penny says. "But let's go call the Black Panther office first before we go all the way down to Oakland." Then holding tightly to his arm, she guides him across the street and through the people milling around in front of the pizza shop, the sidewalk tables on the corner, basking themselves in the warm sun, and out onto the terrace in front of the pool hall where they move foot by slow foot through the crowd of students, hippies, blacks and bikers to the wall phones by the door.

Roger drops a dime in the coin slot, sure he is just wasting the money to call, as a three-man squad of riot cops ambles down the sidewalk by the terrace, helmets on tight, eyes taking everything in, and the one passing closest to Roger stares at him with anonymous gray eyes, stares until Roger turns away with the sound of a girl's voice on the phone: "Power to the People. Black Panther Headquarters. Yes?"

"I've got this article, an open letter to the movement. Would you be interested in publishing it?"

"Read it to me," the voice says, and clearing his throat, he begins to read but hears a click on the line as if someone has picked up an extension and is listening in. He covers a paragraph before he hears a man's voice mumble: "Tell him the paper has already been set up."

"Excuse me," the girl says, stopping him. "The paper has already been set up."

Roger waits, hears the man's voice mumble again, and says, "Oh, yeah?"

"Yes. Why don't you try the *Gadfly* or the *Daily Cal?*"

Struck by her mention of just the very two places he has just been to, limp fingers linked with Penny's, he moves away from the wall phone, past the sidewalk tables packed with customers, through the noisy, milling crowd on the sidewalk, after Omar trotting up ahead, disappearing between all the legs, then appearing on the corner sniffing rears with a black dog, tail vibrating, next to three young black guys who are smiling at the dogs, and one says to the other, "I'll blow it up! I'll blow up Cody's if he don't try!"

"What did you say?" a tall thin riot cop asks, bony-faced and alert.

"Nothing," the husky black kid says, hands on his hips, as if ready to rip off a hook with either hand, muscular as Mr. America in his torn T-shirt and as muscular in the face as the body, with thick jaws, flat nose, heart-shaped, puffy lips.

"I.D." the cop says as his partner, heavy as a bear in his blue padded jacket, steps up behind him, gripping his club, and reaches out and grabs the arm of the tall black with the fuzzy hair, as he tries to step away. "I.D.," he says.

The tall black spins around to wrench his arm free, his lips twisting with anger, then leans away from the cop and looks down on him with heavy-lidded black eyes, a cold expression on his dusky face, his whole attitude prickly and angular as his body.

"I.D.!" the cop repeats.

"It's just a joke," the third black guy says, standing behind his friends with soft brown eyes and three chains of hippy love beads hanging from his brown neck, as his tall friend pulls his ID card out of his wallet.

But the cop snatches the card from the tall guy's fingers, staring at him instead of the card as if to see how he'll take it. But the tall guy just looks at him, smoldering darkness still in his eyes, and the cop glances at the card and hands it right back, pinching it a little so the tall guy has to tug on it. Then both cops turn and move off through the crowd and off across the street, their bubble blue helmets seeming to float above their bodies.

"That cop didn't even look at that I.D.," Roger says in a tight voice. "And the first cop didn't even make you show your card at all, huh?" he says to the husky black kid. The black kid with the beads smiles and nods his head, and Roger suddenly hears himself say, "Hey! How would you guys like to hear an article I wrote all about this? The *Gadfly* doesn't think black people will like it and won't publish it."

All three guys turn full toward him and Roger sees Penny frown, and he wonders if he is making a mistake, falling into a trap. But the guy with all the beads and soft brown eyes smiles and Roger says, "If you guys don't like it, I'll throw the sonofabitch away. What a ya say? Wantta hear it? It's one way of fighting back."

"Sure," the guy with the beads says, and Roger catches a glimpse of himself in the glass window of the Forum on the other side of the terrace, a small man in dark glasses and long dark sideburns standing in front of three black guys, waving some white papers in the air and a girl standing slightly behind him squinting.

And when he sees Axel glance out his second story window to peek through the branches of a tree as they cross the lawn and walk up the stairs to the *Gadfly* office, he feels he is going to fight a losing battle.

"These cats would like to talk to you about the article, Axel," Roger says, and Axel turns slowly away from the wall of copy slots, a smile spreading across his face as if he hasn't seen them from the window and is pleasantly surprised.

"Tell him what you told me, man," Roger says, and Mister America takes one more step toward Axel and standing before him in a faint reek of sweat, his dirty T-shirt torn and sagging off one shoulder like he has just finished some playground ball and couldn't care less how he looks, he says, "I think that this article is important. It's important that people know what's going on under cover so we can keep things free."

Axel says, "Well," then glances at Roger and even at Omar, who pants in the crowded little room, then eyeglasses glinting, grinning again, he grabs Mister America's hand, shakes it, and says, "Well, alright. I'll think about it."

But Mister America pulls his hand free and says, "Let the people know the truth. Let them make up their own minds."

"Yeah," Beads says. Tall Man nods slowly from up near the top of the doorway, and Roger begins to hope they might make a difference.

Axel looks down his beard, fingers a curl, then grins at Mister America, and says, "Well, you know, I have a responsibility to my readers."

"I'm your reader and I think it's important that you publish this article."

"But you're not my reader. I sell to students and street people and the white people in the hill sections, not to the black ghetto."

"Ghetto?" everyone says together, and Axel starts fingering his beard again.

"Man, the people in the streets, especially the Panthers, would be astounded to hear their great white radical friend talking about them like that, Axel," Roger says.

"I've got certain responsibilities to certain groups and classes of people, some of which are black and . . ." Axel's voice trails off. "But I can't use it."

"You're a cop-out, Axel," Roger says.

But Axel just shrugs his shoulders and starts sorting through the sheets of copy on his work-counter, and Roger says, "Let's get the fuck out of here, you guys. It smells of fink."

But thumping down the stairs with his gang, he feels like he is falling deeper and deeper into frustration, that he is caught in the cops' net with every step he takes in any direction, and when he steps outside, onto the porch, he looks up and down the street both ways to see if he can spot his tail: some kind of man, no matter how he was dressed or what age, who would keep looking at him. But he sees no one and walks off the porch and across the lawn, keeping himself from looking up through the tree branches to see if Axel is looking, but is intensely aware of the black guys walking with him. He can sense that they are working with the Man. He feels oppressed as they step up to him, as if he can see the deceit in their gestures, as if the lie they are hiding comes off them like body heat, like some kind of glow that depresses him because it is so inevitable, so inescapable. The cops know how to play all sides. They can stop the publication of the article and make him trust the black cats, too. Even Penny, who comes up and takes his hand, who has been by his side all day, she, too, might now suddenly make some suggestion or move that will fit into the pattern of suppression and corruption. He feels like killing himself. A deep, hopeless feeling covers him as darkly as if he were in a hole or cave with no sign of light anywhere. His whole life is bound to be like this. Never able to enjoy a real love or have a single friendship the cops won't corrupt.

"Why don't we light up!" Mister America says, and Beads smiles and Tall Man dips his head slightly. But Penny frowns and says, "Shouldn't we go home for dinner?" and Roger wonders if she is trying to warn him.

He looks from one to the other, then up and down the street again, guessing that if they are working for the Man then someone else is around to cover, to protect them, just as they protected Axel. It might be the same two guys. There is always the possibility that the cornered rat might turn and kill. But it irks him having to worry about it, to always weigh the chances of everything he does against the unseen presence of the police, to try and interpret in their terms the significance of every act and every word spoken to him. He wants to just stand up and shout and tell them to go fuck themselves, show the anonymous men who shadow and control his life that he hasn't quit, and he nods at Mister America and says, "Let's go."

They walk around the corner and down a side street with brown shingle, two-story houses and a line of maple trees on each side, walk toward the Berkeley hills green with thick foliage, the wide windows of the Lawrence Radiation Laboratory on fire with the sun, giving a rosy mellow tone to the whole hillside and the leafy streets they walk on. He pulls a yellow joint out and lights it, takes three quick tokes and hands the joint to Beads next to him, touching his brown fingers.

"We ought to throw a picket line around Axel's office with signs saying, 'Fink! Stoolpigeon!' " Roger says in a tight voice to keep the smoke down, then laughs hoarsely, blowing out some smoke and can't shake the sense of cops, of being vulnerable, of risking himself like a fool.

"And toss some Molotov cocktails through the windows!" Mister America says, and Penny stares at him, her face puckered and worried.

"And wouldn't the *Oakland Post* like to publish that!"

Beads says and smiles at her until she smiles, too, and says, "And get attention to the Open Letter that way," and Tall Man snorts and reaches out a long black arm to take the joint.

Roger doesn't care. He wants to risk it, to prove that he is still free, to keep his spirit high, literally, with booze and pot, to survive. He is conscious of a lull in the day, in the events that have caused him so much misery all afternoon, when the breeze is still and the sidestreets, as usual, are clear of traffic. It is an existential moment of pure bliss, when all his senses are refined and heightened by the grass and seem to open and tune into a slight hum of sound and slightly unreal light, a sensory tone that gives him pleasure and makes him believe once more that he has a purpose, that there is good in the world, in the very fact of existing, of being, of staying alive and believing in tomorrow, in some other day when things will be all right, a moment when he rejects suicide, an act which will rob him of all this, just this moment in the middle of the day when it is so good to be alive. And he starts humming with excitement when they circle back to the main block of Telegraph at Haste with cans of beer, and he sees the cops in riot helmets pushing their way through the crowd in front of the sidewalk tables and the cop cars driving by every other car or so with four riot cops inside. He is conscious of the quick beat of his heart and the energy that fills him, as if the pressure that has built up through the disheartening day is ready to burst loose. And though he is outwardly calm, watching Omar take a piss around the newspaper racks, his head is floating and churning. He wants to immerse himself in the wild scene and let off some steam in spite of the cops, because of the cops, all cops, seen and unseen, no matter what the cost, and he snatches a leaflet from a short-haired student and gets provoked by the very first lines: "Don't let anyone provoke you into violent action. The fuzz wants you to fight so they can crack skulls. We'll pick the time to fight, not them. This is our revolution."

He gives that to Penny and takes another one from a black guy with a wild natural and stares at the picture of the black panther stalking across the top of the page with Huey Newton's face and skims the writing to some lines which say, "Now let all those bad-talking white radicals lay their bodies on the line. Let them come forth and show what kind of revolutionary brothers they really are. Get it on right now. Right on!" Roger feels a twinge of bitterness shoot through him at the uptight righteous attitude of the Panthers he now suspects play cop games themselves. Yet, he feels like he wants to blow his top and raise some hell, too, run up and down the streets, at least taunt the cops if not try to kill them, and he looks up, alert, ready for some action with the sound of a screech and a commotion several feet away.

"Oh, my dear! My Dear, you look soooo cuuuuute!" a slender, graying, forty-year-old homosexual dressed like a raggedy thief out of the Middle Ages says to a squad of bubble-helmeted cops pushing their way through the crowd in front of the Forum, making everyone around him laugh.

"All right! Break it up! Break it up!" a fat cop says, pushing into everybody in front of him, the crowd barely parting, his voice loud and mechanical as if not really expecting anyone to obey his command.

"How many cops are on the street?" Roger asks and a plump reporter Roger knows from the *Gadfly*, his big blond beard covering his wide chest, steps up on the curb from the street and says, "There's five hundred cops in the underground parking lot at San Francisco Civic Square alone."

"Wow!" Roger says and the whole group including a couple of strange hippies standing near them steps in close to form a small circle around the reporter.

"They come from Southern Alameda County and Brisbane down on the Peninsula and even from Santa Clara County and all of them are specially trained riot cops who are ready to come to Berkeley to avenge the shooting of the pig last night, they say, but really to justify martial law on the streets of Berkeley while they're at it. We're going to do a story just on the witnesses who say he shot himself."

"So that's why all the cops are out on the streets," Roger says. "What do you think we should do, man?"

"Well," the reporter says, sounding like Axel. "You ought to go home and keep off the streets. Everybody really ought to get off the streets."

"Hell, no," Mister America says. "That's letting them run us away."

"That's clearing the streets by intimidation," Roger says.

"You've got something there. But the alternative is letting them beat us all up for nothing," the reporter says, then turns around to see why everyone is looking past him.

Four musclebound karate types with huge chests and arms are shoving their way through the crowd, knocking against everyone near them with their shoulders, bumping into big blacks and Hell's Angels, pretending to be drunk, and Roger guessing they're out to start trouble steps quickly back out of their way when they push near him. But Tall Man is staring up the street and the last muscleman in a tight blue T-shirt elbows him in the belly as he brushes by and Tall Man's hands come up quick to fight.

"Hold it, man!" Roger says and jumps in front of him with spread arms, keeps them up until the guy steps off the curb with his three buddies and starts across the street into the shadows of Cody's Book Store, its two-story high windows reflecting the last rays of the sun, near the roof, then drops his hands and says, "Those guys are cops, man. They probably teach judo at the police academy. They're trying to start trouble so they can have an excuse to crack our skulls, just like that leaflet said."

Tall Man stares over his head at the musclemen and doesn't answer, continues to stare across the darkening street, silent, his eyes smoking under his dark lids, a dull glow that reflects the street lights when they come on, his lashes a dusky color, his hair frizzy on top, and trying to make up, Roger says, "You're sensitive, man. You go through much pain. I used to do that all the time."

"Don't talk about it all the time, man," Tall Man says.

"Don't misunderstand me, man," Roger says. "I'm just trying to love you."

"Don't try so hard, man," Tall Man says.

"Don't you love me, man?" Roger asks, hurt.

"Hellll, no, man! I don't even love myself."

"Oh, don't say that," Penny says, reaching out and touching Tall Man's arm. "You've got to love yourself. Roger is right. You're sensitive. Love yourself."

She looks up at him with the street light on her face, her eyes all curling lashes and the hard glaze goes slowly out of his eyes. They become soft and melting, moist, simmering with booze and pot, and Roger feels she has healed the breach between them when some guy near him shouts, "Fuck you, pigs! Fuck you! Fuck you!" at a cop car driving by.

Roger senses something familiar about him from the back, then realizes it is the gray color of his khaki workclothes. They are police department issue. And suddenly the guy's figure becomes a two-dimensional cut out, a jigsaw puzzle piece in a police pattern, that began with the leaflet warning of provocateurs, and his body quick with energy, Roger jumps out into the street behind the man, cups his hands to his mouth, and shouts, "This guy's a cop! This guy's a cop!" And he keeps shouting until the man turns around, then he jumps up on the curb slightly behind Penny and Tall Man to keep the man from getting a good look at him, yet still shouting, "This guy's a cop! Provocateur! Cop! Cop!"

Penny then joins him, jabbing her fingers at the cop, shouting in a high, sharp voice: "Cop! Cop! Cop!"

The man glances at Roger and Penny, then over the whole crowd on the curb as if he is scared and steps quickly down the street a few feet and shouts, "Fuck you!" at the next cop car.

But Roger and Penny jump out into the street and follow the man, pointing their fingers at him, shouting, "Cop! Cop! Cop!" and everyone on the curb turns to look, and the man hurries a few feet down the street and without looking back, steps up on the curb and disappears into the crowd. Roger stands on the curb staring down the street in the darkening twilight, all figures and faces vague, gray and shadowy, waiting to see if the man will try it again, step back out on the street and shout at the cop cars, when he suddenly realizes that there isn't a moving car on the whole block, that the street is empty when it should be full of cars with people going out to dinner, coming down to the Avenue for pizza and chow mein, tacos and steaks, hamburgers and beer, and that the only cars he can see are a line of cop cars, all a uniform cream color, stopped across Dwight Way a block below him, waiting for the traffic light to change before they move up the empty street, a street dark with sinking night, just a faint glimmer of street lights shimmering off it. Then he realizes that he has only been seeing cop cars for a while now and he leaps up on the base of a street pole and with one arm around the pole and balanced by his toes on the ridge of the concrete foundation, he holds one hand over his eyes and strains to see down Telegraph as far as possible.

A tiny glimmer of red flares, just barely visible, is stretched across the road about four blocks down the street, and checking once more to make sure of what he has seen, he cups his free hand over his mouth and in the momentary lull between groups of cop cars, he yells, "Hey! Hey! Everybody! They've blockaded the street down by the *Gadfly!* Only cop cars are coming through! Dig it! Dig it! Blockade! Blockade! Look! Look!"

People turn and frown at him, then when Penny and Tall Man and Beads and Mister America crowd around below him and step out into the street to look, two waves of people step off both curbs to stare down the dark street, many crossing over to see past the slight bend in the Avenue below Dwight Way. Quickly, people are standing on car fenders and bumpers, pointing their fingers down the street at the red flares.

"The cops have blocked off the street now that the shoppers have left and might try to get us. And look, Penny." He points to the dark, high windows of Cody's and the dark store fronts of the bakery, Moe's Used Books, and all the small storefronts that stretch down both sides of the street all the way to the campus. "All the stores are closed but the restaurants."

But the traffic light down on Dwight Way changes and a half a dozen cream-colored patrol cars start gliding slowly up the street with their lights on and the crowd that has scattered off the curbs into the streets to see the red flares makes no attempt to move out of the way for them and some stand directly in the first car's path.

"Don't let them provoke you! Don't let them get you mad!" Roger shouts and jumps down from the pole, runs out into the middle of the crosswalk to shout, "Don't let them beat our heads in! Clear the street! Clap for the tough guys! Clap for the big heroes!"

Then waving his arms for everyone to clear the street, he starts backing up and clapping for the cop cars and Penny and Tall Man and Beads and Mister America clap with him and are joined by all the people around them and then, as if on signal, the crowd in the street picks it up and backs out of the way of the patrol cars, clapping and cheering for the cops, too. And the cheers and claps and whistles rise to a roaring peak all along the sidewalk as the cars pass by and ripple off as they move slowly up the dark, crowded street.

They clap for the next group of cop cars that come up the block, too, the sound rising, rippling with the slow creeping movement of the cars, reaching a screeching, shouting, whistling peak at the intersection by Roger and his group, then carry on up the next block and die out at the end of it as each new wave of cop cars brings a new wave of noise from down by Dwight Way.

The cops in the first group of cars stare with wide eyes, then sit back stiffly without looking around, just stare straight ahead as if they are embarrassed, and Roger can only see their profiles as they pass. But the cops in the next group of cars start smiling. Roger can see their open mouths and faces creased in grins, although he can't hear any sound of laughter, the noise of the cheering crowd is so deafening, and he isn't sure whether the cops are laughing at the street people in defense or are genuinely amused by them. But the next group of cars convinces him that they are really laughing. The cops have wide grins on their faces and many of them are leaning over the seats to laugh with their buddies, not even watching the crowd anymore, completely relaxed and enjoying themselves, and all the cop cars that pass after that are filled with laughing cops, and laughing, too, her eyes glittering with streetlight, Penny hugs Roger and says, "We're beating them, Roger! We're beating them!"

"You're right! We've won! We've won!" Roger shouts and Beads grins and Mister America nods and lights up a joint and Tall Man claps and grins and waves at the cops in the very next car that passes by.

Gary and the Cops

"Man! What in the hell is all this?" Roger says, turning in a circle in Gary's parlor, sweeping his arm out at all the mens' suits, sportcoats and slacks hanging from every ledge in the room, even from the curtain rods and wall trim, snazzy-looking jackets and pants, dark blues and browns and tweeds, spots a coat arm just visible behind a door, switches on the light in the bedroom and sees more clothes, including sportshirts and overcoats spread across the wall.

"Man, this is really weird," he says and switches the bedroom light off again, and sees in the dark outlines of the suits men hiding in the shadows like cops.

"Talk about the handwriting on the wall. Something's really fishy."

"Come on, Roger," Penny says, dropping her hands with a slap.

"What a ya mean 'Come on!'? It's them! They've always got some phoney thing going, always up to some trick, some way to run my life!"

"Please, don't," she says, and turns away and starts taking her clothes off, ignoring his mumbled words: "I ought to get out of here right now."

She avoids his glance, keeps her sweeping lashes down over her eyes, her silence like anger in the room, and undresses, exposes her white breasts, pulls her levis down, and starts to slip on her pajamas.

"What's the matter? Why are you so uptight?"

"Who says I'm uptight?" she says, but still won't look at him.

"I do," he says as she kneels with her back to him and flips the sleeping bag cover back, then lays down under it with her back to him, her long sandy hair spread out over the mattress behind her.

"Well, what's bothering you?" he says. "What's on your mind? I'm not supposed to complain, huh?"

"I didn't say that," she says and twists her head around to see him.

"You might as well. You'd be more honest."

"Why do you have to make everything a big mystery? Why

do we have to leave just because Gary's got some clothes hanging around?"

"Because it's so *mysterious*, that's why!" he says and waits for her reply. But she just turns her head around and faces the wall, tucks the sleeping bag under her chin, and, after waiting a few moments, he starts to untie his boot.

He lays on his stomach, pulls the felt lining of the bag close around his neck and tries to relax. His legs are tired, his eyes sagging, yet his mind flits from one image of the long day to the next. He sees no escape anywhere. But he needs to relax, turns over on his side and tucks his knees up, aching inside, until drowsiness and darkness finally come over him. He drifts off to sleep only to be awakened by a loud bark and Omar rising up like a lion next to him in the darkness.

"Stay!" he says and grabs Omar's thick mane, feels the tense shoulder muscles under the fur strain to pull away and tremble with another deep growl as someone runs up the stairs.

"Gary?" he asks over another bark, holding tightly to Omar's fur.

"Yeeeeeaaaah?" Gary answers from the darkness.

"Turn on the light, man, so Omar can see you," Roger says, pats his dog with his free hand to reassure him, and sees Gary standing at the top of the stairs with a suitcase in one hand and an overcoat in the other, then Karen, Gary's girlfriend, pops into the hall behind him, a purse and a suitcase in her hands, her freckled face wrinkling with a smile.

"Hi!"

"Hi!" he says and sees Penny staring at Karen, and wonders what kind of web is being woven now. But he rolls over and falls asleep again, then hears, much later, the faint sound of sobbing in the other room, sounds out of the darkness that blur with the shifting shapes of dreams. He wakes as footsteps come back once more into his dreaming mind, move slowly about the rooms, heavy steps that fade away, then come close and wake him with a start, trying to make the dark shape near him come into focus.

Gary stands near him with a couple of suits in each hand; all the walls of the room are bare of clothing.

"What's happening, man?" Roger asks.

"Moving out," Gary asks, softly.

"Maybe I better get out now, too," Roger says, lifting up.

"No-no. Stay here," Gary says. Roger props himself up, sensing something important, and Gary says, "You don't have to leave. Stay here and do your writing."

"I'd like to think about it," Roger says, and lies back down, pulls the sleeping bag cover back over his shoulders and closes his eyes as Gary goes down the stairs again, comes back up once more, then goes down and closes the door. A few seconds later, Roger hears his volkswagen start up and drive off. And with the warmth and darkness, he drifts off to sleep again, only to be awakened in what seems moments by the rachet sound of the phone being dialed in the next room. He tenses with the sound of Karen's voice, tiny, like a chick peeping in the darkness, though he can see light in the kitchen—meaning it is much later in the morning, and he feels an inner quirk of shame for eavesdropping, feels it deepen as her soft voice begins to plead, and he pulls the bag over his head when her voice gets thick and close to sobs, then freezes under the bag, his legs stiff and pointed, when she begins to sniffle as if trying to hold the tears back, then rolls over on his face and pulls the bag close to his ears when she begins to sob and tries to shut the sound out. Finally, she hangs up the phone and stops sobbing and he drifts back into a half-world between sleep and waking until Omar's bark at the back door wakes him completely.

He waits for a moment, expecting to hear sobs, then sleepy-eyed and hair wild and curly, he gets up and walks barefoot into the sunlit kitchen, his eyes smarting at the glare, and stops at Karen standing by the sink, staring at him with bright eyes, ginger-haired and rosy in a red jumper, hints of soft freckles all over her clean-scrubbed cheeks.

Roger is amazed that there isn't a trace of redness or puffiness to her eyes from crying but he steps past her and lets Omar come swishing in with the sinuous movement of a snake, wagging his bushy tail and rippling over to his plate for water, then begin to drink with loud slurps.

"We'll leave today," he says, standing in his blue dacron pajamas, sure he looks puffy-eyed and ugly.

"No-no, stay!" she says and reaches out and touches his shoulder, and he tries to connect the green-eyed, vivacious girl in front of him with the peeping, sobbing voice in the darkness, so totally unable to that she seems unreal to him, though he knows he can reach out and put his hand on her breast, caress the bulge of her red jumper at will.

"Thanks," he says, and steps back into the parlor and lies down on the mattress again, pulls the bag back over his head and closes his eyes and rolls over on his stomach and tries to go back to sleep again, but sits right up as soon as he hears her close the front door behind her, and says, "Wake up, Penny! Let's get out of here!"

"What for?" Penny asks. "What's wrong? Tell me!"

"Gary's trying to get me to make it with his girl," Roger says, expecting her to immediately react with jealousy. But her small chin wrinkles into her neck like a prune and she stands up and stepping past him says, "You might be wrong, you know."

"Whaaat?"

"You're not always right!" she says and stomps away down the hall, her arms and legs ticking like a watch in his old pair of baggy pajamas.

"What do you mean 'Not always right'?" he says and jumps up.

But she turns into the bathroom without answering and he hurries after her, saying, "They're trying to get a fucking sexual scene going, get me liking it and keep me in line with it, even use it against me in a morals case if they have to. What do you mean 'not always right'?"

But she doesn't answer and he walks into the toilet to find her squatted on the seat, primly peeing, knees together, hands resting on her thighs, mouth tightly closed, tiny as a bird's.

"Do I have to be able to prove it in court? Can't even *you* tell that something's going on? Or do you feel guilty, too?"

But she just blinks her eyes at him as if he can think what he wants and looks straight ahead while her pee tinkles into the bowl.

"All his clothes are gone. He moves out and she moves in! And after I take my shower, I'm moving out, too!"

"Well, I'm not! I'm getting tired of running around like a rat every time you get another paranoid idea in your head!" she says, rips some toilet paper off the roll, wipes herself with one swipe of her hand, drops it in the bowl, pulling her pajamas up as she stands, flushes the toilet and ticks out past him to the rush of the water.

"What in the hell do you mean paranoid? Do you think I like being chased like a rat? And a trap set for me every time I turn around? Huh?" he shouts, and follows her barefooted down the hall into the parlor again, where she drops her pajamas on the mattress, her body very white, and slips on her light blue jeans, blue blouse, and sandals. Then, still without speaking, arms and legs ticking, she marches back to the bathroom and washes her face, splashes water lightly under her arms between the opened halves of her blouse, her pale breasts swaying, the nipples smooth and pink, then dries herself with quick movements, as if hurrying to get away from him.

"Answer, Goddamnit!" he yells. "Don't you realize that this whole scene here in Berkeley is an attempt to make me stop writing such dangerous shit and get me to take out my do-gooder impulses on a social worker's job? Keep me from writing about revolution? Don't you know that?"

"No!" she says and hangs up the towel and faces him with her hands on her hips. "No! I don't know that!"

"Uh— Uh—" he says, then shouts, "Well, I do! And I'm getting out of here! Do you think this is fun?"

"No! And I'm not! I'm going to the store for some milk for breakfast," she screams back at him, then pushes past him and stomps back down the hall again, and he stands in the bathroom listening, his face pale, and hears her roll up the sleeping bag in the parlor. Omar whines and rears up on his hind legs and paws Roger's chest, then, still whimpering, licks his mouth and pants,

"Ha-ha-ha!" showing all his teeth, blowing warm breath in his face, as he looks right in Roger's eyes with his own soft pale brown ones. Roger smiles, sniffs his black muzzle and slaps his solid ribs through the thick fir. Then Omar drops back down to all fours and trots down the hall to Penny.

Roger takes off his pajamas and gets in the shower, reaching around the plastic curtain to pick up his razor and shaving mirror from the rim of the tub, then hooks the mirror to the shower curtain bar as the back door closes and the jingle of Omar's collar and Penny's footsteps go down the back stairs. He tilts the mirror to look at his face, trying to avoid the slight puffiness and morning wrinkles under his eyes, trying to keep himself from falling into gloom again. But the mirror's edge is beginning to lose its silver paint from so many wettings and is turning black as ink on the edges of a blotter and rings his face with a cancerous black noose. The small section of his face which shows in the noose looks lined and worried. His brows are furrowed. There are dark circles under his eyes. He is in deep trouble and he knows it.

He is not even surprised when Omar, a bright glob of blood beneath his eye, yelps and barks as he limps in the back door. He leaps up on Roger, pawing his chest, then yelps in a high, sharp, painful cry, and drops down and rolls over on his back, showing his furry blond underside.

"Easy! Easy, Omar, easy!" Roger cries, and drops down to one knee, grabs his dog's head to hold it still. He sees with a pulse of hope that the huge globs of blood are spilling over the lower lid like tears but that the eyeball isn't punctured, then starts stroking his thick coarse fur to calm him as Omar chews the air in silence, then begins to cry "Awrrr! Awrrrrr! Awrrrrrr!"

"Oh! He had a fight! These dogs! Two! Three! They jumped out on him all at once! And they were big! Big!" Penny says, crouched down next to Roger, her face white, her mouth open. Then, suddenly, she stops and squints at Roger and he guesses it was a deliberate trap and that she is either in on it or feels guilty for letting Omar get hurt. But Omar is yelping and twisting and trying to roll back over on all fours, and Roger tries to hold him down to search through the fur around his neck for puncture wounds, sees a blood spot on the outside of his hind leg, and, spreading the fur, finds a half-inch pink hole in his thigh.

"Where are they?" he asks.

"Why?" she asks.

"Because I'm going to get those motherfuckers, that's why, and teach them not to mess with my puppy. This is deliberate. Somebody set them on him and if the master jumps in, I'll take him, too. Tell me!"

"Don't, Roger," she says, and Omar is suddenly quiet, looking at them. "The owner already took the dogs back. He ran after them when the dogs chased Omar." She stops and looks closely at him as if afraid of his reaction. "Omar ran from them."

Roger glances from her down to Omar, who is still lying on his back, his paws tucked into his chest, his head up, watching Roger as if aware of what they're talking about, and Roger says, "What do I care if he ran? I want my dog safe, not showing how tough he is! Tell me where they are."

He stands and she does, too, saying, "Wait! Don't make it worse!"

Omar still on his back, blood trickling from his eye, yelps once, sharply, and gnaws the air with pain, and Roger jerks open the kitchen door, and ignoring Penny's cries of "Stop! Don't go, Roger! Stay here!" and the sound of Omar's yelps, "Awr! Awr! Awr!" and only vaguely aware of where he is going, stomps down the rickety old brown stairs, past the packed garbage cans at the bottom, and out to the sidewalk in front of the house, where he looks up and down for some dogs. But he can't see any, then starts searching through the weeds along the curb for rocks and finds a broken piece of concrete to throw when Penny comes running out the front door.

"Don't go! You might get hurt or get in trouble!" she says, glancing at the concrete in his hand, reaching out for him.

"I'll hurt them," he says, turning to avoid her reach, not trusting her, afraid she might be in on it, anger lines, faint and fine, winging down from his nostrils and around his tight mouth like parentheses. "The cops'll never let up anyway. Don't you see? I'm going to fight back every step of the way. They killed my first dog. I'll kill me a dog. I'll smash his skull in," he says, and starts searching through the weeds for another rock.

"Please, Roger," she says, and grabs his arm, tries to stop him.

"Those fucking dogs will know what it's for," he says, jerking his arm loose, and picks up a smooth garden rock, balances its heavy gray brown shape in his palm and straightens up again to start down the street when Omar comes limping out of the house, rolls over on his back in the weeds in front of Roger, blood staining his blond cheek, glistening on the black muzzle, and tucking all four paws against his body, cries, "Awrrr! Awrrrrrr! Awwwwwwrrrrrr!"

"Please, don't, Roger," Penny pleads. "Not if you love Omar."

"What are you talking about love for?" he shouts, raising both fists, clenching the rocks.

"Roger," she says, and clutches his arm. "Let's get out of here like you want, instead," and he lets his arms sink slowly down to his sides.

There is a sickness in his gut, a tense strip inside him from the pit of his belly to his adam's apple as he dials the phone in a nook in the wall of a short elevated hall between the bedrooms of Craig's house in the Sunset Heights District of San Francisco.

As he sits on a small stool next to the tiny phone table, he is able to see Omar's swollen, reddened eye and the iodine stain on his leg as he lies on the cool stone of the fireplace in the front room. The sight aggravates the irritation he already feels toward Gary. He is afraid it is just a matter of time before they really hurt Omar to stop him from writing his controversial articles. For the article, his open letter, now seems to be missing, which he discovered when Craig asked what he had been doing in Berkeley that would get his dog attacked like he said, and he said, "I'll show you, if you really want to know."

But he could not find it in the basement garage where Craig had laid out an old mattress for them and he had stacked his bags at its foot. He had emptied the briefcase on the rug, tipped the knapsack over, and scattered his clothes out on the mattress with a hopeless sense that he would never be able to get away from them, that they would force him to play their game whether he liked it or not, tried to escape or not, fought back or not. He was homeless and hunted in an almost surreal sense, turned down every time he tried to publish the article, followed by cops on Telegraph, angered by Gary's suspicious actions, the attack on Omar. Yet what made it so horrifying to him was that every event had a real reason for occurring and it was only the outrageous pattern of events that allowed him to see the subtle, insidious attempt to control him, his mind, his emotions, his art. It was 1984 for real for him.

Finally, after Penny had told him she had last seen it on the floor of the MG and they had searched it, too, and she had said, "Gary must have it or you left it at the flat," he had hurried upstairs to call him, swearing under his breath, feeling like a worm on a hook, watching himself squirm, knowing that he could never wriggle free and was forced to cooperate with his tormentor just to keep from being swallowed bit by bit.

He holds his breath in the split second between the phone being picked up, the knock as if the mouthpiece has banged the desk and Gary's smooth voice asking, "Yessss."

"Do you have my article, man?" Roger asks without introductions.

"Is this Roger?" the voice asks in a melodic lilt, stalling.

"Yes, this is Roger, Gary," he says, the phone clenched in his fist. "Do you have my article?"

There is a long silence on the line, then, "Welllll, yessss."

"What did you take it for, man?"

There is another short silence and Roger stares hard at the phone numbers scribbled all over the wall of the nook before he hears, "I saw it in your car this morning and thought I'd read it."

"Without asking me or even bothering to tell me?"

"I can bring it out to you, if you like Roger. Where are you?" Gary asks in a very sweet voice and Roger feels as if he's been struck, the words hit with such an impact. He can't escape!

"Why don't we have dinner together? I'll get a girl and come over as soon as I get off work, which isn't too long now."

His voice is high-pitched and enthusiastic, as if he really hadn't meant anything wrong by taking the article and wants to make up for it.

"She's pretty," he adds, as if to tell Roger it isn't someone he knows, either Karen or Lydia.

"Alright," Roger says, determined to get his article back, thinking of the trouble it will save him. "Come over to Craig's pad in San Francisco. You've been here before. And don't hang me up, man!"

He puts the phone down on the base without saying good-bye, with a pessimistic feeling in his chest that he is in for a long night's bummer and walks over to the wrought-iron railing that fences in the elevated hall and the short curving staircase, stops and stares over the heads of the seated people, out the window at the Golden Gate Bridge poking up between the green wooded hills of the Presidio army base and the barren hills of the Marin coast. Everything is a rosy hue in the sunset, but Roger suddenly realizes that the whole room is quiet, that no record is playing and that everyone in the front room is looking up at him as if they have heard the conversation.

He skims their faces, sees the expectant, waiting expressions, the assorted eyes staring at him, waiting for an explanation. But he hesitates, afraid to speak, a lingering unease in his gut, a sense that in the middle of this calm, this apparent congeniality in the soft shade of the room, his whole life is being manipulated; that, undercover, all of them are in on the attempt to get him to relax and trust them and tell them everything that has happened to him over the article and what he thinks about it. If he keeps quiet, he will keep them in doubt. Then they can't act so surely. He has to save himself, even at the cost of not being frank and open. He feels they know everything that has happened to him. He has this thing with patterns. He can see things coming down around him, pick up on what somebody says or understand how it fits in with a previous event. He doesn't need proof, just signs. That's all he goes by. He has been an outlaw, been hunted for so long that his catlike senses are as developed as a jungle creature's. Sometimes he scares dogs he moves so fast to pet them. He often leaps in the air and comes down with his fists up when surprised. His senses, his emotions are so finely tuned and synchronized from the long hunt that they ring like bells when a hostile vibration touches him.

Like now, he thinks, standing in the room in what already amounts to full seconds of silence, his mind flashing from the quick in his gut, as if a wave of blood has pulsed up there from a belly twinge, hipping him to the fact that here, right here is trouble. Sensitive artist that he is, when he became an outlaw over politics and weed he also became more receptive to sensory signals of danger and now has partially regained what man had lost when he came down out of the trees and put on clothes, what woman has since she doesn't have muscles and has to survive by her wits in a man's world—intuition or just plan animal sense, the intelligence which comes from the senses, the actual five senses of the body.

"It seems Gary took the article without telling me," Roger finally says. "But he's coming over for dinner and bringing it with him. How about a giant pizza?"

Craig wiggles his eyebrows and Roger looks away, knowing how, because he's so intellectual, Craig wants to live desperately, to feel and be emotional and sometimes overreacts. But Roger suspects Craig knows how to use his own mannerisms to conceal something else about himself, some game, so far unsolvable. They were always one step ahead of him.

Ruth is watching him from a cushion with her dark blue eyes, a deep blue darkened by the shadow in the room. The Golden Gate Bridge is lit by the last rays of the sun in the wide window above her. Her black hair waves back into a bun. The small white lobes of her ears are dotted with golden nuggets, a golden locket hangs from her long neck. He turns away from her to see Penny watching him from a cushion against the wall. Her green eyes narrow, cloud up behind the web of her lashes. He goes down the stairs to sit by her, and his mind perking slowly on pot, the pain of his stay so far in the Bay Area lessened somewhat by the calm narcotic haze that seems to envelop everyone in the room, Richie Havens' velvety voice filling the room with misty tones as time passes, and he jumps up with the ring of the phone.

"I'm on my way to the girl's house now," Gary says, oily-voiced. "Pick her up and be right over. She's nice."

He pauses as if waiting for Roger to say something. But Roger stares at the scrawled numbers on the wall and fights the urge to ask him why he's stalling, finally takes a deep breath and says, "Okay, man, we'll order some pizza."

"Why don't you wait until we get over there so it won't get cold?"

"Why don't you get over here in time to eat the pizza hot? It's long after seven, man."

After another pause, Gary says, "Alright," then raising his voice so it sounds light and unconcerned, adds, "I'll be there!"

There is a certain horror that Roger feels as he waits in the front room, pot clouds hovering, music playing, his friends idly talking, his girl sitting quietly near him and Omar lying on the cool stone of the unlit fireplace, a horror in the fact that while he lives he can never escape the control of the police, that in the light of the political system as it now stands, with the police holding all the power, controlling the money strings as well as exerting a powerful influence over the radical groups, there is only one way out of their grasp and that is suicide. The greatest horror is living in a web of intrigue where every possible outlet is controlled by the police, even love. Suicide which he should fear becomes the only possible chance of escape. He smokes heavily when the pipe comes around, drinks another can of beer, and, his girl on one side of him and his dog on the other, he waits. The phone rings again and knowing it is another stall from Gary he goes to answer it.

"Hello? Roger? Ha-ha! Ha-ha! On my way over, man. Ha-ha!"

But Roger just stares at the dull yellow wall, the crossword puzzle of names and numbers in the nook, a hap-hazard pattern as irritating as Gary.

"Are you there?"

"Yeah, I'm here, man, and the pizza's on the way. Why don't you get over here and quit messing around?"

"Alright," Gary says in a deflated voice and hangs up without another word.

"Where's my article, man?" Roger demands as he opens the door for Gary, eleven o'clock at night, the pizza long since eaten.

Gary stands in the doorway next to a girl in a gauzelike minidress, her dark hair done up in a little girl style, drawn to the top of her head in a short ponytail and tied with a big yellow bow, striking with her pale complexion and large dark eyes. Then, pushing the girl before him, Gary says, "This is Ruby. Thought you'd like to meet her," and steps in without answering, forcing Roger back out of the way, the girl smiling at him, and he sees the dark bra, bikini panties and pale blue tights through her transparent yellow dress as she faces him and spreads her coat to take it off. But he steps around her, and, holding out his hand, says, "The article, man."

But Gary turns away from him and helps the girl take her coat off, ignoring Roger, who waits until the coat is in his hands, then steps in front of him again, saying, "The article."

Gary leans to one side as if to free the inside pocket of his sport coat, letting Roger glimpse a folded sheet of paper, reaches in to pull it out but drops it back out of sight and straightens up, saying, "I'd like to talk to you about it a little later. Give it to you then."

"Give it to me now," Roger says, and reaches under Gary's sport coat for it. But Gary jerks back, laughs, "Ha-ha!" and pushes Roger's hand away.

"I'm serious, man," Roger says, and reaches for the article

again, but Gary blocks his hand with the girl's coat, then pulls the article out himself and hands it to Roger. Then, flipping through the pages to make sure he has them all, Roger turns and says, "I've got the article. Who wants to hear it."

Many things flit through his mind as he reads, but the distrust grows into a need, a need for pure friendship, for a true love, for just one relationship of trust, a need which seems to ache inside him, a need which builds up a strain in his voice with paragraph upon paragraph. He longs to see, most of all, a star of pure love shining down upon everybody, twinkling in their eyes with the lamplight, like the visible glow of friendship. But he can only see a blur of light and shadow on their faces, quivering like transparent pools of water, and deep inside he becomes disheartened, his voice sounds false to him, quavers with expectations of their disapproval, sure he can catch glimpses of it on their faces, in the shadow of the room, just beyond his pages, and he strains to get control of his unhappiness, his voice rising higher and higher, coming close to cracking, and he sweeps the pages back from his face and straightens up with a deep quavering breath and stands stiffly in front of them, waiting for somebody to say something. But no one speaks. He can only see a bunch of bowed heads below him, and hurt, he asks, "Doesn't anybody have anything to say?" and drops his hands, the pages slapping against his thigh.

"It's powerful," Craig says from a cushion, tilting up his nose as if trying to keep the blond lock that always falls across his forehead out of his eyes, eyes now bloodshot from the grass behind his plastic-framed glasses, weird eyes that never really looked at anyone, eyes that had seen death when he fell from a cliff at eighteen and changed from a fraternity boy to an aspiring writer, trying to find some consolation for death in a world now filled with the fear of that fall, a doom he had escaped but must someday meet again.

Mollified a little but still feeling that no one is facing what he has to say, Roger asks, "What about you, Benny?"

Benny sits up, so close to the lamp on the coffee table that the glow lightens the wispy patches of hair he combs from one side to cover his balding crown and says, "I don't think Roy Soames will like that."

"Nor the white radicals," Marcia, his wife and Ruth's older sister, says. Roger nods. He likes both of them, and thinks that she is a better natural writer than Benny. Shadow softening her face, blurring out the pimples that flaw her fine features, she does dazzling tricks with language like a lariat twirler keeping a lasso of words spinning around her as she hops through it, dances next to it and under it, spinning it over her head, moving the story all the time on the level of personal experience where the life is, not like Benny, Master of Arts in Creative Writing, with a JC teaching credential who is always hung up on the level of abstract ideas, the significance and meaning of symbols, and a little jealous of her, Roger feels, a horrible fate for a writer and a good Jewish boy married to a Jewish mother.

"What about you, Kent?" Roger asks.

Kent looks up with watery blue eyes from his cushion on the rug. His thin mouth is tight and lipless under the hook of his hawk-beaked nose. A wiry little guy, he is built wide and rangy across the shoulders, and dressed in jeans and boots, he looks like the woodsman he thinks he is rather than the graduate student in creative writing already teaching his own freshman English classes. "It's controversial," he says grudgingly, then looks down again at his bony hands clasped in his lap, his wavy brown hair falling onto his forehead, a worried expression on his face, one that usually makes him seem so sensitive, prematurely wrinkled from working too hard as a boy because of a drifting, itinerant father.

"What's the matter with you guys?" Roger says. "Don't you like me telling how everybody plays games with the pigs? How the police control even the so-called revolutionaries? Do you think it exposes you? Is that what's bothering you? Would you rather live with a lie so you can conceal your own dirty lies?"

"You lie, too!" Kent shouts, and Roger is speechless for a moment, seeing the truth of the accusation.

"But there's a difference in our lies. Your lies support the secret police! I lie by not exposing you every time you lie to me! I lie just to survive! To keep from fighting with everyone I know! Just to have a person I can talk to somewhere on this earth! To be able to even stay in the same room with people! You lie against me first and I lie, secondly, after the fact of your lie! Just to stay alive under your lies!"

Suddenly he is really angry and he waves the papers in his hand and swings his arm in a sweeping gesture and shouts, "All of you! You all cooperate with the FBI against me. Yet the FBI will enslave you, the educated, by playing on your patriotism and fear! by getting you to play stoolpigeon for them, to subvert the constitution! to acquiesce in the murder of our president! who dared to take on the FBI and the CIA! You all help suppress me, an artist, in our so-called free society! You're all nothing but a bunch of collaborators with the enemies of your country! with traitors!"

They are all staring at him, mouths open, shocked by his charges. He jabs a finger at Gary and shouts, "You, too, Gary!" and Gary ducks his head between his knees.

"Who doesn't then?" Kent shouts. "Who doesn't?"

"What?" Roger says, then hears himself say, "I don't! I'm the only person who doesn't!" and Kent's wife Lucille's lips curve up thinly at the corners in a sardonic, disbelieving smile. Plump, buxom girl, her luminous, virgin-like face is as pale and sensitive as a wood nymph's, which she believes in. A perfect poet's wife, she leans slightly against Kent, barely touching arms with him in the gesture of a true mate.

"That's the truth!" Roger shouts, waving the pages. "Every person here is cooperating with the secret police who run my life! who got my puppy attacked! who are keeping my article suppressed right now!"

No one looks at him. The room is quiet. The soft light seems to stifle sound. He hears Omar stir slightly beside him, hears the thump and rustle of his tail. His own breath is loud in his ears, heavy, his chest rising and falling. Finally, Kent raises a sober, whitened face, his cheeks splotched with red, and says, "I'm getting my students to read Che Guevara and Herbert Marcuse now."

"What about you? Why don't you practice what you preach? You've even worked in a nuthouse where they teach people to conform, crush individuality and eccentricity and destroy artists like me who might educate the public to what's going on!"

"That's not true!" Kent shouts, but there is no anger in his voice and no tension in his face. "I was only nineteen then," he says in a softer voice. "And they were going to fire me for not having the right attitude. Right now, I'm trying to write about it."

Roger opens his mouth to tell him he worked in the nuthouse only the summer before when he was Roger's reader, at twenty-six, but touched by the regret in Kent's words and hurt himself by the desperate lie, he says, "Well, if a guy's trying to write about his experiences, trying to face them, to make some good out of them, he's on the right track."

He then crosses the room, holds out his hand to Kent, lying by omission—just like he said he lied—for the sake of peace, and they shake hands stiffly but Roger feels that nothing is really settled between them.

Tight movements here and there in the lamplit room. Craig's slow reach for a beer can. No sounds. No one speaks. Roger, the article still clutched in his hand, is suddenly conscious of how he has cut himself off from everyone. He sees how accusing them has isolated him completely. He wants to call out that he is sorry, that he doesn't want to make everybody suffer, that he only wants everybody in the whole world, not just them, to love each other. But the tension is too tight, he can't back down. Everything, his life, his country, the whole world, the freedom of generations to come is at stake, and stepping to the dining room table, he lays the article down and says, "I guess that's that!"

Gary gets to his feet and helps his girl up. Her short, gauze minidress rises up her rump as she kneels over the cushion to stand, then blinks her long, curling lashes at Roger and smooths her dress down carefully over her hips.

"We've got to go now," Gary says, and Roger catches his breath to speak, wants to say, "I'm sorry. Please stay. Stick around. Drink some beer. Smoke some grass. Have a party. Let's be friends. You just got here." But he only nods and follows Gary and his girl across the room as the Beatles' album, "The Sergeant Pepper Lonely Hearts Club Band," starts to play.

He reaches slowly for the door knob, wanting to ask them to stay, when Gary pushes the girl's coat at him and says, "Help her, will you?" and strides back across the front room as if he has forgotten something. Roger takes the coat and steps behind the girl to slip it over her shoulders and feels a cushion of air between her back and his chest as he reaches around her, filling the space inside his arms, keeping him from touching her, yet almost embracing her. He can smell the sweet scent of her body, the flesh of her neck when she leans back into him, her buttocks to his crotch, and drops the coat over her, but she turns before he can pull away, her breasts against his chest, her big brown eyes staring, her full lips close to his, and waits. Craig is shuffling through the records three feet away, Penny is just out of sight in the front room near Omar. Somebody is in the bathroom and its light falls across the curving stairs touching his feet. The sound of the music is loud. She leans into him and lets her lips touch his softly and he starts to pull her to him and kiss her when he hears a step behind him, feels a hand clap on his shoulder, and hears Gary say, "Ha-ha! Got you!"

Shadow under his high cheeks, cupped in his heavy upper lip, his face tense and unhappy as if the taut skin is just barely stretched over the inner pain, feeling used, hurt, and humiliated, Roger tries to relax a moment and get control of himself before he steps back into the front room, when the door suddenly jerks open and Gary bursts into the foyer, runs into the front room and shouts, "Hey! The cops are outside!"

"What?" someone shouts, and everyone jumps to their feet, seems to stand suspended around the coffee table. Yet Roger still doesn't get that fear like falling that comes with a bust, the moment of truth when the cops break in through the doors with drawn guns and the women scream and the men turn pale.

"A strange car followed me around the block and there was an unmarked car with two plainclothesmen in it down at the second corner of the curve, Roger," Gary says, and Roger, afraid it might be true, says, "Clean up, then! Turn off all the lights and cover the windows and lock all the doors!" and doublelocks the front door himself as everyone starts rushing through the house with a rumble of footsteps and lights go off and shades come down and the whole house is suddenly dark.

Roger moves down the steep small basement steps, holding tightly to the wooden rail with one hand, squinting, trying to spot any cops who might have already slipped into the basement or who are waiting outside. The whole house is a darkened place of scurrying sounds, footsteps, whispers, drawers opening and closing, rustling bags. He feels his way in the unfamiliar places with his feet, straining to see, afraid of tripping on one of the many boxes scattered around the darkened floor. Penny whispering, "Get your grass!" pulls the curtain closed over the dim light of the basement window. Omar whines. Roger digs under the clothes in his knapsack for his big paper bag and pulls it out. The strong, moldy smell of clean earth sharp in his nostrils, then picks his way to the garage door, pushes a couple of boxes in front of it, though aware it can still be sprung with a good shove.

Omar trots over whining, his face silver in the pale light from the little window next to the door, his ears flattened against his head.

"Stay!" Roger says, and hurries down the long basement, into the back rumpus room, peeks out onto the well-kept lawn to see if there are any cops among the shadows, then hurries out the door and down the wooden steps, down to the second lawn, past the small fish pond and up to the old wooden fence. He leans over it and throws his sack into the blackberry vines that grow wild in the no-man's land between the back fences of the houses on the hill, then turns and hurries back into the house without once getting that hollow feeling of despair down in his chest that comes with a bust. He is playing the game of scare just for safety's sake, knowing the cops are much better and faster than this.

He opens the door onto the main floor of the house to find Craig silhouetted by the big picture window, standing in the middle of the front room with a bag of dope in his hand, his eyeglasses glinting with jerky movements of his head as if he is looking for someplace to put it.

"Go throw it in the blackberry bushes," Roger says. Craig walks by him, his back hunched and his head hanging forward as if pondering something, but avoiding Roger's eyes in the darkness, another shield besides his plastic-rimmed glasses. Craig's light-brown eyes, usually hazed as if his mind is somewhere else, looks out from the inner world as if there is a split, a doublevision in the iris itself.

Everyone else is milling silently about in the darkened front room, with all the windows covered except the picture windows that stretch across the whole back wall of the upper floor. Yet Roger can imagine a cop placing a ladder against the house and climbing up to shine a flashlight through one of them, and whispering ludly, he says, "Those windows are scary."

"Should we go into my bedroom?" Ruth asks, and when

several people answer "Yes" at once, everyone creeps past the front door, up the steps to the short hall and down to the bedroom where some sit on the bed, the spring creaking loudly and dangerously. Others stand along the wall as Roger slides the fancy purple drapes over the windows and glass doors of the Spanish balcony that overlooks the front lawn.

He then sits down on the floor to wait the whole thing out, a small knot of uncertainty in his stomach. He no longer even remotely believes in the outright bust, but is still afraid some special trick might be pulled and he has to take precautions or leave himself wide open. Omar whines and paws at him and Roger presses him down to the floor, then presses his muzzle to the floor and whispers, "Quiet," then remembers that Craig hasn't come back yet and gets to his feet with the first real fear he's felt since the scene started.

"Checking on Craig," he whispers, and opens the door, closes it softly behind him, starts quietly down the hall, taking short slow steps, his eyes switching back and forth, scanning the dark room ahead of him, the faint glow of light from the picture windows at the opposite end, the blackened doorway to the basement, when the bedroom door opens behind him and in the blurred light from the picture window, he sees Penny's vague shape behind him.

He waits by the stairs until she reaches him, checking to make sure she closes the door behind her, worried by Craig's absence, since it only takes a minute to throw the bags in the vines, and they can bust him back there without anyone in the house hearing. With Penny close behind him, he creeps quietly down the three steps, and, almost holding his breath, tiptoes past the front door, fearing a loud knock and an official announcement of "Police!" in spite of the fact that he can still not really make himself believe in the bust. He walks slowly, softly over the front room rug to the small window next to the picture window, where he can peek out with less chance of being seen. But he can't see well through the dirty window and pushes it open like a door, trying not to make noise, strangely afraid, his hands sweating, his breath short, and he gasps with fright when the window squeaks and a man's face looks up from the lawn below.

He freezes like a wild animal, cringes, his belly kicking over with a pang, expecting the beam of a flashlight on his face, dying of dread in the fraction of a second before it hits him, sure he is busted.

But no beam of light glares in his eyes. Nor is there any sound below as he stares down. Unable to believe that he hasn't been seen by the man and sure there is still a dark figure on the lawn, he whispers, "Craig?"

But there is no answer, just the glimmer of light on the man's spectacles, and his belly sinks. He can picture the guy's cold eyes and clear, official features. But still no light shines up, no flash of gunmetal nor any command to stay put. And he drops back out of the window as if he has not been seen, as if he still has time to fade back into the front room where no flashlight beam can reach him, fighting the urge to close the window after him, to risk making noise by pulling it in, and bumps into Penny behind him just as a voice says, "Yeah?" and his blood comes pounding back into his body with the heavy beat of his heart.

"Man! You scared me!" he says with a heavy sigh and leans out the window. "Come up!" he says, and pulls the window in with shaking hands, then leaves it slightly open when it squeaks and jams.

"Why didn't you tell me it was you, right away?" he asks when Craig steps into the foyer.

But Craig steps by him without answering, then only stops to ask, "Where is everybody?"

Roger stares at the blank circles of glass that blur Craig's face, then says, "Up in your room, man. And you might as well tell them to come down into the front room and get comfortable. There's nothing happening anyway."

Craig just shrugs his shoulders and turns and moves up the stairs and down the dark hall.

Sitting in a circle with the others by the light of the big picture window, listening for the noise of cops prowling around, a knock on the door, watching for the sight of a flashlight beam to shoot in through the big windows and make them cower, Roger now believes by Craig's behavior that the whole thing is a plot to scare him, to play cat and mouse with him, and convince him that Gary is being followed, too. Yet his common sense makes him go along, keep his suspicions to himself so he'll have the leeway to pull a switch and escape, if and when the cross comes down. Every once in a while someone shifts or moves around or sticks their legs out or leans back and lays down on the rug. Finally, he asks, "Just what did happen out there, Gary?"

Gary suddenly leans forward, with his hands cupped on his knees and drops down to speak in a low voice, his girl Ruby's hairbow a big lump in the picture window, and says, "An un-marked cop car with two plainclothesmen in it followed me for a couple of blocks, then disappeared. Then a zipped-up hot rod with high orange fenders followed me when I came back to tell you, and then parked down on the corner. Do you think we all ought to go out and get in our cars and leave all at once to confuse them?"

"There's not even any dope in the house, man, and with all the lights out, as far as they know, we're not here. Outside, all they've got to do is block each end of the street with a cop car and they'll catch us all like sitting ducks," Roger says, figuring that this is a trap.

Gary doesn't press it but after a few more minutes of charged silence, people begin to shift and change their positions and whisper to each other. Roger finds himself wanting the knock of a cop's fist on the door, just to end the tension, to make the impending trap snap shut so he can at least adjust to it.

"Listen, it's late and I've got to get home," Gary finally says. "Why don't you all go out and get in your cars and give me some cover so I can get away."

"Good enough," Roger says. Although still frightened by the multiple possibilities that can happen out there, he wants to end the long, boring, tense and unhappy wait, and he gets to his feet with everyone else, with much sighing and yawning and stretching of arms.

Sure that the trap will now be sprung, his legs tight, ready to jump at any sign of cops, he holds onto Omar's collar and opens the door and steps out. But there are no cops and he gets in Craig's car with Penny and Omar, figuring he has a running chance in someone else's car and none if stopped in his own. He does not think that anyone is in danger but himself and feels no shame at protecting himself.

Backlights flashing red, headlights on, puffs of exhaust, all four cars pull out at once and the whole string of them head around the curve in synchronized slow motion. Roger sits up alert when they near the star-shaped intersection by the small park, fearing the sweep of cop cars down around them, his hands sweating. But his scalp tingles with a horror he hadn't anticipated when they round the curve at the top of the high hill and he sees a hot rod with high orange fenders and big back wheels like a pickup truck sitting under a streetlight on the other side of the curve, with two young men in it, just like Gary said. It looks so strange and unreal, he feels a sense of hopelessness and doom. There is no exit. Reality itself is twisted and stacked against him by an absolute force and there is absolutely no chance that *they* will not get him. But he has to fight back or die and he twists around in his seat as they turn down the hill until they lose sight of the car. Then checking every cross street and checking behind him, too, to see if they are being tailed, he sees Kent turn off in his old car at one intersection and Benny in his Volkswagen at another—to confuse the cops, like Gary said. Then checking down the steep hill ahead, he stiffens and catches his breath at some red lights on a corner a couple of blocks down.

He swallows and, with a weakness in his knees, leans over the front seat to jab twice with his fingers at the lights, then drops his hand and tenses himself for a bust, ready to explode with pressure when they reach the lights. But he feels as if he is going through another strange, surreal sensation when he gets close and sees an unmarked cop car parked on a corner under a streetlight, with its passenger door wide open and all its lights on inside and out, and a plainclothes cop sitting behind the wheel and another big beefy plainclothes cop standing at a blue call box, talking over the phone. The whole scene is as stiff and still as a tableau under a stagelight. The cops don't even look at them as they pass by. Yet the whole thing has a chilling effect on him. It is a warning of what's to come if he keeps up his rebellion. He wants to shout at them, to curse. And he fights the urge to hate Gary, too, whose tail lights blink red with the touch of his brakes at each intersection down the high hill. He fights it because it will only get him in trouble, because it will make him do something he can be put away for, like punching on Gary.

When they reach the crowded flat streets next to Golden Gate Park, Gary turns down Lincoln Avenue and heads straight toward the Bay Bridge as if he doesn't need them anymore and Roger says, "Turn off, Craig, and go back." Then, all the way up the mile-long hill, he keeps seeing the cops on the corner and expects to see them on other corners, then sits up tense and alert when Craig levels off at the top and he sees the hot rod with the orange fenders parked at the other end of their block now, in the middle of the street, not quite blocking their way but forcing Craig to touch the curb with his rear tire when he makes the right turn.

"What are you guys doing on this corner?" Craig asks and stops the car next to the hotrod.

"What'd you say?" the husky, black-haired guy standing outside the driver's door with his foot on the running board says, and turns toward them as his friend opens the driver's door to get out. Sure this is it, the trap he's been waiting for, Roger nudges Craig in the back and sticks his head next to Craig's window, saying, "Can we help you guys in any way?"

The guy stops and stares at him from a square, hard-lined face. His friend's bony face is visible over his shoulder.

"Looking for an address or something?"

"Naw," the guy says and continues to stand there, his big muscles showing under his rolled-up shirt sleeves.

"All right then," Roger says and nudges Craig in the back again to get moving. He keeps quiet until Craig has pulled around them and is far enough down the street to be safe, then turning to watch them out the back window, he says, "Don't mess with guys like that, man. They're tough and like to fight."

Craig's eyes stare at him from the rearview mirror with no sign of emotion, a glimmer of glass in glass, just as silent and motionless as he was on the lawn, and Roger believes he is in on it, that he has tried to start a fight to either get Roger hurt or cause a commotion that will get them thrown in jail.

The next morning, the musty smell of the cold basement air filling his nostrils, he opens his eyes on the boxes of personal junk, unused belongings, golf clubs, and old clothes hangers scattered around the damp cellar, pushed in front of the garage door, and the gloom from the fake bust the night before fills his mind. There is a big emptiness in him, a sense that he teeters on the edge of nothing, of blackness, the void, with only jail or suicide or surrender on the other side, like a long drop down. There is no escape. He feels as if he faces a force as absolute as Greek fate or God. There is no escape. They are always on him. They will never let up. He will probably never see his open letter in print. Suddenly his eyes widen. The open letter? Where is it?

He bunches his legs with panic and rolls off the mattress to keep the bag down and the cold air off Penny and runs across the cold basement floor, in and out of the boxes of junk and up the basement stairs. But when he steps into the cold, dingy front room, he stops and shivers, trying to remember what he did with the article, then remembers the dining room table, and rushes across the room only to find nothing on the scratched wood. Then he remembers Gary coming back to the table when he left him with his girl at the front door and he runs across the room, leaps up the steps to the hall, grabs the telephone and dials Gary's number, his lips pursed, breathing heavily through his nose, still shivering. After four long rings, he hears Karen's sleepy "Hello?" and pictures her soft, freckled face.

"Roger. Is Gary there?"

There is a small pause, then her voice: "I have a number you can call if you like."

"Thank you, very much," he says as soon as she finishes, and dials the number she gave him with a shaky finger, shivering badly in the cold hall, his toes curling up from the icy floor. The phone rings and rings and rings until he counts thirty-three rings, and completely chilled, his nose plugged and starting to run, he slams the receiver down and steps into the toilet, avoiding his angry moon-faced image in the mirror. He blows his nose with shaky hands, throws the paper in the bowl and goes out to dial the number again.

But there is only the monotonous, dragged-out "Hmmmmmmmmmmmmmmmm-pause, hmmmmmmm-pause," but he hangs on until the phone is beginning its fifty-sixth ring and someone picks it up. He hesitates, waits for the person to speak, but no one does and finally he asks, "Gary?   Gary?"

After a moment there is an oily, "Yeeeeeah!"

"It took you long enough, man," Roger says, not bothering to identify himself. "Where's my article?"

"Your article? I don't know. I just woke up. Ruby's still asleep," he says, and is quiet as if to make sure that Roger doesn't miss the point of what he's been doing during the night.

But Roger says, "Did you or did you not take my article off the dining room table last night?"

"Oh!" Gary says, then is silent as Roger stares angrily at the scrawled phone numbers on the wall. "Let me go check," he says, and waits for a moment as if waiting for approval, then puts the phone down.

Roger waits for several minutes, fuming, expecting only a lie and he catches his breath, ready to shout when the phone is picked up again.

"Must have picked it up without realizing it," Gary says, then adds, "Say? Can I get this to you later sometime? Not today. I'm going to be with Ruby."

"You chickenshit motherfucker," Roger says. "Mail it to me," and hangs up.

Ruth

Roger pulls the bag up over his head, hears a pit-pat, pit-pat of bare feet crossing over his head into the bathroom, and throws the bag down from his face, still too angry at Gary to fall back to sleep. Omar is asleep only a touch away, drugged and exhausted from the medicine and the fight the day before. His eye is half-open, the ripped outer lid of his right eye is bright red and ugly. The pus in the corner is already an ugly greenish white. Roger starts to reach out to pet him but stops himself and lets him sleep, then hears the toilet flush and footsteps again. Penny lies next to Roger on her stomach, her porcelain pink face turned his way, eyes closed, hair flaring out over the bare mattress, looking so much like a child that the very thought of her getting busted makes a wave of emotion in him. He has to go out in the daylight and get his grass out of the blackberry bushes, too, and the whole hillside is visible to the back windows of both rows of houses. There is a weakness in his arms and legs. He aches with a heavy sense of persecution. He gets up and puts his robe and mukluks on right away to keep from getting chilled, glances down at Penny and feels a pain rise up in him at the sight of her below him. He misses her as if he was already busted and he feels an urge to lie down and hug her, but Omar opens his eyes and leaps to all fours, and wagging his bushy tail, licks Roger's hand. Then, tail swishing like a plume, he prances through the boxes to the garage door to be let out as if he isn't even sick, and Roger feels a spasm of joy in the middle of his misery. He tiptoes through the boxes and pulls the garage door back, making the cardboard boxes scrape on the cement, and lets Omar out onto the dew-wet lawn.

The morning sky is gray. He closes the door and turns away, glances down at Penny again and walks slowly through the boxes and up the musty stairs to the bathroom. But he stops just as he reaches for the knob of the slightly open door, puffy-eyed and sleepy, as if he can sense that somebody is behind it, though he can't hear a sound, not a sound. He takes a half-step forward, but stops again, his fingers resting on the knob, the sight of the grimy shower curtain and pink tub all he can see, yet some animal sense warns him. He suspects a trick, but wondering if he is just too apprehensive over the bust, he pushes lightly on the knob and watches the door swing slowly open upon Ruth standing on a towel, nude, with her buttocks to him. She spins around to face him, her mouth open as if she is going to cry out. But she keeps silent and nude before him, with heavy white breasts, a wide, dark pubic triangle between her legs, then suddenly turns and runs out of the bathroom and into her room, her bare feet thumping across the floor.

He sees her nude again when he steps out of the study after writing all morning, depressed, wondering where everybody is, since he hadn't heard a sound in the house the last hour. He stops at the sight of her lying on her bed about fifteen feet from him, with the sheet covering her from the crotch down. Craig is sitting on the foot of the bed with his dick sticking out of his white shorts. The drapes are open behind her and she glows in the light like some Renoir nude, though much more slender. The light behind her highlights her long neck, makes a pale globe of her right breast. Her black hair is very black and her blue eyes are striking. The whole upper part of her body seems to bloom before him. He cannot take his eyes off her.

"Just had a quickie," Craig says and stands up, letting the head of his prick drift back into his shorts. He stands next to the bed with his body flexed, powerfully built from a family strain of German peasants. His father is principal of a high school and yet still hits his sons when he's angry and Craig hits Ruth, too, sometimes, when he gets frustrated at her games.

She lifts the sheet, exposing her whole body, and, staring at Roger, throws the sheet back and sits up on the edge of the bed, her legs spread. Then, still staring at him, Craig standing silently, she gets up and walks through the doorway and into the hall up to him, then stops just in front of him and stares.

Roger can see the blue veins in her heavy breasts, the slight track of hair that leads down from her belly button into her pubic hair, conscious of Craig watching, yet feeling his dick throb in his pants. There isn't a sound in the house. All three stand motionless. He wants to reach out and stroke her body. But he feels no affection in her stiff pose. She is not giving to him, she is watching him. He can't move.

Hamburgers are sizzling in the frying pan. The strong smell makes his mouth water. But all three stop talking and concentrate on their eating when he comes in. Penny looks up from the kitchen table and her face under the light is slightly puffy and sad. Craig lifts up the corners of his mouth in a slight smile but doesn't really look at him. And Ruth smiles very broadly at him, showing a row of nearly perfect teeth, saying, "I wasn't very scared last night at all," then looks quickly down at her fruit salad, bits of nuts, orange parts and banana slices.

"Where's Omar?" Roger asks, ignoring her remark, sensing

another trap. He fumes silently at the way they torture him, so middle class, so genteel, yet so ruthless. *Ruth-less.* He thinks about that name. She pretends to be so nice to him, so tempting, yet helps keep him under total lock and key, total surveillance, total manipulation, total tyranny.

"He's outside," Penny says, "Here!" and scoops up a hamburger patty, places it on a slice of french bread already spread with mustard. "Put some lettuce and tomatoes on it," she adds in a concerned tone as she hands it to him. He takes the sandwich from her with a grateful glance, but she looks away as Craig says, "Penny knows how to take care of her man. She keeps the kitchen nice and clean, too."

"What's that supposed to mean?" Ruth says.

"Oh, nothing," Craig says.

Penny turns away and busies herself at the stove, turns the gas off, moves the frying pan, while Roger lays lettuce leaves and onion rings and a slice of tomato on his open-faced sandwich, wondering if they're up to something new.

"Then why did you say it?" Ruth says.

"Well, you are kind of sloppy," Craig says. "And this is the first time the sink has been clean in a while."

"Oh, fuck you!" Ruth says, then shoves her chair back and stomps out of the kitchen, across the foyer, up the stairs and down to her room, where she shouts, "Fuck you, you bastard!" and slams the door.

"Hmmmmmm," Craig says, and then swallows his food.

But Roger can't believe it. Something's really up, and he's sure it has something to do with him having sex with Ruth. She brushes up against him when nobody's around, sometimes kisses him on the neck, makes eyes at him and sits on the couch with her legs spread, and when Craig is there, lifts up her dress to pull up her pants in front of Roger. And on top of what has happened today, he wants no part of them. He keeps his eyes down to avoid Craig's eyes, spreads mustard on another slice of bread, acting as if the little scene has no effect on him, trying to show by his indifference that he doesn't believe it.

"Hmmmmmm," Craig says again, and when neither Roger nor Penny comment, he puts his sandwich down and, without looking at either of them, walks out of the kitchen and stiffly up the steps to the hall, then hardheels it down to the bedroom door. Roger can hear him try the knob, then hit against the door with a soft thump and a creak as if he has hit it with his shoulder. Finally, there is a knock and his voice: "Ruth? Ruth?"

Roger glances at Penny, who is busy laying lettuce leaves and tomato slices and rings of onions on her bread, and shakes his head. It is hard for him to tell whether the scene is another game on him because Craig is so simple with girls and believes that life exists on the level of debatable ideas, while Ruth runs circles around him and he doesn't even know it. Still, it is hard for Roger to believe that Craig will go for such an act in front of them, that he'd play such a sucker's game.

He listens as Craig knocks again, harder this time, and when he gets no answer, tries to force the door by throwing himself against it, grunting with the effort. Then, he finally bangs and kicks on it, shouting, "Open up, Goddamnit!"

"Fuck you!" Ruth shouts from inside the room, and Roger hears Craig suddenly run down the hall and through the bathroom to its bedroom entrance. But Ruth runs across the floor, too, and beats him to it, for he rattles the knob and pounds on the door and shouts, "Open up, goddamn you! Open up the goddamned door!"

There is a long silent pause, then his footsteps come back out of the bathroom, down the hall stairs, and out the front door. He is muttering to himself, Roger catches a glimpse of his green plaid woolen sportshirt before he slams the door and his footsteps skip down the concrete stairs. Roger and Penny are silent. She sits across the table from him, chewing seriously, swallowing, sipping from her glass. Suddenly, there is a scuffling in the bedroom, feet scraping, Ruth screaming, "Stay out of here, you bastard!" Craig shouting, "Let me in, goddamn you!" and the door to the balcony, which Craig must have reached by climbing from the landlord's porch next door, slowly creaking open.

Roger and Penny sit up and look at each other. The door bangs against the iron bed. There is more foot scuffling, her screeches and his grunts as he fights to overpower her, then finally her loud scream, a long moan, and her voice breaking into sobs, and a moment later his voice saying, "Gee! I'm sorry, honey! I'm sorry!"

Roger and Penny both look at each other but sit in silence, chewing as the sobs slow and stop. There is a long silence, the sound of bedsprings, more silence, then in a few moments, the creaking of bedsprings, slow, then fast, and then faster, accompanied by her pants, her gasps, and, finally, a long moaning, "Oooooooooooooh, it feels so gooooood!" and Roger now knows what it's all about. It is a moan out of a sex act so patently staged it is hard to believe, a lousy attempt to trap him through sex. Even love is under police control. He is as good as locked up.

Penny

The slam of a car door. Somebody running down the walkway. Then Penny's face outside the study window, saying, "Omar's gone!"

"Whaaaat?"

"I said he's gone!" Snapping her lips shut, she stares at him through the window, the plain underside of her face puffy and sullen, making him doubt her, yet fear her words.

He stands up, a numbness sweeping over him, afraid it is another trap, another trick, and seems to sleepwalk up the steep stairs to the hall and down to the front door, where she waits for him with one foot in the hall, a frown on her face, sunlight bright on the white stucco wall behind her.

"Hurry up!" she says, and he grabs his coat from the wall hook. Afraid to show his feelings, afraid if he says it's a trick he'll hurt Omar, he follows her all the way to the car without speaking.

He watches her get into the driver's seat, turn the key on and kick the motor over, then back up and pull out and drive quickly around the slowly curving street with stiff motions. Her turned-up nose points at the windshield; she never meets his eyes except in a glancing way when she turns right down the hill at the star-shaped intersection and has to look past him for cars, squinting, her eyelids slanted nearly closed. She turns the wheel with her whole upper body as if it takes all her strength and concentration, then starts down the steep straight avenue of the mile long hill towards Golden Gate Park, a broad swath of green at the bottom. Her head switches from side to side all the way down the street, checking both ways at all intersections, never meeting his eyes, and he watches her with an almost objective detachment. Except for the fear in him, it is like watching a play, but a stage performance that makes him suffer. He is both an unwilling actor and a captive member of the audience. He is both watching the play and performing in it. He is split down the center of his being, unable to detach himself or give himself to the play. He has not suspended disbelief. He is in purgatory.

"Check that street there!" she says, and he looks in spite of himself, searching for the wolf-like shape, the shaggy fur, the blond, pluming tail. But there is only a broad, treeless and barren street, all concrete and asphalt paving.

"Where'd you lose him?" he asks.

"By the door of the supermarket."

"Why don't you go there? He should be where you last saw him," he says.

"He might be heading home."

"Get down to the supermarket, then down to the park if he's not there. To where we played frisbee with him."

"He might be heading home," she says, driving at a slow, maddening speed. "Goddamnit!" he shouts. "Drive by the supermarket, then down to the park! So we can find him, if he's really gone!"

She glares at him with his last words but drives straight down the hill to the supermarket, where she slows down, pulls into the crowded parking lot, points to the glass entrance doors, and says, "Get out and clap for him."

Roger steps out and raises his hands above his head and claps sharply several times, knowing it will carry far and bring Omar from a block away, while she lets the car motor idle. Faces go up on a young couple walking by. A middle-aged couple in a car stare at him. Two men step out the glass door and stare at him, and though they have sportshirts on, they look so big and beefy and conventional, he thinks *Cops!* And dropping his hands, he steps back down into the MG, slumps down in his seat, slams the door and says, "Fuckit! Let's go back home!"

"Why?" she asks but her eyes are gray and cloudy.

"Because this is all a game, that's why!" he says, slipping into a slight tone of self-pity, without the courage to accuse her straight out of being in on it.

But her face goes through an instant change. Gone is the sweet little girl from next door. Her mouth twists out of shape, one eye wrinkles up, and she screams, "You egotistical maniac! What right do you have to say that?"

Her whole head is vibrating. The cords in her long neck stand out and her mouth twists weirdly as she struggles for more words, then blurts out, "I hate you! You— you hear? I hate you! You always think of yourself! You think everything is planned to revolve around you! Just you! I hate you! I ha-a-a-a-ate you!"

Her head keeps vibrating. Her cheeks are splotched with red. Her mouth is puckered. He is shocked, but he gets control of himself, saying softly: "You don't have to go through this act. You can leave if you want to. That's what this is all about anyway."

"You sonofabitch! You cocksucker!" she screams, shaking her head at the windshield, literally pulling her body off the seat with her stiffened arms, holding herself in the air by her grip on the wheel. "I hate you! I really hate you for this!"

Roger is really shocked, yet there is something forced to it. He has seen her really flip out when she thought he might leave her and she fell into a quivering mass on the floor, kicking and screaming, and he has seen her really angry at him, too, when she screeched at him with high, piercing cries, but nothing so guttural and hoarse as she grits her teeth now.

"All the bad vibes have come from you," he says. "There hasn't been an ounce of real worry for Omar since you showed up. Just hostile commands, that's all. Not a true feeling for Omar."

"You dirty bastard! You filthy bastard! I hate youuuuuu!" she screams but looks out the windshield, not at him, and he says, "Please don't try to make me feel guilty. And you don't have to either."

She turns and stares at him, surprised.

"Don't hate me just to have an excuse to leave. You don't need a reason. If this life is too much, if you suffer so terribly, leave. You don't have to get me mad enough to chase you out, to drive you away, so you can then blame me and feel better later."

"Ooooooooooo!" she says, sucking air through her puckered lips, then suddenly leans over the wheel, vibrates slightly with the idling motor, as if to get directly in front of Roger, then looks directly into his eyes, and says, "Do you know that I hate you so much your body repulses me? Do you know that your body's repulsive to me?"

She is staring closely at him as if she doesn't want to miss any of his reactions, her mouth trembling, and his belly tightens with anguish when she twists her lips and says, "Do you know that I haven't come in a . . . in . . . a month? Do you know that I've been pretending to come for a month now? Do you know that? Do you know that I hate your body so much I can't come?"

She leans over closer to him when she sees the hurt, sagging look on his face and in a low, hissing tone says, "Do you know that I've been lying to you, Roger? Do you know that?"

"Too bad, man. She got a ride. You're too late," the student says, music and voices and the sound of laughter from the flat behind him. Roger can see red-haired Karen, a former student and one day lover in the room, too, with a glass of red wine in her hand, and feels an urge to go talk to her. But she doesn't see him, and he walks back down the dark stairs, wishing he hadn't come to pick Penny up, to try and apologize to her, thinking the place looks more like a party than a poetry class.

He drives down Haight Street with his head full of forebodings, imagines her making love in a car to the young poet she talked about, searching for her now, as well as Omar, and though there are few cars on the street so late at night, the sidewalks are crowded with hippies, blacks, bikers, and straight people. He skims the features of the people by streetlight, noticing costumes, long hair, long skirts, cowboy hats, knapsacks, sleeping bags, crowds of hippies outside donut shops, print shops, small clusters of guys and girls sitting on doorsteps next to the busy sidewalk smoking dope, a group of black cats blowing some drums, three sailors standing around a young hippy mother with a small baby in her arms, her long skirt down to her ankles. But he doesn't see Penny.

When he passes the Park Police Precinct, he curses at the barred windows, convinced she has been put up to it to punish him for blaming her over Omar. But he can never really put his finger down on any of her actions or anybody's actions in the end. He can see what happens to him and guess the pattern but he never knows how *they* really work, what they tell his friends and what they don't, and where the line between fact and his imagination lies, finally, in the end. He could go crazy over it if he wasn't so convinced they were really around him, in the shadows of his life, just out of sight.

His stomach is fist-tight when he parks the car on the darkened street on the hill and sees no lights on in the Spanish style stucco. He walks into the dark house listening carefully for her, sees that Craig's bedroom door is shut and that he and Ruth are probably in bed though it is only a little past eleven and they rarely go to bed before midnight. He washes his face and brushes his teeth in the bathroom without turning on the light, then hurries down into the cold, dark basement, straining to see if she is in bed, then puts his pajamas on and lays down under the sleeping bag cover. He lays there a long time, listening to every sound, hearing an occasional car go by, holding his breath to hear if the car will stop, not breathing again until it moves away, then breathes slowly after it drives past, missing her, sorry he hurt her, jealous, too, and realizing how much she fills his empty, almost loveless life, which is mostly a series of misfortunes caused by cops.

He stiffens under the bag when a car comes to a stop, its motor idling, then shifts gear, pulls into the curb, and stops. He hears voices and footsteps that draw near and make him stiffen under the bag again, anticipating what she will look like and what he will say to her. But the sounds fade away. A door closes. Silence. Darkness. A faint glow of light from the small garage window. He remains tense and alert for a long time, alternating between anger at her and love for her, fighting a picture of her getting screwed in a car, panting as she comes.

Another car comes down the street. He hears it slow down, stop, idle for a few moments, a door open, close, voices: "Bye!" the car drive off. Light footsteps come down the walk, past the window with the closed drapes next to the mattress, then up the front stairs, into the foyer and up the hall steps to the bathroom. Flush of the toilet. Water running in the sink for several minutes.

He is sure it is her, although it could be Ruth. He is afraid she is washing herself off after screwing. The water stops. Footsteps in the hall, down the stairs to the foyer and the basement door. He tenses as she walks softly down the darkened stairs.

"Penny?" he asks.

"Oh! Hi, Roger!" she answers as if there are no problems between them. And stunned by the false sound of her voice, he watches her dark form move slowly through the boxes on the floor, faintly touched by the dim light from the garage window. She slips out of her clothes, her nude body glowing vaguely in the darkness, then steps over him onto the mattress and slips under the sleeping bag. But when she slides over to him and puts her arm around him and tries to cuddle up to him, he says, "Got a guilty conscience, huh? What have you been doing? fucking?"

"No!" she says, and jerks her arm away, then rolls over to face the wall.

"Where have you been?" he asks, and grabs her shoulder, jerks her over on her back and presses her down.

"Nowhere! Oh, nothing!" she says, her face white and clear, then suddenly sticks her thumb in her mouth.

"Answer me, Goddamnit! Who have you been with? Who brought you home?"

"Oh, Roger, hug me! Make love to me!" she says, and tries to put her arms around him.

"I'll make love to you all right!" he says, and throws himself on top of her, forces her legs apart and starts pumping heavily, feeling her pelvic bone every time he hits her, trying to hurt her, to degrade her, making her grunt and catch her breath with little cries, just close to sobs, but hurting himself, too, making his balls ache; then he has to stop, and grabbing her by her hair, jerks her head back and sits back on his heels and says, "Tell me who you've been with! Tell me!"

"Owww! Owwwww!" she cries and tries to pull his fingers loose, but he bends her head back even further.

"You're hurting me! You're hurting me!"

"Tell meeee!" he says through his teeth. "Tell me who you were with!"

"Oww! Owwww, Roger!"

"Where have you been since class let out? Kissing, huh? Fucking that poet you told me about?"

"He didn't touch me! Owwww! You're hurting me, Roger!" she cries, then suddenly starts sobbing and gasping for breath, sounding like a handsaw, "Huh-uh! Huh-uh! Huh-uh!"

"Tell me what he did!" Roger says. "Tell me where he touched you! I'm not going to let you go until you tell me!"

"He just kissed me! He didn't touch me, Roger! Oh, stop, please!" she cries, then begins to sob again, but shutting out her sobs, he asks, "Tell me! Did he finger you! Answer!"

"No, no. He doesn't even know how to kiss. I could feel his teeth on my lips. He opened his mouth like he was going to take a bite. That's the truth, Roger! Please, oh, please!"

"Aaaaah, you kissed him! You made love to him! Admit it! He fingered you! Didn't he! Didn't he!" He shouts, and shakes her back and forth by her hair and, in the din can hear the bed creak upstairs, voices and bare footsteps on the floor above.

"Owww, Roger! Please, oh, please. He didn't. I just went home with him because I was sad over you and because he offered me a ride. I didn't know he—— Owww!"

"Liar! Liar! You knew what you were doing! That's why you went along! He screwed you, didn't he! Didn't he!" he yells and jerks her back and forth again, sobs hiccuping out of her, hands prying at his fingers, her screams cutting into him, making him feel guilty for not loving her enough, for not being able to trust her enough. Yet her sobs increase his anger, his sense of being betrayed, of being made a fool of by her and the police and he stops, still holding tightly to her hair, when Ruth's voice calls, "Can we help you guys? Can we be of any help?"

He turns his head to see weak light filtering down the steps into the dark basement and unable to see Ruth, he answers, "No! Penny just let some cat play with her tits tonight, that's all," then jerks back on her hair.

"Ow!" she cries, but doesn't sob, and Ruth says, "Alright," and closes the basement door, shuts them into darkness again, and walks barefoot across the upper floor to her room. Tired, spent, Roger throws Penny's head back down on the mattress, stares at her hunched, sobbing form, and asks "Do you want to leave me?" holding his breath, waiting for her answer.

"Huh-uh?" she asks, with a sob, lowering her hands to look up at him, her eyes luminous with tears.

"Do you want to leave me?" he asks again, trying to sound strong enough to let her go.

She sobs, then catches her breath, and lifting her face up, tears spilling out of her eyes, cries, "I don't knoooow!" and hides her face in her hands again, sobbing heavily, and Roger lets himself fall back on the mattress, his stomach a tight, aching knot.

He tenses with the sound of the basement door opening, then closing. He lifts his head off the mattress to hear better, hoping she is coming down to be with him. He clasps his hands behind his head when her steps touch the cement, then watches her walk through the boxes of junk toward him, stop next to the mattress and stand without speaking, purse in her hands, her face sagging into her doublechin. He holds his breath and waits for her voice, afraid she is going to say goodbye. But she doesn't speak. They just look at each other in silence, no words broken by a sobbing breath. No sound. Nothing. She just looks down at him with gray eyes. They are gray in the shadowy basement. He waits for her words like Judgement. She stares at him. Then, almost imperceptibly, her lips quiver like a rubber band, and filled with love for her he hears himself say, "I'm going to try and not let myself get bitter, Penny. Because if I do I won't make it. When Bootsy died last year I almost quit. I thought they killed him, slowly. I wanted to die, to jump off the bridge. I lost my wife and my dog. I don't want to go through that again. I can't let myself give up just because Omar's gone and you . . . might . . . go. Life gets too hard. I've got to let myself believe that he might come back, and no matter what I think or suspect about the cops doing it, being responsible for it, I'm no fool. I'll never rule out the possibility that somebody did, really did take him who had nothing to do with the police."

She seems to search his face as he speaks, then asks, "Do you mean that?"

"Yes, I mean it," he says.

She sits down on the mattress, tucking her shoes under her, and looks into his eyes. Her hair falls down from a part in the middle of her head, thinning her cheeks, making them trim and delicate like her tiny chin, like her tiny mouth which seems taut enough to quiver again.

"I've been searching for Omar," she says.

"I know," he says.

"All morning," she says.

"I know," he says.

But she still doesn't reach out, still doesn't touch him, keeps her small hands in her lap, and he, though he wants to badly, doesn't reach out either. With an ache in each of them, a tense feeling in each gut, they keep their arms down at their sides, keep them from hugging each other. Finally, she stands up again, hesitates, her lips part, she sighs, they close, and turning away from him very slowly, she says, "Bye, Roger," as if she is going away forever, not just upstairs, and with her first step away from him, his belly tightens like it's all over.

He stands in the foyer in the middle of the house, daylight waning, pockets of weak light coming from the picture windows, giving a bleak tone to the gray walls and worn-out carpets. Head cocked, dark glasses in his hand, he strains to hear some sound of someone's movement, but hears only the sigh of creaking wood and hum of wind. He is vaguely aware of some special moment of existence, some pause in the turn of time, when alone in a silence like death he stands in a house in which all the people are gone, in which he is the only one left. He is alone. He has been alone since he fought with her. He is alone in the small foyer, the focal point of the whole house, with access to all doors, all rooms. He is above. He is alone. He is alone after searching for Omar all day, alone. He stirs. He takes a step toward the open door of the basement, stands at the top of the stairs for a moment, then walks quietly down the wooden steps, his eyes taking in the shadows in the basement, searching for her, then for her things, and his hopes rise when he sees her knapsack and cosmetics bag still stacked at the foot of the mattress. He looks for a note now, some word that she cares and will stay with him, then spots one on the sleeping bag cover, a folded piece of typing paper. He picks it up. He reads, "Roger. I went to school to study. I still might go home. Penny." There is not one single word of love.

The Primary Campaign

Roger looks out the big picture window. Dark strips of clouds run through the gray sky like streaks of marble. A solitary tree sticks up on the hillside. Steep, empty streets. Telephone poles. Rooftops. A small patch of blue in the east. A silver melancholy tone flickers in subtle lights and shadows on his ivory-toned brow, the hollows of his cheeks. He sees Omar in his mind come prancing into the house with the morning paper, lifting his paws like a thoroughbred stallion, neck arched, ears flattened, tail curling up like a plume, proud, proud as he circles the room. And where is Penny? And his article? He sighs. Muffled sounds from outside, the tiny peep of voices from somewhere near the house, the tap-tap-tap of someone hammering, distant horn-honk, and the slightly stifled hum of the city noises, fused into an indistinct sound. He hears the front door open.

"I've been down to McCarthy Headquarters and got some material on the Democratic Primary Campaign. I've been thinking of working with them, uh—" Craig says, then covers his mouth and coughs. "Why don't both of us work for McCarthy? For peace?"

Roger suspects a trick but sees the suggestion as a good idea, a chance to do something political that might pay off, though the odds are against McCarthy and on Bobby Kennedy.

"Sure," he says, but feels a pressure rise up in his chest and he has to cough to get the wheezy feeling out.

"Gee! You're getting it, too," Craig says.

"Man, I haven't had a cold since I first got out of the nuthouse," Roger says, suddenly scared they might try and get him sick. They'll do anything. He tries to let Craig know what's coming down without accusing him of it. "A few months after I got out I got the flu badly two times in one month and almost died, like I had a death wish since I wasn't loved by anybody."

Craig just stares at him, his eyes shielded by his glasses.

"You see when I was in the nuthouse for smoking grass, I figured they were either trying to break me, make me conform, or put me away for life, and I used to keep my fear hidden. But when I went to sleep, I sweated like I was in a steambath. That's anxiety but they call it schizo-affective, not fear and not crazy but a split from my own senses. Wow! They had me coming and going."

Craig grins.

"I'd get up in soaking pajamas every morning and my bed would be a damp hollow. I had to wear silk pajamas to keep from rotting the sheets and I was prone to colds. And also when you write you usually sit down and don't get much blood circulation. That's why I stand up now when I can, to make my legs pump my blood around, fill my head with it and help me think faster and that's why I try to exercise every day, too. Most writers are prone to sedentary diseases and juice when they're through writing to get the blood moving, to feel warm and good, and I used to keep the house warm during the damp morning hours and this was, of course, called schizo-affective too by the psychologist they forced me to see for about a year."

"Hmmmmm," Craig says, nodding his head like it is a serious story.

"And working on my first novel, I didn't get much exercise and would put the heat up at night and make it too hot for the weather outside and then would catch colds easy when I went out. But this was called schizo-affective, too! And so when I finally left home for not being loved anymore, my family playing games with the Man even after I got out, I wrote standing up, didn't put the heat way up, didn't suffer over living with a family that didn't love me, and didn't catch a cold for two years now. Now what's schizo-affective?"

"Hmmmmm," Craig says, then hacks, makes a squinty face at Roger, opens a bag he's carrying, and pulls out some Contac cold capsules and Vitamin C, though Roger hasn't seen him show one symptom of a cold but the fake coughs.

"How come sick all   of   a   sud   den . . . ," Roger asks, but his voice fades off. He tries to say something else but only a hoarse sound comes out. He takes a sip of beer, then a deep swallow, and tries again but is only able to whisper.

Craig stares at him. The house is silent, with no music or voices, without speech, without the actual vibrations of his own speaking voice in the air, without sound waves in the lull about them tying them together, the day outside the window seems very gray and cold to Roger. Bare sidewalks, telephone poles and wires, concrete and brick are all he can see. Everything is bare outside as only a San Francisco neighborhood without trees can be, and he feels haggard, as if his eyeballs are falling in and the flesh is sagging off his cheekbones, pulling down at the corners of his eyes like hot, slowly slipping wax. It's as if all the running and hiding and worrying and beer and pot are finally catching up with him, and he coughs again with a hollow sound from deep in his chest. Then in the silence, the vague, tense hum of the city is punctuated by a dog's bark, then another dog's bark, and Roger can suddenly see another vision of Omar, lying out on the lawn in the sun, raise his head at the distant bark, his large ears peaked, his brown face marked by the dark worry lines of his brow, but cute, belying the ferocious, answering rumble from deep in his golden throat, with the wide mane of blond fur around it.

Craig puts two blue cans of beer and a half-dozen sandwiches down on the end of the long conference table between them, and says, "Have a beer." Roger stares into his pale brown eyes to see what he's up to, guessing it was in this way Craig infected him with cold germs. He glances down the long table at Penny to see what she thinks. They are in a big modern office with glass walls in a highrise building on downtown Market Street. There are large pictures of Senator Eugene McCarthy on every window and on every spot of wall space and about a hundred people spread around the large room at various desks and tables, working busily at clerical tasks, some writing, others using phones and inserting envelopes like the people at their table. But Penny doesn't seem to notice.

She had smiled when he agreed to go, but didn't sit close to him in the car or speak to him on the drive or when they hurried down the windy street to the building. Roger sniffles, still cold from the icy wind that blew down the concrete canyon of Market Street. He was afraid he might catch a real cold if he went out to work at night. He had already seen the big refrigerator filled with stacks of salami sandwiches and cases and cases of Hamms beer in frosty blue cans, red cans of Coke and orange cans of soda, but feeling Craig's supposed cold ready to worsen in him, already making him sniffle, and fearing the beer might run his resistance down, he doesn't drink anything. He looks at Craig, who sits down in his chair and writes out some more names on envelopes and doesn't look up for a few minutes until, his mouth full, the bread dough flashing white inside his mouth, he asks, "Why don't you have a sandwich, anyway?"

"I might have a bite," Roger says, and takes one of the sandwiches and eats it as he works, writes names on envelopes, puts invitations to the "Victory Ball" inside, seals them and puts them in a box. But the sandwich tastes so good, he has another, then another, and then gets thirsty and asks the girl across the table: "Is there something warm around here to drink besides coffee? Some tea maybe?"

She smiles, shakes her head and says, "Try the beer, it's warm."

Craig pushes a can of beer that has been sitting by his elbow at him, and Roger, afraid he is making a mistake, glances over at Penny again. But she has her head down, addressing envelopes, and doesn't even seem to notice what is going on. He feels the can with his hand, and seeing that it is not very cold, drinks some. But the swallows don't quench his thirst and he drinks it all down at once. Then he takes a deep swallow of the second beer Craig puts by his elbow, and drinks that down. Then, still working hard, he starts on a third beer but has to stop and blow his nose, then blow his nose again, and keep blowing his nose until he uses up all the napkins and tissue paper lying around the table. Then he asks where the men's room is, goes in, comes back with two big fistfuls of toilet paper, catches Penny's eye when he sits down, then addresses more envelopes, eats more sandwiches and drinks more beer, blowing his nose and blowing his nose.

"Gee, I hope you don't get sick," Craig says.

A pressure seems to puff up like a balloon in Roger's head before he has walked more than three or four steps from the MG with Penny, heading toward the first address on a long list of Democratic voters, a big red white and blue identity badge on his chest. He is very warm in a turtleneck shirt and green cardigan sweater and is drugged with cold pills and aspirin, but still has to stop and blow his nose. He feels so weak down in the muscles of his arms and legs, in all the joints of his body, his knees, his elbows, his shoulders, that it takes an act of will to start walking again. All he really wants to do is lie down and rest. He pulls some tissue paper out of a back pocket, blows his nose, then wipes the tip of his nose off and drops the wet, sticky tissue along the curb in front of his car, feeling like a litterbug for dirtying up the clean, middle-class neighborhood. It's mostly white stucco homes stretched down both sides of the wide San Francisco street to the ocean shimmering with sunlight above the distant roofs a couple of miles away.

He steps back from the curb, fighting resentment against Craig, determined to go through with the canvassing. He feels that he owes it to society as a citizen and is also unwilling to let any avenue of political work go unused, anything that can possibly work, even if he doesn't have much faith in the philistine voter.

Penny takes his arm, looks anxiously in his face, and walks up the concrete steps of a yellow stucco duplex with him. He is torn between admiration for her help, since she knows very little about politics, and her willingness to try and save what is left of their tenuous love affair, and a suspicion that she is going along to help the cops make him conform. He rings the bell, tortured because he will never know where the line really is between love and betrayal.

"Yes?" a wall-eyed young woman in a flowery dress asks, opening the door.

"I'm with the McCarthy campaign and I'd like to talk to you about your vote in the Democratic Primary on June 6th," Roger says, trying to spot any suspicious movement or gesture that will tell him if the house is staked out. He's suspicious immediately when she says, "Wait a moment," and steps back into the hall, disappears into the front room, and reappears in a moment with a green-eyed teenage daughter who looks like her but is prettier.

"Talk to her. She knows all about it," the woman says, smiling, and walks away.

"What's McCarthy's stand on the street riots?" the girl asks.

"He backs efficient police protection, of course," Roger says, aware of how middle class the neighborhood is, and immediately on guard, sure the girl is a decoy.

"What about the domino theory in Southeast Asia?" the girl asks, her smooth, sweet face as bright as a cake of Lifebuoy soap. He tries to think of an answer to her right-wing question, guess how the question can fit in with a police plan to make him reveal himself and respond to the innocence of her face, too.

"He doesn't accept the domino theory," he says, "and points to—"

"What about the draft? How does he stand on military conscription?" the girl asks, and Roger knows he is in for an exam. He wonders who has drilled her, got her so sharp, but tries to answer while Penny watches. The girl cuts him off with question after question, ranging from the welfare rolls and the black man to the shape of the table at the Vietnam Peace Talks in Paris, pinning him down on every point of domestic and international policy, and making him thankful that he has studied the pamphlets and mimeographed sheets the crew leaders passed out.

"Thank you very much," she finally says, and blinks her bright green eyes at him, and closes the door.

He turns away, feeling like he has just been through a third degree, and fatigued but his mind simmering even if his body is weak, with Penny holding onto his arm, he walks down the stairs and into the warm sun with wobbly but determined steps.

He lays on the mattress next to Penny in the cold basement, one nostril clogged, a cough growing in his chest, the sleeping bag pulled up around his neck. Thoughts begin to take shape like actual experiences in his mind, the first hints of dreams, when there is a sudden roar of a crowd, the shouted name, "Kennedy!" and he wakes completely up but can still hear the crowd roaring, an announcer trying to speak above it and the buzz of the TV set.

"Penny!" he shouts and sits up. "Something's happened to Bobby Kennedy!" He throws the bag cover back, jumps to his feet, and runs through the dark basement up the stairs and into the front room and over to the TV set, where Craig is standing in his white jockey shorts and T-shirt, looking silver as a ghost in the glow, his glasses frosted with light, pointing at the picture on the set.

"Fuck! Fuck! Fuck!" Roger says, seeing the last chance of a democratic election lost and a fulfillment of Martin Luther

King's prophesy of a right-wing coup in America right there on the TV set in front of him, in the best American news fashion: Bobby Kennedy sprawled on the floor. A blurred look in his eyes. His slightly crooked teeth showing in his open mouth, his boyish shock of hair standing on end as if he's just been slapped. And some man putting a rosary in his stiffened hand.

Pain splitting, pulsing like shafts of lightning through his ringletted head, thoughts blurred by weakness and cold pills, sniffling, snorting to breathe, his body soaked with sweat, he chills quickly with the cold basement air if he dares to lift an arm out from under the sleeping bag or stick a toe out at the bottom when the steaming body heat gets too oppressive. He had stayed in front of the TV set, barefooted, sniffling, shivering and coughing, refusing to believe that Bobby Kennedy was dead—even when everyone in the hotel lobby dropped down on their knees to pray for him. Only when the newscaster announced that Kennedy was still alive an hour later, then still sniffling, shivering and coughing did he go to bed. He didn't want to look at the headline:KENNEDY DEAD Craig brought down either and wouldn't look at the funeral on TV nor read the paper that said, THREE PEOPLE KILLED BY FUNERAL TRAIN.

He just lays on the mattress and does nothing, absolutely nothing. He doesn't even think, all thought is blurred, as he sinks into sickness, his mind stupefied, too weak to even lift his head, stomach curling with nausea. He's filled with a wish to just drift away, to just fall asleep and slide into death, not to ever move again, to drift into oblivion, into nothing, nothing, where there is no secret police to steal his dog, to take his article, to suppress it, to corrupt his friends, to coarsen his woman, to destroy his family, to harass him until he explodes into fits of rage, and to kill his President, too, and his brother, the next-to-be president, and the greatest black men the country has produced.

He lies cold, cold, chilled from his clammy skin deep into him, deep into his stomach, his intestines, his chest, the joints of his knees, his elbows, chilled stiff with a deadening pain in his heart as if he lies in snow, shot down in some cold mountain range, with rings of light radiating from his body, rippling the snow around him like white waves, like his life force ebbing away. He can feel himself lift into space, feel the space spread out around him, from him, from his body. He can feel his life energy pushing out around him, forcing the icy snow, the world out from under him, away from him. He can feel the world getting further and further and further away until he is floating in space and knows he is dying. He knows it. Yet, he doesn't care. He does not panic. He merely tells himself he is dying. He, Roger Leon, is leaving life, and he doesn't care. No, he doesn't care. Yet there is a sadness in him for all the lost things of his life, his family, friends, dog, woman, place in a society he had once lived with in some harmony, murdered President, Bobby Kennedy, Martin Luther King and Malcolm X and Bobby Hutton, deep sadness like the deadening icy pain in his heart, a deep, deep sadness.

A dog's howl pierces like an electric current through rings of light, rings like a bell in him, sound of Omar calling him, wanting to come back, and his body shivers and his limbs jerk with a rush of blood, a painful thumping of his heart with the hope that charges through him, and he wakes late at night, sweating and shivering under the sleeping bag.

"Is that Omar?" he asks. He hears himself ask it. He hears the words come out of him and resound in the cold darkness of the basement. There is a movement at his side and he can feel Penny throw the sleeping bag back and stand up on the mattress, feel her body weight shift on the surface. He can hear the drapes slide back and the window screech when she lifts it, though he can just vaguely see her, cannot really open his eyes, does not even know if his eyes are open or if the basement is just dark, really dark.

"Omar! Omar!" her voice calls, and his body heats with hope, waits for the sound of his dog, for his whimpering, for his scratch at the door, for him to leap up through the window and land on the mattress, to curl around him, his thick wolf's fur carrying with it a current of cool wind and fresh-cut lawn and little white daisies. He can smell the fresh air he has brought in with him. He can smell his dog, the scent of bacon in his ears and the good dry smell of his paws. He can smell him. And he can feel the cool current of wind as Omar curls around him with a low, moaning groan. He can smell him and hear him but cannot see him. It is too dark. Yet he is sure that if he can only make himself reach out from under the bag into the chill basement air, he can now stroke his wet fur. For it has been raining outside. He feels Penny lie back down next to him and he asks: "Is it five o'clock?"

"Yes," she answers.

"Omar's crazy," he says.

"He sounds like a ghost," Penny says, and Roger feels himself drift off again, still worried about Omar, still not sure he's lying next to him, though he can smell him. He can definitely smell the fresh clean air that clings to Omar's thick fur, even as he sits with Penny at the outside table on the veranda, across a light-well from an Italian restaurant, with a large dance floor, and they listen to an argument. A bald, fat maitre d' in tuxedo and bow tie, red cummerbund, is shouting at a plump waitress with long dark hair in a white peasant blouse and full red skirt who shouts back at him from a table by the dance floor. There is another waitress on the other side of the maitre d'. There are no customers in the room, which Roger can see through an open window

142

of the restaurant, not more than eight feet from him.

Suddenly the woman starts screaming and trying to get away from the maitre d', who pulls on her while the other waitress screams and shouts too, though Roger cannot tell which one she is shouting at. But the first waitress suddenly breaks away from the man and leaps up on the window sill, stands there as the maitre d' and other waitress scream at her not to jump. She hesitates up there, her face contorted with grief and fright, but when they rush to grab her, she jumps to the screams, her arms spread, and flies toward Roger at his table. But she drops and strikes her head on the ledge of the veranda, which is now a window, gashing out a piece of skull with blood and hair on it on the window hook, which is on the outside of the window instead of inside as it should be, on her way down, then falls to her death at the bottom of the lightwell to the screams and shouts of the maitre d' and the other waitress.

Roger stares at the piece of skull and hair and blood oozing and dripping off the finger hook of the window and is too afraid to look over the edge of the veranda at the body a couple of stories below. He fears it. He won't look. There is much talking and screaming by the excited people crowded around the body down below, but he won't look over.

Though he goes to the funeral. It is at his grandfather's ranch where he spent summers as a little boy. He can see his Uncle Willie with his pinkish skin and pale eyes, his reddish hair, dressed in a brown plaid sportcoat, rushing around in the wide dirt yard, trying to get things organized. Roger points out to Penny the land and the barn and the church on the property, the dirt road that curves between the bare, slightly rolling hills touched with green, with only scrub brush and cactus, when he notices about five hundred people out in the yard before the church. Then they are in the church and he looks for his grandfather among all the people to point him out to Penny—he is very proud of his grandfather—while Omar runs around the church, through the pews, and splashes back and forth in the half-foot deep puddles on the church floor. Still trying to spot his grandfather and point him out to Penny, Roger finds himself seated on a bench at a table along the inner wall of the church, talking to a lady who might have been his grandfather's woman after his grandmother died. She is a pretty little middleaged lady of Spanish descent with fair skin and light eyes, who smiles at him and points to his head when he asks her what she is smiling at, and he realizes that he is wearing a hat peaked like a candelabra, with large white candles, like those on an altar, sticking up on it and that he has chosen it rather than a hat with a white donation bucket on it, which a woman tried to put on him, making everyone smile.

But he is still trying to point out his grandfather to Penny, still trying to find him among all the well-dressed people. The men are in white dinner jackets and the women are in formals as if it is going to be wedding instead of a funeral. Finally, he sees a man he thinks is his grandfather and he pokes his finger at him, where he stands at the head of all the people, leading them down the center of the floor, the seats now gone except for a few along the edges, facing the aisle rather than the altar. The man has fair, pinkish skin with graying, thick, wavy hair.

"That's him! That's my grandfather!" Roger says, and the man looks at Roger at the table and nods at him, then hooks arms with the man and woman on each side of him, and they hook arms with those on the sides of them, and all the people in the large, well-dressed crowd hook arms with everyone else and start pushing forward, almost marching, in a zigzag manner, from one side of the church to the other, but in a tight, clumsy way, almost stumbling over their feet.

But Roger stares at the man and realizes that he is not his grandfather but his grandfather's eldest son, his dead mother's brother, who looks a lot like his grandfather but is stouter, and that he cannot ever see his grandfather because his grandfather is dead. His grandfather is dead just like Bobby Kennedy and Martin Luther King and Malcolm X and John F. Kennedy and his mother and his brother, all dead, dead, dead, and he throws his arms in the air like the waitress when she jumped to her death and screams and screams and screams, and the scream rings and rings and rings in his ears, and he wakes to find Penny's face blurred in front of him, calling, "Roger! Roger! What's wrong? What's wrong?"

A rainspout is dripping somewhere as he sits up on the foot of the mattress, leans his head against the window frame, and looks out the basement window at the walkway down the side of the house which is lined with bushes and small trees, still wet from the morning rain, and at the house next door, where they as hippies are intensely disliked. The dark boundaries of damp, graded dirt that separate the cultivated plots of up-turned earth and the close-cropped lawns make him feel lonely and alien as if in a land of Greece or Turkey. The whole backyard is shadowed from the overcast sky, damp and gloomy from the rain, bare next to the other treeless backyards which stretch far down the hill and finally blur out in a landscape of rooftops, telegraph poles, and streaks and streaks of wires. Dark blood and skull and hair ooze off the window hook, drip, drip, drip in his mind. He hears the rolling crunch of Penny crushing marijuana seeds in a shoe box with a jar, kneeling on the outer edge of the mattress with her back to him. Her hair hangs low, close to her ass, which he swears is heart-shaped, in dark green levis. He wishes he could be happy with her alone and to hell with the whole world, its causes, cops and murders, its finks, its killers. He wishes he could really trust her. Suddenly she turns her head and looks over her shoulder at him. Her arms are still out in front of her, hidden from sight by her body.

"Why are you looking at me like that?" she asks.

"Because you're pretty," he says in a weak voice.

"It doesn't look like it," she says, and her small mouth quivers.

Someone heavy-footed comes down the basement stairs and Craig comes around the corner of the basement wall and smiles, raises his hand when he sees Roger, his glasses flickering with the gray light. He moves along the little path through the boxes.

"Not feeling too well yet, huh?" he asks, and stands by the edge of the mattress trying to look concerned, his brows furrowed, a lock of hair resting on the white plastic frame of his glasses. Roger shakes his head, his full mouth shut and sagging.

"Let's smoke a pipe. That ought to make you feel better," Craig says, and sits down on the edge of the mattress. In the silence, the rain spout dripping somewhere on the other side of the wall, he pulls a small plastic bag of grass out of his levi pockets and starts packing Roger's waterpipe with neat, methodical motions, nodding his head while he works as if to reassure himself.

Roger watches him, looks at his new, fuzzy brown beard, the colorless tone of his complexion, of his eyes, and sees that he does not sniffle nor sneeze nor show the slightest symptom of a cold.

Craig lights up, takes a deep drag, then hands the pipe to Roger as a mushrooming cloud of smoke puffs up from it. Someone starts down the basement stairs as Roger takes a deep hit from the pipe, fills his lungs, which ache a little from the congestion of the cold, then holds the first drag in as Ruth walks through the boxes over to them. She is wearing a blue man's sweater and levis, her eyes dark blue and her hair jet black in the basement. She stops next to the mattress, puts her hands on her hips, and looks down at Roger. A black camera she has borrowed from school for her photography class hangs from her neck. But she looks off when Roger looks up at her, turns away and stares out the window, then pirouettes slightly, self-consciously on one toe, walks around Craig, and looks around the basement like she is trying to keep from looking at Roger, who feels ugly with his hair wild and curly from sweating in bed for days, his face puffy and covered with beard stubble. Yet, when he takes a second toke of the pipe and starts to hand it back to Craig she suddenly says, "Oh, Roger! Let me take your picture!" and unsnaps the camera case, while Craig stands up and steps behind her.

Roger still has his hand out with the pipe in it, reaching toward Craig, and for a moment he is caught between giving him back the pipe and wanting to tell her to stop. But Craig keeps his arms at his sides and avoids Roger's eyes and, turning his back, doesn't turn around again until he is standing behind her.

"What in the hell's the matter with you, man?" Roger shouts, then jabs his finger at Ruth, commanding: "Don't take my picture!"

She drops the camera which was already aimed at him, and turns away with a stiff face to look out the window, her blunt-tipped nose, the only flaw in her beauty, stubbing her profile.

"Listen, Craig," Roger says, his breath quickening, his tone hardening. "I really don't like your coming on with me like this." He stops and barely suppresses an urge to accuse him of infecting him with the cold, knows it's too far out to be proven, and that it will weaken what he has to say. They are both stiff and still.

"And I don't like the way you asked me a few days ago over your probably tapped phone to give your stranger friend a stick of marijuana either."

Craig frowns. His shaggy head hangs down. His elbows in his blue wool shirt stick out at his sides awkwardly.

"You know, man. You're a dangerous cat, regardless of what your motives might be. And if you get me busted some day, you might get hurt someday, too. No matter how many years later. Remember that!"

Roger has one hand down on the mattress, ready to push himself up and start punching if Craig wants to fight over it.

"You're not saying that he's trying to put you in jail, are you?" Ruth asks.

"I'm not talking about what he's trying to do," Roger says. "I'm talking about what he *might* do to me and what *might* happen to him for it. Fuck what his reasons or excuses are." He jabs his finger at Craig. "And don't ever, ever try to make me pay for my share of the dope with a check again, man, and I mean it."

Craig winces, pulls his elbows in close to his sides as Ruth blushes.

Roger leans his head against the burlap drapes and looks out the damp window. The rain has stopped for good it seems. Light reflects from the shiney wet stones of the garden walk and shimmers like guitar strings on the ceiling. He watches a silver dollar-sized puddle of rain water on the slanting oily surface of the walkway suddenly spill out the lower side of its circle as if too full for itself and trickle in jerky, zigzag motions across the slick texture, down to a shallow puddle as big as his palm.

"Look, Roger!" he hears, and he turns to see Craig holding up a newspaper.

"CLUBBING AT STATE COLLEGE SIT-IN," the headline reads with a picture below of Slugger Moynihan lying on his face outside the ad building, a girl standing behind him with her mouth open in shock, and cops in riot helmets standing around them.

"Why don't we go to the sit-in?" Craig asks, trying to appear serious and earnest, and the word *trap* flashes in Roger's mind. He starts to shake his head, not wanting anything to do with Craig, but takes the paper when Craig hands it to him, looks at the picture of Slugger lying on his face, the cop with his club above him, and suddenly angry, he sniffles and says, "Fuck it! If the right-wing is going to void the electoral process by murder, then I'm going to join that sit-in! Civil Disobedience is better than nothing! than being sick! than dying for nothing!"

And he jumps up on the mattress and starts bundling himself up in ski underwear, a turtleneck shirt, slipover sweater, boots and coat, with quick, coordinated, electric movements, there's a smile on his face; he's alive, his face flushed with enthusiasm, his cheeks burning, striking with the sallow color of his sickly complexion, his hazel eyes on fire with yellowish sparks, exciting Penny, too, who had started to object but closes her mouth and reaches for her peacoat. Rain clouds bunch over the sun, dark as asphalt paving, yet Roger can see a long, jagged scratch of blue way out over the rooftops and somewhere over the sea.

PART THREE Strike
Sit-In

Caught on the outskirts of the crowd, cheeks burning, eyes glistening, Roger can't see what is going on in front of the President's door, and can't understand the man's words over the mike there is so much noise in the big hall of the Ad building—the whinnying voices of the women, their "Oooohs!" and "Awwwwwwws!" at the speaker's words, the several debates going on in small circles outside the main crowd. The circles suddenly break apart and scatter, then gather quickly into other circles, while cameramen move up and down the hall behind the TV cameras snapping pictures with flashes of light. But all movements are very tight in the crowded hall. He finds it hard to move. Dosed with cold pills and vitamin C and hot tea, he is tense, nervous. A sharp voice near him flashes in his brain and he jerks his head around toward it as if an alarm has gone off.

"Ey! Ombre! Ven aqui!" a young black man says from above him, straddling a big waste bin against the annex wall. He blows his heavy beer breath down on Roger and motions for him to move up on the bin next to him. And as Roger moves toward him, he's suddenly filled with an urge to jump up next to him and warn everybody, try to save them, tell them what is happening in America, tell them that Martin Luther King was killed only three days after he warned of a right-wing coup in America by 1970, and that the coup took place only a few days ago with the murder of Bobby Kennedy. He wants to warn them that traitors are murdering the liberal leaders and destroying the democratic process under the guise of fighting communism, and if they don't support the sit-in, civil disobedience, the right wing will make it guns from now on, that this is the only chance for a peaceful change in America.

But he stops. The guy looks too much like Roy Soames, the black writer he wrote of in his open letter, and it makes him suspicious. He looks the guy over. He is his own size and has yellowish brown skin, a long, beard-stubbled jaw, and a banditto mustache as if he is trying to pass for a Mexican. Roger doesn't like the guy speaking Spanish to him either, as if he's trying to put him in his version of a little brown bag, where he can treat him as a stereotyped abstraction instead of a human being. He looks at Penny to see what she thinks, dependent upon her since she has been so loving and caring to him since he got sick. It seems to have brought them back together. But she is looking at a small group of people arguing near them and he notices that Craig has already disappeared. He stands on his toes to look for him and finds that he can actually see over the heads of the crowd next to the TV cameras to the students bunched up on the floor thirty feet away, like a big wave splashed up against the President's door, where the leaders and speakers of the sit-in are standing, a bunch of white faces, mainly, when he hears the black guy say, "Hey, man! Come on up!"

He turns back around and stares up into the yellowish brown eyes to try and figure the guy out, then realizes that he, Roger, has long Spanish sideburns growing down to his jawline and that Carlos Chavez and his grapestrikers are big on the campus and that the black guy can honestly think he is a spic and is just trying to be friendly to him.

"Thanks, man," he says, and gripping the bin with both hands, he leaps lightly up on it, straddles the three foot hole with his hiking boots and finds he has a balcony seat on the whole sit-in. He can see right over the TV cameras and crews and the heads of the hundred or so noisy people bunched up around the crews to the carpet of squatting students and the cluster of people surrounding the mike in front of the President's door and even into the adjoining hall, packed with sitting students, which disappears off to the left at a right angle from the main foyer. He is also in a perfect position to see the deans moving back and forth in the annex hallway below him, and he motions to Penny to come up with him. He hooks hands with her and pulls her up on the bin with him, where she leans against him for balance, and he leans against the wall of the closed information booth behind him. But he ignores the black guy when he tries to start a conversation, stares straight ahead, and pretends to be too engrossed in the speeches and songs to talk. He wants to stay happy. He doesn't want to have to worry about cops or informers. He wants to enjoy himself, enjoy being with Penny and with people who believe as he does, who dream like he does and want to try and make those dreams come true. He wants to be part of it, the whole sit-in, a part of life not death, not isolated and alienated and thinking of suicide. And he so completely ignores the black guy that he finally gives up, gets down from the bin and walks out the glass door of the main hallway into the night. Roger feels immediately better though a little sorry he has had to snub the guy.

"Why don't the professors meet with each other instead of trying to get us to meet with them?" a big blond student says, his soft belly popping out in his T-shirt. He stalks back and forth in the tiny clear space in front of the President's door. "Fuck them! Why don't they do what we're doing and discuss the issues?

149

That's what I'd like to know."

A big cheer goes up along with a lot of clapping and whistling and Roger and Penny clap too until the portable microphone changes hands and the noise dies down. Roger sees Bob Dilman, head of the creative writing department, stop Dr. Morganthal, head of the poetry center, and say, "Come on, Dick. Let's do what the students say and go have a meeting in the Board of Publications Room to discuss the issues."

Though Roger can see that they cannot fail to see him up on the bin above him, neither of them speaks to him, though he knows them well: two Jewish intellectuals in their fifties; Dilman, plump, bespectacled, and balding, who sells tight, light, well-written short stories to the big slick magazines, and who believes that the book should be kept as a barrier between the professors and the students; and Morganthal, a veteran of a German prisoner-of-war camp who, except for his silvery hair, looks like his brother Eddy with his high forehead, bulbous eyes, and hooked nose. But their snobbery doesn't surprise him; he has such a bad reputation as a rabble-rouser. He is so pleased to see them both turn and gesture to other men in dark suits and all of them go around the corner of the annex hall that even though he does not want to draw any attention to himself, he feels that what what has just happened is so important an indication of the effect the students can have on the faculty that he cups his hands to his mouth and, in a loud voice, says, "For anybody who cares! The professors have taken the suggestion of the last speaker and have gone to meet and discuss the issues!"

A big round of applause crackles in the hall. Faces look up at him. In the bright glow of the TV lights another person begins to speak. But for a moment, with all the faces turned toward him, Roger feels conspicuous and keeps his face set and serious, dark circles under his eyes, a sallow, bloodless color to his brow, a feverish glow to his cheeks. He doesn't want to grandstand. He is too aware from too many demonstrations and crowd scenes how the desire for attention can spur a person to foolish actions and he only relaxes when everybody turns to look at the new speaker. Penny, who is now standing on the bin next to his where the black guy stood, looks into his face as if aware of his tension, then reaches out and touches him to show her sympathy, and he squeezes her hand and feels very lucky to be alive, to have her, and to be doing something important that he believes in.

But another busy dialogue begins in the annex hall below him. A handsome, middle-sized man in his forties, whom Roger recognizes as President Wintergreen, comes walking slowly down the hall talking to two students, and stops next to the waste bins. Wintergreen's wavy brown hair is sprinkled with gray and his face is just beginning to wrinkle with age, but he is still slim in his gray-blue, conservatively cut suit as he concentrates on the young man who is talking and then says, "Yes. But how do I grant their demands when the State College Commission has ordered me not to?"

He then looks up at Roger as if speaking to him, too, and Roger says, "Do it anyway. Do what's best, what your conscience tells you to do. Don't just follow orders."

Wintergreen grimaces as if the problem is now too clear to him and he turns and paces a few steps down the hall, stops, puts his hands in his pockets, then paces back. He seems so genuinely concerned that Roger feels sorry for him. He remembers how Wintergreen appeared in a peace march only a couple of months before, carrying his small daughter on his back, and got his picture in the papers, which gave the anti-war movement a boost in the Bay Area. And when Wintergreen stops and, frowning, tries to answer another student's question, Roger feels he is caught between pressure from Reagan, a right-wing governor who got elected because President Johnson split the California Democratic Party over *his* Vietnam War, and the students, who are forcing him to back up his liberal beliefs with real action. And he wonders what Wintergreen is going to do next, when he walks off down the annex hall, still looking worried but boyishly innocent, and turns the corner, since he seems to sympathize so much with the attitudes of the students.

Just then there is a big cheer over some speaker's words as Bob Dilman's wife comes in the door from the campus side of the main hall, then moves around the cameras and crowd over to the bin by Roger, who wonders if she is up to something.

"Hello," she says in a mild tone, her soft, dark eyes meeting his, though her pale face remains expressionless. She is a plain-looking though personable housewife starting to middle age, wearing a warm street coat of the functional kind that Roger's older sister would wear. But besides being his sister's age, she even resembles her in a general way with her dark hair and pale skin. He has met her only once in her home at a cocktail party and likes her, thinks she is sweet and unaffected, though he believed then that he was only being invited because the State was trying to rehabilitate him when he got out of the nuthouse.

"Hello," he answers in the same subdued tone that she uses. He still believes that Dilman has brought her with him on purpose to keep him liking something about the English department and the school, since he is supposed to get along so well with women, has a Don Juan complex by nuthouse standards and a man's nature by Latin ones, and that *they* are still trying to fit him into the existing social structure so he will stop causing so much disharmony, he is grateful to her for her politeness. And though the hall lights imbedded in the ceiling give his face a vivid, white, sickly look, with burning cheeks and hollowed eyes, as if he is churning inside with resentment and anger, he only feels warmth toward her. He only wants to love her, to love everybody, and he turns toward the sound of raised voices and a cluster of people around a man with golden, ringletted hair and broad shoulders, wearing a blue tweed sportcoat, who is asking some students on the fringes of the crowd for something. His voice saying, "Betty Morales and Jorge Enriquez!" carries up to Roger when he turns away from the students and meets Roger's eyes.

"Say!" he says, smiles, and steps over. "Could you do me a favor? The professors who have just met would like to speak to Betty Morales and Jorge Enriquez. I can't get word through to the mike for them." He waves at the blockade of people and smiles again.

Roger stares down on the man as he speaks, feeling Penny's weight on his hip, guessing the guy is a campus cop, but knowing, too, that it is for Betty Morales and Jorge Enriquez, he says, "The professors would like to speak to Betty Morales and Jorge Enriquez." Then, feeling the need to justify his interruption, he adds, "To get their side of the story."

People in the hallway turn to look at him, and a tall, thin, dark kid with a very short haircut and blackrimmed glasses, whom Roger assumes is a Third World leader, repeats the call for Betty Morales and Jorge Enriquez over the mike. A thin, dark man jumps up from a bench in the annex hallway behind the cop and looks questioningly at Roger, as if he recognizes him as the wild, radical teacher of creative writing who never went into the faculty cafeteria and always hung around with the students. But Roger recognizes him, too, in his impeccable, conservative green tweed suit and vest, Oxford thin tie, straight black hair hanging over his ascetic face, as the Mexican-American professor he had seen around the campus and whom he always avoided and suspected of being a police collaborator merely because the guy always stared at him whenever he saw him. Still, he looks at him now and points at the cop, who turns around, a surprised expression on his face that he walked right past the man he was looking for. He hurries back down the annex hall and starts talking to Enriquez as a dark, fairly tall and very pretty blackhaired girl stands up by the President's door and begins to pick her way across the sitting students with careful steps of her shapely legs. Slim, with very fine features and brown skin, she is almost out of the mass of students and about to step into the crowd around the cameras, when she suddenly glances up at Roger. Then, head down, she meets with the curly-headed cop and Jorge Enriquez, and talking together, all three make their way down the annex hall and around the corner.

"Help me down. It's too tiring up here," Penny says, and Roger grips her hands and holds them until she is safely on the floor. He hears a cheer from the crowd, and has just straightened up when the cop appears below him again, smiling up at him as if they are old buddies, looking very friendly with his freckles and gingery hair, hints of gray at the temples. "Could you ask for Melchior Chow, President of Third World?" he asks.

Roger knows that he is being used, but he also knows he can do some good for the sit-in. So, he nods, and feeling some hint in the back of his brain that he is pleased to be playing his brief but important role in the sit-in, he calls out: "Would Melchior Chow, President of Third World, please go to the BOP room, where the professors are meeting?"

But the student speaking over the mike, a long, thin, beardless hippy, spins around and, with his long hair flying, shouts, "You tell the professors to take care of their sit-in and we'll take care of ours!"

His face is twisted with anger and his mouth is a black hole. Some people break out clapping, and Roger, stunned as if he had been slapped, shouts back: "Are you more interested in shooting your mouth off or in settling the problems we're sitting in for, punk!"

The clapping stops and the student shuts up as a short, Filipino student with a smooth, gentle face gets up from the floor near the President's door and, glancing at Roger, picks his way through the students' bodies, glances again when he gets past the TV cameras, then hurries down the annex hall.

Everyone is quiet. Many people are staring at Roger. Bob Dilman's wife has her eyebrow arched as if she is now convinced for herself that Roger is the foul-mouthed gang leader and no-good street kid most of the faculty think he is. Roger resents the false reputation, which he knows is based upon his outlaw heroes, but he feels shame burning in his face as well as the fever, and he shifts uneasily to relieve the ache in his feet when he hears: "Give up this unlawful assembly and work through the normal democratic processes of the student government!" He suddenly feels the shock all over again of Bobby Kennedy lying dead on the ballroom floor, with crooked teeth and blurred eyes, and he shouts, "No! No! Noooooooooo!" until he runs out of wind. Most of the people at the back of the crowd in the main hallway turn to stare at him again and a man standing only a few feet from him in a blue windbreaker and a short, black crewcut shouts, "Shut up!"

"What do you mean 'Shut up!'?" Roger asks, wondering if the guy is a cop, he looks so much like a jock, the only thing missing is his block letter.

"Just shut up!" the guy says.

"I can disagree if I want to," Roger says, and he shouts again, "Booooooooo!"

"I said shut up!" the guy says, steps in front of the bin below Roger, and glances at his legs as if he is thinking of grabbing them and pulling him down.

"Hey, man! I can yell if I want to. Your team's rules don't count anymore, buddy. That's the whole object of this sit-in: to stop the game!" Roger says and shouts even louder: "Booooooooo!" until his face turns hot and his eyes feel like they are going to pop out of his skull. The blue-jawed guy frowns, takes another step closer, then suddenly turns and marches off down the hall. Roger keeps booing at his back until he disappears, determined to spend the rest of the night on the bin and say anything he wants to, regardless of what anyone thinks, when a tall, blond, country-looking student with a boney face and silver-rimmed spectacles suddenly appears below him and says, "Say! How would you like to come back and join the sit-in?"

Agents Provocateurs

Students walk up and down the narrow hall through the trail between the feet of the students, spread out on sleeping bags like Roger and Penny. Cameramen come by. Men in conventional suits and sportcoats crowd up on the trail, going in opposite directions. A TV personality who interviewed Roger on his show about his first book smiles and says, "Hello," as he passes. The microphone keeps changing hands. Most speakers talk about what the students should do now that the sit-in has gained momentum, how to out-guess the administration, force them to meet the students' demands. Someone gives the latest news on the battle to reinstate Jorge Enriquez and Betty Morales. Professors speak, most opposing the sit-in. Students from other campus strikes speak, too, rebels from Columbia and Stanford with long hair and hippy clothes or with short hair and blue jeans like workers, who call the students brothers and sisters like the Black Panthers. Everyone shouts and cheers and boos and claps and laughs and sings songs.

But though he is excited and happy, Roger cannot shake the metallic eyes of the monitor: short blond hair sticking up in back, above his skinny neck, who brought him back to the sit-in. He is sure the black guy on the bins was a plant and that he had allowed the freckle-faced cop to use him in such a way that even if the cop had not meant it he got him in trouble with the steering committee, who sent the monitor around to bring him back to the sit-in proper and under their control.

He doesn't blame them. It just means that he is already in a bad conspicuous position. And he gets suspicious when a girl, who has flirted with him for over a year, squeezes in right across the narrow hall from him, sits down on her rolled-up sleeping bag next to her boyfriend, smiles at Roger, and keeps stealing glances at him with her big brown eyes, smiling each time their eyes meet. He knew her long before he knew Penny, and she still turns him on with her creamy white skin and her long black hair, her big luminous eyes. But he i afraid she is now a plant and feels uncomfortable, yet has to smile back when she does and is grateful when Penny says, "What's so funny between you two?" He is happy she loves him enough to care, and she makes the girl quit staring. He presses next to her to let her know how he feels but tightens with fear when a speaker says, "Attention! The Mayor's tactical squad which translates as riot cops is a hundred strong in the service garage of the Park Apartments across the street!"

A big gasp goes up from the crowd, trill of girls' voices, some moans, a sudden pause as if breath is spent, then a lot of excited chatter, a loud din that rings in the hall. Students stand up and start shouting at each other and waving their hands, cheeks flushed, mouths open, eyes wide.

"Please don't get excited! Don't get excited! Stop! Stop! They're merely there! No one has said anything about them coming after us! Please quiet down! Be calm! Stop talking! Please, shut up! Shut up!"

The noise dies down a little but doesn't stop and someone calls over the mike: "Can we have a vote on the motion to adjourn into service committees? So we can get busy on the tasks we need to complete if we're going to continue this sit-in? It's been seconded. All those in favor say Aye!"

"Aye!!!!!!!" many call out and no one answers to a no vote.

"Meeting adjourned!" someone says, and all the students rise to their feet, voices ringing in the hall as they move in different directions to join their committees, though Roger and Penny stand up not knowing what to do.

"What are you striking for?" the blond girl with the dutch-boy bob says and points her finger down at the redheaded girl with all the freckles and the blue knit cap with purple pompons who sits in the circle of students in the basement hall.

"Yes! Have you really considered your motives? Aren't they a little self-indulgent?" says the blond boy with the junior high school haircut, who looks just like the girl, both in the neat, conventional clothes of business administration majors, looking like the Bobbsey Twins. Roger can see them both in FBI literature, with ROTCuniforms, talking to J. Edgar Hoover to show what nice soldiers clean-cut college students can be. The girl only lacks a girl scout uniform. They had stepped into the hall just after the poster committee voted to make slogans on butcher paper and stopped the only constructive activity Roger has seen since the announcement that the Tac Troops were across the street changed the sit-in into a jabbering, milling mess. Though he was pleased by the announcement because he now had allies against a common enemy, and he joined the poster committee full of enthusiasm.

Several students in the circle speak up to answer them, but they keep their eyes on the redheaded girl, who, short and slim, rolls her deep blue eyes up and opens her mouth to speak when the girl says, "Don't you think the majority of students have the right to decide whether they want to go to classes or not?"

"Yes! And not have you decide for them!" the boy says, and the redheaded girl's pompons jerk from side to side as she looks from one to the other, the freckles standing out on her face as she moves her lips but only gets out, "Uh— Uh—" Roger, as stunned as the rest of the students, but angry at the way the couple has attacked her, says, "What are you two anyway? Agents provocateurs? Are you trying to destroy our confidence? Our unity?"

The blond girl and boy both blush deep red and, with mouths shut tight, train identical sets of pale eyes down on Roger. They both turn away toward the red-headed girl again. administra—"

"No-no!" a dark girl, who seems to be the committee leader, says, and shakes her finger at Roger, and before he can defend himself, the blond couple step around the circle of sitting students and walk off down the hall as Penny touches her fingers to her lips to quiet him.

A little student about five foot three with a Van Dyke beard, pointed nose and hair combed down over his forehead like an elf, comes staggering around the bend in the hall as if he's drunk, bumps into girls down on their hands and knees over strips of butcher paper, coloring in the letters of their slogans with different colored marking pens, steps on their posters, then walks right down the middle of one poster as if it's a hall carpet. Roger checks an impulse to yell at him to get off, to keep from getting caught in the middle again, and watches as the girl in the red bandana says something to him and the student stops on the poster and says something back. Then the redheaded girl in the blue knit cap and purple pompons says something to him, too, and Roger, down on his knees over his own poster, trying to spread the red coloring of his felt-tip marker over the last word in his poster, ducks his head and keeps coloring in his letter, forcing himself to keep out of their business though he feels like leaping up and rushing over to help.

He is working hard on his letter when the student's legs come into view, staggering his way, though he doesn't stop coloring until the legs stop on the redheaded girl's poster. Then, with his pen still touching the paper and his head still down, Roger watches her freckled face lift up, her mouth pucker, and some quick but calm words come out of it. She makes no attempt to push the student off, just sits waiting for him to move.

Although the guy sways slightly, Roger doesn't think he's animated or loose enough to be drunk and keeps working on his poster. But he stiffens when the guy's dirty tennis shoes walk down the hall and stop right next to his poster, then start shoving it away from the wall, dirtying it, wrinkling it, almost tearing it, as the student slides down the wall to his butt, legs sticking straight out in front of him.

"Hey, man! Don't rip that poster!" Roger says, but the little student only leans his head back against the wall and peers through slitted eyes at him. Roger slides the poster out into the middle of the hall and tries to press the wrinkles out with his hands, barely keeping himself under control, but still not believing the guy is drunk.

The student hiccups, lifts his hand and waves it in a loose-wristed romantic way, then lets out a sigh, sticks his hand in his back pocket, pulls out his billfold and shows Roger his pink student body card, his hand waving back and forth so Roger can't read the card even if he wants to.

"Get away," Roger says, and aware of Penny watching him from her poster, he jumps to his feet and bends down, feeling the power in his arms, then grabs the student and jerks him to his feet, shoving him against the wall. He feels no trace of fatigue from the sickness, his breath snorts out his nose clear and dry from the cold capsule, and he has the urge, just for a moment, with the guy pinned against the wall, to drag him out the door and dump him in the bushes.

"Hey! Hey!" the student says, struggling to get away, scraping his shoes over the poster. Rogers lets go of his arms but grabs him by the shirt collar, and pressing his fists into the guy's neck, his face only a few inches from his, he says, "Man, if you step on my poster again, I'm going to bust you in your mouth! And don't forget that I'm small, too, so don't be playing that picking-on-a-little-guy shot!"

"Don't hurt him! Don't hurt him!" the girl in the bandana says, and Roger jerks him away from the wall, shakes him once, then sets him down on his heels, and pushes him away with a little shove.

"Get lost, man!" he says, then suddenly realizes that the student is just another provocateur who has come downstairs to cause a disturbance just like the Bobbsey Twins. And he is cautious when they go back to their sleeping bag on the main floor and the girl across the hall smiles at him again. He notices how curvy her body looks even in the blue denim shirt and blue levis and the long white slope of her neck was just made for kissing, but Penny is watching him closely and he doesn't want the girl to provoke her. He is afraid that the sit-in is just another arena for the police to get him, and he is suspicious when the TV commentator, oozing good-natured charm, with a smile that could be a toothpaste ad wrinkling his lined, handsome face, asks, "May I sit down?" He then bends his expensively slacked legs and drops down on the bag next to Roger, and says, "I'm doing news commentary now, Roger, and I'd like to ask you what you think is the most important issue at stake in the sit-in?"

"Gee, Steve, I really don't know. This is my first night here. Though I could take you to a guy who's supposed to be in charge of publicity. He's one of the leaders, he'd know. Do you want me to go find him for you?"

"Well, uh . . ." Steve says, and he tucks his cleft chin in and frowns, then sticks it out again and says, "Alright," and starts getting to his feet.

"Wait a minute, Steve. Wait here. I'll be back in a minute," Roger says, and he hurries down the hall, tiptoeing between students' feet, legs, sleeping bags, stepping high over a shoulder where a circle of students block the hall. Then he hurries down the back stairs where he has seen the guy leading a publicity committee, blaming himself for being so paranoid, telling himself to fight any egotistic impulses, keep from attracting attention to himself, and above all do something constructive for the sit-in. He must not seek glory for himself. He must think of the sit-in, not his name in the papers or his picture on TV. But there is no one at the bottom of the stairs and there is no one at all in the basement hall where the poster committee had met, and dreading the fight through the main floor hall again, he runs down the basement hall and up another flight of stairs that lets him out right by the President's door, where he asks the girl in the red bandana for the publicity committee leader.

"You mean Chuck?" she asks, squinting up at him.

"I don't know. Whatever his name is."

"Thanks," Roger says, and he runs up the stairwell thinking of the suspicious look she gave him, then trots down the second floor hall until he finally recognizes the guy by his shoulder-length brown hair, cut off even with his unshaven square jaw.

"Say, there's a TV man downstairs who's trying to find out about the sit-in. Would you come and talk to him? He's waiting for me now."

Chuck looks at him, his thick, rugged features belying the long, light, girlish hair, as if he is thinking more about Roger than what he said, then says, "I don't think so. Let him talk to the students."

"He seems to be having problems about that and it might do the sit-in some good, keep them from broadcasting the wrong information, you know, distorting the facts like the media does," Roger says, speaking up to be heard over the loud noise in the hall, hurt by the guy's rejection but respecting his humility, too.

"Go with him, Chuck," says a girl who could have been his sister with light brown hair and eyes, cute plump cheeks, square build, like his. "Okay," Chuck says, and he follows Roger back down the crowded hall, down the stairs, and into the main hallway so crowded that Roger has to pick his way carefully down it, saying, "My sleeping bag's right around the corner."

But when he turns the corner, no one is there, not the TV man nor Penny nor even the cute girl across the hall. He stares at the sleeping bag, then turns in a circle, steps back and peeks around the corner to see if he passed the man by, then says, "He was right here, man." But Chuck just looks at him and doesn't speak.

"Where were you?" Roger asks when Penny comes back.

"I just went to the ladies' room," she says. "What's wrong?"

"Steve disappeared before I came back. A lot of strange things are happening. Too many strange things. We haven't even seen Craig since we got here."

She looks away, seems to search the hall for Craig.

"I searched all over the building for you and him. Then I had to go back and tell that guy, Chuck, that I couldn't find him. He looked at me like I was a cop. I think the heat is messing with me."

He stops, not wanting even her to know what he really thinks, not wanting to start an unhappy conversation either. She'll try to talk him out of it regardless of what has happened. He can't rely on her to take his side. He's all alone. He feels like he is sinking into quicksand. Every move he makes traps him more deeply.

She reaches out and runs her fingers over the waves of his temple, trying to console him. She likes to fuss with him when they are getting along and even peels the dry skin off his feet if he'll let her. He jerks his head away from her though and she leans over and stares in his face, her eyes green and serious.

"Why don't we go home and come back tomorrow? So you can get away from here and not have to worry about everything. That TV man might have just wanted to interview a personality! And he was disappointed when you were so modest and sincere and left. He knows you'd be good on TV. You can get some rest, too. Keep you from catching cold again. There's not much else going to happen tonight. Let's go, okay?"

The soft tone of her voice soothes him and he nods and says, "Okay. You might be right. Let's get out of here before something really bad really happens."

160

Vote of Confidence

Students pour into the hall to join those already packed in by the President's door. TV cameras are already set up between the glass doors of the exits in the main hall. People from radio stations move around with tape recorders and mikes held out in their hands to catch the conversations, debates, and speeches. The noise in the hall is like a prolonged shout. Tom, an old radical acquantaince from the early peace movement days, in a neat green suit and short blond hair, nods hello to Roger and Roger is immediately on guard. He had doubts about Tom in the peace movement days and now remembers all the strange things that happened the night before. He glances at Craig, who is crowded against the wall on the other side of Penny. He still looks like a fraternity boy in his blue wool shirt and levis, even with his fuzzy brown beard, and Roger remembers his weak excuse about having a headache and taking a bus home. He feels edgy, nervous, afraid of getting set up again, and he wishes he knew what he was doing, what it is all about.

"No more songs! Let's discuss the issues!" he shouts when the black-mustachioed leader of SDS in levi jeans and jacket starts to sing, "There's a tree that's standing by the wa-ah-terrrr."

"Not enough people know what's going on! Let's discuss the issues! Not just the steering committee! No more songs!"

"Atta-boy!" Tom says, raising his fist. "Discuss the issues! Discuss the issues!"

"Discuss the issues! Discuss the issues!" Penny and Craig shout, too, and people up and down the hall start shouting: "Discuss the issues! Discuss the issues!" until the SDS leader stops singing and asks in a hoarse voice: "Do you want to sing or discuss the issues?"

"Discuss the issues!" many people shout.

"All those in favor of discussing the issues raise their hands!" he asks, and so many hands go up that he says, "No need for a no vote. Break up into little groups with the people around you and start the discussions." He then turns off the mike as students start forming circles up and down the hall.

"The main points of the sit-in are the rehiring of Professor Enriquez, reinstatement of Betty Morales as a student in good standing, the hiring of ten Third World professors, the admittance of one thousand minority students regardless of whether or not they meet the academic standards, and the kicking of Rotsee off campus," says the pretty girl who had sat across the hall from him, and Roger says, "Wow! You sure did tell me the issues, didn't you!"

But he is even more suspicious of her since she crowded into their discussion circle. He remembers how she had come to his poetry reading on campus, had had coffee with him once and had flirted with him the night before. She has such luminous dark eyes he is afraid to look directly at her. He doesn't want Penny to get jealous and unhappy when she has been so loving to him.

"What should we do to get these demands?" Tom asks.

"Keep within the legal boundaries," the girl says, raising her voice when some guy in the circle behind her shouts, "No! No!" to some point made in his group and she almost shouts herself: "And force the Administration to recognize our legal right to sit-in."

"That sounds like the words of the chairman of the Young Socialists Club," Roger says, and points at the President's door, where the chairman is deep in dialogue with some other leaders, making some point in his calm manner, his blue levis bagging on his wide hips, pushing the dark brown hair that falls into his face out of his eyes, his full jowls and paunchy belly slightly visible from the side. He's the real administrator of the battle, Roger thinks, quiet and unassuming, very serious, and not the least least bit concerned with personal glory. He is a parliamentarian capable of any sharp trick to keep things going his way according to the rules, a pragmatic battler unconcerned with the symbolic protest tactics of the little guy from the SDS in the black banditto mustache, who is more to Roger's liking so far in the sit-in. "It would be much better to wake the administration and the whole country up to what is at stake here with a giant arrest like Cal's in '64."

"Let me finish," she says.

"We should threaten the administration with the biggest weapon this side of violence possible. Seize the building, maybe, and make them arrest us!" Roger says.

"Let her finish, man!" says the tall, husky blond student withthe paunchy belly who said the professors should have their own meeting the night before. "Wait your turn. This should be run by parliamentary rules so that everybody gets a chance to speak and—"

"Why don't you let the discussion go where it wants to go, man?" Roger cuts in, leaning over towards the guy. "Let the discussion have its own natural organization and form and maybe we'll get answers instead of playing rule games and just giving everybody a mechanical turn to speak."

"Nobody'll get a chance to speak but the loudest, then."

162

"Not true," Roger says. "That might be the case where the whole sit-in is concerned, man, but not in this small group. We don't have to observe mechanical rules for large bodies of people when we can pierce right to the point like this girl here, who gave me the answers without having to raise her hand and be recognized by the chairman, whom we'd elected first, etcetera, and maybe all of us forgetting what the question was by the time we got through the formal process enough to even discuss the question. We don't have to have rules between us. We don't have much time! We've got to wake up the whole country! We've got to save it! We've got to sacrifice ourselves for it! We've got to take advantage of this one chance before school lets out, win or lose, and make a bang so big everybody in the whole country knows what's going on!"

Penny's hand on his makes Roger stop and realize he's been shouting and that the girl's face is flushed and the guy's lips are shut tight and bloodless. He holds up his hand to apologize when the microphone begins to stutter, squawk and cough above the rumble of voices, then a voice says, "An important announcement! An important announcement! Would everybody please be quiet! Be quiet please!" Then as voices drop to a whisper here and there in the hall and everyone turns to face the microphone, Melchoir Chow, the slender, dark president of Third World, his eyes slightly hooded, his complexion slightly sallow, steps out of the standing crowd of leaders, and says, "We've just received word that President Wintergreen and the Deans are close to some decision on the issues and we think we've got them where we want them. But I can't tell you where we stand, what points are at stake, because it might hurt the ad hoc committee in their bargaining."

The whole hall rings with cheers, clapping, whistling, and everybody jumps to their feet and pushes toward the speaker. Roger and his group have to press up against the wall to keep from getting pushed away, but they cheer, too, until Tom suddenly starts shouting, "Boooooo! Booooooooooooo!"

Roger is shocked by his first cries, then feels disloyal when Tom prods him, and suddenly full of mistrust for the leaders, the same kind of guys who have played games with the cops on him before, he shouts, "Let the students decide! Let the students decide! Booooo! Booooooooooo!"

"Shut up!" the blond student says, "Don't do that!"

"Don't be so divisive to our cause!" the pretty girl says, and Roger stops, torn between his fear of a sell-out by the leadership and fear he is at fault. But other students in the hall shout, "Let him speak! Let him speak! He's right! Let him speak!"

"If you've got something to say, come up to the mike and say it," Melchoir Chow says.

"Just tell the students what's at stake and let them decide

what to do about it. That's all," Roger says, shaking his head to the offer, not wanting to get trapped into drawing more attention to himself, feeling like he is getting boxed into a corner. And in the lull, with everyone staring and waiting for him to go up to the mike, the skinny, gawky party member with the steel-rimmed glasses, who had led him back to the sit-in the night before, suddenly raises his fist, and jabbing it into the air, shouts, "Three cheers for the steering committee! Ray! Ray! Ra-"

"What in the hell's the matter with you, man?" Tom yells, and the guy's fist goes down and nobody joins him.

"I repeat," Melchoir Chow says. "If you have anything to say, come and say it into the mike. Come on!"

Roger leans back against the wall, having said all he wants to say. But students all around him say, "Go on up and speak! Go speak! Go on!" and glancing around him, he meets the glance of the pretty girl from his group, who says, "If it's for the good of the sit-in, go ahead and speak," and he pushes off the wall and makes his way through the students, who drop down to sitting positions again. But Chuck grabs the mike from Melchoir Chow just before he reaches for it.

"I've got it," Chuck says. "Wait your turn."

"What?" Roger says and looks at Melchoir Chow, who says, "Take it."

Roger snatches the mike out of Chuck's hand, and facing the students and TV cameras in the foyer, the lights glaring in his eyes, he says, "The whole sit-in has to be open and free so that the students can decide the issues. Otherwise the whole thing can degenerate into something in which a certain vested group can grab control and then sell-out, for whatever reasons, the rest of the students. At Columbia, the Black Students Union took over one of the buildings and wouldn't let white students leave the whole weekend, and backed this up with force. Then they surrendered the building without a fight as soon as the police appeared, leaving the white students to get arrested. If everything is kept out in the open and the students decide everything by democratic vote this sort of thing won't occur."

"Racist!" Chuck's girlfriend yells.

"We've got to keep all the decisions in the students' hands if we want the sit-in to stay honest and democratic," Roger says, trying to ignore her, his voice weakening, and a few students clap. But the girl, who is only a few feet away from him in the foyer, shouts, "What are you, a cop?"

"Shit!" Roger says, spinning around toward her, glancing at Slugger Moynihan, the sit-in lawyer, standing by the TV cameras, whom he has known for ten years, and his voice rising with anger, knowing he is blowing it but unable to calm down, says, "You blew that one, baby. I've been in and out of jail probably more times than anybody here. And many people know me. But that's

164

not the point. The point is that the students keep control of their own movement, their own sit-in—"

He stops, feeling that the words have fallen flat, that he has made a fool of himself again, and handing the mike to Chuck, his face pale, the shadows from the sickness heavy under his eyes, he picks his way to his place through the students as if he is stepping carefully over rain puddles, and sits down against the wall between Penny and Tom.

"Good, Roger," they both say, although it doesn't make him feel any better. He is exhausted, weak in his limbs, and sorry he has even come to the sit-in. He sniffles and searches in his pocket for some kleenex, then blows his nose twice, afraid he is going to get sick again.

"There's been a motion for a vote of confidence in the ad hoc committee meeting with the President. Who'll second it?"

"I will!" Chuck's girl cries, and Melchoir Chow says, "All in favor of a vote of confidence in the committee raise their hands and answer aye!"

"Aye!!!!!!!!!" everyone in the hall but Roger's group seems to cry.

"All against say no!"

There is absolute silence in the hall as everyone turns to look at Roger, who doesn't say a word.

"You're a wonderful bunch of students," Melchoir Chow says. "Now we'll call a break for the afternoon so the steering committee can meet with the ad hoc committee and find out where we stand. All other students report to their committees after the break."

The whole hall fills with noise again as the students get to their feet and start talking and moving away, but the pretty girl with the luminous eyes turns her pale face toward Roger, and, catching his eye, and shaping her words slowly with her mouth to be understood in the din, asks, "Don't you trust them?"

"A little bit," Roger says, making a small space between his thumb and forefinger.

He can feel many eyes upon him as everyone heads in different directions for the break, but when he turns to meet them, he only sees the back of a head or a profile, a cold cheek or a shoulder or back. He cannot meet one person face to face. He feels oppressed and confused, certain he has made another spectacle of himself. But unable to verify it with his eyes, he tries to slip through the dense crowd and into the foyer for cover, and runs right into the light-haired girlfriend of Chuck. She pretends she doesn't see him but he knows, just knows, she has been planted there by the steering committee to stop him.

"You've really got me wrong, baby," Roger says, stopping. "I'm no racist and I'm no cop. I've probably been busted more times than anybody here."

She whips her face around toward him, her long hair sweeping in the air for a split second, then falling lightly upon her tanned bare shoulders, exposed by a low-cut peasant blouse. Then, forcing a smile, she says, "Oh, I didn't really think that. I shouldn't have said it. I apologize. You're okay, but the guy in the suit and tie . . ."

She frowns and holds out her hand to take his, making Roger think "Sex Bait." But in earnest, the yellow flecks of his eyes alive with light, he speaks up in a high voice as if he had no mistrust of her at all, saying, "Tom's okay, too. He's an old leftist, works with black students in a high school or something."

He drops her hand, turning to introduce her to Tom but can only see Penny right behind him and Craig behind her, with no sign of Tom. He turns back to the girl, who is still standing right in front of him in the middle of the busy, noisy foyer, a stiff expression on her mouth. He searches for some manner of escape when she makes no motion to move and spotting Slugger Moynihan, Marxist to the core, surrounded by students only a few feet away, he says, "Got to say hello to Slugger."

He waits for Slugger to finish speaking to a student, hoping the girl is watching so she can see he is really a political oldtimer and not the racist cop she had called him, then says, "Hello, Slugger," and reaches out to shake hands with his old leftwing sometime acquaintance, fellow boxer, and political enemy.

Slugger leans forward politely to take his hand, his cut eyebrow puffed up, purple, and aflame with a bright orange swab of iodine that dyes his sandy hairline red.

"You used to win them all before," Roger says, trying to make a joke out of it, referring to the cut from the cop who clubbed him as well as the two or three times Slugger has been arrested for felonious assault and his long line of bouts as a Cal boxer.

But Slugger just looks at him with pale expressionless eyes, hard as his punch-thickened features, freckles standing out on his pink complexion like a mask. Roger remembers how he fought the Moynihan family politically when he tried to organize the big peace rally, how Slugger had appeared almost everywhere he went when he first got out of the nuthouse, which made him suspect they were trying to get him to join the Communist Party so they could control him and teach him to play the game, quit being so idealistic, more practical and corruptible. He remembers, too, how the different sons of the Moynihan family were elected president of the Cal Law School, a post they couldn't even have run for if the police hadn't given their okay in those days, meaning they felt the family—Communist or not—was safe and not a threat, like Roger, meaning the family cooperated with them.

He drops the cold hand and starts moving slowly through

the crowd toward the glass doors on the street side of the foyer, when the redheaded girl with the blue stocking cap suddenly steps in front of him, her pale eyes as bright as her freckles, and says, "Say! Who are you? Let me see your student body card!"

"I won't show you a damn thing!" Roger says, though he is a part-time student, taking a film writing class from a member of the Hollywood Ten, as several people turn to watch. "But I will tell you that I'm an ex-lecturer in English who got run off the campus in part by an administration girl student masked as a Mao Tse Tung radical. And I'm a part-time student now and a hot-headed motherfucker who'll fight any sonofabitch going given the right cause!"

She blinks, bit-bat of her light red eyelashes, and seems unable to answer. There is silence. Everyone is waiting for her reply. But remembering how she had been dumbfounded by the provocateurs in the basement, Roger feels sorry for her, and he puts his arm around her and says, "I just want this thing to stay pure. I'll tell you, I've been in a lot of demonstrations."

She lets Roger hug her for a moment, then pulls herself away and says, "Well, uh, okay. But kind of take it easy and see what's going on before you start attacking again, huh?"

"I agreed with you in the end," says the blond guy who had argued with him in his discussion group. "But I wish you had chosen another way to do it."

"I didn't think of how to do it, man, or of what I was doing, I just did it," Roger says. "Excuse me now. I'm getting out of here."

He faces the publicity committee above him at the turn of the stairs, Penny and Craig beside him, the whole turn of the stairs in shadow, and sees the rugged face of Chuck before him, the bristles stiff and brown on his chin, his light hair falling across his craggy-boned face, a large head on a stocky, long-waisted body. "We've already completed our work for the time being," Chuck says, and Roger notices how carefully unexpressive his eyes are. Normally a soft brown, they are nearly orange and opaque and slightly glazed, like the outer surface of a marble. Roger is aware of all the other faces of the students all fixed on him. He's aware, too, of Craig in his blue Pendleton shirt and levis at his side, and Penny on the other, her face as serious as his own must look, her eyes fixed on Chuck like his eyes are fixed on Roger, who knows he is being rejected. He guesses that it's because of what he has said and how he has snatched the mike from Chuck to say it, as well as the mysterious disappearance of the TV announcer the night before. Roger is caught again between the two forces of power, the police and the radical organizations, voicing a third view of freedom, of democracy, of political power with the people rather than with the rulers, suspected as a fink or a police agent while still being constantly persecuted by police agents, and still expecting to find some proof that the student leaders are working with or will work with the police, the very enemy, all against all, divide and conquer, and keep everything under cover, if they can.

"I'm not going back anymore," Penny says. "And why should you? You saw the way they rejected us and the way they attacked you just because you led some dissenters against their rule!" Penny says.

"They have a right to be suspicious, Penny," Roger says. "I'd be suspicious of them, too. We've just got to prove by our behavior that we're only interested in student control over things, that we want democracy."

"Well, I'm sick of it," she says. "I'm not going back anymore."

"I'm going to stick it out, Penny."

"Go on, then. You're a glutton for punishment."

"We just can't quit because the people in power object to our stand!" he shouts.

"I can!" she shouts.

"I'm not," he says.

"Go on back, then, sucker!" she says.

Cop

"Shut up, you!" the girl with the pompons says, her frizzy red head down between her shoulders like a cat about to strike. She makes a face, bares her teeth at him, then slides over as if she doesn't want to get contaminated.

"What?" Roger says. He can still hear the speaker saying, "You should respect the other students on the campus who are trying to study and stop this sit-in and try to work through the regular channels," and still wants to tell on the guy, tell everybody that he *isn't* a music major at all and *hadn't* given his real name. Roger knows he had registered as an English major in his class last spring under another name, but he's too afraid to bring everyone down on him again. He had felt better when many other students in the hall joined him in booing. "What's the matter with you? Why are you angry at me for booing at such reactionary talk?"

"You're a dirty cop!" she says, eyes stony as gravel pebbles, and Roger jerks away from the wall with his fist up and says, "If you call me that again, you little bitch, I'll bust you in your mouth! I don't care if you are a girl!"

She jerks back and blinks her eyes, clamps her thin mouth shut, her nostrils pinched white, and Roger lowers his fist, leans back against the wall of the hall and says, "How's that for irony, Craig? I'm the biggest outlaw in this fucking school and she's calling me a cop."

"Hmmmm, yes," Craig says and nods his head, purses his mouth. But the girl says, "Show me your student body card! Prove you're not a cop!"

"I'm telling you, baby!" Roger says and falls away from the wall again, fist up. "If you call me a cop once more, I'm going to blast you in your mouth."

She leans back again with a tight white face, her mouth set straight as a ruler, as a new wave of students coming back from dinner flows into the sidehall, fills out the lines on both sides to where Roger sits, doubling up, bunching up down by the mike where the side hall meets the foyer, blocking the whole hallway except for a narrow path between the legs and feet, leaving hardly any room for those still coming in to pass.

Roger sits quietly but simmers inside, bubbles of bitterness popping up from the murky currents to the surface of his mind, aching, his stomach tight, his lips curled with a bitter taste in his mouth, when he sees the redheaded girl scooting down the hallway, moving on all fours like an Indian sneaking up on a fort in a movie, and he sits up. He watches her stop a few feet from the mike, and still down on all fours, whisper in the ear of the girl in the red bandana. He starts scooting down the center of the packed hallway, skimming over legs, trying to get there in time to catch them together, and almost does until she sees him and pulls back from the girl with the bandana, her face pale with fear. He pushes past her and says to the girl in the bandana: "You told her I was a cop, didn't you?"

The girl ducks her head, blushes a deep ruddy color.

"You don't have any right to do that!" he says, trying to be heard over the speaker's voice without shouting.

"No, man," the girl says, looking up at him with big, brown eyes. "I only told her you acted funny, that's all."

"Listen. Here's my student body card. I'll prove I'm a student," Roger says and pulls his cardholder out of his back pocket, shows her his pink student body card. "Read it!"

But the girl won't look at the card, and he turns to show it to the redheaded girl. But she is already crawling back to her place in line, and he puts his card back into his back pocket with a sinking feeling in his gut that Penny is right and he is through with the sit-in, his only chance to do something politically worthwhile. Suddenly angry, sick and tired of always being put down by both sides, he crawls over some sudents' feet to Melchoir Chow who is acting as MC, and asks, "Say! Can I use the mike soon?"

Melchoir Chow gestures at the student already waiting, but, his face smooth and gentle, says, "Sure," and motions for Roger to wait.

He speaks so decently that Roger squeezes himself in against the wall, right in the middle of a group of committee leaders, and waits his turn, as several of the leaders turn to look at him. The chairman of the Young Socialists, a lock of brown hair falling in his face, studies him carefully, as if trying to figure him out. When the student stops speaking and Melchoir Chow turns around and reaches out to hand the mike to Roger, the chairman leaps up from his sitting position and grabes the mike out of Melchoir's hand, falling over a girl in front of him. And with the mike held up in one hand like a hot cup of coffee, he raises himself slowly up to his full height, and turning his back on Roger, says, "I'd better give this some parliamentary order. There's too many people waiting to speak."

Roger sits back down by the door in the big guy's place, knowing he is trying to keep him from speaking, and watches his wide back in a striped workshirt as he calls on students in the hall and foyer for suggestions about some point Roger hasn't caught. Several times, Roger gets the urge to stand up and ask for the mike but lacks the confidence, is too sure he won't be believed. Even if they aren't collaborating with the cops, they don't trust him. But when no other students raise their hands to offer suggestions, he stands up finally, but the guy turns his back on him and quickly hands the mike to the redheaded campus cop who had gotten Roger into trouble in the foyer.

"I would like to announce," he says without identifying himself, "that this being Friday and the administration offices being closed on Saturday, this building must be vacated by nine o'clock or the occupants will face arrest for trespassing on state property." Then he hands the mike back to the chairman as gasps and cries and worried voices fill the hall.

"Hold it! Hold it! Hold it down!" the chairman cries over the mike, but the noise keeps building and many of the students begin to stand up and mill around and talk excitedly with each other as if they haven't even heard him.

"Would somebody please make a motion to adjourn for fifteen minutes so the steering committee can meet and discuss the warning!"

"I make the motion!" some student calls out, raising his hand.

"I second it!" a girl next to him shouts.

"Meeting adjourned for fifteen minutes!" the chairman yells and turns off the mike as everyone stands up and starts scattering in different directions, leaving Roger by himself near the President's door.

"Hey, Karen!" he says, suddenly full of energy when he sees his former student say something to the girl in the red bandanna, who turns around to face him, her eyes large and frightened. "She thinks I'm a cop!"

"What? He's no cop!" Karen says, and the girl's face turns a deep red. But she still doesn't say anything and Roger says, "Hey, Slugger! She thinks I'm a cop!"

But Slugger glances over his shoulder at Roger, his swollen, purple eyebrow giving his pale green eyes a merciless look, and walks off down the sidehall without a word.

In the garish light from the TV cameras, the group of steering committee leaders, bunched up in a huddle, stand out above the seated students as if they are on stage, and there seems to be a lot of confusion and noise as if the fifteen minute break was not enough for the committee to come to some decision on the official order to leave. They make Roger uneasy, though he is already uneasy over Craig's failure to return after the break, as if he were part of a set-up to leave him neatly alone with Karen, who might be another decoy. But he can feel her body between his legs as he sits on a rolled-up sleeping bag, resting easily, intimately up against him, as if they are lovers, and he feels a deep need for her, for somebody to care for him, to ease his unhappiness with his girl, with the people he lives with, with the leaders of the sit-in, with the citizens of the country who allow their best men to be murdered and do nothing about it. He slides his hands under her arms and around both sides of her waist to her stomach and she presses back against him and raises her face to his and slips her tongue into his mouth when their lips touch and he catches a glimpse of heads going up swish, swish, swish, swish at the end of the hall. But suddenly Melchoir Chow steps out from the huddle, pushes up his sweater sleeves to expose his long, graceful wrists and hands, and looking very middle class with his white dress shirt open at the neck, white duck pants and saddle shoes, announces, "We've just received word that fifty Tac Squad members have just been seen a block from school on a street in the Park Apartments facing the main entrance to the Ad Building."

A spasm of fear tingles in Roger as cries go up from the girls, deep moans from a lot of guys, and Karen looks up at him with fearful eyes, then presses up closer to him and pulls his arms around her. Roger feels torn between bitterness toward the leadership for spreading the word he was a cop and the need to fight back against the police, who got him into trouble with the leadership in the first place.

"Quiet down, please! Quiet down! Quiet down!" Melchoir Chow pleads, and when the noise drops, he says, "We don't have to fear them. We've got a choice. We can evacuate peacefully and come back fighting Monday or go to jail now for our beliefs and strike a moral blow!"

Loud cheers and clapping fill the hall and Roger hugs Karen closer to him, ready to join them in whatever the students decide, then sits up with interest when the big, paunchy chairman takes the mike, and stepping out from the group of leaders, says, "I'm against committing a merely symbolic action, tying up all our money and all our time the whole summer and the whole fall fighting court battles. We should beat a tactical retreat instead, come back to get them Monday, then go on to build a movement at this school that will last from semester to semester, gaining and accumulating movement rather than going down from legal action each semester."

Loud cheers greet his words and Roger cheers, too, believing in the chairman's logic if not liking his treatment of him. And with his arms around Karen, Roger feels as if he shares something with the other people at the sit-in. They now have, temporarily, the same enemy, an enemy who makes Roger's own diffference with the leadership much less important, but he still doesn't want to go to jail either, especially with people who call him a cop.

Yet when the SDS leader with the black banditto mustache takes the mike and says, "No one can object to the chairman's good sense, but speaking for myself not SDS, I'd like a compromise, in which a majority of the sudents leave the premises but a token force of us volunteer for arrest so we can take a practical and a moral stand, too, and since I've already been busted fifteen time, I volunteer first!" And when in the middle of the burst of cheers, the pretty girl who has been flirting with Roger shouts over the mike: "I second the motion and volunteer, too!" and a dozen other people stand up and shout and raise their hands to volunteer, he has an urge to go join them, to sacrifice himself, do something to stop the murder machine, and maybe, too, become an accepted part of the sit-in. But when the redheaded security officer takes the mike and says, "You have exactly five minutes to vacate the building or face arrest for trespassing on state property," and in almost total silence picks his way through the sitting students it is so quiet that Roger, halfway down the side hall, can actually hear the man's footsteps on the floor.

He knows he will only submit to arrest if all the students do. He stands with everyone else when the chairman says, "Let's sing 'A Tree That's Standing By The Water' for George from SDS, one of the finest young revolutionaries I know," and marches out with all but the volunteers, feeling inspired and a small but genuine part of the sit-in, even though he is the most hated person outside the cops and the administration there. And he vows to defend democracy when he marches outside into the crowd of two hundred or so students jammed up outside the main street entrance, spilling out into the wide street and onto the concrete dividing strip down the center of it, where breath steams up like fog under the tall light poles, and the chairman cries, "Clear the area! Clear the area! Get off school property! Clear the area!"

Roger sees the cops come marching down a narrow side street from the Park Apartments toward them, their white riot helmets and plastic visor guards glimmering like window reflections in the distance. Fifty white bubbled heads moving like spacemen above black jerk-jerking shapes and the smack, smack, smack of boots. As they pass under the small trees on both sides of the street, their plastic heads moving on a black-clothed current appear bodiless, and their marching feet, pulsing down below them, like the deep undertow of a river at night, throbbing, flowing, perpetually moving, but barely seen. And when the first row of riot cops move out from under the trees a half a block away and come into the glare of the streetlight ten at a time, with the smack, smack, smack of boot leather, their polished clubs held out like rifles in front of them flash like gun metal.

Roger gasps with the crowd and tightens his grip on Karen's hand, and has to remind himself of the vow he has just made.

And he is deathly silent as all the others when the cops stop in the middle of the wide street, a command cracks across the silence, seems to reverberate over their heads like a rifle shot, and the last column of cops falls away and spreads out down the block to provide an obvious flanking movement. Then another command cuts the air and the main body of men starts straight across the dividing strip toward them, and Roger jerks on Karen's hand and hurries down the strip out of their way, watches them pass and stop in front of the ad building, and with another command, another column of men falls away and spreads itself down both sides of the campus sidewalk. Then on another command the main body of thirty men in riot helmets and padded bullet-proof vests marches up the main entrance to the foyer, marching six abreast for five rows toward the lighted hallway where the volunteer force of a dozen students wait arrest, forcing the last students back and out of the front entrance, when a sudden cry from the megaphone: "Let them pass! Clear the property! Let them pass!" seems to break the spell, and someone shouts, "You fucking pigs!" then all the students join in, jeering, "Pigs! Pigs! Pigs! Pigs!"

Roger jerks on Karen's hand and pulls her down the center strip until they are beyond the last cop, who stands under a small tree, club ready. He sees that the redheaded girl is near him as well as the dark girl in the red bandanna and another girl with short black hair and dark skin who looks like the girl spy who wrote Mao Tse Tung propaganda in his creative writing class. They all are staring at him and Karen, making him suspicious of the whole thing, then glad the girls can see him with her, since she is a committee leader, too, and will make them doubt he is a cop. And when the group around him starts jeering, he glances back at the cop beneath the tree and shouts, "Pigs! Pigs! Pigs!" for the first time in his life.

He shouts, "Pigs! Pigs! Pigs!" with all the others as the main body of riot cops marches up the walkway to the steps of the main entrance, the students filling in the street behind them like floodwater, bunching up under the glow of streetlights, climbing on bumpers, trunks, hoods, and fenders of cars, then falling back when a white paddy wagon comes up the wrong side of the street, pulls into the brightly lit parking lot, and backs up near the steps of the main entrance.

But the jeers stop when the first prisoner appears, silhouetted in the doorway, flanked by two cops. The doors open and the cops march him down the floodlit steps, and the students break into song, "Weee shall not, we shall not be moved! / Weee shall not, we shall not be moved!" when everyone recognizes the little SDS leader. And they keep singing as two more cops appear with the pretty girl and march her, too, down into the paddy wagon. And they continue singing until the last four prisoners are driven away in the last wagon and they finally break into a loud and prolonged cheer. And Roger's heart seems to swell in his chest, and with a tense but sweet knot of pain in him at the beauty of their sacrifice, he swears he is going to live a free man's life in American someday, a life based upon the philosophy of the Bill of Rights and John Locke's tenet that everybody has a right to pursue happiness as long as he doesn't interfere with the happiness of others. He swears it to himself, and squeezes Karen's hand as she turns quickly to look in his face and smile.

With the rasping cry of the bullhorn to "Disperse! Disperse! Disperse!" growing fainter in the darkness, caring for everybody in the sit-in, the school, the country, the whole world, wanting to love them and be loved by them, aching with this unfulfilled love, and wanting to fill this ache, this unhappiness with love, he turns to Karen, the bond of opposing the cops, of working on the sit-in, and the beauty of the sacrifice of the volunteers still strong between them, and stops her on the sidewalk, and throws his arms around her slender body. And bending his head back, he pulls her to him so that she bends in all the right places, waist, neck, back, knees, to fit right to him, then kisses her hard, twirls his tongue around hers, presses tight against her and feels a rising tension in his groin, pleased, so pleased to be holding her, to be deep in the act of love, and she moans and shoves to meet him, her hump just fitting over his like a slot, and starts running her fingers through the long waves at the back of his head, pressing her face into his, their mouths cupping to cushion the force, her tongue curling into his mouth, until he pulls free and says, "Wait. Let's get in the car!"

But his key won't start his car. He jams it forward again, but it still won't go in. Then while she sits next to him, running her fingers through his hair, he turns on the dash lights to see in the dim glow that somebody has jammed and twisted the ignition out of shape with either a screwdriver or a chisel.

"What the fuck!" he says, and Karen stops playing with his hair and leans over to see what's wrong, her face a soft pink, sensuous with shadow in the dim light, and he is sure she hasn't had anything to do with it. But he immediately thinks "cops" and that he isn't going anywhere—not even to make love—until he gets a tow truck and that means going back to the campus to find a phone, or to a service station glowing a block or two back in the darkness. At the campus he will be attacked, called a cop, and dragged deeper into the muck the cops have already stirred up around him, ruining any chance for making love to Karen, ruining all the good feeling he still feels for the sit-in.

"What's the matter?" Karen asks, and tangles her fingers in the waves at his neck. "Going to have to call a tow truck?"

He looks at her, thinks of the stories about love she had

written in his class, mostly about a girl who seeks love and motherhood but gets abandoned by her lover, and remembers how she would wait for him in the hall after class but was so shy and sensitive she'd turn away without speaking to him, and he still feels affection for her in spite of the jammed ignition.

"Yes," he says, finally answering her.

"Forget it right now," she says, and he slides his arms around her, pulls her to him, and kisses her long and deep, lets himself forget everything but that she is in his arms, a girl who cares for him, who wants him, who proves to him that they can't control everything, especially a girl's emotions.

He lies with his limp prick still in her, their bodies interlocked, her legs still around him, a deep feeling in his groin where their pelvic bones brace against each other, where most of their lower weight meets, his weight resting on hers, where they are joined together, his plug deep in her socket as it should be. Their chests touch on one side, her left breast flattened by his rib cage, rising and falling with her deep breathing as if she is asleep, their faces pressed together, a strand of hair in his eyes, perspiration on his forehead, damp in the hollow of his back. Darkness. The need for love now satisfied. Then a moment of sadness. Nothing has changed. There is still no way out. She stirs beneath him, pulls her cheek away from his, her curly hair out of his eyes, and asks, "What's wrong?"

"What?" Roger asks, raising his head and pulling back to see better in the darkness. Her face is a soft shadow next to his with a small hint of light in her eyes.

"You seemed to go stiff," she says, and starts caressing the waves behind his ear.

"Nothing, really," he says, and she smiles, showing the slight imperfection, the small slanting inward of her two front teeth, as if she came from Southern people who don't put braces on their children's teeth. But he is touched by the way she cares, and wanting to do something for her in return, he says, "When we were together at my apartment and you came out of the shower and dried yourself in the front room by the windows, your red hair was slightly wet and your green eyes were sparkling as if you were really happy and the colors in contrast with your milky skin made you look beautiful. I almost told you so right then. I wish I had."

She stares at him a long time as if to see if he really means it, then says, "I wondered if you ever thought of me again, if you ever wondered about me. But you're the one who's beautiful. You're *really* beautiful." She cups his face in her hands and says, "You're so sexy. Your face is so striking and unusual, so strong and yet so fine. You must take beautiful pictures. Please keep coming to the sit-in even if that girl called you a cop. I have to come to return a wallet I found. There might be a big demonstration Monday and I love to get my picture taken."

She then kisses him and as he squeezes her nude body up against his and lets her searching tongue curl around his, he wants to pull away and get dressed, bothered by her last comment, suspicious of her now, and worried that he might get caught by a patrol car or a campus guard with his pants down.

"You smell like pussy," Penny says after he lays down next to her. The drapes are open and allow enough street light in for him to see her and to know that she can see him and his frizzy hair. "Who did you fuck?"

"Don't ask me that," he says.

"Why not?"

"Don't force me to lie to you," he says.

"Where have you been the last two hours?" she asks, and he stares at her in the darkness, her face a blur except for a faint plane of light on her cheek.

"We don't have much love together anymore so what do you care?" he says, but sees her cheek quiver and quickly says, "Somebody jammed my ignition and I had to wait for a tow truck. He towed me up here now. I'll have to coast down the hill tomorrow and get it fixed. How did you know I wasn't at the sit-in?"

"It was on the eleven o'clock news," she says. "With the news that Wintergreen gave in on most of the demands when he heard that students had been arrested last night."

"Is that right?" he asks, propping himself up on one elbow to see her face.

"That's why I was worried," she says. "I was afraid you might have been arrested, too."

Roger looks at her lying next to him in the darkness, her face in semi-profile, up-turned nose, perfect little lips, realizes how important she is to him, how much more important than the sit-in, where he is suspected of being a cop, and where he doesn't even trust Karen. He lays his hand on her shoulder to turn her a little toward him so he can see her eyes and says, "Penny?"

"What?" she answers, her voice thin and trembling.

"I won't go back to the sit-in, even if they keep it going. They're winning anyway and they think I'm a cop besides. And I don't trust them. So there's no use my even being there. You were right, I shouldn't have gone back, they attacked me as a cop, even called me one. I won't go back."

She doesn't answer but her eyes seem to glow in a sad, somber way, and she reaches out and touches his cheek and says, "I'm glad, Roger. Just write, Roger. You'll do all the good you want that way, eventually."

Mill-In

"Wintergreen's been fired!" Craig shouts, standing by the dining room table, looking as brown as his old leather jacket with his brown beard and brown hair.

"What?" Roger says.

"Yes! And he's just flown to India for the Ford Foundation. Some kind of educator's job. A Deans' Committee has taken over until a new president can be appointed. No chance of getting one before the term's over though, with finals starting tomorrow."

"So there won't be anybody the students can deal with personally," Roger says, shaking his head, but then purses his mouth with a small sense of satisfaction that even the mighty can be hurt by the Man, not just himself.

"How about the issues he's supposed to have granted?"

"All void," Craig says. "There's going to be a mill-in at one in the administration building. The rally's already started. Do you want to go?"

"Not me, man," Roger says, shaking his head again, feeling a bitter twinge of self-pity. "I'm not wanted and I don't go where I'm not wanted."

Penny reaches across the table and touches his arm, her face heart-shaped and tender, and feeling very virtuous, he says, "Besides, I told Penny I wouldn't go back."

"But you *are* wanted," Craig says. "You know that red-headed girl who called you a cop? Well, she gave me these letters when I got to the Commons where all the students were waiting for the rally to start."

He hands Roger three hand-written notes in an envelope and Roger snaps them open and reads each one quickly, each one asking him to come back and join the movement now that everything they have fought for has been lost. But he is still hurt over being called a cop, for being treated so coldly when he had been fighting for the cause, and hands each one to Penny as he finishes, then asks, "Who were the other two girls?"

"The girl with the red bandanna and the pretty little girl who sat in our discussion group. And while I was there today, Melchoir Chow got up on the mike and told the crowd that one kid who had been called a cop had broken down and cried and that the accusations had to stop or they would break our solidarity and the administration would win."

"Is that really true?" Roger asks, his voice rising with hope.

"Yes it is. The atmosphere's changed. The Steering Committee must have held a meeting and talked about you, too. Come on. They need all the help they can get."

Roger studies him and Craig meets his gaze, quite capable of looking into his eyes, and Roger is unable to understand where he stands, whether he is a police agent or whether he believes in the cause. He sees Penny hesitate, then look at Craig, then look back at him and nod, her cheeks bright and pink as if she has caught the undercurrent of excitement, and Roger shoves his chair back and hurries across the front room to get his sweater off the coat hook. But when he reaches for it, a pulse of fear twitches in the pit of his stomach, a funny feeling, like some premonition that he shouldn't do it, that he should stay home or be sorry, and he stops with his arms still out, still capable of not going, when Craig opens the front door and says, "Come on, Roger, or we'll miss the rally."

But he's inspired by the big roar of applause that goes up from the crowd seated on the commons lawn in front of the cafeteria, followed by the spontaneous chant: "Off Rotsee! Off Rotsee! Off Rotsee!" accompanied by a thousand fists jabbed into the sunlit air, at the big paunchy chairman on the small portable stage, with his big fist in the air and his dark hair in his eyes, and Roger jabs his fist up, too, and feels the thrill of belonging tingle over his flesh. Then he sees Karen in her pale pink levis, picking her way through the seated students on the outskirts of the crowd with her long stilt-like legs, in something akin to slow motion, floating over the heads of the students like some slender pink flamingo, her red hair combed out long now and bobbing behind her, catching the sunlight like a rippling wave, a flaming bird plume. Not once looking in his direction, she holds the wallet she had shown him in her hand, as if it's a signal he could have made money if he had played along with her, and he remembers her mysterious words about getting her picture taken—but even she doesn't weaken his spirit.

"Remember when we get up into the ad building you can make noise, create a disturbance, and engage whoever you want to in dialogue but do not destroy anything! No trashing! We've got to keep this mill-in on a strictly non-violent basis so no charges can be brought against us for destruction of property, so the Deans' Committee can have no reason to put the Tac Squad on us or deny any of our points. Now let's go!" the chairman cries, and singing "This land is your land. This land is my land, from California to the New York Island," he steps down from the stage and starts across the commons and the whole crowd rises and joins in singing and starts moving slowly and then with more and more speed toward the yellow administration building, and Roger steps up the pace so fast that Craig has to take longer steps and Penny has to run a little and skip a step or two and then grab Roger's hand to keep up. But just inside the glass doors, when the singing students ahead of him split in opposite directions, some going right toward the President's door and some left into the annex, Roger, his hands sweating, his mouth dry, doesn't know which way to go, and hesitates, and breaks his step, his head swinging from one side to the other as a strange sense of anxiety seizes him, a fear of something momentous about to happen, some dangerous risk and loss of control over his own life.

He stands there, blocking traffic, as students pour around him, and stares out the glass doors of the front entrance some fifteen feet away to the street beyond, with the concrete divider running down the middle, the tall silver lightpoles, and the white stucco Park Apartments in the background, as if it is the last glimpse of freedom he will ever see. Then Penny tugs on his hand and he sees her, a step in front of him, with a quizzical, slightly worried look to her face, and with a shove in the back from someone behind him, he wakes from his trance, then turns with her toward the President's door, where a couple of students with long hair are pounding with the flats of their hands on the glass window.

Their action sparks him, and he moves straight through the crowd and starts pounding on the wall with them, feeling immediately better with the first slap of his palms. But there is so much noise in the hall with students pounding on the walls and others crowding by singing, moving up the stairs to the top floor or down to the basement, that he can't hear his own sound, and he grabs a metal stand built like a stool with a boxlike container for the school newspaper in place of a seat and starts pounding out a conga beat on its flat top, getting a deep resonant sound which fills the foyer and gives some soothing rhythm to the jarring noise around him.

Penny pulls over a tall trash can with a swinging peaked top and starts doing a rat-a-tat-tat conga rap on it as a guy with a guitar joins them, then another guy with a guitar, and many students line up against the walls and start pounding in time to the rhythmic "Bob! ba-ba-bop-bop! Bop! ba-ba-bop-bop! Bop! ba-ba-bop-bop!" And other students still filing in the campus side-doors pick up the beat and carry it down the halls with them, pounding on the walls and clapping their hands in time, and the foyer fills up with students pounding out the beat to the melodic accompaniment of the guitars and TV cameramen and news photographers and students with cameras take pictures and soon everyone around them is smiling and singing and pounding. And as the percussive song rolls on, shaking the halls with its sound, the little

SDS leader smiles brightly under his banditto mustache and the big paunchy chairman smiles at him, too, and Roger is so inspired that he gives a swinging rock to the beat and pounds until there is a great sound that causes more and more people to crowd around, to pound on the walls and clap their hands as movie cameras whirr, flashbulbs pop, TV cameras train on the crowd around Roger, all grinning and happy, all pounding harder and harder and harder until they reach such a peak that they can get no louder, and Roger, whose big bass beat is carrying everybody, suddenly finishes off with a "Bam! Bam! Bam!" and everyone lets out a great loud cheer and hugs everyone near them.

"Let's move!" Roger yells when the cheering stops, then grabs a waste basket and leads about fifty students down the hall, pounding out a beat as he moves to the accompaniment of strumming guitars, of whistling flutes, feeling truly inspired and truly a part of the sit-in now, no longer an outcast, an under-cover cop, but part of a movement that is trying to do something about democracy, about freedom, and the good of his fellow man. And pounding on filing cabinets as they move, on walls, windows, and wastebaskets, their metal bottoms giving off sharp, resonant sounds like good trap drums, Roger and Penny and a group of musicians and students varying from ten to fifty at times, move down the main floor hall, past other groups and isolated students, go in and out of offices, never let the noise up, stop in the hall at times to play with a group of students when the moment seizes them and the sounds get good, sweep into the accounting office with its score of young women, and one black woman smiles and points out the good places like filing cabinets and desk tops to get good sound, then taps on a metal box with an eraser herself when they get a good strong beat going, the students chanting nonsense sounds, then up the back staircase to the top floor, meet some former students of Roger, who laugh and grin and nod their heads when they see him, as if they knew he would be in on it, then join him as the group moves slowly in and out of every office on the floor, picking up noisemakers who want to help make music and add their sporadic rumbles of noise to the greater, more melodic one, everyone grinning and making the sour faces of some employees turn to grins when the rocking beat and the pleasant strummings of the guitars giving a sweet melody to the "Thump-thump, thump-thump," finally gets to them, the group varying the tempo at times when one person or another, guitarist, drummer, or flutist, starts up a rhythm he wants, sometimes quick and exciting, sometimes slower and more basic, deeper in tone, then finally down the front staircase to the foyer after a busy, noisy, exciting hour or more in the main administration building.

In the annex hall, squatting down, his back against the wall, his butt balanced on his heels, pounding out a popping beat on the bottom of a wastepaper basket, Penny clicking two coke cans together with a counterpointing latin swing near his ear and keeping herself between him and the pretty girl with the luminous eyes who had been arrested and who has been following him around for over an hour, Roger picks up signals like a radio antenna, as if he is electric. He can smell the scent of sweat and hair and body heat in the air around him as he drums and watches the students fill the dark hall, pound on desk drawers and wastebaskets, coke cans, walls, the glass windows and metal partitions of the office on the inner side of the annex hall, as if he is watching a movie, as if he is seeing some exciting performance, figures shadowy and their drumming hands a blur of fluttering wings against the square of light from a large picture window at the far end of the annex hall. The premonition of fear he had felt has long since been lost in the joy of action, in the success of the noisemaking, in the flow of happy vibrations that has caught him and all the other students up, that has swept them along for a good part of the afternoon, and perspiring, his hands so loose from the wrist that there is no more fatigue in his arms, long past the point when they got tight, but having to change from the flats of his hands to the fingertips to ease the pain, a full afternoon of beating on hard surfaces making them swell on the bottoms, a blue line across the heel of the palms where they have been hitting the rim of the wastebasket bottom, the warmth that fills him from the exercise and the emotion keeping away any symptoms of the cold, Roger raises his hand on the upbeat to Bob Dilman, head of the creative writing department, who comes walking by, his eyes not so cold now, more curious to see Roger there, a former student and teacher, the first to rebel in the department, and now without any respectability at all, creating a disturbance again. He lifts his hand and gives Roger a snappy salute as he marches by, his body plump but still straight-backed and strong, a gesture of respect, Roger feels, out of another age, his time, when men like him went off to fight the Second World War and Hitler, a hand to his rising forehead that told Roger he had fought fascism in his way, too, and it seems a good omen, that what Roger is doing and has risked will pay off for everyone, and possibly, even himself.

But out of the large milling crowd making noise down at the far end of the hall, their figures cast in shadows and silhouettes from the light of the big window, comes Dr. Morganthal, the late-blooming poet and director of the poetry center, who now lifts his nose up as he walks by Roger and Penny, who still clicks her coke cans together, smiles and lets out a high trill with her tongue when Roger smiles and yells, "Yi-yi-yi-yi!" and pounds harder on his wastebasket. Then slowly and rhythmically, Roger and Penny and the pretty girl and twenty or so more students move down the far hall of the annex, with its yellow plaster walls, wind in and out of offices, keeping up a rinky-tink beat, backing out of the student job placement office when a group of girls tells them they have engaged the staff in debate, move from there at a leisurely pace into the Student Psychiatric Center, where Roger was taped without his permission by a psychologist who asked where his grass was hidden five years before, and there in the pleasantly colored office, with its soft pastel shades, its soothing paintings, he picks up a wastepaper basket, and sitting down in a chair, starts tapping out a beat with the tips of his fingers, and is joined by the rest of the group, mostly girls, Penny dropping into a chair next to his, the rest filling up the whole waiting room, making a rough circle of students, and gets a good sound going to the head shakes of the receptionist in high heels and pancake makeup and the hard glare of a man who looks like an accountant in a white shirt and tie, who stares at Roger with arched eyebrows, and in a shrill-pitched voice shouts, "Do you realize that the students are having their last interviews with their counselors before summer vacation?" and Roger stops drumming and stares at the man's soft round face, full cheeks and paunchy belly, and as everyone else stops, too, and watches, he asks, "Is that right?"

"Yes, that's right!" the man says, straightening himself up to full height, and nodding curtly as if to dismiss Roger, his powdery cheeks quivering.

"Then good," Roger says. "Because if there's one place in this school that I can really do without, it's this fucked-up counselling office that turns students into middle-class robots in white shirts and ties like you, brother!" then starts pounding out a deep bass beat on the tin bottom of the waste basket that makes his hands sting, to a big cheer from the students who start knocking the place apart with percussive noise as the guy puffs up fuller and fuller, turning a deeper and deeper red. Then around a corner they go, to the windows of the admissions office which stretches the entire length of the annex, and up to the long counter for filling out forms against the glass wall, where he starts pounding out a deep, basic, rocking beat, a "Ta-tat! Ta-tat! Ta-tat!" that carries everyone up on its swell like a gigantic wave, causing them to line the counter next to him and line the wall of windows next to the counter and line the frosted glass windows that stretch the unbroken length of the offices on the inside of the hall, and join him, pounding with the flats of their hands, tapping with coins on the glass, carrying a long, long beat with many chanting sounds, someone yelling every once in a while, with not a space against the windows of either wall free, the percussive beat exploding like an unbroken series of concussions, rattling the windows, yells splitting the spaces in the beat, a hall full of people grinning, happy, having fun and making noise, pounding on the glass doors and windows, the thin metal wall partitions of the portable offices that occupy the annex floor, Roger stripped down to his T-shirt now, his turtleneck wrapped like a sweater around his waist, his cardigan sweater in the car, sweating, rocking his shoulders, dark curls bobbing, Penny next to him, pounding out her good bongo tap-tapping sounds, grinning, too, the grin vanishing every time the pretty girl gets near him or smiles at him, but Roger, smiling, happy that he is liked, pounds and pounds and pounds, cups his palms sometimes when the sting gets too bad, spreads them flat when he gets a good rock going with an earth-quaking "Boom! Boom! Boom!" letting his head hang back and wobble loosely to the beat, curls bobbing, face up, eyes nearly closed, daylight from the windows filtering through his lids and eyelashes to a watery bright blue, suddenly touching a deep, rolling beat that swells toward a climax and everyone picks it up, realizes that they are getting there, tension growing, smiles tightening, bodies crouching, movements stiffening, elbows bending and sticking out as louder and louder and louder the sound grows and up and up and up the tempo swells until everyone is right at the edge of their feelings, then Roger ends it with a "Boom! Boom! Boom! Boom!" and stops, and after a split second of complete silence, everyone screams and yells and whistles and claps and hugs each other.

War

"Hey! Stop!" yells the country-looking rube with the metal-rimmed glasses who led Roger and Penny back to the sit-in on the first night as fifty or so students pound on the door to the graduate dean's office and on cans and wastebaskets and shout and chant and tap with coins on his window. "Nobody's in there! Don't waste your time!"

A lot of students stop but in the diminished noise, the thin kid with the long hair who shouted at Roger answers, "That's not true! They're in there. I saw a dean go in," and the noise level rises again.

"They're not in there, I'm telling you!" the country rube says again.

"The hell they aren't!" the pretty girl with Roger yells and within seconds everyone stops pounding, and, sensing something important, crowd around the arguing students, bunch up tight, shoulder to shoulder, chest to back, blocking all passage in the annex hall.

"No, they're not in there!" says the heavy blond student who insisted the professors hold their own meeting the first night. But the pretty girl yells, "They are too! This guy saw a dean go in!" And everybody starts talking and yelling and arguing all at once, shouting and screaming so that no one can be heard, packing in so close that there is no room to step or even lift an arm without having to wiggle it free first, faces turning red, mouths opening and closing and not a single voice clearly heard.

"Get order! Get order! Melchoir!" Roger shouts at the small Filipino student who has a bullhorn in his hand. "Tell us what to do!"

"We'll decide, not him!" yells the pretty girl, and Roger keeps quiet because that's what he's been fighting for since he arrived. But Melchoir stares at him with his soft dark eyes as if really surprised at his willingness to accept his formal authority, then puts the bullhorn to his mouth and calls out, "Would everybody please sit down! Please sit down! As Roger says, if the deans are really in there, we need order to come to some decisions on what to do! Please sit down! Please sit down and keep quiet!"

But more and more students pour into the hall from other

parts of the building, packing it from both ends, all of them shouting and arguing over what to do, and pay no attention to Melchoir's words. Roger notices Dr. Morganthal trying to push his way through the crowd to stand between the students and the dean's door, where Roger stands. And seeing that he is stuck in the crowd and unable to move only a person away, Roger reaches up and taps him on the shoulder, and when his dead brother's eyes turn on him, he shouts, "Why didn't you say hello to me, Jeff?"

"Oh!" Dr. Morganthal says, but doesn't answer.

"Why don't you tell me what's really bothering you?" Roger shouts, but too loudly, for there is a sudden lull near them and his words sound like a challenge.

"I don't like the idea of non-students coming out to our school to start trouble," Dr. Morganthal says, then turns his face away. Shocked, not sure if he means him, Roger has no time to think of an answer before the big chairman's voice blasts over the bullhorn: "Please, sit down! Please, sit down! Sit down, please!" and a ripple of bodies sinking down to the floor spreads all the way to the ends of the hall in both directions, maybe a thousand students squatted down next to each other, up tight, shoulder to shoulder, knee to back, arm to arm. Besides the chairman, only Dr. Morganthal is standing, and he steps over the seated students to the dean's door where, his wrinkled white shirtsleeves rolled up to his elbows, he crosses his arms and stands in front of the door with a sagging face.

"I suggest we find out if the deans are really in there before we start making suggestions about what to do," says the heavy blond student, his head sticking up above the heads of the students around him.

"They're not in there!" shouts a student with a heavy black beard.

"They are too!" shouts the pretty girl sitting next to Roger. "One guy saw a dean go in."

"Hold it! Don't shout! Wait until you're called!" the chairman says, holding up a hand to calm them down. "Who saw the dean go in?"

"I did!" the student with the long hair says. "He went in through the secretary's office when nobody was in there. But I saw him from the hall."

"Do you know who he was?" the chairman asks.

"No, but he was a dean and I could see the other deans sitting around a table just before the door closed."

"That's settled, then. Let's get on with the suggestions," says the pretty girl.

"Let's just start pounding on the walls of the room, inside and outside, until we wear them out, make them quit and leave the building," Roger says, and the pretty girl jams her hand in the air and says, "I second that!"

"Alright. Everyone in favor say aye!" the chairman says and a huge "Aye!!!!!!!" fills the hall.

"Okay, split up. Some go outside. The rest stays here in the hall and let's have some noise!!!!" the chairman shouts, and everyone leaps to their feet with a big cheer, and spreads out down both sides of the hall, while others pour out both ends of it to go outside and pound on the windows of the room. Roger pulls a drawer out of a counter, and squatting down against the wall, starts pounding out a bass beat with the flats of his hands, keeping his tender heels and swollen fingers up, smacking only the very center of his palms against the wooden bottom as Penny sits next to him and does the same.

A huge tapping roar fills the hall as students line two and three deep against the wall of the graduate offices, reaching over each other's shoulders, and single file down the hall to both ends, those pounding on the windows using coins and those pounding on the walls the flats of their hands. TV men and news photographers about fifty strong move up and down the hall, in and out of the crowd, taking pictures, bright flashes going off everywhere, people shouting and cheering, mouths open, heads back, the noise going on and on and on and on and on until the hall seems to explode with blasts of air that rattle the glass and shake the walls like an earthquake that won't stop, until Roger's ears ache and throb. When he's sure he cannot stand it anymore himself, let alone the deans trapped inside the room, it explodes yet into an even louder roar and the dean's door finally opens. The students bunch in close to block their path and a few drop down to a sitting position to block the hall with their bodies and keep the deans trapped.

But only Professor James, who ran the summer school English department Roger's first semester of teaching, steps out, squeezes next to Dr. Morganthal and closes the door behind him. But he finds himself unable to move, and stands in front of the door in his rimless glasses and apple pie look, clean-shaven face, dimpling around the belly of his starched white shirt. He finally takes a step over the shoulder of a guy near him, and everyone in the hall stops pounding and drops down to completely block his path and force him to tiptoe over the crush of bodies. As the pounding goes on outside, they watch in silence while he lifts his legs high, one at a time, as if trying to keep his balance on slippery rocks in a rushing stream, trying to get his toes into the holes in the web of legs and arms and feet and heads around him. He balances awkwardly on one leg at a time, his arms spread to keep from falling, but missteps, tilts way over, wobbles on one leg, and starts to fall over, his arms waving frantically, his mouth opening as he realizes he is going over, and Roger jerks up on his haunches and sticks his hand up and out for Dean James to grab just in time to stop his fall. Roger keeps his arm stiff as a pole until the professor can balance himself, put his other foot down, and holding onto Roger's hand like a cane, take another step, then another, until he reaches a spot where he can get his footing. He pushes up to a full standing position again, where he stops and sighs and says, "Thank you, Roger," with a small twitch of his soft mouth, then pushes off through the crowd as the pretty girl next to Roger turns an angry red.

For a moment, all the students are quiet and still as if all the air has been let out of them by the anti-climactic nature of one dean leaving so quietly, until one student suddenly shouts, "Let's get all the fucking deans out of there now! Let's drive them out of the building!" And all the squatting students jump to their feet, and, shouting and screaming, start pounding and kicking on the door and the walls, beating, beating, beating as if they will pound them down in their anger, catching up everyone in an orgy of noise and action. And the furious pounding goes on non-stop for minute after minute after minute until Roger's ears ring and his throat is hoarse from yelling and his arms ache and his hands sting and he can see the wide screaming mouths and bodies of the students around him jerking and moving, arms flailing as if everyone is a victim of St. Vitus Dance, seeing the turmoil, hearing the roar around him as if he is in the center of a riot, exhausted and spent but unhurt and still able to pound, still able to pound when a strange, hollow noise seems to rumble like an echo over the explosive pounding and screaming and he tilts his head back and lightens up on his beat to listen, then stops drumming altogether when Penny stops, and, her eyes gray and distant in the shadowy hall, looks off toward the window at the end of the hall some twenty feet away as if she has heard it, too. But the sound disappears in the clamor of yells and cheers and slogans and unbroken pounding, and Roger starts to pound on the wall again but hears the sound once more and stops. A couple of students stand still near him as if they have heard it too, and though it disappears, they all stand listening until it comes back again, and other heads start turning in the direction of the big window at the turn in the hall. There is a perceptible drop in the noise around them as everyone at their end of the hall stops pounding and waits—so silently the clicking of coins on the window panes outside the building can be clearly heard.

"Shhhhh! Shhhhh!" people say, fingers to lips, and the hoarse sound becomes that of some voice over a bullhorn making some kind of an announcement, stopping between words, and Roger holds his breath until he hears it again. It seems to stop altogether, then suddenly blasts out at them from close range as the top campus security officer appears by the hall window only a few feet from them in his brown uniform, his eggshell eyes white and glaring over the orange mouth of the bullhorn, making all of them jump with fright, and Penny grabs Roger's arms with his words: "Attention! Attention! You have five minutes to clear the building or the Mayor's Tactical Troops will clear the premises and arrest all who refuse to leave. Five minutes! Five minutes!"

"Fuck you, pig!" the pretty girl shouts.

"Fuck you! Fuck you! Fuck you!" comes a chorus of cries, then everybody in the hall starts shouting, "Fuck you! Fuck you! Fuck you!" and starts pounding on the walls and doors again, the defiant sound booming like an explosion in the hall, reverberating and reverberating, and the cop steps back, the bullhorn still to his mouth, his eyes bright under the cap brim.

"Fuck you! Fuck you! Pig! Pig! Pig!"

Then there is the smash and tinkle of glass to a loud cheer, then the smash of more glass and the cry, "Fuck you, pig!" and when the cop turns and steps out of sight, Roger grabs Penny's hand and with a jerk of his head motions for her to follow him, sure there will be trouble now. He starts in the same direction as the cop, moving slowly in and around all the students who are screaming and shouting so loudly that they hurt his ears. But when he gets to the bend of the hall and starts to turn down it, he remembers he dropped his turtleneck shirt against the wall by the dean's door. He turns back to get it, still holding Penny by the hand, and when he finally gets back to the door and picks the sweater up, ties it around his waist, and turns back toward the bend again to get out of the building, the sound of marching feet, a "hut, hut, hut, hut!" resounds in the foyer. He stops, tense and listening, watching, until a girl screams and a column of blue suited tactical cops, two-wide, come around the corner of the hall with their clubs held out in front of them, clasped with both hands like rifles, their plastic visors down, their jaws bound shut by helmet straps, their badges glinting on the dull blue padding of their bullet-proof vests. They charge into the students in front of them, swinging their clubs with sickening smashes to the skull and back, knocking down a newsman taking their picture, smashing his camera when he falls, then pound on his back to keep him down. Then, clubs flying up and down, they drop students all around them with screams and groans and a scramble by other students to get away, knocking each other down, trampling on each other, tripping over those who fall, as Roger jerks Penny into a broken-field run down the hall, around students in front of him who look to see what he is running from, then start running, too, as screams and groans and yells and the thump-thump of clubs on flesh and bone fill the hall. He keeps running until he reaches the hall at the far end of the annex, then starts running toward the street exit to get off campus when he hears screams in front of him and sees another squad of cops come around the streetside hall swinging their clubs, dropping students in front of them. He turns around, Penny right behind him, and runs back toward the campus exit with the crowd and out the glass doors into the square between the main campus buildings, running until he is deep enough into the campus to escape any cops who might charge out of the annex. He sees that there are no police around, then slows down and stops. He looks at Penny, her eyes bright green in the sunlight as she gasps for air beside him, and takes a deep breath himself, turns toward the annex to watch for more cops, remembering his premonition when he left the house, and the fact that Dean James left the office just before the warning and that he was the one who probably told the security officer to order the students out. Roger hears a helicopter and looks up to see it hovering directly above him, and though his heart is pounding and his breath is puffing out of him, he feels momentarily safe, with cars zooming by and housewives with shopping bags calmly standing on the streetcar island in the street. Until there is a scream and a rush of students away from the glass doors of the annex, and cops come running out, clubs up, and blue-suited reinforcements pour out from between all the buildings and fan out in all directions in the square, clubbing every person in front of them, and he jerks Penny into another run with a huge crowd of students, who shout, "Fuck you, pigs! Fuck you! Pigs! Pigs! Pigs!" And mouths wide open with their cries, some girls pull out clumps of grass from the lawn and throw them at the cops, most falling harmlessly on the concrete, as a voice keeps croaking over a bullhorn: "Clear the campus! Clear the campus! This is illegal destruction of property! There are no innocent bystanders! There are no innocent bystanders! Clear the campus! Clear the campus!" Faces and figures shimmer in the windows of the Park Apartments, and people stand on roofs and garages and houses across the boulevard, where cars speed by. Cops pull back to the one-story annex, dragging fallen students with them, and spread out in a line across the small square between the annex and the humanities building, while a helicopter chop-chop-chops overhead. Roger reaches the boulevard, holding Penny tightly by the hand, feeling safe until a flash of gunmetal catches his eye. A rifle goes up and fires, and a teargas shell arches through the air toward them, and the crowd splashes apart like water when a rock hits, leaving a bare space on the square where the shell hits with a pop and spins in a circle, spewing thick clouds of gas, billows of smoke which cover everything around them, and irritate the throat, making Roger take short painful breaths, as it floats up in the branches of the giant sequoia trees.

"Pepper gas!" someone yells.

"That helicopter is helping direct their fire!" Roger shouts, pointing up at a cop leaning out the open door to point at them. Roger watches as a long-haired student runs out in front of them and grabs the spinning teargas canister, heaving it back across the square into the line of cops, making some jump out of the way to a loud cheer from the students.

"Look out!" someone yells, and everyone ducks to the ground, but the cop fires at a group of students in the doorway of the humanities building, and the missile flies low over the square and smashes into the wall above their heads, making them scatter, then drops on a student who is sitting on a step, engulfing him in fumes. His hands come up to his face and he jumps to his feet, staggers with one hand held out in front of him, takes a couple of steps down the sidewalk and falls to his knees in the middle of the fumes, his tongue out, coughing, his hands over his eyes. Roger jumps to his feet, runs across the square into the gas clouds, squinting and holding his breath, his eyes stinging and watering, and grabs the guy by the hand. Then he leads him out of the gas onto the lawn to the cheers of the crowd, and sneezing and coughing, joins Penny with a group of students around the flagpole. The stink and sting of tear gas spreads in thin clouds over the annex and the humanities building, over the sneezing students, when suddenly one, two, three teargas shells are fired, one shell smashing into the base of the flagpole, nearly hitting Roger. And his anger seems to explode in him, anger at the cops for firing at the students, at Dean James for sending the security officer after he kept him from falling, at Governor Reagan for firing Winter-green, at all the radicals who cooperated with the cops for their own interests, at Craig, who was nowhere around.

"You dirty motherfuckers!" he shouts, and Penny close be-hind him, he dashes out from under the gas and into the protec-tion of the grove of Giant Sequoias on a corner of the campus. Then grabbing some rocks out of the flower beds with other stu-dents, he runs around the trees to where he and Penny are alone, and when the cops in the square aim their teargas guns at the students throwing rocks at them from the flagpole, he lobs one, then two heavy rocks at them, then jumps behind a giant tree to hide, without waiting to see if any hit. He waits until the cops fire another salvo of shells at the students by the flagpole, then steps out and lobs one, two rocks again, sees them float over the lawn, over the small trees at the corner of the annex, a quick flurry of cops' legs scattering apart where he aims, and then ducks behind the tree again to wait. Penny presses against him until "Pow! Pow!" two teargas canisters hit a tree nearby and spew gas on them, and peeking out from around the tree, he sees a cop on his back by the corner of the annex. Up above the trees he hears the chop-chop of the helicopter, and looks up to see another cop leaning out with a pair of binoculars trained on him. He jerks Penny by the hand into a run from giant tree to giant tree, trying to stay under the thick branches so the cop can't pinpoint them, realizing as he runs that war is a battle over patches of land, and that the cops are able to drive them out of the building but they can't run them off the campus or even away from the annex. Finally, he reaches a group of students who have taken cover in the grove of trees, and notices several well-dressed, middle-aged men hovering around the group like military observers. He moves away from them but barely gets to the other side of the group, many of the students heaving rocks, shouting, "Pigs! Pigs! Pigs! Oink! Oink! Oink!" when a loud cheer goes up and he sees three guys hauling down the American flag from the flagpole only fifty feet away, two white kids with long hair and a black kid who looks like a high school student and who pulls out some matches and lights one. "Don't burn it!"Roger yells. "Don't burn it! You'll only turn the workers against you!"

"Shut up!"some student yells.

"Fuck you, pig!" a girl shouts, then screams as a group of husky jocks come tearing through the crowd and slug the three guys around the flag, knock them quickly to the ground, fight off a weak attempt by a few guys to take it back, then kick the black kid in the mouth when he starts to get up. Then, after they kick another kid in the nuts, they start to move backwards toward the annex, but are followed at a distance by a group of students, who suddenly double in number and charge down upon them when "Pow! Pow! Pow!" teargas shells land among them, and a big cry of fear goes up as a squad of cops, fifty strong, gasmasks on, clubs raised, come charging through the grove of trees and drive everyone in front of them deep into the square. And no longer holding hands, Roger and Penny run past the flagpole with some students, coughing and rubbing their reddened eyes, trying to run around the humanities building, afraid to run out in the street where cars are speeding by, when a scream and a shout stops them as another squad of cops comes running around the building
toward them, cutting off escape, encircling them, driving all of them down into the square in a wild, chaotic scramble, as more cops from the annex move up in an unbroken line to trap them, gasmasks on, clubs raised.

Students go down on the fringes, others jam up in the middle of the square or shoot out in fast runs, trying to break through the circle of cops, some making it. Roger starts to dash toward the street where the line of cops is thin, but can't see Penny, turns and spots her running with some other students toward the basement entrance of the humanities building further down the slope, where they jerk on the doors one after another but can't open them, and they turn and scream as cops charge down on them.

"Run, Penny!" he shouts, and she turns toward his voice but moans, "Nooooo!" and crouches down with her arms up as a cop charges her, and Roger feels a shock of fear spurt through him, paralyze him, then suddenly spark him into action at the sight of her so totally helpless only a few feet away. And all fear gone, he runs at the cop, rams into his side just before he reaches her, hits him in the padded ribs with the heels of his hands, knocks him over on the porch, then grabs her arm as the cop goes sprawling out on his back. But he sees her stare past him and scream again and "Bam!" a flash of lightning shoots through his head and he staggers back with rubbery legs, sees the cop who hit him raise his club again, but can't make his legs carry him away or even get his hands up high enough to block the club, and watches helplessly as the monstrous figure in the gasmask and visor steps toward him and brings the club down again, catching him on his half-raised arm, staggers him backwards off the porch, and drops him on the lawn as the cop on the ground leaps to his feet. But the sight of the cop jumping up fills him with energy and coordination again, and his head suddenly clear, he pushes off the ground with his hands, and jumps to his feet in front of the charging cops, clubs raised, their eyes wide with surprise behind their masks. He starts running with an insane energy, spurting ahead of them toward the giant sequoias on the corner, amazed that he has gotten so far, beginning to believe he can make it by the cheering faces of the students between the trees who are heaving rocks at the chasing cops, and running like fire, heartened by the cheers, he dashes to the trees, runs in and around them, sees the students backing into the boulevard ahead, and though still running hard, almost clear of the trees, he picks a gap in the crowd that is falling back to let him through, even takes a deep breath the last twenty feet or so, when he sees just a hint of a shadow at his side, then a quick flash like a cloud closing out a sunspot, and a blinding smash in his head again, which knocks him off his feet, topples him headfirst onto the concrete, a terrible pain like fire in his head, and he tries to cover it with his arms, to soothe the fire and hide his head down between his legs, as a long moan comes out his mouth from deep inside his body like some stranger's voice. He writhes, feeling like somebody has plunged a hot soldering iron into his brain, splitting it in two, feeling whacks to his back and shoulders, legs, and sure he is about to be killed, desperate, he screams and starts running on all fours, lifts to his feet as he runs, but sees the clump of trees in front of him instead of the street and realizes that he is running the wrong way too late, feels a painful thump on his back, then another to his head with a smash, a flash, and splintering stars, horrible pain, and the trees blacking out like a movie screen, and he falls again, a numbness coming over him, the thump of more clubs on his back and ribs, then a blurry sense of fatigue, no sight, his body deflating as the air passes out of him, a blurry darkness, a heaviness at the back of his head, then nothing, neither sight nor sound for moments or minutes he cannot tell, can only feel his body roll over and over as if buoyant and under water, his head hanging, wobbling loosely, as if his neck is broken, then wet, wet lawn in his face. His brain sputters, fuzzes with flashes of light, and he floats somehow, sharp winces of pain shooting through his brain with a jog-jog-jog, and he catches his breath, feels like he's falling, tries to throw his arms out to stop his fall, but catches his breath again with panic for his arms are locked behind him, his wrists cut by sharp metal, and he falls, rolls onto wet lawn with a big moan in his ears, then crash! like a wave breaking, noise comes pouring into his head and he wakes to the shouts of the crowd, opens his eyes and looks up from the lawn, sees through the blood the students backing up, their mouths open, fingers pointing at him, yelling, the chop-chop-chop of the helicopter, screams, great din of noise, the sound of sirens screaming in his head and the flash, flash, flash of red lights.

Busted

Clang of a cell door. His eyes open. He is on a jail bench. His head rests against the steel wall, throbs with pain. Chin on his chest. Blood drying on his face, stiff and sticky on his cheeks, caked into ringlets in his hair. He reaches his arm up stiffly, slowly, afraid he is still handcuffed, and touches the mat of sticky blood on his head, presses the itchy cut, but jerks his fingers free with the lightning shock in his scalp that burns deep in his head; he winces, squints.

A student with long dark hair sits on the bench against the opposite wall. The faint glare from a small bulb in a wire cage on the steel gray ceiling gives a bloodless tinge to his face. He is the kid who yelled at Roger for making announcements for the professors the first night and who tried to burn the flag. His jacket is ripped. His lip is cut and swollen. He stares back at Roger with circles under his eyes and hollows in his cheeks. His eyes are watery from either teargas or crying. There is no recognition of him in them. The sharp features of his face look bleak, almost skeletal.

Roger closes his eyes but he can still see a faint rose glow through his lids, can feel the throb of his pulse like a soft, steady drumbeat in his skull, and a queasy nausea in his gut like he is drunk and about to vomit. He had to keep his head up in the paddy wagon to keep it from bouncing, to stop the sharp pains from shooting through it. The drone of the motor. The sweet, sickening smell of the exhaust, the dizzy rocking that made him wish he'd pass out and slip past the suffering that gripped him into oblivion. It ached to move when the paddy wagon stopped, the back door clanked open, and the cop's voice said, "Get out!" He had let his feet fall off the edge of the seat to give him ballast, tip him upwards, then worked his way up to a sitting position with his hands, his elbows, pressing against the side with his back. He had wanted to fall over and vomit, but pushed himself off the panel wall with his back and hands to a standing position, swayed, sharp pains shooting through his head, everything off-kilter and blurry. He stepped out of the wagon and almost fell, hit with a jolt, winced, and had to grab for the door frame. Hard edges of concrete and steel all around. Nausea. The smell of oil and sweat.

A sob comes up and his blood-coated head jerks up and

down on his chest like a hiccup with the thought of Penny crouched down, screaming, and warm tears run out his closed eyes. His throat tightens as he fights to keep down the sobs, holds them in, swallows as a sense of guilt floods over him. She is caught in the middle. They both use her against him and torture her, too, like everybody who loves him, like Omar. She is probably in jail. She might be hurt. She could even be dead. Her whole life is ruined. Her family has good reason to hate him now. Sound of keys. He opens his eyes. Scuffling. A cop cursing, "I'll kick your ass!" A scream, "Owwww!" then "Pig! Pig! Pig!" Clang of a cell door. Footsteps. Silence. Then the soft sound of sobs. The light bulb goes out. Shadow fills the cell. There is only a faint light through the bars. He shivers with a sharp pain in his chest, the left side, a spasm of his heart muscle. Deep sadness fills the empty hollow inside him, the void. He lies in a void. The cell is a void. Empty darkness. The world spins in empty darkness. The whole universe is in a void. He can make out the young student opposite him, sitting up, his back against the dark wall, his eyes closed as if asleep. Faint light from the hall throws steep, slanted, bar shadows across him as if he is already in the stripes of a convict, as if he is bound by those stripes, as if his thin body is roped by them. The skinny arms that stick out of the short-sleeved shirt are so undeveloped and childish, without any muscular definition on them at all, that a wave of pity sweeps over Roger. He is sorry he argued with the student, a boy, really, and he feels a great need to touch him, and with that touch, bridge the chasm that separates them, that surrounds them, the void, the hole they sit in, and save them both. He forces himself to look at the bloody cut on his puffed lip though it turns his stomach, just as he had made himself look at the swollen corpse of Bobby Hutton. The sight brings a fresh wave of tears to his eyes. They have been hurt fighting the same battle together. They have shed blood together and the blood has made them brothers. They are in the same cell, the same hell together. They are brothers just like all men but it has taken a crisis, a life and death fight to make him realize it. He wishes he were on the same bench with the student so he could clasp his hand in a gesture of brotherhood. But he is too weak, too beat up and nauseous to stand up and cross the cell, and he hears himself say, "Hey!" in a rasping voice, and feels everything sway around him. Stripes shift across the thin body. Nausea rises up in him. Pain throbs in his head. He swallows and tries to focus his eyes on the student's eyes but can't and doesn't know why until he sees them open and stare at him.

"Looks like we ended up together after all, huh?" Roger says, and tries to smile, but his blood-coated face twists weirdly and his lips spread in more of a leer than a grin, and the student does not answer or smile back. Roger squints to see if the student's eyes are really open. But there is the shadow of a bar across them and Roger's own sight blurs. But when the student blinks, he says, "Say!" again, and fixing his eyes on the student so he won't look away, he lifts his hand slowly, feebly, and holds it there, trying to get a response, wanting a response, needing a response. But the student just sits with a blank stare in his eyes, and Roger lets his hand drop with a soft pat back down on the bolted bench.

"Can't you talk?" he asks, a hurt tone to his voice, trying to keep the bitterness down that wells up with a new wave of nausea.

"Not to pigsssss," the student says in a low, sullen voice, dragging out his words, showing his bottom teeth, and Roger's whole body stiffens with pain and anger. But the student's face is so thin and long and drawn, his eyes so dark-hollowed and sad, so empty of any kind of hope, so defeated, that Roger lets his body sink back down against the bench with a sigh, the pain and anger settling into a sad, dull ache.

"Listen, man," he wants to say. "I'm not a cop. I'm fighting for what you're fighting for. I'm your brother. Can't you see that?" He actually says the words to himself and tries to catch the student's eyes. But they are closed and he says nothing, watches the stripes rise and fall with the student's body, as if he is so unconcerned about him that he has fallen back to sleep again. He notices the bar stripes across his own legs. They can be shackles they bind him so tightly. They are as good as steel bonds across his chest. They are crushing his heart, imprisoned in his chest like his body is imprisoned in the cell, because he cannot love. Because he can never really trust anybody and no one will ever really love him because of that. Penny might have even set him up. She ran toward the police not away from them like he did. She may not even have a mark on her. And he had cried for her only a few minutes ago. He is in a cell even outside a cell. His whole world is as dark and shadowy and gray as a cell, this cell. There is no win for him.

He has risked his life, even his chances for love for the sake of a better world and lost. His head has been busted in and the student still calls him a pig and doesn't even care if he gets mad or tries to hurt him over it. There is no escape to any country or to any revolutionary group either. They all play the game. They all cooperate with the secret police. Black Muslims, white segregationists, Cuban exiles, and Arab nationalists had helped them kill Malcolm and King and both the Kennedys. Expediency rules the day. Even the kid opposite him might be used after they get out of jail, after they leave this very cell. The cops will not pass up such a good chance as this, to turn somebody he thinks is straight against him later. The steering committee probably got those girls to write those notes in cooperation with the police. The red-headed girl and the girl with the bandanna and the pretty girl all hugged him during the mill-in. And the cops know how he likes girls. The cops will never let up. They will manipulate him for the rest of his life. His life will only be a lot of suffering for nothing and there will only be emptiness and oblivion and nothing in the end. After a lifetime of pain, nothing. Just death after a lot of useless suffering. The students have lost the strike and he has lost all chance of love. He gets it both ways, all ways. The cell looks horrible to him. The bars press in on him. The shadows fall across him like weights.

The cell is closing in on him. The gray mass sinks down to suffocate him like the padded cell when he was eighteen. The bars seem to shake with his short breaths now, shiver and jerk with the gasping breaths he takes and the pounding of his heart. His heart pounds in his chest like a heavy drum beat, like doom, like it will crack his chest. He feels like he is going to die. He opens his mouth and tries to take deep breaths, but nausea gags him and his stomach buckles as if he's going to vomit. He closes his eyes to stop the spinning and keep the walls from closing in on him, to keep from being crushed, but he is falling into blackness, like a drop in an elevator, falling, falling, down, down, down, and he throws his arms out to stop the fall and opens his eyes, and his left foot falls off the bench, touching the concrete floor, resting upon it. But sadness wells up with a choking sensation in his chest and throat, gagging him, and he lifts himself to relieve the pressure, so he can breathe. Then, bracing his hands against the bench, he pushes himself up, creaks to a sitting position, and with both feet on the floor, spreads his arms and leans back against the steel wall to keep himself up, wincing with pain, his body aching all over, whoozy, the bar stripes blurring across the floor, running off into the dark wall of the cell, shadows floating around him, unreal, without substance, but shifting, causing the walls to pulse with heavy breaths, pulsing, pulsing, like some horrible creature that will smother and kill him. He will only die in the end. The sinking gray shadows cover him like a shroud. He is as good as dead. His chest aches with a low, persistent pain around his heart. A sharp pain twinges through it and he moans, making his head bob on his chest. His neck aches. Pain throbs in his skull. His body is sore all over.

His life is sore all over. Everything he has attempted has backfired. He has lost Penny's love. He has lost faith in everything. There is no hope, only emptiness and certain doom ahead of him. There is nothing but a long, lingering death left, without spirit, without joy, without love. He is too tired to fight anymore. He realizes that he is halfway there, that he doesn't have to wait for the cops to kill him slow bit by slow bit, that he can take one final act of freedom, that there is one thing he can still do, that they cannot stop him from doing now that there is nothing else to live for. He can do that. Yes, he can.

He looks at the student, who still seems to be asleep, takes a deep breath to keep the nausea down, strengthens himself for what he has to do, keeps himself moving so he won't back down and quit and continue his slow crucifixion. He'll end it himself, be his own master, decide his own execution, and bracing one hand against the wall, he stands up, swaying, his hair curling stiffly around his face, his eyes large and intense, as he faces the bars and steadies himself. He then slides his wide leather belt out from his waist, trying to figure out in his foggy mind how to do it, thinking bitterly that he should know since so many of his friends and members of his family have committed suicide. He stares at the cell bar in front of him to force the dead corpse of his brother out of his head, and sucks air in through his teeth, tightens his chest, and strains with flexed muscles to keep himself from breaking down. But he can't keep the tears from welling up in his eyes and blurring his sight, then remembers how Dr. Morganthal had said in a poetry class that suicides suffer from self-pity, and he blinks his eyes, purses his lips, straightens his back, and says, "Fuck this feeling sorry shit!" under his breath and gets control of himself. Then, holding the belt in his right hand, he takes a step toward the bars, but gets dizzy and has to reach for the wall to steady himself and wait until his sight clears. Then he reaches out in front of him and takes two small steps and catches hold of a bar, then takes another step to the door, grabbing the bars with both hands, and pauses there to get his balance. Then he reaches up as high as he can with a trembling hand to grab a bar. His grip is slippery. His hands are sweating. He is scared. He can feel fear trembling all through him now, a weakness in his knees, in all his joints, in the pit of his stomach. He takes a quavering breath, tastes blood in his mouth, and lifts his leg to set his foot on a crossbar. It shakes badly. But he pushes off the floor anyway, and holding the belt in three fingers of his right hand, grabs a bar with his thumb and forefinger, brings his wobbly right foot up level with his left, and stands trembling on the lowest crossbar.

He is shaking all over, and though still dizzy and weak, he can see clearly, can make out the cell doors across the hall though they are in shadow, and the only light comes from a faint bulb down at the end of the short hall as if his last glimpse of the world is going to be especially acute. But his head hurts, and though he doesn't want to take any chances of falling, he is still too close to the floor. He needs at least another foot to make sure that his feet don't touch after he drops and cause slow strangulation. He wants to break his neck and put himself out fast. He lifts his right foot, finds the next crossbar, and lifts himself up, keeping his left foot on the bottom crossbar for support until the last moment, so weak, he's afraid he'll fall. But he makes it, yet shakes so badly that he has to hold onto the bars with his wet hands for a moment before he is able to reach up and slip the belt buckle around a bar over the top crossbar. He takes a deep breath, then hooks a finger through the dangling buckle and pulls it down, hooks an arm around a bar, leans back and buckles the belt with clumsy fingers, It is an awkward position and a hard job. He pauses again when he finishes, then twists the belt so that it makes a lopp and slips it down over his head with one hand, wincing when he rubs a sore lump, but gets it to the back of his neck and stops to rest.

There is a great crippling weakness in him as if the fear that he has forced out of his mind has merely sunk down further into his body. He feels an urge to quit, to not go through with it, the weakening fear growing in him. His lips tremble. He fights to keep the self-pity down, strains with all his strength not to give into the weakness, and his head seems to swell with throbbing pain, the pain thumping like a hammer, and he feels himself swoon, grow dizzy, and start to lose his balance. He twists his upper body around quickly to face the cell, the belt loop under his chin, his heart pounding, his brain pulsing with a deep throbbing pain, a great fear sizzling in him, in all his limbs, his joints, deep in his chest, scared, scared, but knowing this is it, now or never, he twists his hips and throws his feet out from under him, his arms to his sides, and drops, his teeth clacking together, his eyes blinking, and his hands flying to his throat with a squawk as the belt catches on his adam's apple and his head smacks against the cross bar behind him with a blinding smash.

Bailed Out

A hoarse squawking splits his head from the back of his aching skull to the furrow of his blood-caked brow. He hears his name called as he comes back to blurry consciousness, and the student's face far above him shifts and waves like a shadow in front of the lightbulb. He sees the benches on both sides of him, and wonders why he is on the floor and what he is doing in a jail cell. Then he sees his belt dangling, unbuckled from the student's hand, and remembers what he has done and what he has failed to do, and all the misery floods back into him. A deep sadness saps his strength, his will. All he wants to do is lie on the concrete floor and die, close his eyes and float away, forget it all, not have another thing to do with living. But the student squats down and shakes him, rocks him back and forth and forces him to open his eyes again.

"What did you do? Try to kill yourself?" he asks.

Roger blinks his eyes and tries to nod, but can only swallow, feeling a soreness in his throat.

"You're Roger Leon, aren't you?" the student says. "You better get up. They called your name over the loudspeaker."

Roger listens, his throat aching, expecting to hear his name called, and notices the fine, pointed nose of the guy, the smooth hairless chin, and thinks of how soon the face will be rotting in the ground, dirt in the nostrils, maggots in the soft whites of the eyes, and he feels an immense pity for the guy, because of the death he is doomed to. He doesn't even care that the student knows his name, meaning he is well known among the people at the sit-in. He only wants to tell the student how sorry he is that they have fought and that the student will die soon, like all of them. He only wants to tell the student that he loves him and that he doesn't care if the student called him a pig.

"Did you really try to kill yourself?" the student asks, and Roger nods slightly and blinks his eyes for an answer, his throat hurting too much to speak, afraid he will break down and cry in front on him.

"I heard a thump in my sleep but didn't think anything of it after all the noises I've heard all night. But when the loud-speaker started squawking, I woke up and saw you on the floor and the belt dangling from the bars and realized what had happened. It's a good thing you fell out of that loop or you might be dead now."

The concern in the student's voice touches Roger, seems to give him strength, give him a reason for moving, and he lifts his head up with a sharp pain, forcing himself to move, realizing that he has to do something about himself whether he wants to or not.

"Don't tell the cop. They'll send me to the nuthouse. Please!" he says, struggling to prop himself up, his head splitting with every vibration, turning to squint out the cell door at the sound of footsteps, the jingle of keys coming down the hall.

"I'll help you up," the student says, hooking an arm around Roger and pulling him into a sitting position, and Roger grabs his wrist and squeezes it, holds onto the thin limb, his long fingers going completely around it. And wanting to show that he appreciates the help, he holds on too long as if his grip can keep him from drowning, from dying, and the student has to pull himself free.

But sitting up, everything seems so much brighter and unreal to him. The cell benches stand out from the wall with hard edges. The bars seem two-dimensional and frosted with light as if they are flat, not round. The student's face above him is a sickly white like a mask, in stark contrast to his puffed, bloodied lip. And everything pulsates, seems to breathe back and forth, in and out in front of him, with the pain throbbing in his head. He feels like he has a hangover, and reaches up to touch a knot at the back on his skull, then tenderly feels two more bumps, all sticky with dried blood. He is still alive but everything looks strange, as if he has come back from the grave and cannot only see everything in its place but the space around it, the void, the black nothing hovering over everything, ready to engulf everyone in darkness. He can see death everywhere. He can see the skeleton in the student's body. He notices the knuckles holding the belt and the prominent bones of his thin head, the hollows that the pale skin just barely covers. When the student looks away as if embarrassed, Roger appreciates the movement, the life in it. He is glad the student is alive.

"Morning?" he asks.

"About seven or eight o'clock, I guess," the student says, and looks up at the bars with the sound of footsteps, the jingle of keys close to the cell, and the sight of a cop's pantlegs which makes Roger's aching head throb with fear.

"Who's Leon?" the cop asks, bars across his heavy blue body and bald head. His clean-shaven cheeks, fleshy and full above his thick neck, seem to vibrate with his words, his pale eyes are gray as the walls. Roger lifts his hand.

"Hurry up!" the cop says, and rattles his keys as he fits one into the lock.

"He's hurt, can't you see?" the student says, and pushes his hair out of his eyes. He bends down to grab Roger's arm and helps him up, and a wave of emotion and love rises in Roger's chest. He is so sorry now for calling the student a punk the first night, he wants to throw his arms around him and beg his forgiveness. He wants to tell him to keep living, to keep caring, that he is precious, that the cop is precious, that they are all precious, everybody, every living thing.

"Shut up!" the cop says, and opens the cell door. But Roger wants to hug him too, and when he takes his belt from the student, and mumbles, "Thanks," his lips twitch with a weak smile, and he reaches out and touches the student's bare arm, trying to apologize for not being his friend from the beginning. Then he turns away, feeling like he has wasted part of his life, that too much of his life has been a series of missed friendships, of lost loves, something he never wants to happen again as long as he lives. And though he squints with the pain that throbs in his head with every step he takes down the corridor, he searches for every student in the cells, some staring back at him, some sitting on benches, some standing, some lying down as if they are all in coffins practicing for dying. He wants to show them that he cares for them, that he wants to do something to help them, and he waves at one student who waves back at him when the cop stops to unlock a solid steel door at the end of the corridor, and he wants to wave at the cops in the big booking room, too, which he vaguely remembers from the day before, and those at the high counter he's lead to, where he can see the freeway through the barred window behind it, cars already streaking by, the early morning sky pale blue and spotted with a few, low, lonely looking clouds. But the glare of the daylight hurts his weakened eyes, makes them blink and water, and he has to look down at the counter to ease the sting.

"You've been bailed out, Leon," says the desk officer, a handsome blond man, then looks at Roger as if waiting for some reaction, as if he knows him, and his lips part again as if he is going to say something else. And Roger waits for him to speak, wants him to speak, wants to share some brotherhood with him before it is too late, but the cop and the counter shift a little, white sparks glitter around him like fireflies, and he feels himself sway. He grabs the edge of the counter with both hands to steady himself, suddenly conscious of how he must look with blood caked and sticky all over his head and face.

"Sorry about this," Roger says, waving his hand at his face, wanting to say that he holds no grudges, that he knows the cop is just doing his job. But he's aware that he has said something that is somehow ridiculous, and he signs when the cop pushes a paper form and a pencil toward him, then takes the cardholder, keys and five dollar bill the cop dumps out of a manila folder onto the counter. He smiles, though, when he follows the cop's thick finger to the door, and smiles at the balding cop who opens it for him, though neither of them smiles back, and the balding cop looks quickly down as if he can't stand to look at him. And he smiles when he sees Penny step through some parked cars toward him, the dew still sparkling on their metal roof tops, cold blue shadows slanting away from them, coughs and sees goose pimples on his arms when he realizes he is just wearing his green T-shirt. And he feels a wave of tenderness for her when she moans at the sight of him and lifts his arms to embrace her, his belt dangling from his hand, realizing how much he loves her, that he almost lost her forever.

But she approaches him so carefully, takes such small steps toward him, and tucks her arms close to her ribs as if she is afraid to get near him, acting so guilty that he begins to suspect her again, and drops his hands to his sides. He is afraid he is back where he started, that nothing has changed, except to get worse, for he now has a trial to face. And he deadens his feeling toward her to keep himself from caring too much, to keep them from getting another way to subjugate him, concious of holding the belt in his hand, standing in a parking lot next to a police station, in the middle of a city, on the edge of an ocean, under a sky stretching away into nothing above him.

"Got a busted skull," he says, sniffling in the chill air, and points at his head so he will have something to do with his arms and can keep himself from throwing them around her, forcing himself to keep away from her. Yet he sees death in the dark circles under her eyes when she gets near him, sees how fragile she is, and thinks that she can disappear off the face of the earth today and by tomorrow she won't even be missed, gone like his mother and his brother, like the Kennedys, like Malcolm and Martin Luther King, and wanting to hug her, wanting to love her, wanting to never let her go, he stares so hard at her she breaks step and lowers her eyes and doesn't look up until she is directly in front of him and he can see the pink tinge to her eyelids, the bloodshot streaks through the whites of her eyes. Her face is a pasty white.

"You bail me out?" he asks, though he already knows it, and follows her through the parked cars, across the gravel lot to his MG, where he opens the passenger door and drops into the bucket seat with a heavy sigh.

"We've got to get you to a hospital. Your head looks horrible," she says, squinting her eyes as if it hurts to look at him, the tires crackling over the gravel as she drives out of the lot, and he turns the rear-view mirror his way and raises up in the seat to look at himself. His head is crusted with blood, plastered down on top and sticking out at the sides in wild ringlets. His face is streaked with dried blood, too.

"Where are you going?" he asks, dropping back into the seat, hurting over the way he looks, at her rejection of his love for her, as she drives onto the freeway, heading west toward the ocean.

"To the medical building at school," she says, glancing at him, and then at the freeway again, staying in the slow lane, moving away from the city with the light traffic.

"I don't want to go. I don't want anything to do with that school or you," he says, without any thought of saying anything like that.

"Why?" she asks, but closes her mouth and appears to sit straighter, to harden a little and occupy herself with her driving as if she regrets the question.

"Because it's just a complete waste of time, of everything," he says in a low monotone. "I'm getting out of here, out of this town. I'm splitting."

Her face wrinkles up as if she is going to cry and she slows down to drive off the freeway onto the boulevard only a few blocks from school, but doesn't say anything, and her silence infuriates him, makes him want to hurt her enough to upset her and make her tell him the truth.

"Craig cooperated with the pigs and the steering committee to get me back to school and you probably set me up for that charge, got me this knock on the head and got off without a mark yourself."

"That's not true, Roger!" she cries, her mouth quivering. "When they chased you, I ran the other way to get away, that's all!"

"Liar. I wanted to hug you and kiss you when I just came out of that jail, but you acted so guilty you turned me off! Take me to the pad so I can pack. I hate everybody in this fucking world! I hate you, too! I even hate myself!" he shouts, his head throbbing, wanting to punch something, to smash out all the windows with his hands, to explode, to destroy everything including himself. But a cold, deadening sense that it is all useless keeps him from punching, keeps him cold outside, though he is hot inside, like hot ice.

"Listen, Roger. Please listen to me," she says, and puts one hand on his. And when he turns to look at her, his face stiff with a grimace and caked blood, the cuts in his skull throbbing with his heartbeat, she says, "I've been waiting for a chance to tell you. I was going to tell you right away to make you feel better, but when I first saw how badly you were hurt, I couldn't talk. I felt guilty because you got hurt over me. I was afraid you might think I set you up. I wanted to hug you, too. I was just afraid you didn't trust me. The administration has given in under pressure from the faculty senate, which was called after the police beat and arrested over two hundred students. They've been meeting all night and allowed students to testify and forced the Dean's

Committee to grant all the points we sat in for except Rotsee off campus or they'd strike during finals."

"Whaaaaat?" he says, his head throbbing, looking carefully into her eyes to see if she is lying. But she meets his gaze and says, "Yes. And right now there's a rally going on down in front of the ad building to celebrate the victory and take up a collection to bail out all the students who don't have the money and make plans for next semester."

"Is that really true?" he asks.

"Yes," she says, and squeezes his hand.

"Then let me see for myself. Drive by there on the way to the medical building," he says.

"Don't you even believe that?" she asks, shaking her head.

"I just want to see for myself," he says as she stops at a red light, her mouth quivering, her eyes filling with tears. She lets out a low moaning sob, turns the corner and drives down past the lawn on the corner of the campus, and pulls into a red zone directly in front of the main entrance to the administration building, where a crowd of a hundred of more students are massed in front of the steps and the SDS leader is waving his hand and shouting over the bullhorn: "And we won't quit until we've brought a working democracy back to this whole country, until the power belongs to all the people, and the wealth of this land is shared with all its citizens and the exploitation of the rest of the world is stopped forever! And I mean forever!"

There is a big cheer with shouts and whistles and much stamping of feet and Roger sits up, rolls the window all the way down, and his head pounding with pain, eyes squinting at the glare of sunlight off the yellow walls of the building, hearing the prolonged cheers through the slight ringing of his ears, with proof that some good has come from all the pain, all the suffering and misery, he leans his head out the window and jabs his fist into the air, jabs it, jabs it, jabs it, and shouts in a hoarse voice: "Power! Power! Power! Power to the people! To the people! To the people!" then turns and throws himself on Penny and hugs her to him, hugs her as she sobs and hugs him.